"BELIEVE WHAT YOU WILL. Only I know the truth of what lies inside me."

"I'm not certain you do." Trembling fingertips fluttered along her neck. Her pulse leaped in response, and she sucked in a breath, the hiss loud in the dark. "You cannot stand there and tell me you feel nothing."

Oh, she felt, certainly—too much and the sensation was altogether too enticing.

"You cannot convince me you'd be willing to enter a marriage with no tender feelings at all."

She reached out, hoping to placate him, but immediately balled her fingers into a fist. Best not to touch him, not while he was in this mood. "I would not be the first to do so." Mama, for one, had entered into just such an arrangement. "Nor would I be the last."

"Then you'd be missing the best life has to offer."

"And I'd save myself a great deal of pain when it all came crashing down."

"Some things are worth the pain. They're most definitely worth the risk."

In the dark, she missed the movement, but the emotion pulsing from him had heightened the rest of her senses. The only warning she received was the whisper of fabric. Before her brain had a chance to process the meaning of that sound, he took her roughly by the shoulders and crushed his lips to hers.

A Most Scandalous Proposal

ASHLYN MACNAMARA

BALLANTINE BOOKS • NEW YORK

A Ballantine Books Mass Market Original

Copyright © 2013 by Ashlyn Macnamara
Excerpt from *A Most Devilish Rogue* copyright © 2013 by Ashlyn Macnamara

Published in the United States by Ballantine Books, an imprint of The Random House Publishing Group, a division of Random House, Inc., New York.

BALLANTINE and colophon are trademarks of Random House, Inc.

This book contains an excerpt from the forthcoming book *A Most Devilish Rogue* by Ashlyn Macnamara. This excerpt has been set for this edition only and may not reflect the final content of the forthcoming edition.

ISBN 978-0-345-53474-3
eBook ISBN 978-0-345-53475-0

Cover design: Lynn Andreozzi
Cover illustration: Gregg Gulbronson

Printed in the United States of America

www.ballantinebooks.com

9 8 7 6 5 4 3 2 1

Ballantine Books mass market edition: March 2013

To Marian, for all your encouragement,
for recognizing in me, over ten years ago,
a talent I am loath to recognize in myself,
and for always reminding me
to make things worse.

To the rubber chicken, just because.

A Most Scandalous Proposal

CHAPTER ONE

April 1816, London

William Ludlowe wagers five thousand pounds that Miss Julia St. Claire will become the next Countess of Clivesden.

Benedict Revelstoke reread the lines in White's infamous betting book. What the devil? His fingers constricted about the quill, just shy of crushing it. Right. He'd been about to sign on his friend's wager. Some idiocy, no doubt—hardly worth the bother now.

The book's most recent inscription was scrawled, for all the world to see, in gold ink, no less. How fitting. Gold ink for Ludlowe, whom many of the *ton*'s ladies dubbed their golden boy. The man's lack of a title did nothing to diminish their opinion.

Upperton nudged him. "What's the matter? Your feet coming over icy all the sudden?"

Lead blocks would be more accurate, but Benedict was not about to admit to that. He laid the quill aside and jabbed a finger at the heavy vellum page. "Have you seen this?"

The page darkened as his oldest friend peered over his shoulder. "Clivesden? Thought he was married. Ludlowe's a jumped-up bacon brain. And what's Miss Julia got to do with either of them?"

"I've no idea, but I intend to find out." He released a breath between clenched teeth. "Appalling how so-called gentlemen will lay bets on young ladies of good reputation."

"Young ladies in general or Miss Julia in particular?"

Ignoring the gibe, Benedict turned on his heel and strode down the steps to the pavement. A glance at his pocket watch told him it was ten minutes past eleven, still early by the *ton*'s standards. That was something. At least he knew where he'd find Julia at such an hour.

He sighed at the prospect of dodging a passel of marriage-minded misses. But he'd be damned before he let some idiot besmirch her reputation.

JULIA stiffened her arms, but her dance partner refused to take the hint. Dash it, he held her too close for propriety's sake. Hang propriety—on that last turn, he'd actually tightened his grip so much her breasts grazed the front of his tailcoat. Too close for her comfort. So she did what any self-respecting young lady would do and trod on his toes.

"I do beg your pardon, my lord." The lie slid easily from her lips.

Lord Chuddleigh's smile faded, and his grip slackened along with his jowls. "Not at all."

Thankfully, the final notes of the waltz rose to the high ceiling of Lady Posselthwaite's ballroom a moment later, and Julia backed out of her partner's greedy embrace, stopping short when her skirt brushed against a dancer to her rear. "If you'll excuse me."

Chuddleigh eyed her up and down, before his red-rimmed gaze halted at a spot several inches below her chin. "Are you engaged for the next set?"

What could he be thinking? The roué. He was forty if he was a day, and a strong hint of brandy surrounded him like a cloud.

Julia made a show of consulting her dance card. "No.

I actually find I'm rather exhausted," she added before he could ask her for the next dance.

"It's the crowd. Dreadful crush as it is every year, of course. Perhaps a turn on the terrace?"

Drat. The man was relentless. Julia cast a swift glance about the ballroom. Unfortunately, Lord Chuddleigh was right about the crush. So many members of the *ton* packed into one spot, the men in starched linen and intricate cravats, the ladies in pastel ball gowns, it was a wonder anyone could move at all. Attendees wove past one another with polite smiles and quick *pardons*, intertwining like maypole dancers.

Convenient for Lord Chuddleigh, though, if he wanted an excuse to brush against her a bit more. Not that he had to expend much of an effort the way his paunch preceded him. She should never have agreed to the first set, but he'd seemed a safe enough choice when he asked. At his age and still unattached, she'd expected he wouldn't turn into a serious suitor.

Apparently, Chuddleigh had formed other ideas.

The crowd made it impossible to pick out a convenient means of escape. Her father was too occupied in the card room to concern himself with her dance partners. The ballroom—the marriage mart—that was her mother's exclusive domain. Papa was all too happy to leave Mama with the responsibility of landing wealthy, titled husbands for Julia and her sister, while he gambled to increase the family's meager earnings. Alas, for Mama aimed high in the hopes of giving her daughters what she had never had—social standing and influence.

In short, power. But such power came at the price of keeping up with fashion and maintaining a house in Town.

"I think a lemonade would be quite sufficient," she finally replied with a weak smile.

Lord Chuddleigh pressed thick lips together but acquiesced with a nod. "Do not move from that spot. I shall return anon."

The moment he disappeared behind Lady Whitby's bright orange turban, Julia elbowed her way in the opposite direction. She'd left her older sister amid a group of twittering hopefuls in their first season. With any luck, Julia could use them and their mamas as a shield against any further unwelcome advances.

She discovered Sophia next to a potted palm, deep in conversation with the dowager Countess of Epperley. Between the plant's fronds and the matron's ostrich plumes, Sophia was well camouflaged.

On Julia's approach, the dowager snapped a lorgnette to her face and eyed her from her sleek, honey-colored coiffure to the tips of her silk-clad toes. A frown fit to curdle new milk indicated Julia had passed muster.

"Oh, Julia." A rosy glow suffused Sophia's normally pearl-white complexion.

Julia pasted on a smile, knowing she was in for at least half an hour's worth of gushing, and that was just in public. Depending on what time they made it home tonight, Sophia could easily chatter away the remaining hours before dawn in her ebullience.

As long as she didn't end up sobbing herself to sleep, as had happened all too often in the past. So full of affection, Sophia. If only she hadn't bestowed her heart on a man who only occasionally acknowledged her existence. On such evenings, the urge to pull her sister into a hug warred with the desire to give Sophia a stern talking-to.

Tonight, apparently, was one of those evenings.

"My lady," Sophia breathed, "you simply must repeat to my sister what you've just told me."

The dowager pursed her lips and subjected Julia to a second inspection, as if she might find evidence of Julia's unworthiness to hear the latest gossip. Defensively, Julia spread out her fan and held it in front of her bosom, before Lady Epperley concluded her gown revealed too much.

"There's no need to sound so pleased about it," the old woman huffed. "You young chits, you have no conception of the serious nature of events."

Julia cast a sidelong glance at her sister. Such high color in Sophia's cheeks was normally associated with only one person.

"Then I shall have to tell her myself," Sophia pronounced.

"You shall do no such thing." The dowager harrumphed, setting both her jowls and plumes a-shudder. "It's a perfect tragedy, I tell you. It must be announced with the appropriate solemnity. It isn't as if we were exchanging the latest *on-dit*."

"What's this about the latest *on-dit*?" growled a familiar voice.

Julia smiled warmly at her childhood companion. Thank goodness. Better Benedict than Chuddleigh turning up with the lemonade.

At his appearance, Sophia inclined her head.

"Ah, Revelstoke." Acknowledging Benedict with a nod, Julia suppressed a jolt of surprise. She'd become so used to seeing him in his scarlet uniform that his bearing in eveningwear and starched cravat startled her. By rights, he should have looked like any other man of the *ton,* but the black superfine of his coat, matched to his ebony hair, only served to set off his dark complexion and sparkling blue eyes.

Snap! The lorgnette put in a reappearance. The dowager's frown lines deepened as she inspected the new arrival. Her gaze lingered on his sharp cheekbones, square jaw, and shaggy waves of hair that hung nearly to his shoulders, too long to be fashionable.

Or, for that matter, respectable.

"In my day, a young lady would never dream of addressing a gentleman in such a familiar manner. Why, I never called my husband by anything other than his title in all the years of our marriage, even in the most intimate of settings."

Benedict's shoulder brushed against Julia's as he leaned close and whispered, "That was more than I needed to know about their marriage."

She ducked behind her fan to hide both her grin and the blush that suddenly heated her cheeks. And why should she blush over Benedict of all people? She'd experienced the warmth of his breath wafting just beneath her ear on any number of previous occasions. She ought to be long accustomed to his brand of cutting commentary.

The dowager let out another harrumph, raised her considerable chin, and sailed off in a cloud of ostrich feathers and plum-colored silk.

"I believe she overheard you," Julia said.

"Without a doubt. The old dragon just trod on my foot."

Sophia giggled into her fan.

He turned his gaze on Julia, and her heart gave an odd thump. Normally, when he had a chance to seek her out at these functions, it was for one of two reasons—to save her from overzealous suitors or to escape from the pack of society mamas and their daughters. They might pass an agreeable hour or two on the sidelines exchanging pithy observations on the *ton*'s foibles, laughing together as she tried to match him in wit.

In all the years of their friendship, she'd had occasion to witness many moods etched on his face. Rarely had he turned so serious an expression on her, and never this strange intensity. *Thump*. Another pang in her chest. And where was that coming from?

Rather than press her fan to the spot, she tapped his forearm. "What's happened?"

He opened his mouth to reply, but Sophia chose that moment to interrupt. "I suppose I'll have to tell the news myself."

Julia turned to her sister. She watched as Sophia's features suddenly bloomed with renewed excitement. Something else was amiss there. Julia craned her neck. Had William Ludlowe actually put in an appearance?

"What news?" Benedict leaned closer. "What's going on?"

As if on cue, a collective sigh passed through the room, emanating from the females in attendance. A late arrival stood between the plaster columns of the entrance, his tall form easily visible over the heads of lesser men. Waves of golden blond hair flowed neatly back from an even-featured face that set feminine hearts to racing all across the room. The snowy linen of his artfully tied cravat stood in stark contrast to the austere black of his eveningwear.

Elegantly coiffed heads tilted toward each other, and the twitter of conversation increased its pace, punctuated by giggles. Sophia's smile broadened, and her fan fluttered double time, while the rosy glow on her cheeks extended to her forehead. On Julia's other side, Benedict let out a groan.

An easy smile graced the newcomer's lips as he nodded to an acquaintance. His gaze glided over the room to alight almost immediately in Julia's corner. Sophia grasped her arm, and her fingers tightened until Julia was sure she'd be sporting bruises tomorrow.

"Oh," Sophia sighed. "He's coming this way. How do I look?"

Julia didn't spare her sister a glance. With her neat golden hair swept off her lovely face and an ice-blue gown that, despite its age, displayed her figure to its best advantage, Sophia set a standard of beauty to which most of the *haut ton* could only aspire. If not for their mother's humble origins and the hints of scandal surrounding their parents' marriage, she might have been declared an Incomparable in her first season. Still, she'd turned down enough offers of marriage to cause their father to pull out what little remained of his hair.

"You look perfect as always."

The ragged edges of Sophia's fan flapped so fast that the breeze cooled Julia's own skin.

Benedict tugged at her other arm. "Might I have a word? In private?"

Sophia's eyes went round. "Not now. You cannot just leave me here. What if I faint?"

Faint? In five seasons, Sophia had yet to succumb to that particular malady. "Do not be ridic—"

"Then Ludlowe can catch you." Benedict's response was clipped. His fingers curled about Julia's wrist. "I really must insist."

"What is the matter with you tonight?" Julia whispered to Benedict. "You're behaving so strangely, if I did not know better, I'd say you were foxed."

"Believe me, Julia, I'd like nothing better at the moment."

She stiffened at the use of her given name. They'd known each other so long, the address came naturally in private, but it was unlike him to forget himself in the middle of a ballroom.

"Oh, M-mr. Ludlowe," Sophia breathed.

Julia turned her attention to the man before her. His smile might have bedazzled the dowager Countess of Epperley into forgetting her lorgnette—or snapping it out for a better view—but it had little effect on Julia.

"Good evening, ladies. Revelstoke," Ludlowe added with a nod in Benedict's direction. "My dear Miss Julia, I must say you look particularly enchanting this evening."

For a moment, she didn't react. She couldn't have heard right. But then he reached for her hand as if it were his due. Belatedly, she disentangled her arm from Sophia's death grip and allowed him to brush his lips against the back of her glove.

"Mr. Ludlowe." She deliberately flattened her tone to coolness, hardly what anyone would term friendly.

After another moment, he dropped her hand to turn his considerable charm on Sophia. Julia could feel its effect radiating off her sister in the form of heat. A dazzling smile threatened to split Sophia's face in two.

"A pleasure, as always, Miss St. Claire."

If Sophia noticed that he paid her beauty no compliment, she hid it well. Dipping her head, she dropped into a curtsey. "My lord."

Julia's mouth dropped open. *My lord?* The evening was growing stranger by the minute.

Ludlowe's chuckle rumbled, low and smooth as hot chocolate, over their corner. Even the potted palm perked up. "Now, now, Miss St. Claire, let's not be overly hasty. Nothing's settled as of yet."

Beside her, Benedict held himself rigid, the tension seething in the air around him.

"What isn't settled?" Julia's question floated free before she could stop herself.

Ludlowe turned back to her. His smile would have melted butter. "You haven't heard of my good fortune then?"

"No, I haven't."

The fine lines on his forehead smoothed to solemnity. "It's quite boorish of me to refer to it as good fortune, actually. Do forgive me. My fortune is another family's tragedy, you see."

What on earth? She frowned, resting her fan against her bosom. "Oh dear."

"The Earl of Clivesden has met with an unfortunate accident. Horrific, really."

Foreboding settled over her. "Accident?"

"Poor man. He should never have ventured out on those winding Devonshire roads. Entire carriage tumbled off a cliff into the Channel. His young son was with him."

She pressed suddenly icy fingers to her lips. "How dreadful." At the same time, she noted Sophia's lack of reaction. This must be the news Lady Epperley had imparted to her sister, doubtless with the proper ceremony.

Benedict's lip curled. "I fail to see how such a tragedy might turn to anybody's advantage."

Ludlowe had the grace to avert his eyes. "There's an appalling lack of male issue in that line. They had to trace the family back four generations to find an heir."

"You'll forgive me," Benedict said, his words clipped to the point of rudeness, "but what's that got to do with you?"

Ludlowe sketched them a bow. "My great-grandfather was the third Earl of Clivesden's younger brother."

Benedict surged forward with such force and suddenness that Julia laid a restraining hand on his forearm. "*You?*" he snarled. "You're now Clivesden?"

Ludlowe's smile did not falter for an instant. "Not yet, but my claim is solid. I daresay the Lord Chancellor ought to accept it without delay."

"As long as the former earl's widow isn't in a delicate condition, you mean." Benedict seemed to be forcing the words through gritted teeth.

Julia slanted her eyes in his direction. What she could see of his neck above his cravat flushed red. Beneath her hand, the muscles in his arm had turned to steel. Why was he so upset over the circumstances? While tragic, to be certain, none of them had actually known Clivesden well.

Ludlowe's smile remained fixed. "Of course."

He stepped closer to Julia, and the muscles beneath her fingertips jerked.

"I had hoped to keep the news quiet a bit longer. I might have known gossip would foil my plans." He acknowledged Sophia with a nod, and she beamed at him from behind the protection of her fan.

"Ah well, *c'est la vie*." Ludlowe shrugged. "I hadn't come over with the intention of discussing this matter. I was wondering if Miss Julia would care for the next dance."

If he hadn't been looking her in the eye, Julia would never have credited the notion. When Ludlowe turned up at a ball, he remained decidedly ensconced in the card room or on the sidelines. He chatted with the ladies, he flirted outrageously, he might disappear into the gardens for long stretches, but he rarely danced.

The lilting strains of violins in three-quarter time met her ears. Goodness. Ludlowe certainly never waltzed.

An expectant silence fell over the group, while the music swelled around them. She couldn't possibly, not with her sister standing right there, deflating a bit further with each joyous note. "I'm terribly sorry—"

"She promised the next set to me," Benedict said over her reply.

"I'm sure Sophia would be delighted," Julia added quickly. "That way, no one is disappointed."

Ludlowe hesitated a second too long before nodding. "Your servant. I must insist you save another dance for me later."

He didn't wait for her reply. Offering his arm to a glowing Sophia, he led her to join the whirling couples already on the dance floor.

Julia rounded on Benedict, who bent his left arm in invitation. "I believe this is our waltz."

She ignored him. "Are you planning to tell me what that was all about?"

He held her gaze, the breadth of his shoulders blocking the flickering light from the crystal chandeliers. That disturbing intensity still lit their depths. And where had it come from along with his, well, protectiveness? She pressed her lips into a line and shuffled her weight from one foot to the other.

"After this set. Meet me outside. For now, we'd better make a proper show of dancing. Just so no one is disappointed."

She took his arm, and he set off at such a clip that she stumbled after him through the crowd until they found a spot among the dancers.

"Why can't you tell me now?" she persisted. His brows lowered in disapproval, but she ignored the reaction. The waltz permitted conversation, after all.

He set a solid arm about her waist, seized her hand, and spun her into the first turn. "Not here. Not where others might overhear." He tipped his chin toward an orange turban swaying not far from them. "Lady Witless, for example."

At the nickname, Julia suppressed a laugh and tapped him on the shoulder with her fan. Benedict had so christened the old gossip two years ago when Lady Whitby's spiteful tongue had run her afoul of a few other matrons who had overheard her and arranged to knock her into the punchbowl. "Stop. You're terrible. By the by, what are you doing here tonight? I didn't even realize you were in Town."

"I only arrived two days ago. I came to have a look at some horses."

"Ah, of course. No wonder you haven't seen fit to call. What's more important than cattle?"

"Quite a few things, it turns out."

"Oh?"

But his gaze settled at some point beyond her. Well. Whatever was more important must have to do with this mysterious discussion he refused to have in the middle of the dance floor. He guided her through the steps of the dance with practiced ease until she felt as if she were hovering several inches above the floor. This was not dancing; it was floating. On every turn, her stomach tripped over itself.

It was nothing more than a waltz. Meaningless. The buoyancy that lifted her heels on every step had nothing to do with the hand planted at her waist, the fingers flexing into every pivot. Those strong fingers, calloused from the constant rubbing of reins, capable of controlling the most hot-blooded of horses, burned through the layers of her ball gown and stays. And his thighs, powerful from years in the saddle, brushed against hers through her skirts. She should not allow herself to think of such things. This was Benedict, steady and dependable, not one of her suitors.

Suppressing a sigh, she tried again. "I had no idea you danced so well. How is it we've never waltzed before?"

He winked. "You've never twisted my arm into it before."

"I twisted? As I recall, this was your idea."

"Perhaps I ought to have ideas a bit more often." His words slipped out easily.

For a moment, Julia was dumbfounded. That sounded rather roguish. "Who are you practicing for?"

"I beg your pardon?"

"You're practicing your flirting on me." Once again, she tapped him with her fan. "I shall not allow it unless you confess immediately who you intend to pursue."

He grinned maddeningly at her. "Then I suppose I shall have to remain woefully out of practice. A gentleman never tells. But if I remain forever a bachelor, I shall lay the blame at your feet."

Out of the corner of her eye, she caught a glimpse of Sophia dancing with Ludlowe. With their matched coloring, they turned heads all about the room. Sophia absolutely bloomed in his arms, the very portrait of an utterly smitten young woman.

Smitten indeed. Julia had vowed never to allow such tender feelings to overtake her. They made her anxious and edgy. Vulnerable. Her fingers curled about her fan until its delicate ribs threatened to snap. She'd witnessed too many others ensnared by what they termed love to aspire to anything more than a civilized, sensible union.

She concentrated on keeping up with Benedict. But for the occasions when he came home on leave, the past few years he'd spent with the cavalry had prevented her from enjoying his company at the *ton*'s events. To think she'd missed dancing such as this, when she hadn't even known it possible.

At long last, the music swelled toward the coda. He leaned down to mutter next to her ear, "I'll be out on the terrace in five minutes."

Heart still thudding, she slipped out of his arms, only to collide with something soft.

"Careful now." Lord Chuddleigh caught her in an enthusiastic grip.

Blast it all. She cast a glance about for Benedict, but the crowd had already swallowed him. Why couldn't he have said his piece now, rather than playing games? Surely, they could have found a quiet corner away from overzealous ears.

She pressed her fingers to her temple. "Your pardon, my lord. I'm afraid I'm not feeling at all well. If you'll excuse me."

With that, she wove her way through the crowd in the general direction of the ladies' retiring room. Just before stepping into the corridor, she glanced over her shoulder.

Fan a-flutter and rosy with excitement, Sophia still chatted with Ludlowe. Thank the heavens. Perhaps something good would come out of this evening, after all.

Five minutes later, Julia found herself second-guessing that prediction. Benedict led her into a quiet corner of the garden far from prying eyes.

"I want you to stay away from Ludlowe," he said in a harsh voice and without preamble.

A shiver prickled along the back of her neck. Never once had he seen fit to give her orders, as if she were one of his men. In the darkness, half his face lay in shadow so that he appeared as some creature of the night.

Puzzled, she frowned. "But why does it matter? It's not as if he makes a habit of attending these things. He's made a career of avoiding marriage." Unfortunately for Sophia and her hopes.

"He's about to inherit an earldom. His priorities have changed."

"It hardly signifies. Besides, we've managed to arrange things so he's spending time with Sophia."

Benedict stepped closer to her and placed his hands on her upper arms. The heat of his palms permeated his gloves and seared into her bare skin.

"He hasn't got his sights set on Sophia. He's set them on you."

CHAPTER TWO

Ever since her first season, Sophia had dreamed of this night. William Ludlowe had actually asked her to dance. She didn't count the first time, although that had been a waltz, because Julia had practically pushed him into her arms.

A reel, of course, was less romantic and hardly conducive to conversation, but no matter. The second time, his invitation had come without a prompt.

The jaunty tune wound to a close, and Sophia's heart thudded in her chest. Under the cover of her fluttering silk skirts, she crossed her fingers in a silent plea for him to remain by her side.

As she straightened from her low curtsey, she smiled and snapped out her fan. "Gracious, that was vigorous." With any luck, he'd take the hint and offer refreshment.

"It was." His elbow angled toward her, and she laid her hand on it, her fingers tingling beneath white gloves, as he led her off to the side. "I say, I haven't seen your sister for a good while now."

Sophia's smile wavered. Why should he care about her sister? "I've no idea how anyone can keep track of a single person in such a crowd."

Besides Mama, who, even now, watched Sophia through narrowed eyes. Assessing as always, calculating the chances along with the potential income. Perhaps the

news about Ludlowe had already reached Mama's ears.
For once, Sophia was on Mama's side.

"You'd think we'd have seen her on the dance floor
before now," Ludlowe went on. "You do not think she's
fallen in with the wrong sort, do you?"

Sophia wafted her fan before her heated face. "What
sort is that?"

"Why, the sort to lure her out into a secluded corner
of the gardens."

"She has more sense than to do such a thing. She val-
ues her reputation too much." She didn't have a choice
there. Neither, for that matter, did Sophia. Not when,
as their mother constantly reminded them, the St. Claire
family had fought for years to attain its current social
status, and even then they remained firmly on the
fringes of the *ton*. A title in the family would go a long
way to solidifying their position.

An odd, almost possessive gleam came into his eye.
"Yes, she does, doesn't she?"

Sophia's fan continued to flutter with barely a hitch.
Thank goodness. She feared her smile, however, had
become rigid. Her cheeks certainly ached with the effort of masking her disappointment with a cheerful appearance. When would she learn?

"Of course, if you're really that concerned, we might
take a turn on the terrace ourselves. See if we can't spot
her." She kept her gaze fixed firmly on the corner where
her mother stood on the edge of a circle of other society
matrons, in the hopes that the view would prevent the
color from rising in her cheeks. Such a bold proposal,
but after five seasons of nurturing a fruitless *tendre* for
Ludlowe, her desperation had reached its limit.

Ludlowe stiffened. "My dear Miss St. Claire."

"Yes?" *Please agree. Please.* She turned toward him,
peeping reluctantly over the fraying lace that edged
her fan.

"My dear," he repeated, and her pulse raced ahead of her rational thought. "I'd never dream of putting a lady of your standing in such a position."

She ducked her head, as shame heated her cheeks. "Forgive me. My suggestion was rather forward. I don't know what I was thinking."

Once more, she glanced in her mother's direction. Slender, her skin still a flawless porcelain, Mama had bequeathed her beauty to her elder daughter. A smile lingered about her lips. Wonderful. Now her mother believed something might be afoot, something that would, at long last, press the reluctant Sophia in the direction of matrimony.

If only. She would sell her soul for the chance to marry William Ludlowe. He'd come to her rescue in her first season, when several other girls had disparaged her mother's more humble origins. He'd overlooked them all and escorted her to dinner. Her. The looks of jealousy and disbelief on the other girls' faces had made their ridicule worth the pain. On several other occasions he'd smiled, winked, shared a joke with her. He had a gift, it seemed, for sensing when her spirits needed a lift.

In five years, her feelings toward him hadn't changed, to the point where she'd refused several advantageous offers.

His gaze softened. "Your suggestion was quite sound, as long as you do not accompany me."

With that simple pronouncement, her racing heart turned to lead and plummeted. "Oh. Oh, of course."

Full lips stretched into a dazzling smile that showed off a perfect row of even, white teeth. That smile set many a lady's heart to pounding. Sophia's flopped back into its usual position and began a hopeful patter. He reached for her hand, and the patter accelerated.

Bending at the waist, he brushed his lips across the

back of her glove. Lucky, lucky glove. "Never fear. I shall see to your sister's safe return."

Before he could turn away fully, someone pressed against Sophia and elbowed her way next to Ludlowe. "My goodness, what a crush."

The newcomer, a dark-haired beauty, turned a bright smile on Ludlowe. Her white gown hugged generous curves. A heavy cloud of cloying floral scent assaulted Sophia's nostrils.

Ludlowe returned the lady's smile with a lazy bow of his lips.

Sophia frowned. On other occasions, she'd been the object of that smile.

"Indeed," Ludlowe said. "And how are you enjoying the evening's festivities?"

The newcomer flapped her fan, wafting another cloud of scent in Sophia's direction. "I might find them more diverting if my dance card were fuller."

Gracious. Such a brazen hint. Worse, Ludlowe didn't seem to notice anything amiss about her behavior. Sophia took in her dark head of curls and her wide, brown eyes. Something familiar about her. Ah, yes. Lady Whitby's niece—Eleanor, that was her name. Gossip pinned her as betrothed to Lord Keaton's heir, minor enough in his own right, but well connected through his mother's side of the family. Eleanor had no business flirting with William.

And flirting she was. She leaned her head toward him, and he inclined his head right back. She took a step toward the wide double doors that led to the hall, and he followed. Sophia wasn't about to stand for it. As they inched away, she moved right along with them, wincing when her foot crushed something soft and yielding.

A heavyset baronet let out a yelp.

"I do beg your pardon, sir."

The man pulled out a quizzing glass, the better to inspect her. "I should say so. You young chits these days, always in a hurry. If you'd learn to watch where you were going, these things might not happen."

Blushing, she inclined her head. "I shall endeavor to follow your advice in the future."

"Hmph. See that you do."

By the time she'd finished apologizing, her quarry had disappeared. Drat.

As much as Sophia was loath to admit it, Eleanor had been right about one thing. The Posselthwaite ball *was* an absolute crush. Various scents vied with each other amid the smell of perspiring bodies. A point behind her right eye began an ominous pulse.

What she wouldn't give for a breath of clear air. A cool draft drifted in from the hallway, and she followed it. A few steps farther on, she wished she hadn't. Eleanor and William stood just ahead, partially concealed in an alcove.

What was he doing? Didn't he know she was betrothed?

"I say," she called out. "I don't suppose you've heard the latest." Not the most original interruption, perhaps, but at a pinch, it would have to do.

Eleanor turned and eyed her from head to toe, as if Sophia were some urchin on Bond Street. In another moment, the brunette might look down to make sure she still carried her reticule. "Have we been introduced?"

Face aflame, Sophia pulled up short. Naturally they had. And William simply stood there, smiling benignly, as if that hussy hadn't stopped just shy of giving her the cut direct. He might say something, might cover the moment.

Not this time. This time, he was all too happy to let her twist in the wind. She searched for something, anything, she might say to save face. Not a thing came to her. Nothing beyond a lungful of that strumpet's awful, awful perfume.

He leaned in close and said something straight into Eleanor's ear, his lips forming words that caused her to giggle and simper behind her fan.

Sophia's stomach did an uncomfortable flip that set its contents to churning. The air in the hallway turned stuffy, sending a cold trickle of sweat between her shoulder blades. Her fan was of no use. She needed the ladies' retiring room.

She backed along the corridor—away from William and his latest distraction. A glance revealed them still conversing. The girl threw back her head and let out a peal of laughter. *Ee-ee-eeee.* Like the drawn-out call of a particularly annoying kestrel.

In a whirl of ice-blue silk, Sophia forged ahead, and ran smack into another obstacle—a soft, spongy obstacle. "I do beg your pardon."

A mass of curls and purple bombazine quivered in her path. Lady Wexford, one of Mama's acquaintances, or more accurately, a lady whose friendship Mama had sought to cultivate. The woman's frown set her numerous chins to trembling.

"Oh dear," Sophia whispered. Nothing more would come out. Her stomach seemed to be blocking her throat.

Lady Wexford's opinion might well decide whether or not the St. Claire family received any future invitations. She held enough social power to have their Almack's vouchers revoked.

The heat in the corridor pressed down on Sophia until she struggled to draw in air, but the only breath she caught carried that scent. She tried to blink the spots from before her eyes, but they grew until they consumed her entire field of vision. Not now, of all times! In the next moment, everything went black.

* * *

"Miss, miss . . . Is everything all right?"

Sophia wrinkled her nose and coughed at the assault of ammonia fumes beneath her nostrils. A low snarl of masculine voices, terse, coiled with tension and punctuated with curses, invaded her mind. That couldn't be right. No gentleman would dream of using such language in the presence of a lady.

She shook the lingering cobwebs from her mind. At least the air here was clear. Not the slightest hint of floral scent, thank goodness.

"Sir, I believe she's coming round."

At that pronouncement, the men broke off abruptly, but the heaviness in the atmosphere remained, a low storm cloud on the horizon. Neither voice sounded completely familiar.

"Where—," she began.

A hand took hold of hers and patted enthusiastically against her glove. "Don't ye leave us again now."

The uncultured accent betrayed the female voice as that of a servant. Sophia opened her eyes, and her suspicions were confirmed. A mobcapped girl of about eighteen hovered over her. Somehow she'd been spirited into a drawing room. The silk-covered cushions of a stiff-backed settee supported her shoulders and feet.

She pushed herself up on one elbow. "How—" Her head swam, and she sank back onto the pillow.

"I would not get up too quickly if I were you."

She blinked at the man who had spoken. His deep, resonant voice washed over her in soothing tones. The lines at the corners of his dark eyes were deeply etched. Neatly trimmed brown hair showed hints of gray at the temples.

"I beg your pardon if I've inconvenienced you in any

way." She paused. "Forgive me. Have we been introduced?"

He sketched a stiff bow. "You will forgive my forwardness if I introduce myself. Rufus Frederick Shelburne at your service."

Sophia drew in a breath, and a hint of sandalwood cut through the lingering odor of ammonia. "My lord."

Her glance settled on a thin scar that bisected his left cheek from ear to chin. Everyone in society knew how the Earl of Highgate had come by his wound, just as everyone knew he preferred to keep to his country estates. She stopped just short of embarrassing herself by blurting out an inconsiderate question.

"You, of course, are Miss Sophia St. Claire."

She snapped her gaze back to meet his. Unwavering brown eyes regarded her solemnly. The measure of sadness filling their depths awakened a sudden urge to smooth the lines on his forehead with her fingertips.

She curled her hand into a fist. "How did you know?"

"My sister is an acquaintance of your mother's, and she pointed you out to me." His voice rumbled over her, the kindness in his tone at odds with his ravaged face and the snippet of masculine conversation she'd just overheard. If, indeed, she had overheard it. Perhaps the presence of another had been a figment of her imagination.

"I see." She didn't. Not at all, but she couldn't ask what he was doing at Lady Posselthwaite's ball without appearing rude—or overly interested. Unmarried gentlemen didn't often attend these events unless they were in the market for a wife.

A sharp image leapt into her mind, and she straightened. William was in attendance. He'd danced. Of course, he usually put in an appearance, but soon he'd hold the responsibility of a title. Her heart skipped ahead of itself until she fought to draw breath. William was in the market for a wife.

As if her thought had summoned him, William's perfectly sculpted face floated into view. She placed her hand over her suddenly racing heart, while heat crept up her cheeks.

"Goodness." She swallowed. "My goodness, you came to my rescue when I fainted, didn't you? I don't know how I could possibly thank you."

"Ever a pleasure." He placed a hand on his chest and bowed.

Highgate fixed him with a weighty stare. "You mean to—"

But William went on as if no one had interrupted. "You look as if you'll manage from here. We sent the ladies to fetch your mother, but they don't seem to have found her yet." He snapped his fingers at the maid.

"Begging your pardon, sir." The girl bobbed a curtsey.

"Go and summon Mrs. St. Claire immediately."

"She cannot leave us alone!" Sophia burst in. "It's unseemly."

One side of William's mouth raised in a half smile, but he gave no reply. Instead, he leaned toward the girl and murmured something too low for Sophia to catch. The servant's head ducked once again, and, color rising in her cheeks, she darted out the door.

"Here, now. What do you think you're about?" Highgate spit each word, his voice shaking slightly as if he'd rather use far franker language. "Do you mean to take all the credit?"

William grinned, but the line of his jaw betrayed a tension, as if his teeth were grinding together. "If you'll excuse me, perhaps I ought to try to find your sister. If I'm quick about it, there's no harm done."

With a bow, he swept out after the maid.

Stunned, Sophia stared at Highgate. Could she trust

him? She'd never heard the least insinuation that Highgate was a rake. Quite the opposite, in fact. And William! Why on earth would he have contrived to leave the pair of them alone?

"What have you done?" she gasped.

"What have I done? It's all on that bounder." Brows lowered, he lurched in the direction of the doorway. But then he glanced at her and paused. "Are you sure you're feeling quite the thing? You look pale."

"I'm not about to faint again, if that's what you're hoping," she replied, unable to keep the tartness out of her tone. The man must think her the greenest girl in London. "Goodness only knows what might happen next."

One heavy eyebrow arched above his left eye. "At my age? A young miss like you?"

At his age, indeed. She could not recall any gossip pinning a precise age on him, but he had to be closer to forty than thirty. Yet his gaze traveled over her figure in slow appraisal. A blush raced back to her cheeks. Had she thought him kind? She would not make that mistake twice.

She fixed him with a glare. "I hardly think it proper you remain here with me, my lord. I assure you I'm quite well enough to be left alone."

"And risk the vagaries of whoever might venture into this room next? Perish the thought. You might find yourself in the presence of a true debaucher." A line formed between his brows. "Like Ludlowe."

She struggled to her feet. "Sir, you are impertinent!"

Highgate crossed his arms and tilted his head slightly. She didn't like his assessing look, not one bit. It saw too much; it laid her bare. "Nursing a *tendre* for the man, are you?"

"That is none of your affair. Now, if you'll excuse me—"

She made to step around him, but his hand shot out and pinned her wrist. "Do not waste your life pining after the likes of Ludlowe. He'd break you within a year."

She tugged at her arm, but his grip held firm as an iron band. She wanted out of this room, away from his disturbing perception. As a stranger, he had no business looking into her heart and divining all her private desires and fears.

More than that, he had no business holding her gaze with such unfathomable eyes. She couldn't miss them—they lay on a level with hers.

Only William had a right to capture her attention like this. Except by now William was probably out on the terrace with Eleanor, darling Eleanor, that strumpet, all thought of finding Julia conveniently laid aside.

Sudden tears welled in her eyes, and she blinked, breaking the spell. Long fingers uncurled from about her wrist, but somehow an impression remained on her skin. She suppressed the urge to rub the spot, as if she could brush away his touch.

"If you'll excuse me," she murmured. The point behind her right eye had begun to pound. Fruitlessly, she pressed the heel of her hand to it. She wanted nothing more than to go home and forget this night had ever happened.

He inclined his head, and she scurried toward the corridor. On the threshold, she came face-to-face with her mother.

Mama reached out and rubbed a hand along her arm. "Sophia, dear—"

With a glance beyond Sophia's shoulder, Mama stopped short. She gaped for a moment or two, before the fine line between her eyebrows sketched itself more deeply. "What is the meaning of this?" she hissed. "How long have you been alone with this man?"

"I was not alone," Sophia protested. "Not completely. Mr. Ludlowe sent a maid to fetch you, but beyond that, both he and the maid were with us the entire time."

Behind her, Highgate heaved a sigh, then came to stand at her shoulder. "Madam, the fault is entirely my own."

Mama's nostrils flared as she looked him up and down.

"Ludlowe thought it best to inform Miss St. Claire's family of her malaise. But he left us rather abruptly, or I would have withdrawn at the same time."

Mama's jaw firmed. "You ought to have at any rate. You've given no regard to the consequences."

"On the contrary. As long as nobody else learns of this, there is little chance of damage to Miss St. Claire's reputation."

Splendid. Sophia leapt on the idea. "Mama, no one knows of this but us. I'm sure we can count on Lord Highgate's discretion as a gentleman. What harm has been done here?"

Pale blond curls softening to a silvery gray quivered as Mama drew herself up. At her fullest height, she was nearly as tall as Sophia—and Highgate. "Plenty, if word should get out. Do not forget the maid, who saw fit to inform me of your whereabouts in front of Lady Whitby. You're fortunate I was able to convince the shrew her presence was not required here. But as things stand . . ."

Mama let her voice trail off into menacing silence. Sophia well understood its import. What Lady Whitby couldn't gather as fodder for gossip, she'd willingly invent.

Sophia's head spun, and her knees turned to rubber, as she fought off insensibility for the second time that evening. All she needed was to swoon into Highgate's arms in front of the wrong witnesses, and they'd find themselves exchanging vows under special license within a week.

The entire corridor, awash in the portraits of generations of Posselthwaites, swam before her eyes. Her hands turned to ice. "Mama, I do not think—"

"Miss St. Claire, are you certain you're feeling quite the thing?" Highgate's voice seemed to reverberate along the empty hall. "You've gone pale."

"I should like to go home now." She forced the words past the constriction in her throat.

"I shall send for my carriage at once."

Her hand fluttered in an ineffectual attempt to wave Highgate off. "No, not—"

Ee-ee-eeee.

The distinctive laugh cut off her refusal. At the far end of the hall, the faces of two new arrivals blurred. William and the strumpet. Why had he brought her back to witness Sophia's downfall?

The floor beneath her feet heaved. Not again! In spite of her efforts, the corridor constricted to a tiny point, and for the second time in an hour, she fainted.

"REALLY." Rufus's sister, better known to society as Lady Wexford, approached from behind Mrs. St. Claire. "Two spells in one night? That's rather much."

He shifted his weight, the better to support Miss St. Claire's limp body. After all, it would hardly do to let a young lady of quality slump to the floor, most especially while wearing such a fine ball gown. At least, that was what his sister would tell him.

Mariah was a stickler for the finest points of protocol. She'd happily spent all thirty-seven years of his life terrorizing him on such matters until they were drilled into his being. He'd always thought their father would have made a sound investment in buying her a commission—preferably in India.

Said sister now advanced along the corridor, rather like an Indian elephant, less the trunk, of course. Cloaked in disapproval, she came to stand beside Mrs. St. Claire.

"Rather than tutting over this turn of events, you might lend a hand." He shifted Miss St. Claire in his arms, and soft curves pressed into his chest. If his sister divined the direction of his thoughts, she'd berate him for that, too. "Ring for a footman, carry her off yourself."

Mariah's lips disappeared entirely as she pressed her mouth into a rigid line. "I would not make light if I were you."

"I say, what seems to have happened?"

He jerked his head up to find Ludlowe strolling toward them, a woman on his arm. Capital. Just like the man to return to gloat. Hadn't the bastard done enough damage? The evening just kept getting better and better.

Ludlowe craned his neck to peer at them. "Why, that's Miss St. Claire."

Rufus barely spared him a glance. "Perceptive of you."

Ludlowe's companion let out an awful trill of laughter. Rufus narrowed his eyes. He'd spent ten years avoiding Town and most especially the season, but if he knew Ludlowe, this dark-haired beauty, whose low-cut white gown set her assets on display, was no doubt the wayward wife of some peer or other. Mariah could certainly tell him which peer, should he care to ask.

"You might make yourself useful and call for the St. Claires' carriage," Rufus added.

"Highgate!" His sister's tone took on a low note of warning. "This is a highly serious matter."

He suppressed a sigh. *Only among ninnies.*

"Indeed it is." Mrs. St. Claire nodded slowly. "He has

compromised my daughter. As soon as Mr. St. Claire hears of this, he shall demand satisfaction."

Rufus stiffened at the implication. "I hardly think there's any call to take matters quite so far."

Mariah turned her imperious gaze on Mrs. St. Claire. "Compromised? I refuse to believe it."

Mrs. St. Claire jabbed a finger at Rufus's forehead. "Then explain to me how I came upon the two of them alone."

Rufus glared at Ludlowe, who was whispering behind his hand. His companion giggled. What was his game? If anybody in this corridor was apt to compromise marriageable misses, it was that beef-witted bastard.

"We weren't alone," Rufus protested. "Not entirely." He nodded to his sister. "You witnessed Miss St. Claire's fainting spell. You know Ludlowe, here, assisted me."

"Mr. Ludlowe was no longer here when I arrived," Mrs. St. Claire insisted.

"He'd only just stepped out." If he'd had a hand free, Rufus would have pressed it to his forehead. He was going to have to break down and appeal to a cad's sense of honor. "Ludlowe, why don't you tell her?"

The man had developed a great interest in his fingernails. Filthy hypocrite. "I honestly cannot recall how long it took me to return here after a fruitless search for Miss Julia. Horrid crush as usual. Impossible to get through."

"I still cannot believe it," Mariah interjected. "No, I will not have it. Of all people, my brother knows better than to embroil himself in such doings."

Mrs. St. Claire shot her an ugly look. "We did have to make our way back through the crowd. That took rather a long time."

The burden of the others' collective scrutiny weighed him down more than the girl in his arms. Ludlowe smirked knowingly, while his companion sniggered behind her fan.

An odd gleam shone in Mrs. St. Claire's eye. Triumph, perhaps? No doubt the woman was typical of the *ton*'s mothers, ever scheming to land her daughter the best possible match. Somehow Ludlowe must have guessed it. And now this particular mother was angling to entrap him. *Him*. He loosened his grip on the poor girl in his arms. No point in bruising her on top of everything else.

He avoided Town for this very reason—any vicious gossip could turn the least likely event into a scandal. Judging by Mariah's imperious expression, she was ready to turn the situation into an even greater spectacle, and there was Ludlowe's companion to consider. She practically glowed with excitement, as if she could not wait to pass on this juicy bit to all eager ears.

Mariah had badgered him into attending tonight's festivities so he could investigate the possibility of selecting a bride. If he didn't tread carefully now, he'd be forced to remarry—a complete stranger, no less.

Remarry! As if his first marriage hadn't been disastrous enough. Best to put an end to the spectacle now, before they drew a crowd.

"Well?" Mrs. St. Claire took a step forward, raising her chin. The gesture managed to make her appear taller. "What are you planning to do about this mess?"

"I daresay, madam, my first order of business is to see your daughter safely home," he drawled. To the devil with the lot of them. They obviously cared more for propriety than for the health of the poor girl lying limp in his arms. "She is quite apparently in no condition to enjoy the rest of the ball. Shall I send a footman for your carriage? Or perhaps you'd rather we did this up right, and I'll see her home myself."

Both Mrs. St. Claire and Mariah inhaled sharply at

that statement. Feathers, ruffles, chins, all trembled. The air around them expanded with the heat of their indignation. Ludlowe's companion let out another high-pitched twitter.

Rufus shifted his burden, drawing that delicious body more closely against him, and held up his hand. "I will, of course, call on Miss St. Claire tomorrow at the earliest possible convenience."

CHAPTER THREE

"Oh, Julia, it was perfectly dreadful." The bed ropes creaked as Sophia sank to the mattress to sit next to her sister. Julia had returned from the ball to find a red-nosed Sophia already in her night rail, blond curls straggling, dabbing at her eyes with a lace-edged handkerchief.

Julia shifted sideways and pulled Sophia into a warm hug. "There, there."

How many times over the last five years had she repeated those very words, in this very room, still decorated in the pastels more appropriate for schoolgirls than grown ladies? Certainly enough to convince her of their uselessness. But her heart ached for Sophia, and the simple words, like an oft-repeated litany, seemed to lend comfort.

Sophia sniffed against the pale silk of Julia's ball gown. "I haven't told you the worst. Mama claims I've been compromised."

Julia's hand froze, halfway to her sister's hair. "What?"

"I fainted, you see." Sophia's cheeks reddened, and she kept her gaze pinned on her handkerchief. "That . . . that awful woman was more than I could stand, and . . . Surely you must have heard something."

"Not a word."

"Really?" Sophia raised her head and dabbed at her swollen nose. "Perhaps it will not be as bad as Mama thinks. If it's kept quiet, there cannot be a scandal, and everything will be fine."

Julia tamped down the urge to sigh. Her sister was ever constructing castles in the air, the largest a monument to William Ludlowe that rivaled Windsor in size. "I must admit I wasn't in much of a position to hear any gossip."

Sophia lowered her handkerchief and arched a pale blond brow. "Where were you then?"

"On the terrace." The second brow joined the first, and Julia hastened to add, "With Benedict."

Sophia threw herself back into the pile of goose-feather pillows. "Only Benedict. Still, the terrace." She rolled to her side and propped her head on her elbow. "You must've been out there for quite a while."

"He had a good deal on his mind," Julia hedged.

"Like what?"

Blast her sister's curiosity. At least Julia had distracted her from her tears, but the truth would only release a new flood. She must dissemble, if only to spare her sister more pain. "Oh, the usual. He went on awhile about some horse he'd seen at Tattersall's."

"How utterly boring." Sophia's look sharpened. "Are you sure that's the truth?"

"Of course," Julia replied. Too fast.

Sophia's lips stretched into a grin. "If you ask me, there's more to it than that. Come now. I tell you everything. Can't you confide in me this once?"

"I confide in you all the time."

"Not when it comes to matters of the heart."

Julia released a breath. She had good reason to keep such things to herself. The subject inevitably led to Ludlowe, which, in turn, often led to upset. Most evenings, Julia preferred not to encourage her sister's *tendre*. Tonight, that went double. "Lord Chuddleigh made an utter nuisance of himself."

"Lord Chuddleigh indeed." Sophia ran her finger along the lace edging of the coverlet. "You know, Julia, the more you dance around the topic, the more I think you've got something to hide."

She did, but not anything she wished to confess to her sister. "Nothing where Benedict is concerned."

Her smile widening, Sophia pushed herself upright until she sat eye to eye with Julia. "I do not believe you. Benedict is in love with you."

"Oh, pish-posh." There Sophia went, building another of her fancies.

"He is."

Benedict? In love with her? Then Julia caught the glint in her sister's eye. "Stop. Why do you insist on teasing?"

"What makes you think I'm teasing?"

Julia stood and began loosening her gown. "Because I know Benedict, and if he is in love with anybody, it is most likely his horse."

"Haven't you ever imagined what you'd say if he proposed?"

Julia's gown pooled at her feet. "Of course I haven't."

The last thing she wanted was to set aside the suit of an old friend, but if what Sophia said were true, she'd have to do exactly that. If she married at all, she refused to do so based on the brittle frailty of sentiment.

She presented her back so Sophia could help unlace her stays. "At any rate, I shall never have to concern myself with a reply."

Because he'd never ask. Growing up on neighboring estates, they'd played together. Lord only knew they'd landed each other in enough trouble over the years. As a child, she could dare him to do anything, even jump from the high hayloft in his father's stables. He took her up on the challenges without question and to devil with the consequences. Later, after he'd left school and joined the cavalry, his occasional letters had recounted all manner of amusing anecdotes about the other members of his regiment. Hardly the stuff of passion, that.

"What a pity." Tone light, Sophia finished loosening Julia's stays and stepped back. "I happen to think he's perfect for you."

"Miss, you have a caller."

Julia studied Billings's stiff posture, compensating, no doubt, for yet another overenthusiastic bout of tasting the St. Claires' dwindling wine stores. From across the morning room, it was impossible to tell whether the old butler had addressed her or Sophia.

Next to her, Sophia shrank down in her seat. "Already?"

Her curiosity aroused, Julia sat straighter. Sophia? Dreading a caller? Whoever it was must have something to do with her mysterious claim she'd been compromised. Sophia, drat her, had been all too successful in her attempt to divert Julia's attention from the subject last night. "Who is it?"

Billings marched forward and presented a calling card on a tarnished salver. Red, spiderlike veins stood out on his overly prominent nose. Julia took the stiff vellum in hand. "Sophia, it's Ludlowe."

Sophia inched to the edge of the brocade chair, her hands fluttering about her face. "Oh my." She pinched at her cheeks. "Do I look all right?"

"Stop. You're already bright red. Do not make it worse." Julia hopped to her feet. "Show him in, Billings. I've suddenly recalled I left my embroidery in the library. I simply must get at it."

Billings paused mid-bow, wavering slightly as he straightened once more. "But miss, Mr. Ludlowe has requested to see you."

There was no denying it this time. Billings fixed watery blue eyes directly on her. From this distance, even his wire-rimmed spectacles couldn't hide the direction of his gaze.

Julia slanted a glance at her sister. In an instant, Sophia's complexion went from glowing to ashen.

"I've no idea what he could possibly want with me," Julia murmured for her sister's benefit. If there was anything to what Benedict had told her last night, she knew exactly what he wanted.

Marriage. With her.

The reason why he'd chosen her out of all the eligible young ladies of the *ton* remained a mystery—Benedict hadn't been exactly forthcoming on that score. Nor, for that matter, had he mentioned how he'd come by the information.

She sank back into her seat. "Very well. Show him in. And you stay right where you are," she added to Sophia. With any luck, she could contrive things to her sister's advantage yet.

A moment later, the butler ushered Ludlowe into the morning room. Julia straightened her back in an approximation of Billings's usual stance—officious and distant. She set her face in rigid, unwelcoming lines that she refused to soften, not even when Ludlowe favored her with a smile so dazzling, it drew a breathy sigh from Sophia.

"Miss Julia, how radiant you look this morning."

Ludlowe's blue eyes fixed solidly on her. She thought of the time she'd decided to eat a lemon and pursed her lips accordingly, a simple inclination of her head her only response.

His smile did not fade. If anything, it broadened into a grin, or perhaps a leer. Challenge accepted. Hang it all, that was the last thing she wanted.

"And Miss St. Claire." He nodded to Sophia. "I must say you look equally lovely."

Sophia positively glowed beneath the compliment. More than that, she blossomed. "How kind of you, my lord."

With a chuckle, he lowered himself into a mahogany chair, one hand braced on the silver knob of his ebony walking stick. "Now, now, none of that yet."

A rosy blush staining her cheeks, Sophia leaned toward him. "Shall I ring for tea?"

"Do not bother, my dear." Her lips parted on a gasp at the endearment. "I shall be but a moment."

"Then why have you come?" The coldness of Julia's tone bordered on rudeness, but she didn't care. How could he? How could he miss Sophia's obvious affection for him? She took no pains to hide it. She might as well lay her beating heart in his lap, and yet . . .

And yet, according to Benedict, he'd set his sights on Julia.

Ludlowe caught her eye. Objectively, Julia could point to his even, golden features, his clear blue eyes, his easy charm and state he was handsome. But his looks left her completely indifferent.

He smiled, and her heart continued its steady, even pulse. "I've come with a proposition for you."

Julia caught her breath. He couldn't possibly. Not so soon. Not in front of Sophia. The Bath buns she'd consumed at breakfast shifted uneasily in her stomach.

"Yes?" she grated. Experience had made her adept at putting off suitors who displayed overly large quantities of sentiment.

"I was wondering if you'd do me the honor . . ."

"The honor?" A welcoming smile brightening her features, Mama sailed into the room.

Julia twisted her ice-cold hands into the pale green

muslin of her morning gown. The last thing she needed was her mother's interference.

Ludlowe cleared his throat and rose to his feet. "Good day, Mrs. St. Claire. I was just asking your daughter if she'd care to come riding with me in the park. With your permission and a proper chaperone, of course."

Sophia let out a tiny whimper. Blast the man, couldn't he show a little tact?

"My goodness, I couldn't possibly," Julia blurted before her mother could intervene.

His eyes widened, and his nostrils flared. Julia bit back a smile. He hadn't counted on her turning him down. She was possibly the first woman in England ever to do so. "Tomorrow then," he said smoothly, "if you have an engagement?"

Mama pinned Julia with a pointed gaze. "She has no engagement that I'm aware of."

"But Mama." She cast a telling glance in Sophia's direction before turning to Ludlowe. "I'm dreadfully sorry, but horses make me sneeze."

He raised a tawny eyebrow. "They make you sneeze?"

She wanted to kick herself. Surely she could have come up with something more convincing. "Indeed. I'm sure Sophia would be delighted to accompany you on such an outing, but I fear I cannot."

"Perhaps a simple walk then?"

Julia pushed herself to her feet. Naturally, he wouldn't give up so easily.

"I trust *I* do not make you sneeze," he added.

She made a show of coughing. "I fear I may have caught a cold."

Mama glared at her. "What utter nonsense. You were perfectly healthy until this moment."

Ludlowe's smile indicated he knew just what she was up to. "I shall be honored to escort you on any other occasion of your choosing."

She looked him in the eye and firmed her chin. "I regret that I must decline."

Before he could utter a word of protest, her mother's hand clamped itself about her upper arm. "If you'll excuse us for but a moment, I require a word with my daughter."

Ludlowe bowed his head. "By all means."

Julia made no reply as Mama frog-marched her toward the door.

SOPHIA exhaled at the sight of her sister's retreating back. The sourness of acrimony burned through her veins. Of all women, why did Ludlowe have to choose Julia? And Mama's encouragement was another betrayal. Now he'd decided to seek a wife, it was unfair of him to overlook her. Dash it all, she'd been waiting for him ever since her first season. Her own experience had proven him an inveterate flirt. How could he overlook her open response?

He cleared his throat and shifted his weight forward. No. She would not let him take his leave. Julia had made her lack of interest clear. Now he could deuced well consider the girl sitting directly under his flawless, straight nose.

She pasted a smile on her face. "Shall I ring for tea?"

"No, thank you."

Drat, she'd already offered tea, hadn't she? And he'd turned it down the first time.

But then, after five long years, God smiled on Sophia and produced a miracle. Rather than rising to take his leave, Ludlowe rested his back against the carved flourishes of his chair and cast her an assessing look. "It occurs to me, now that I'm here, there's a matter we ought to discuss."

She straightened and folded her hands in her lap, the epitome of a demure, marriageable miss. Mama would be proud, if only she weren't currently occupied with Julia in the doorway. Suddenly coated in perspiration, her palms slid against each other. "Yes?"

"You'll pardon me if this is none of my affair, but I cannot stand by and allow such a lovely young lady to throw herself away on the likes of Highgate."

At *lovely,* her cheeks heated, but then the remainder of his comment sank in. "But—I've done no such thing."

How dare he question her actions when the entire situation was his fault? He'd left them alone so he could run off and answer the siren call of that strumpet.

"That isn't how things looked last night."

She opened her mouth to protest, but he held up his hand. "You were in a swoon for a good deal of the conversation, so you cannot know what was said. Your mother has all but sealed your marriage contract."

She clutched at the simple pendant that hung from a gold chain about her neck, while her breakfast threatened to put in a reappearance. With difficulty, she swallowed the obstruction in her throat and fought to maintain her composure.

"Fortunately, such are things of the past." To her own ears, her voice sounded thin, but at least she'd managed to quell its shaking.

"You may have no choice in the matter, should Highgate make an offer."

Her backbone went rigid. "His would not be the first proposal I've refused."

"You'd have done well not to put yourself into that position in the first place."

The hand on her pendant trembled, and she tightened her fist. "*I*'ve put myself in no position, as you are quite aware. You were there. You know nothing untoward happened."

"Indeed I do." His voice rolled over her, smooth as honey, just as sweet and slightly sticky. "But it is very difficult to stem the tide of gossip and scandal once it begins."

"Yet it can be stopped with the truth."

He regarded her for a long moment, his expression inscrutable. "I shall endeavor to do what I can. You may count on that."

She dropped her hands into her lap and folded them. "Thank you."

"Be that as it may, I'd tread carefully, if I were you."

She twisted her fingers together. "Pray, what is that supposed to mean?"

"I suppose you're too young to have heard the rumors." His gaze raked over her, but his eyes remained steady and cold. "Yes, you'd still have been in the schoolroom."

She forced herself to meet his gaze, even though it chilled her. Why couldn't those vivid blue eyes soften a bit and twinkle with warmth? "What rumors?"

"You certainly can't have missed the scar on the man's face."

"What of it?"

"He claims to have come by it in the accident that killed his first wife."

"So all of society says." She waved a hand. "But you do not believe that?"

He leaned forward, and his walking stick hit the floor with a crack as he repositioned it. "I've heard more than one rumor where Highgate is concerned."

She blinked. "The *ton* is full of rumors and gossip."

"Indeed. Only some hold more than a grain of truth." He pressed to his feet. "His wife is dead under horrific circumstances, and he's holed himself away at his country estate, long past the accepted mourning period. Whatever his involvement in the affair, I daresay it cannot be anything good."

* * *

CLUTCHING Julia's upper arm in a death grip, Mama halted at the very limit of propriety—just inside the door to the morning room—and grated, "What do you think you're doing?"

Julia cast a glance in Ludlowe's direction. "Discouraging some unwanted attention."

Mama raised her chin, and the sunlight filtering in through the windows glinted off her carefully curled silver-blond hair. "You're hardly in a position to discourage attention at your age. Between you and your sister, I do not know which of you is worse, refusing perfectly good matches. And now there's to be a scandal. Do you realize Sophia was caught alone with a man last night?"

Julia folded her arms beneath her breasts. "Which man was that?"

"Didn't she tell you about it? Too ashamed, I suppose."

"Ashamed? Why?"

A grim smile pulled at Mama's lips. "I ought to be grateful. At least we'll have one of you properly settled. Now go back and entertain your guest. I'll not have you embarrass your father and me with your boorish behavior."

"Mama, it's Ludlowe. He came to call on me. *Me*. And you want me to go sailing back over there, knowing how Sophia feels about him, and bat my eyelashes as if I'm delighted to catch his eye?"

"Just so."

"Mama!"

Mama stepped closer and lowered her voice. "Your sister's feelings in this matter do not signify."

"How can you say that?"

"Due to her behavior last night at the Posselthwaite ball, it can no longer be helped. She can never be for

Ludlowe. He would not have her now. Gracious, he witnessed it himself."

"Witnessed what, exactly?"

Julia could not credit her mother's story. Sophia had always been careful to preserve her spotless reputation. For her, it was a simple enough matter—she was saving herself for Ludlowe, and if she couldn't have him, she'd happily live out the remainder of her life in spinsterhood.

Or perhaps not so happily.

For the last five years, Julia had watched her sister pine away for that man, witnessed the pain and tears when Sophia's hopes came to naught. Oh, she'd attempted to entertain the attentions of other men, but none of them had ever measured up in Sophia's mind. Bearing witness to that pain was enough to make any girl guard her heart against more tender feelings.

And when Julia considered the rest . . . If she accepted Ludlowe's attentions, she'd be adding to her sister's misery. As silly as her sister might sometimes be, she couldn't compound Sophia's hurt, whether or not she had been compromised.

"No matter now." Mama nodded decisively. "What's done is done. But if Mr. Ludlowe is interested in you, then, by gracious, you will go back in there and behave in a manner that befits your station. Surely you've heard the rumors." She leaned in, as if to deliver the juiciest tidbit of gossip. "This is your chance to become a countess."

"I'm not particularly interested in becoming a countess."

Two red blotches spread over Mama's flawless cheeks, and she opened her mouth to retort. Julia braced herself for the familiar verbal barrage. Over the past several years, she'd had it badgered into her that a woman's place in society was key.

The beautiful daughter of a wealthy cit, Mama had had her chance at a title in her youth, only the Earl of Cheltenham's feet turned to ice, and he backed out of the arrangement. Mama had settled for Charles St. Claire, a mere mister too far removed from the aristocratic antecedents in his background to possess a title. Because of her lowborn status, Mama had borne the societal brunt of the scandal.

But that only proved her point. Position was everything, and she was determined that Sophia and Julia both attain the status she had never enjoyed.

A title was power. Julia could recite the line as a litany.

However, instead of delivering the expected assault, Mama pressed her lips together and held Julia's gaze. Her tone, when she spoke, was low and urgent. "I did not wish to worry you with the news, but it seems I have no choice."

A shiver raised the fine hairs on the back of Julia's neck. Anything that diverted Mama's single-minded attempts to convince her daughters to wed couldn't be good. "What news?"

"Your father—" With a quick glance about, she took a step closer.

The shiver turned to an outright chill. "What now?"

"He's lost a significant sum recently."

Julia swallowed, while her fingers contracted into a fist. "Again?"

"Yes, again! He'll have us bankrupt before the year is out, but if you were to accept Mr. Ludlowe's suit, you might save us."

"Why Mr. Ludlowe in particular? Why not just set me up on a block at the next ball and offer me to the highest bidder?"

"I will not have this impertinence." Though she kept her voice low, it still carried the force of her temper. "If it hadn't been for the pair of you being so blasted difficult, refusing perfectly good offers for years, we might not be in such a predicament."

Julia opened her mouth and closed it, unsure how to respond. Her mother had a point. Several years' worth of seasons and all they entailed—gowns, fans, bonnets, and a rented town house—had eroded the family's finances. Papa's attempts to replenish the coffers through his card play only added to the burden.

In the next moment, Ludlowe rose from his seat, saving her from having to reply. His walking stick tapping the bare floor, he glided over to bow over her mother's hand. "Good day, Mrs. St. Claire. Alas, I must leave you."

Mama beamed at him like a young lady at her first ball. "You must call again soon."

"I have every intention of doing so. Miss Julia, I do hope you'll reconsider."

Mama had the grace to wait until he had taken his leave before rounding on Julia. "The next time he calls, you will not decline. Do you understand me?"

An audible sniff came from behind. Julia gritted her teeth, turned on her heel, and went to console her sister.

CHAPTER FOUR

Benedict hadn't come to Town to become entangled in the doings of the *ton*. He most certainly hadn't expected to embroil himself with Julia's doings. Damn Ludlowe and his wagering.

With Hyde Park awash in the fashionable out to see and be seen, it was a blessing to escape the crowded paths to the point where Curzon Street faded into Boulton Row. Only a stone's throw from Berkeley Square, the St. Claires' rented town house strained toward the rarified air of more exclusive addresses.

Benedict patted Arthur's glossy chestnut neck and slowed the beast to a walk, though his true destination lay several streets beyond. Beneath his thighs, the horse's powerful muscles strained with the desire to gallop. The sound of iron-shod hooves clopping against the cobblestones echoed through the narrow lane. Arthur tossed his head, sending tendrils of his mane flying.

"Easy, boy. I know you're eager to have your head, but that'll have to wait until we find a place with more room to run."

They would not find it in London. Once he'd taken care of his business, he could retreat to his estate in Kent where Arthur might gallop for miles before they encountered another soul. In the meantime, they were stuck in Town. It was almost enough to make Benedict

wish he hadn't sold his commission several months after
Waterloo.

At the sight of the carriage standing in front of the
St. Claires' address, he tightened his hands on the reins.
He could guess easily enough to whom the conveyance
belonged.

"Ludlowe."

Like the devil himself appearing at the sound of his
name, Ludlowe emerged from the town house. Benedict
reined Arthur to a halt. Something about the future
Earl of Clivesden's gait told Benedict all he needed to
know. The man walked with the stiff-legged stride of
someone who had been refused.

And Ludlowe was not used to refusals. Most especially from a lady.

If Benedict had known with any assurance that Julia
could see him, he'd have tipped his hat to her. With a
grim smile, he wheeled his mount about, urging him
into a sprightly trot. Thank God, last night's warning
had been sufficient. As things stood, he was late for an
interview with a potential replacement for his delin-
quent estate manager. No time now for social calls.

The rumble of heavy wheels to his rear caused him to
spur Arthur to one side. Four blood bays, perfectly
matched down to the socks on their off hind legs and
the stars on their faces, clattered past, their coats glossy
in the watery sunlight. Apparently, Ludlowe had an eye
for flashy horseflesh.

Benedict pressed his lips together. He didn't want a
reason to admire someone who had so arrogantly wagered on Julia and put her reputation at stake. Not
when Benedict had experienced at Eton the sort of man
Ludlowe really was.

He chirruped to Arthur and set off down the row, his
mount's hooves clacking in sharp rhythm against the
cobblestones, as if he could outrun the memories of his

first year at school. Thank God for an older brother who had shielded him from the worst. To either side, houses pressed in, all but obliterating the sky and blocking any hint of a breeze, until the air in Town became stifling.

For the hundredth time, he questioned the wisdom of selling his commission. The war with Boney might be over, but the cavalry offered other opportunities to a young officer. Those opportunities would have taken him far from London, but they would also remove him from the wild pasturelands of the Kentish countryside.

On his return to Kent, he'd discovered his estate manager gone and the property nearly derelict. After seeing to the most pressing repairs, he'd put the stables in order and acquired a stud. Only a stud needed broodmares, and the best place to acquire good bloodstock was Tattersall's. He could have bought locally, but if he hadn't come back to Town, he might never have learned of Ludlowe's intentions in time to warn Julia.

He tightened his thighs on Arthur's flanks at the thought. The horse darted forward, into the wider thoroughfares of Mayfair, dodging carriages and passersby. A shout or two trailed after him, but he ignored the outraged protests.

This city was too crowded by half, but he might have to delay his departure to the estate his mother had bequeathed him, all because of Julia. Months ago, he'd returned from Belgium fully expecting to learn of her marriage or at the very least her betrothal. Yet at her age, she was still not only eligible but, according to gossip, firmly resisting any offers. After all these seasons. And why should he experience satisfaction at the notion?

He shook himself and spurred Arthur toward St. James Street. Her marital status was none of his affair. As long as she did not accept Ludlowe's suit. He'd only reacted out of protectiveness and a long-standing friendship.

And yet, when they waltzed last night, she moved with him so perfectly. His palms still warmed at the memory of touching her, even through the barrier of gloves and gown. He'd touched her before, of course. They'd run wild through the woods together as children, handing each other across streams, boosting each other up trees. He'd helped her regain her footing often enough when she tripped over her skirts trying to keep up with him.

But a waltz was different; a waltz was the next thing to an embrace. Good God, the dance had driven him to flirt with her. With Julia. And that, perhaps, was even a greater shock than returning from the war to find her unwed.

"What do you think of that parasol?" Julia pointed out a creation of peach silk, hand-painted with depictions of parrots and edged in peacock feathers. It dangled from the hand of a giggling young miss a few yards to the left.

Sophia barely glanced at it. "Lovely. Why don't you see if you can find one like it in the shops?"

"Because it's perfectly ghastly."

Besides, neither of them could afford any sort of new accessories. If only she'd seen her way clear to accepting Lord Brocklehurst's suit. She might have saved her family the expense of two years' worth of unwanted ball gowns. As with her other suitors, he'd been too attached for her comfort, too enthusiastic in his courtship. No man would pursue a young lady of no fortune and little enough connections unless he experienced true sentiment. And the depth of ardor in Brocklehurst's eyes had struck a fundamental fear within.

Sophia blinked. "Oh. I suppose it is."

With a sigh, Julia took her sister's arm. "We may as well go home."

A stroll through Hyde Park had done nothing to improve Sophia's spirits. She went through the motions of greeting the fashionable crowd, all the while drifting slowly from the main paths until she and Julia stood on a forsaken patch of grass.

She paled. "Must we?"

Julia leaned close. "I thought a constitutional might serve as a distraction, but it's obviously doing no good."

"Why, Julia? Why won't Ludlowe see me?"

A quick glance revealed several schoolgirls tossing bits of bread to the ducks along the banks of the Serpentine. A few young ladies strolled the paths, showing off the latest style of walking dress, while gentlemen on horseback attempted to steal their attention. None of them, however, were close enough to overhear anything Julia and Sophia might be discussing.

Julia looked hard at her sister. "If I might speak plainly, I cannot help but wonder why, after all these years, you still want him to."

Sophia's lower lip trembled. "Don't you think if I could stop feeling this way, I would?"

Julia tightened her fingers about her sister's arm. "Let's go home."

"No, not home."

She shook her head. "Whyever not?"

"I don't want—" Sophia's blue eyes focused on an object past Julia's shoulder. "Oh no!"

Turning her head, she followed the direction of her sister's gaze until Lady Wexford's frowning face came into view beyond the rim of her poke bonnet.

Sophia tensed further. "Drat, she's spotted us."

Julia swung her head back to her sister. "Why should it matter?"

"You have some nerve showing your face in public after last night." Lady Wexford's hiss of disapproval crashed over them both.

Firming her chin, Julia swiveled to meet the threat head-on. "What is the meaning of this?"

Lady Wexford surveyed Julia from head to toe and then nodded, a single jerk of her head. "It's no surprise she hasn't told you. Hardly a cause for pride, what she did last night. There are ways of capturing the attention of one's betters that do not result in one's social ruin."

The feathers on her bonnet rippled in righteous indignation as she stepped closer. "If you had any sense, young lady, you'd stay out of society until the matter is settled. Why your mother hasn't kept a tighter rein on either of you, I'll never know. She ought to have learned her proper place and taught it to you, as well."

Julia drew in a breath to respond, but Sophia's elbow in her ribs quite deflated the effort. "Please do not involve yourself," she muttered.

"What was that all about?" Julia asked, once Lady Wexford had taken herself off down the path.

"Not here." Sophia cast a worried glance about her. "Mama squawked so loudly there was never a hope of keeping things quiet. Suffice it to say Lady Wexford's connected with the reason Mama believes I'm compromised."

Together they pushed their way toward the perimeter of the park and the road home. Several smartly dressed ladies turned their heads in their wake. "Oh, and now they're looking," Sophia whispered. "They've heard, I know they have."

"Sophia, what connection does Lady Wexford have to the incident at the Posselthwaite ball?"

"She's his sister."

Julia halted in the middle of the path, causing the tide of the fashionable to break and flow around them. "Sister? The Earl of *Highgate* compromised you? Why didn't you tell me sooner?"

Despite his sister's acquaintance with her mother, she

knew only of Highgate's reputation, a reputation that painted him a recluse, rather than a rake.

"Hush," Sophia hissed, but her cheeks burned red. "Do you want them to gossip even more?"

"You know they're going to gossip, no matter what." Julia took her sister's arm and stepped toward the exit. "Lady Wexford certainly didn't help you out just now."

"It's silly. Nothing untoward went on, and it all might have blown over if Mama hadn't made such a fuss." Sophia twisted her hands in her skirts. "And in front of William, too." Ah, and perhaps therein lay Sophia's reticence to recount the story.

"Yes, it is ridiculous," Julia agreed. Her sister's affections for Ludlowe topped even the absurdity of the so-called scandal, but Julia wasn't about to point that out. She'd suggested the walk to take Sophia's mind off Ludlowe's behavior. "I'd go so far as to wager Mama put on a spectacle to manipulate the situation."

Sophia cast her a dark look. "She might have kept quiet. I do not understand her. All she cares for is one's influence on society. She thinks nothing of love, and yet she should remember from her own past. She had to give that up."

"She was jilted. Her earl could hardly have returned her sentiments if he threw her over." Besides, Julia wasn't completely convinced Mama didn't love her earl for his title over all else, but she knew that bringing up the subject would lead to a fruitless argument. Sophia held fast to her assurance that their mother had suffered from the same sort of unrequited *tendre* as she held for Ludlowe.

"Why can these things not work out?" Sophia's voice wobbled. Whatever beneficial effects their walk might have had on her outlook, they were about to be undone.

"I believe they can," Julia affirmed in hopes of staving off another upset.

"You do?"

"I do. Leave matters of the heart aside, and choose your husband from those you admire and respect."

Beneath the overhang of her bonnet, Sophia cast her eyes skyward. "The next thing you'll tell me is I ought to seek a civilized and sensible match."

"Just so."

"And do you truly believe such an arrangement will make you happy?"

Sophia had a point. Such an arrangement hadn't made Mama happy, but then neither had Sophia's infatuation with Ludlowe made *her* happy. Somewhere, amid all this turmoil of feelings and sentiment, there had to lie a middle ground. Julia suspected she'd discover it—in the corner of the ballroom with the other spinsters.

CHAPTER FIVE

Watery sunlight pierced the haze but contributed no warmth. Sophia pulled her pelisse tight against a raw wind that belonged to February rather than April. Its searching fingers penetrated even the town house's tiny garden.

Although spring seemed a distant promise, Sophia crouched to pluck away the previous year's growth. It was time to prepare for the coming summer. In any case, shivering among the rosebushes was preferable to waiting indoors, dreading Highgate's visit.

By rights, he should have paid his call yesterday instead of William. If she stayed out here long enough, patiently clipping dead branches and clearing off dried leaves, she might bring herself to believe Highgate would never come. And if he never turned up, perhaps the entire situation would conveniently disappear.

As if that would happen.

Her secateurs slipped. The sharp blade sliced through the leather of her glove and into the fleshy pad of her forefinger. Blinking back tears, she tugged off the glove and popped the digit into her mouth.

"Blast." Her mother would have fits to hear her utter such an unladylike word. "Damn and blast."

That felt even better—pity Mama couldn't overhear. It was *her* fault Sophia was in this predicament. If only

Mama had kept quiet, they might have hushed up the scandal.

No one could conjure any hope of that given Mama's determination to see her married to a title.

"Is that a China rose?" rumbled a deep voice. *That* voice.

Sophia raised reluctant eyes.

The Earl of Highgate leaned over to inspect the bush she'd been pruning. "Lovely specimen. Very rare, that."

He knelt beside her and snatched her discarded seca-teurs off the pea-stone path. With a few deft strokes, he removed most of the overgrowth.

"There, that's an improvement. They will not bloom properly if you leave all those old branches." He turned and caught her eye. "But I suspect you already knew that. It must be quite pleasant here in the summer, a peaceful little oasis amid the bustle of Town."

She slipped her finger from her mouth. "I'm not usually here past the end of June. We always attend as many house parties as Mama can wheedle invitations to."

He settled back on his heels. "Seems a shame to spend so much time tending roses you're not here to enjoy."

She twitched one shoulder upward in a casual shrug. "I like looking after them. It makes me feel useful."

"And now you've cut yourself."

She glanced down. The throbbing had dulled, but blood oozed in a steady trickle down the side of her finger. Highgate reached into his greatcoat and produced a handkerchief. Without a word, he took her hand in his and wrapped the scrap of fine linen around her wound.

Sturdy fingers closed over her palm. She stared at the deep tan of his glove, her white hand tiny in his.

Ludlowe had all but insinuated he'd raised that very hand against his own wife.

Out of the corner of her eye, she studied Highgate's weathered face. Even-featured, somewhat stern, with deep-set dark eyes and strands of gray in his hair, no one would ever describe him as handsome. Rugged, perhaps, but never handsome, not with that scar slicing across his cheek. A sense of calm radiated from him—or perhaps it was resignation—and when he spoke to her of such mundane topics as gardening, she had trouble picturing him as the sort of person who would commit violence against another.

He was doing her a kindness, applying gentle pressure to her cut—and sacrificing his handkerchief in the process. Even the other night at the ball, when she'd been a stranger to him, he'd shown concern for her welfare.

He seemed a nice enough gentleman, but, Lord help her, she wished he'd remained a stranger. Then Ludlowe might have called on her in all earnestness and not her sister. She tried to push aside the insistent thought that Ludlowe had been overly interested in Julia even before that disastrous fainting spell, but it kept cropping up like a tenacious nettle between paving stones.

Had Julia done something to attract Ludlowe's attention? A chill that had nothing to do with the weather spiked through her gut. No. Julia would never betray her like that.

"Why have you come?" she asked.

He blinked but did not release her hand.

"Forgive my lack of manners," she added quickly. "You've shown me a kindness on two different occasions."

"Perhaps I ought to quit while I'm ahead." Humor sparked in the depths of his dark eyes, and the lines at their corners deepened.

"What do you mean?"

One side of his mouth quirked upward. "Only that if I'd been a bit more coldhearted on that first occasion, you might not be in such a predicament."

"Oh." She slanted her eyes down to the side. Her

glance fell on their joined hands. "You mean you should have left me insensible on the floor?"

His chuckle somehow settled deep inside her. Warmth radiated through the leather of his glove and into her hand. How odd. "Quite selfish of me not to, wouldn't you agree?"

A smile caught at the corners of her mouth and pulled them up. She lifted her gaze to meet his. "I cannot blame you. You'd have had all the society matrons shouting at you for leaving an obstruction in the middle of the corridor."

His smile faded, and a strange sense of disappointment washed through her. If only he'd laugh again.

She couldn't recall the last time she'd laughed with a man for the sheer pleasure of it. She'd spent five years dodging potential suitors and worrying about whether she'd run into William, and if so, whether she'd possess the proper wit to capture his attention—so long she'd forgotten how to relax and enjoy herself.

She wished this occasion might have lasted a little longer.

"Instead, I managed things so my sister took her venom out on you." Bitterness infused his tone. "I owe you an apology for her words to you in the park yesterday."

"Her words? But how—"

"She made certain I learned of the incident. Brazen, I believe she termed you."

She focused on her fingers resting across his palm. Somehow he made *brazen* sound complimentary. "It was nothing."

"It was not, and well you know it." He drew in a breath. "You must know why I've come."

She tugged at her hand, but he tightened his grip. With a sigh, she gave up the struggle. "Pray, say your piece so I can refuse you, and we can have done with this farce."

"Miss St. Claire." His tone was so serious, it compelled her to meet his gaze. "You cannot refuse. You must understand that."

Again, she strained against his grasp. "Why can't I? Do you know how many proposals I've turned down?"

"None of them signify. You cannot refuse this one."

"Why?"

"Do you not realize the damage that has been done to your reputation? I do not trust Ludlowe's companion to keep the matter silent. If you refuse my proposal, you will never get another."

"Perhaps I do not want another." A lie, but a small one. The chances of Ludlowe falling to one knee to beg for her hand were fading as quickly as snowflakes in May. Even she could no longer deny that fact, not when he'd come calling on Julia.

Julia.

All these years she'd wasted on unrequited feelings for the man, and he'd set his sights on her sister. Bile filled her mouth, and she swallowed against its bitter taste.

She waved her free hand. "I'm nearly on the shelf as it is."

"By your own choice."

She shrugged. "I suppose so."

"How old are you?"

"Three and twenty."

"So young," he murmured, low enough that she had to strain to hear him. "I suppose it's natural you do not understand the ramifications."

Her breath caught on a gasp. How could she *not* understand the ramifications? To him, she might seem young, but that didn't make her a simpleton. She yanked her hand from his grip, shot to her feet, and strode away.

Booted feet crunched down the pea-gravel path behind her. In all her dealings with the *haut ton,* she had yet to meet a man who equaled Highgate for sheer arrogance, and that was saying quite a lot. He caught at her arm, and she whirled, her eyes on a level with his. Perhaps he was like Napoleon—what he lacked in size, he compensated for in pride.

"What don't I understand, *my lord*? Please explain in terms I will understand."

He inclined his head. "My apologies. We are essentially strangers. In time, we shall learn to get along."

She raised her chin and bit back a smile of satisfaction when he pushed himself up on his toes to remain on her level. "We most certainly shall not. If I was not inclined to refuse you before, you've just tipped the scales against yourself."

"I see you do not give a fig for your reputation. Have you stopped to consider mine?"

Sudden gratitude toward William washed through her. Unwittingly, he'd given her a weapon to use against Highgate. "Your reputation precedes you, my lord."

He studied her for a long moment, his gaze piercing, assessing. Her blush provided little protection against the feeling of transparency, as if her every last hope and desire were laid bare before him. It stripped her naked. A shiver coursed through her, and she gathered her pelisse more closely about her shoulders.

"So you've heard of my first marriage," he said at last.

Certain victory was near, she allowed herself a smile. "Yes."

He waved a hand. "Rumors, of course. What have you heard?"

Sophia bit her lip. She couldn't come out with an accusation of murder. He was going about in society. Her parents must have admitted him to the house. What William had hinted at yesterday morning could not have been in circulation.

Come to think of it, Lady Wexford would never have let him show his face at the Posselthwaites' if he'd had a hand in his wife's demise. Little comfort, somehow, that thought.

"Rumors, as you've said," she replied.

"If it will lay your concerns to rest, I can tell you what happened. Quite simply, I made what I thought was an advantageous match. But what society deems an advantage and what is, in fact, an advantage in the actual living are two different things. In short, we did not suit, but we did not realize our mistake until it was too late."

A stiff breeze blew into the garden, tossing dried leaves about in a swirl and whipping the points of Highgate's collar against his chin. Sophia hunched her shoulders.

"I see." But she didn't. Not completely. His explanation only covered half the story. But perhaps he'd never heard the darker insinuations. Didn't that fact alone put the lie to them?

"I'm not sure you do. Since that time, I've preferred to avoid another such entanglement, and I've stayed away from society. Gossip, as my sister is ever eager to remind me, has made of my marriage what it will."

"I do not understand. Why offer for me, if you do not wish another marriage?"

He rubbed his hands together. The raw wind had stained his cheeks red. "I must marry. It is my responsibility to leave an heir to whom I can pass my title."

"You do not need me, specifically, for that. Any young miss would do. Even a widow."

His breath released on a heavy sigh. "I have no choice but to offer for you now. Surely you see that. If I do not, any good family will discount my suit, and given my disastrous first marriage, I do not need any further black marks to my name."

Anger seethed inside her, its heat little comfort against the day's chill. "So that's it then. Because of a few moments, my entire life will be dictated to me. I cannot even call it an indiscretion. My goodness, I did not get so much as a kiss out of the evening, and yet I'm forced into marriage with you. A marriage, I might add, that neither one of us wants."

He reached for her shoulders, his hands sliding along her woolen pelisse, up her neck, until they framed her face. Leather-clad thumbs traced her cheekbones.

She pulled in a lungful of cold air. A light leapt into his eyes, an intensity she recognized. She'd seen it before on her erstwhile suitors. Not that she'd ever given in to the temptation to allow so much as a kiss. Whenever she caught the slightest hint of descending lips, she turned her head aside to offer her cheek.

Fending off Highgate would be another matter. His grip burned into her flesh.

"Would you like a kiss from our dealings, I wonder? Or do you find me too repulsive?"

She puzzled over the sudden bitterness behind his words. While she'd never qualify his looks as classic or chiseled, neither did he repel her. The thought shook her to the core. She'd once vowed never to kiss any man but William. But now, as she stood in the garden under a lowering sky, she found herself intrigued.

"I do not think you're repulsive." Her cheeks heated at the admission.

His lips stretched into an ironic semblance of a smile. "How you tempt me to put that statement to the test."

Fathomless eyes focused on her lips, and she tangled her fingers in her skirts in anticipation of the inevitable descent of his mouth toward hers.

Without warning, he dropped his hands. Reflexively, she covered her burning cheeks with her palms, her touch a poor substitute for his.

"Best not give in to temptation," he muttered, "or we truly will find ourselves bound for life."

She shook her head. "I don't understand. Did you not come today to propose?"

"I did, and to salvage your reputation, you must accept. If we are careful, however, we need not carry the charade as far as the altar."

"How are we to manage that?"

"Simple. We will pass a week or two as betrothed, and then, I shall be gentleman enough to allow you to cry off, should you wish it. Is that agreeable, Miss St. Claire?"

BENEDICT rested his cheek against the bay's warm flank and leaned his weight into her hip. With a snort, she lifted a dainty hoof just as she ought. Well-trained, if a bit high strung.

As he inspected the underside of her hoof, he inhaled. The clean, sharp scent of fresh hay wafted into his nostrils. Only a slight underlying earthiness of manure and the tang of urine marred the effect. The stalls at Tattersall's were kept cleaner than many a London stew—or, for that matter, an army encampment—all for the equine elite and noble clientele the horse trader catered to.

Gently, Benedict released the mare's hoof, and she settled her weight on it. Her tail swished at a nonexistent fly. Benedict patted the heavy flesh of her rump. Powerful muscles flinched at the touch.

"You'd have been a real goer at Newmarket, wouldn't you?"

She let out a soft whicker of agreement.

Moving to her head, he reached into his coat and offered a lump of carrot on the flat of his palm. Supple, velvety lips snatched at the treat. As her heavy teeth crunched, she nosed for more, regarding him with intelligent, liquid eyes.

He reached up and stroked the blaze of white that streaked down her face.

"Pity, 'at one." At the groom's coarse accent, Benedict

looked up. "Ye wants a runner, ye'd best look elsewhere. Great prospects, 'at one, 'til she broke down."

"I'm not in the market for a racehorse. I'm looking for breeding stock."

The groom rested an elbow against the side of the stall. "Can't beat 'er bloodlines. 'Er sire won at Ascot five years running, 'e did."

"Are you quite through?" Upperton's bored drawl sounded from the aisle beyond. "I'm sure I've got a pressing engagement or other, one that doesn't involve horseflesh."

Biting back the obvious comment about Upperton's taste in mistresses, Benedict gave the mare a final pat and pushed his way out of the stall, noting in passing the name and lot number. Nefertari. A queenly name for a prizewinner.

Upperton was lounging against the door of an empty stall, arms folded over a brocade waistcoat and one foot propped up. Against the backdrop of rough wood and bales of straw, his polished Hessians, intricately knotted cravat, and artfully tousled sand-colored hair looked rather out of place. The man might well fancy himself a dandy, but Benedict knew him to be a loyal friend in a pinch.

"Since when have you got such an objection to horses?" Benedict asked.

"I've none at all." Upperton kicked himself away from the wall. "I like them just fine when they're winning me bets. I just prefer not to commune with the creatures. If I'm to run my hands all over a female and murmur sweet nothings, I'd rather she be able to reciprocate."

Benedict cocked a brow. "When's the last time a woman let you get that close?"

Puffing himself up in mock outrage, Upperton stabbed a finger in Benedict's direction. Benedict braced himself for a verbal barrage that never came. Instead, Upperton let out a grunt, his gaze fixed somewhere past Benedict's shoulder.

A prickle of awareness caused the hairs at Benedict's nape to stand on end, and he pivoted. Perfect, white teeth gleaming in a wide grin, William Ludlowe strode down the aisle.

"I say there, isn't this a lucky chance?"

Benedict attempted to return the smile, but he feared he'd only succeeded in grimacing. Two encounters in as many days was hardly what he'd term lucky.

Upperton pushed past him, jostling his shoulder with unnecessary force—a warning, no doubt.

"Lucky indeed," Upperton boomed. From several nearby stalls came the restless rustling of hay as their occupants shifted nervously. "Never thought you were much on cattle. What brings you here?"

"I'm in the market for a bit of flash, you know. Something to befit my new station."

"Ah." Upperton didn't miss a beat.

Benedict, on the other hand, gritted his teeth. His grimace must resemble a death mask, his face was so stiff.

"Heard there was a fancy little bit on offer come Monday," Ludlowe went on. "Wanted to come have a look for myself. Name of Neffer-titty."

"Nefertari," Benedict grated.

"That's it." Ludlowe stepped past Upperton. "Groom said she was somewhere around here."

Benedict shifted his weight until he blocked Ludlowe's path. "You don't want that one."

"Oh, I say!"

Benedict inhaled: fresh hay, wood, leather, horse. Ordinarily, he found such scents soothing. Not today. Not now. Rather than point out the obvious, he settled for a gibe. "I didn't think fashionable nobs rode about on mares."

Beyond Ludlowe's shoulder, Upperton arched a brow. "Better listen to him, old man. When it comes to horseflesh, he knows what he's about."

Ludlowe's grin didn't waver. Not a flicker. "Oh, I don't want her for me." He leaned closer, all manly confidentiality, as if he and Benedict were old school chums. "I'm in the market for a wife. Any bride of mine ought to ride in style."

Upperton broke into an explosive fit of coughing. Nefertari pinned her ears back and tossed her dainty head. Down the row, another horse kicked at his stall.

Benedict balled his hands into fists, but he couldn't let on what a complete and utter idiot Ludlowe was if he thought to win Julia over with a saddle horse. "You still don't want this one. They retired her from racing because she broke down. She isn't fit for much more than a sunny pasture and breeding."

Ludlowe tapped his chin with an immaculately manicured finger. "I suppose you would know a thing or two about horseflesh, wouldn't you? Tell me, if you wished to surprise a lady with a really prime mount, what would you recommend?"

Upperton's coughing fit turned into a wheeze. His reddened cheeks darkened to crimson. Was he so childish as to laugh over an unintentional double entendre?

"If you cannot rein in your juvenile sense of humor," Benedict snapped, "would you mind stepping outside?"

Upperton's chest expanded as he drew in a lungful of air. With a series of splutters, he brought his breathing under control. "Go on then," he gasped. "Answer the man's question."

"It all depends on the particular lady. Some prefer to walk. Others prefer carriages."

"Nonsense!" Ludlowe burst out. "They all take to riding eventually. Some just want lessons."

The corners of Upperton's mouth twitched. Benedict

quelled him with a glare. "Subtlety is wasted on the likes of you."

"Oh, come now, Revelstoke. One might say you've misplaced your sense of humor."

"Or one might say I prefer to wait until I'm diverted to laugh."

Ludlowe made another tentative move toward Nefertari's stall. "Do you think I might . . . ?"

Benedict could hardly prevent him. He didn't own Nefertari—yet. Suppressing a sigh, he stepped aside and allowed Ludlowe to pass.

"Ah! And aren't you a fine-looking specimen?"

Upperton arched a brow. "Perhaps they'd like a little privacy."

Benedict might have been all too happy to comply with the suggestion, except he wanted to ensure Ludlowe didn't decide to bid Nefertari out from under him, in spite of her unsuitability. "Be certain to take a good look at her knees."

"Delightful things, ladies' knees," Upperton commented. "You might want to run your hands over them."

Benedict sent him another glare. "If you've got nothing constructive to add . . ."

Upperton shrugged. "Just passing the time until we can get on to something more agreeable."

Ludlowe stuck his head out of the stall. "Run my hands down her legs, you say? Whatever for?"

"Remind me why all the ladies twitter over him again."

Benedict ignored Upperton's dig and stepped back into the stall. Resisting the impulse to shove Ludlowe into a fresh pile of manure, he bent down and cupped his hands about the mare's near knee. "If you know what to look for, you can see she's in no condition for any sort of hard riding. There's swelling in the joints. They're warmer than they ought to be. A nice, quiet life in the country is about all that's left in her, and you might get a foal or two out of her once she's had a good rest."

Or at least that was what Benedict was hoping to get from her.

A jet of warm air shuddered out of Nefertari's nostrils. Shuffling her feet in the straw, she nosed hopefully at Benedict's pockets.

He rubbed a hand down her bony face. "Sorry, old girl. I'm all out of carrots."

"Here." Ludlowe produced a lump of sugar and held it out in his flattened palm. Nefertari shouldered Benedict aside and lipped up the offering. "Suppose I'll be seeing you at the auction, then, Revelstoke."

CHAPTER SIX

JULIA PRESSED her fingers to her temples, but the pounding in her head was relentless. The air in the crowded room weighed on her. If only she hadn't chosen to sit in the middle of the row. Boxed in between Sophia and their mother, she could not escape easily. Henrietta Upperton's rendition of "Believe Me, if All Those Endearing Young Charms" was not helping matters, nor was her younger sister's accompaniment.

The poor girl's voice squeaked on the final note. She cut it blessedly short, while a blush crept up her cheeks. After a few moments' awkward silence, a scattering of polite applause broke out.

Julia nudged her sister. "Pardon me."

Sophia remained in place, her gaze fixed on the matron seated directly in front of her.

"What's the matter with you?" Julia whispered in her ear.

Sophia gave a start and turned a vague glance on Julia. "I'm sorry. Did you say something?"

"I was just remarking on Miss Upperton's lovely voice. Don't you agree?"

Sophia nodded, the golden ringlets brushing the sides of her face. "Oh yes, quite."

Julia wrapped her fingers about Sophia's upper arm and tugged.

Sophia blinked at her. "Oh, is it over?"

"Of course not, but I cannot stand another butchered rendition of Mozart, and you're obviously off in your own little world."

With a quick excuse to Mama and many apologetic nods to the other spectators, she urged her sister toward the back of the room. As they slipped through a paneled door into the main hall of the Upperton town house, Julia cast a final glance over her shoulder.

The reason behind her sister's distraction became immediately apparent. His snow-white cravat arranged in an artfully complicated knot, William Ludlowe lounged against one of the far walls. He caught Julia's eye and acknowledged her with a smile and a nod.

Julia turned her back on him. "Why did he have to choose tonight of all nights to begin attending musicales?"

In reply, Sophia let out a moan. Julia studied her sister for the least sign of illness. If anyone were to express disgruntlement, it should be Julia herself.

"You aren't feeling faint by any chance, are you?"

Sophia waved her fan in front of her reddened cheeks. "Certainly not. I've resolved never to faint in society again. It gets me into the worst sort of trouble."

Julia was about to point out that fainting was not exactly a reaction Sophia could control, when her sister added, "Oh, I should never have come tonight."

"I cannot say I blame you there. The Upperton sisters do seem to get worse each year, don't they?" The strains of a new tune reached the hallway. Julia winced.

Sophia's fan came to rest against her bodice. "I did not mean it that way."

"Then what did you mean?"

"Only I'm not fit to be seen in society now."

"What nonsense. Of course you are."

"But Lady Wexford—"

Julia reached for her sister's arm. "Lady Wexford is

nothing more than a vicious gossip with nothing better to do than create scandal where none exists."

"Be careful who you say that to." Sophia slumped against the fading chinoiserie wallpaper. The faint off-key warbling of some Scottish air drifted from the conservatory. "If she gets wind of it, she'll be out to ruin you, as well."

"How will she get wind of it?"

"You never know." Sophia inspected her nails for a moment. "At any rate, Mama's invited her to dinner on Monday, so be careful what you say."

Julia frowned. "Why would Mama invite her to dinner? Or perhaps I ought to ask why Lady Wexford would accept."

"Something happened today while you were out paying calls." Sophia sighed and stared up at the crown molding for a moment. "I knew I should have gone with you. I might have avoided this mess altogether."

"What mess?" Her sister's face took on a grayish tinge, and Julia grabbed her wrist. "Sophia, what's happened?"

"While you were out, Lord Highgate paid me a visit." Sophia's blue eyes sought out Julia's. "He proposed."

"And?"

"I accepted," Sophia murmured.

"You *what?* Sophia—"

"It isn't as if I intend to go through with it," she rushed to add.

"Good evening, ladies."

Sophia gasped. Julia whirled. Benedict loomed at the far end of the hall with George Upperton. Their heels thudded on the parquet floor as they approached.

A grin split Upperton's good-natured face. "Taking the intelligent route and hiding out in the corridor, I see. It's a strategy that's served me well over the years."

Julia nodded at the new arrivals, while inwardly curs-

ing their sense of timing. She ducked her head to avoid
Benedict's gaze.

"Miss Julia." The gravelly quality of his voice struck
her as somehow different. But why? She'd been hearing
it for years.

She closed her eyes in a vain effort to ward off an
inner prickle of recognition. Drat Sophia, why had she
teased her with the possibility that Benedict was in love
with her? Now Julia would question all his actions
toward her. And what if what Sophia had said in jest
turned out to be true?

*If I remain forever a bachelor, I shall lay the blame at
your feet.* And what, precisely, had he meant by that?

If she had to face his feelings, she might well have to
examine this terrifying and new but insistent reaction
she experienced in his presence. Soon, it would become
impossible to ignore. Years of friendship had proven he
wasn't like the other men of the *ton,* but his experience
with the cavalry had deepened those familiar traits.
He'd grown graver, more earnest. His presence, his person, might swallow her so easily until the essential Julia
became lost, the same way Sophia had lost herself in her
unrequited *tendre* over the past few years.

"With any luck," Upperton went on, "the torture will
be over soon."

"Perhaps next year, you'll convince your mother of
the futility of the exercise," Benedict said.

Upperton plucked at his impeccably knotted cravat,
pulling it slightly askew. "The woman is as tone-deaf as
my sisters. She's convinced they're prodigies. Next year,
I believe I shall sneak off to my club and get thoroughly
foxed."

Benedict raised an eyebrow. "How's that any different from what you do most nights?"

Upperton elbowed him. "Now, now, not in front of
the ladies. I've got a reputation to preserve."

"I'm afraid it's far too late for that." Julia hid her grin behind her fan. "Unless you're referring to your reputation as a wastrel."

He put a hand over his heart, further wrinkling his cravat. "Miss Julia, you wound me." Then he winked. "And you definitely spend too much time with Revelstoke if you're bandying such terms as wastrel about."

"Do you think so?" Over the lace edging of her fan, she widened her eyes. "It seems to me that after the time he spent with the cavalry, he could teach me some more interesting words."

Upperton blinked. Then he threw back his head and let out a hearty laugh. "Miss Julia, I cannot believe some fortunate fellow hasn't yet snapped you up." He offered her his elbow. "If you'd consent to stroll with me, we might discuss a remedy to the situation."

Julia smiled demurely and lowered her lashes. "And put a black mark on your reputation? I would not dream of it."

Benedict arched a brow. "Besides, she has better taste than that."

Upperton's gray glance darted from one to the other. Then with a flourish, he stepped aside, leaving Benedict next to Julia. "Have the pair of you ever thought of making a go of things?"

Julia studied the pointed toes of her slippers peeking from beneath her gown. Blast Upperton for suggesting the same thing her sister had. Out of the corner of her eye, she spotted Benedict's polished shoes—they shifted as he shuffled his feet. A thrill passed through the pit of her stomach, similar to the feeling of whirling in his arms to the strains of the waltz.

Upperton gave a small cough. "Have you considered any children you produced would be the absolute terrors of their schoolmasters?" He stepped closer, his expression imploring. "It'd be perfect revenge. Put their names down for Eton the moment they're born."

Heat crept up Julia's cheeks, and she prayed the flickering candlelight in the corridor was dim enough to mask her reaction. She slanted a glance at Sophia, who was doing a poor job of hiding a smile behind her fan. No help from that quarter.

Benedict's shoes advanced a step. "That will do."

His words held a tone of command that Julia had never heard from him before. She suspected he'd perfected it during the war. Upperton, at any rate, took the hint immediately. "Yes, quite."

Over the rose silk of her fan, Sophia's eyes glittered annoyingly. If they could talk, they would have proclaimed, "It looks as if I've hit on something delicious."

Julia cleared her throat. "The musicale must be over by now."

Upperton put his hand to his ear and made a show of wincing. "Not quite. I almost recognize the last movement to Mozart's sonata in C."

Julia took her sister's arm. "Mama will wonder why we've been gone so long. We ought to get back."

Just as she took a step toward the conservatory, Ludlowe appeared in the doorway. His gaze focused on Julia, and he smiled. "How fortunate, Miss Julia. I thought you might already have taken your leave."

Julia favored him with a curt nod. It was the most she'd allow him. "I'm sure we'll be off soon enough."

"Perhaps we'll run into each other later. Lady Whitby is hosting a rout, and I daresay there'll be a spot of dancing. Might I hope you'll save me a waltz?"

"Dreadfully sorry. I'm afraid I stepped out because I felt a headache coming on. I think it best if I head directly home."

Ludlowe's smile faltered. "Pity. I suppose I'll see you on Monday, then."

With a bow, he turned on his heel and, signaling for a footman, strode toward the stairs.

"The man is making himself a regular nuisance."

Julia felt Benedict's comment as much as she heard it. He'd managed to hover closer in the time Ludlowe took to summon his carriage.

Upperton crossed his arms and leaned back against the wall. "No surprise there, considering."

"Considering what?" Julia asked.

Benedict stepped forward, menacingly in Julia's opinion. "Yes, Upperton, perhaps you'd like to explain." He punctuated this statement with a jerk of his head in Sophia's direction.

Upperton raised a pair of pale eyebrows. "Contrary to popular belief, I do know how to read."

"While that might be true, you don't always use your head, do you?"

Julia stared at one man, then the other. They'd been friends since their school days, and any insults they traded were usually good-natured. Not this time. Benedict was glaring at Upperton.

"I'm completely at sea," Sophia said.

"As am I," Julia chimed in.

Upperton pushed himself away from the wall. "Why should it come as a surprise that a charming young lady of good reputation and family should attract a suitor?"

There was more to it than that, but Julia knew she would not get the real explanation now. Not while Upperton and Benedict continued their silent conversation right over her head.

"What I want to know," Benedict said at last, "is why Ludlowe thinks he's going to see you on Monday."

"Mama must have invited him to dinner," Sophia said softly, the hurt evident in her tone. "She did not tell me."

Julia stared at her sister. Sophia gave a small jerk of her shoulders in reply to her unasked question. Julia couldn't fathom their mother's lack of tact. It was one thing to hold a dinner to announce Sophia's betrothal; it was quite another to invite the object of Sophia's infatuation to witness the proceedings.

Underneath it all, Julia understood what guided her mother's actions. She'd seat Julia and Ludlowe next to each other in hopes they'd get on together. Ludlowe would serve Julia the choicest morsels from whatever rich dishes were closest and charm her with his wit and good looks.

Why marry off one daughter, when she could marry off two? And what's more, to earls, the both of them.

If she dared, Julia could thwart her mother's plans. Benedict would leap at the chance to separate her from Ludlowe. But would he see an invitation from her as encouragement? She stopped herself from shaking her head. She was being ridiculous. Over the course of their childhood, they'd dined in each other's presence on any number of occasions. Surely he wouldn't read anything more into an invitation than simple friendship. Just the way things had always stood between them.

Julia laid a hand on Benedict's forearm. Beneath the fine wool of his tailcoat, solid muscles clenched. "Would you like to have dinner with us on Monday?"

CHAPTER SEVEN

"Now this is a fine specimen of a mare. Lovely lines, healthy teeth, wide-set eyes, and deep chest."

In spite of himself, Benedict tensed. He'd been waiting for this moment all afternoon.

As if she could understand the auctioneer's words, Nefertari swished her tail and held her head high, looking down on the mere mortals in the crowd. Her groom clucked to her and tugged on the lead, but she stood stock-still.

"Excellent bloodlines on this one. Both sire and dam trace directly back to the Godolphin Arabian. Quite a record at the track."

Such a statement was a cue for the groom to jog about the cupola at the center of the ring to show off a horse's gait, but Nefertari remained firmly on the spot, her ears flicking back and forth. Not even a few paces of sideways dancing.

With a smile, Benedict leaned back against a pillar and folded his arms. Such stubborn behavior was likely to discourage most bidders, and if they couldn't see her paces—well. He just might acquire a broodmare for a song.

Unperturbed, the auctioneer forged ahead. "What am I offered for this fine beast?"

Benedict opened his mouth, but another shout preceded his. "Two hundred!"

Damn. Pressing his lips together, he scanned the gathering of men about the perimeter of the ring. The dull day lent little light to the proceedings, but somehow his glance picked out a shock of golden hair on the opposite side. Ludlowe. Blast it all.

"Two twenty-five!" Another voice joined the fray.

"Two fifty!" cried a third.

"Three hundred." Ludlowe. Damn that idiot's eyes.

"Three fifty," called the second gentleman before anyone else had a chance. No matter. The two unknown bidders were likely trying to get a bargain. Benedict could wait.

"Five hundred."

The auctioneer smiled.

Benedict glowered across the enclosure. Ludlowe's jump may have silenced the other two, but if the price kept rising at this rate, Nefertari would be beyond Benedict's means. Time to test the waters.

He settled against the pillar and affected a bored expression. "Five twenty-five."

"One thousand."

Next to Benedict, Upperton let out a colorful string of invective, a sentiment echoed all around the enclosure. A thousand was probably the most Nefertari could hope to fetch in her condition. It was also the upper limit of what Benedict had hoped to spend.

Upperton nudged him. "Where do you think he's getting all the blunt?"

The auctioneer intervened before Benedict could reply. "One thousand once!"

"Eleven hundred!" Benedict shouted.

Upperton raised his brows. "Come to that, where are you getting all the blunt?"

Benedict was on the verge of telling him to shut his gob, when Ludlowe bid again. "Twelve hundred."

Benedict gritted his teeth. Upperton did have a point

about his finances. His father, the late Marquess of En-field, had bequeathed him a decent settlement, and the sale of his commission had fetched him another two thousand or so. Once his stud was up and running, he might count on enough revenue to live quietly in the country. He would never have the sort of funds Ludlowe obviously did.

"Thirteen hundred!" Or Upperton, for that matter.

Benedict turned to his friend. "What the bloody hell do you think you're doing?"

Upperton smiled. "Driving up the price."

"I was bidding on that mare."

"You don't want a bit of horseflesh to drive you into the poorhouse, do you?" Of course, Upperton would have a general idea what Benedict could afford. They wagered on enough ridiculous trifles.

"Fourteen hundred!" At Ludlowe's latest bid, a broader smile spread over the auctioneer's features. Nefertari's former owner would end today quite pleased with himself—and so would Tattersall when he collected his share of the proceeds.

"Fifteen hundred!"

"Upperton," Benedict growled, "you haven't got fif-teen hundred pounds."

His friend shrugged. "Not at the moment, no, but you'll spot a few guineas to an old chum, won't you?"

The deuced man had always been rather reckless where wagers were concerned. Benedict was about to refuse on principle, but the next second proved any pro-test unnecessary.

"Sixteen hundred."

"Why do you think he wants that damned horse so much?" Upperton asked.

"You heard him. He thinks he'll impress Julia with it." Benedict allowed himself an ironic smile. "That or he's a complete idiot."

Upperton rubbed his jaw. "I'd vote for both. What's more, he was a horse's arse while we were at school. I can think of an incident or two I'd like revenge for."

Benedict frowned. So could he—not so much for himself, but for others. Or, more specifically, one other.

"Sixteen hundred once!"

Upperton raised a hand. "Two thousand."

Benedict rounded on him. "Are you mad? That's fully twice what the animal's worth."

"I may be mad," Upperton said with a flip of his hand, "but Ludlowe's madder."

"Twenty-one hundred."

"There you are." A wicked gleam came into Upperton's eye. "Now let's see how far we can push him."

"FIVE thousand!" Upperton plunked his empty glass on the polished mahogany table and sloshed himself another measure of Boodle's best brandy. "Good God. It must be nice to have those kinds of funds to toss about."

His friend could well laugh, but the thought of emptying Ludlowe's coffers, however deserved, did little to lighten Benedict's mood. "You're damned lucky you didn't find yourself with a bill you couldn't afford. Fully five times the nag's worth."

"Nag." Upperton shook his head. "A fine way to refer to a beast you wanted."

Benedict emptied his glass and set it down with a thump. "I'd have had more use for her than Ludlowe. At least I know Julia will never ride her. As long as he doesn't try to impress some other girl with a fancy mare."

"He would not have placed that wager if he was going to change his mind about his choice of bride. No one bets that sort of blunt, not even Prinny."

That was just the problem. Ludlowe had made up his

mind and with his looks, his natural charm, with his usual success in seducing the *ton*'s ladies, Benedict was not sure even Julia could resist a determined assault forever.

Not without reinforcements. Few ladies managed the feat. Ludlowe was reputed to have collected more conquests than Bonaparte and, unlike the Corsican, held on to them.

He consulted his pocket watch. Nearly five, just enough time to drop by his town house and arm himself for the evening ahead. He set his glass aside and pushed himself to his feet.

Upperton eyed him. "Where are you off to? It's early yet."

"Julia's invited me to dinner."

"Ah, yes. Didn't recall you'd have another round with Ludlowe so soon." He tossed back his drink. "Best of luck then."

Benedict grunted. He had the feeling he was going to need all the luck he could get.

"I do not think I can go through with this."

Julia turned to look at her sister through the dressing room door, ignoring the protests of the maid, who was trying to pin up her hair. "Why did you agree to the match then?"

Already clad in a dinner dress of virginal white, Sophia sank onto the mattress. "It did not seem like such a bad idea the other day, when he asked me."

"I think you're more worried about facing Lady Wexford. Not that I blame you there."

"Why did Mama insist on inviting Mr. Ludlowe?"

Mr. Ludlowe? Interesting. At least her sister had stopped referring to the man by his first name. Was it a step in the right direction? Julia stood.

"Miss," Watkins admonished, "how'm I to do yer hair if ye won't sit fer me?"

Julia glared the girl down. "That will be all."

"But miss, I ain't done."

She suppressed a sigh and turned to the maid. "It hardly matters how I look. Tonight's dinner is in Sophia's honor."

Sophia heaved herself to her feet and slumped into the dressing room to take Julia's place.

Julia laid a hand on her sister's arm. "You'll be just lovely, and Mr. Ludlowe will not be able to take his eyes off you."

"It will not matter." Sophia plopped herself into the seat and gave herself over to Watkins. "For goodness' sake, I'm announcing my betrothal to another man."

"A betrothal you're planning on breaking." Julia plucked a diaphanous wrap from a shelf and set it about her shoulders. "What do you think?"

Watkins stifled a screech. Sophia was more forthright. "Perfectly ghastly. You cannot wear a silvery shawl with a peach-colored gown."

"I know." Julia grinned. "That's why I chose it."

"It makes your face look washed out."

"It's perfect, then."

Sophia pressed her lips into a line. "It doesn't matter how much effort you go to, Mr. Ludlowe is still bound to pursue you."

In the midst of considering other accessories, Julia paused. Her sister had sounded almost . . . jealous. She placed a yellowed lace cap that must have belonged to her great-aunt Harriet back on the shelf. Carrying things a bit too far, that cap. "Why must you be so pessimistic?"

"It's the way of things. Even before the unfortunate incident with Lord Highgate, he sought you out." Not only jealous, but accusatory. "And he continues to do so, even though you keep setting him down."

"I'll tell you one thing," Julia insisted. "If he dares propose, I'll turn him down flat."

"You will do no such thing," said a new voice. "Not if I have anything to say about it."

Julia whirled. Mama marched into the dressing room. With a frown, she plucked at Julia's wrap. "And you will remove that awful thing at once. Why aren't the two of you ready yet?"

Julia pulled the silver confection tighter about her shoulders. "Sophia wants to look her best for her betrothed. Don't you?"

Mama advanced on her. "That's no reason for you to take fashion advice from Lady Epperley. Your hair isn't even done yet."

"I was considering hiding it under a turban, actually."

"At your age?" Mama gasped. "Do you want people to believe you're on the shelf?"

"That's exactly what I want." Julia punctuated this statement with a firm nod. "Sophia's bagged herself an earl. Can't you be content with that?"

"What sort of talk is that?" Mama sniffed. "Bagged herself an earl. You have been spending entirely too much time in the company of Lord Benedict and his feckless friends. I shall not rest until I see both my daughters comfortably settled."

Julia exchanged a glance with her sister. "She'll see us comfortably settled, yes," she muttered. "Comfortably settled but completely miserable."

Mama drew herself up. "Why would you think such a thing? As long as you arrange for the proper family connections, you oughtn't be miserable."

"But what of one's personal feelings?" Sophia asked.

"It's a matter of becoming accustomed," Mama stated firmly. "You learn to get on together, and you learn to get on with life. It's the way of the world."

"I could be perfectly contented in marriage," Julia

said, "as long as people didn't insist on love entering into it."

Sophia let out a squawk of protest, but Mama ignored her. "You always were sensible, my dear. Find yourself a man of proper standing. Over time, a fondness will develop. And you'll have children to dote on. Don't you want children?"

Julia looked away. "I suppose so. I just don't want the entanglement the getting of children entails."

Mama stepped closer and gently unwound the wrap from Julia's shoulders. "The entanglement, as you call it, can be the best part."

She meant the physical entanglement. She must. The last thing Julia wanted to consider was the emotional side. "I do not wish to hear this."

"But you need to, my dear. You set yourself on the shelf, and before you know it, you'll have faded away into a corner, unnoticed. Spinsters hold no place in the *ton*."

"Perhaps that's what I want."

"Nonsense, my dear. You give Mr. Ludlowe a chance to charm you at supper and see if you don't change your mind."

Sophia let out a splutter, or perhaps more of a warbling, dangerously close to tears.

Mama turned to her. "Chin up, my dear. In spite of the way you've gone about it, you've done well for yourself. You'll be a countess before the season is over. Society will flock to you for invitations. See if they don't."

With a firm nod, she swept from the room, no doubt convinced her views on domestic happiness were universal.

Julia retrieved the shawl and wrapped it about her shoulders once more. "I do not want to turn out like her."

"How's that?" Sophia replied thickly.

"So concerned about her position in society, she sets

it above all else. She wants to push me at Ludlowe, and the devil take *your* feelings for him."

Sophia pressed her fingers to the base of her throat. "Don't let her hear you use such language."

Julia shrugged. "She'll only blame it on Benedict's influence."

"And if she forbids your association?"

"She can try." Julia smiled to herself. Mama had on any number of occasions, but she'd never taken into account the lure that the forbidden held for two inquisitive children. "But she's never succeeded in the past."

"Does she know you invited him to dine with us tonight?"

Julia's smile broadened. "I don't think she does. I discussed it with Cook directly and swore her to silence. And I'll arrange it so Ludlowe sits with you. See if I don't."

"Oh, Julia, you mustn't. How would it look at my own betrothal dinner?"

"He certainly will not sit with me. You can be sure of that. Perhaps I shall foist him on Lady Wexford."

A line formed between Mrs. St. Claire's brows the moment Billings announced Benedict's arrival. "Lord Benedict, to what do we owe your presence here this evening?"

Quite a cold greeting coming from a woman he'd known since childhood. Of course, if she'd known about all the scrapes he and Julia had got into during the summers in Kent, she might have reason behind her chill. She couldn't know of every incident, though, or she'd have taken firmer measures to prohibit their association.

"I invited him." Julia stood on the staircase, several steps from the bottom. Graceful fingers trailed along the mahogany handrail. Her tumble of honey-colored curls reflected the candlelight. Hazel eyes met his, and she nodded, her head dipping for a second, while the corners of her mouth tipped upward.

Such quiet beauty, and she didn't even seem aware of it. A heavy awareness arrowed downward.

To mask the reaction, he placed a gloved hand over his heart and bowed to her in turn. She clutched at a ridiculous drape of silvery fabric and descended the last few steps.

"My dear," Mrs. St. Claire muttered out of the corner of her mouth, "you do realize we're expecting guests."

"Of course I do. I felt Revelstoke ought to join the festivities. He's known Sophia all his life."

Mrs. St. Claire pressed her lips together. "And how is the marquess faring these days? A pity your brother could not join us in Town for the season."

He smiled at the reference to his older brother, who had inherited their father's title, while Benedict had received the typical second son's lot of an army commission. "I'm afraid he opted to remain in the country with his wife so close to her confinement."

"Quite prudent of him, I'm sure." Mrs. St. Claire lifted her shoulders in a little shrug.

Julia floated down the remaining steps. "Perhaps his fortunes will change, and the marchioness will present him with a son this time."

"One can only hope," Benedict replied.

The line between Mrs. St. Claire's eyebrows, that smallest of flaws, deepened. "You do not aspire to take your brother's title one day should he suffer the misfortune of not producing an heir?"

"And be required to endure the *ton* on a regular basis? Heaven forbid."

Julia's skirts brushed against his leg as she tucked her hand into his elbow. Long, tapering fingers curled about his arm, and he breathed in the hint of jasmine that hovered in the air about her.

He stopped himself from leaning closer. He was here to protect her from a right bastard, not to spend the evening basking in her perfume.

"Now you've done it. You'll set Mama off," she muttered, as, with subtle pressure, she drew him upstairs toward the drawing room. "No one else has arrived yet. Stick close beside me until we go down to dinner. That way I can avoid Ludlowe."

"Has he been making a particular nuisance of himself? Just say the word, and I'll be glad to take care of him for you." Glad. Such a mild word for the pleasure it would give him to see that bastard get a little of his own back.

With a sharp jerk of her head, she looked up. "Nothing that requires you to defend my honor."

He let her words sink in. He'd love nothing more. "You only need say the word, my lady, and I shall gladly take up my lance for your sake."

He twisted his lips into an ironic smile. Her laughter echoed through the drawing room, and he joined her until the realization struck. Overly dramatic phrasing aside, he'd willingly take up arms to defend her, if necessary.

She leaned closer. "If you're to be my champion, perhaps I ought to give you my favor. Isn't that the way they used to do things?"

In spite of himself, he stiffened. The blood drained from his face to pool in his groin. Damn her. This was Julia, and yet, ever since the waltz the other evening, she'd become a regular feature of his dreams.

Her lips hovered inches from his, plump and tempting. His sleeping mind already knew their flavor, their pliancy. In dream-state, he'd already experienced the paradise of her body gripping his in climax.

Her breath hitched, a sharp intake, and the awareness deepened. If he closed those final inches between them—

if he put his fantasy to the test—would she repay him with a slap?

Or would she respond with all the wonder and enthusiasm of the Julia who figured in his dreams?

A commotion downstairs in the foyer interrupted his thoughts. New arrivals, thank God. Given Julia's reputation for spurning all suitors, he suspected his face would have been stinging in another minute or two.

Turning, he bit back a groan. Just visible from the drawing room, Ludlowe appeared ascending the stairs, grinning as if tonight's dinner was held in his honor—his and Julia's. Head held high, he propped his walking stick in a corner.

Benedict ground his teeth. How he'd love to break that shiny oaken staff right over Ludlowe's thick skull.

To make matters worse, Ludlowe's gaze shifted in their direction, and he strode into the drawing room. "Ah, Miss Julia." His smile faded slightly. "Revelstoke. Such a coincidence, you being here. It seems every time I run into Miss Julia these days, you're never far behind, are you?"

Julia's fingers wound themselves into the crook of Benedict's elbow and squeezed a warning. His gaze fixed steadily on Ludlowe, he covered her hand with his. "I'm here as an invited guest."

Julia nodded and leaned into him, a fleeting touch of her shoulder, nothing more. But it left a pleasant tingle in its passing along with a heightened sense of her proximity.

"Yes, well." Ludlowe shifted his weight from one foot to the other, as if, for once in his life, he had no idea what to say. "Frightful weather we're having lately. Hardly springlike at all."

"Indeed." Julia's one-word reply held all the chill of tonight's wind.

Benedict fought off a grin.

* * *

SOPHIA stared at the glass a footman had just pressed into her hand. Deep red liquid sloshed from side to side, emitting a sweet, cloying odor that turned her stomach. She'd never manage a bite when the gathering went down to supper.

Her father raised his glass and with his other hand smoothed the burgundy brocade of his waistcoat over his belly. "A toast. To the happy couple."

All about the drawing room, the others followed suit. Sophia attempted a smile, but she feared it did not come off very well. Her glance darted from face to face. Lady Wexford's frown deepened, even as she raised her glass to her lips.

Ludlowe smiled, actually smiled at her. How dare he encourage her? Not even a week ago, he'd insinuated Highgate had a hand in his wife's death. Now he was actually drinking to her happiness.

Why had Mama even invited him to witness this humiliation? Pointless to ask. She knew very well Mama expected Ludlowe to offer for Julia.

At the thought, she knocked back her sherry. The liquid burned a path to her stomach, where it settled uneasily. She had to believe that Julia, at least, would refuse him. She was already sticking so close to Benedict that they might have been the engaged couple here tonight.

Billings appeared in the doorway. "Dinner is served."

Papa offered Mama his arm and led her toward the staircase. Spine stiff, he plodded down the steps as if he were headed to prison rather than a meal. Julia quickly followed with Benedict, leaving Ludlowe to escort Lady Wexford.

Sophia blew out a gust of air. A few hours more, and this farce would be over. Setting her empty glass on a side table, she turned to find Highgate scrutinizing her. "Aren't you going to escort me to dinner?"

"Not quite yet. A word, first, if I may."

She raised her eyebrows by way of response.

"If you do not at least pretend to play along with the charade, it will not work."

"Oh? And here I thought everyone would be nicely convinced when I cried off."

He stepped closer, his eyes capturing hers. Such a deep, rich brown, those eyes. "The way you're going about things, they'll never understand why you accepted me in the first place."

"Then we can put it about that my father is forcing the match." As if Papa would do such a thing. He far preferred to leave such considerations as marriage to Mama in favor of more masculine pursuits.

His elbow bumped her as he crossed his arms. "No one would believe that when you are of age."

She released her breath in a little huff. "Do you always approach everything so logically?"

He inclined his head. "Logic has never failed me in the past, and on occasions where I haven't let it govern my actions, I've lived to regret it."

The flickering candlelight emphasized the lines about his eyes and on his brow. As it had the evening of the Posselthwaite ball, an urge rose in her to raise her fingers, to smooth those lines away. She curled her hand into a fist and berated herself for downing an entire glass of sherry on an empty stomach.

He betrayed no hint of emotion, except perhaps in his eyes. For a second or two, a shadow dulled their depths, giving Sophia the distinct impression he was thinking of his first marriage.

His wife was dead. There was no questioning that fact. But Sophia couldn't believe society would tolerate a murderer. Had he even cared for his wife, or had the entire marriage been a simple arrangement for appearances' sake?

Just like what he was asking her to embark on. A façade, a fraud meant to preserve both their reputations.

"We ought to go to dinner before your mother decides to send out a search party." An ironic smile twisted his lips. "She catches us alone again, she may take it into her head to procure a special license for us."

"I do not think a ball to announce the engagement would be at all proper under the circumstances." Mariah set down her wineglass and dabbed at her lips with a linen napkin.

It did not happen often, but for once Rufus, Earl of Highgate, agreed with his sister. The more elaborate social trappings he could avoid, the better. He didn't need the attention of the *ton* focused on him. That road would only lead to bitter memories of the last time he'd been subject to gossip.

His sole aim now was to get on with the business of finding himself a new wife to appease the demands of his title. He wanted no emotional entanglements this time. Cold logic, just as he'd said to Miss St. Claire. And given her reticence and her feelings for another man, she seemed the ideal candidate. Her youth, her beauty, her figure were mere bonuses. How he would enjoy schooling her in their marriage bed. If only he could manage to convince her.

Mrs. St. Claire plunked down her fish fork. "Oh, I was so looking forward to hosting a ball in honor of the betrothal. I've waited years for this moment."

With a loud clatter, Sophia dropped a spoon onto her still-full plate. The look she gave her mother was quite telling—all wrinkled brow and reddened cheeks. Under the table, Rufus nudged her with his foot. She turned to glare at him.

"Smile," he said out of the side of his mouth.

She picked up her napkin and made a show of wiping her lips. Beneath the cover, she muttered, "Easy for you to say when they're discussing us as if we weren't even here. And in front of Mr. Ludlowe, no less."

Hurt put a tremor in her voice. His smile faded, and he covered the moment by sipping at his claret. Ludlowe, always Ludlowe. He'd have to have a serious talk with her about the man she'd pinned her hopes on. A long, private discussion where he laid out the list of Ludlowe's sins, at least those he was aware of—a list that certainly must have lengthened in the years since the passing of Lady Highgate. In ten years, the scoundrel had had scores of opportunities to multiply his liaisons.

"Have you given any thought to how you'd like to proceed?" St. Claire's voice broke in on Rufus's musings. The older man blinked at him from behind a pair of gold-rimmed spectacles. "You could get a special license and have it over with before a week is out."

The man sounded entirely too eager to get rid of his older daughter, perhaps understandably, given how many other proposals she'd turned down. Rufus had badgered the information from his sister—four in her first season alone. Quite a *tendre* she harbored for such an unworthy bastard.

He fingered his wineglass. "Would that not give the gossips fodder for speculation—that there's a reason we must rush matters? Let the banns be called."

More time for him to convince Miss St. Claire that marriage to him might be worth the risk.

As a footman removed the white soup and fish, Rufus took another sip of his claret. Decidedly sour and metallic. He pulled a face, and set the glass aside. If St. Claire could afford no better, no wonder he was so eager to marry off his daughter. The financial burden of all those seasons must be draining his coffers.

Across the table, Ludlowe leaned forward, nearly elbowing Benedict in the ribs as he made yet another attempt to engage Julia in conversation. "I was at school with Revelstoke, you know."

At the pronouncement, Sophia sat a bit straighter. "Why, Lord Benedict, you've never mentioned that before."

Benedict set aside his wineglass. "Our paths only crossed for a year. Ludlowe finished his studies after the summer half." His words were clipped and final, as if the topic annoyed him.

"Oh come," Sophia said, "you must have an amusing story or two you could recount. You're usually bursting with them."

Benedict gave a slight shake of his head. "I'm afraid my memory's deserted me."

Mr. St. Claire's fleshy cheeks wrinkled into a grin. "One might think you acted as Mr. Ludlowe's fag boy, the way you're reacting."

Ludlowe let out a shout of laughter. "Oh, no. That was Amherst. Runty little thing. Clumsiest blighter I ever set eyes on. Couldn't even make me a cup of tea before he'd spilt it all over himself." He shrugged. "I wonder whatever became of him."

Benedict shot a dark look in Ludlowe's direction. "He died at Corunna."

Julia let out a gasp. "If you were at school with him, he could not have been more than—"

"He was eighteen. His father took him out of school and bought him a commission. Thought to make a man out of him."

"All these years and you've never spoken of him," Sophia said faintly.

Benedict stared hard at her. "It's not the sort of thing

one boasts of, when one stood by and did nothing while the older boys goaded Amherst into being even clumsier."

"Older boys?" asked Sophia. "But what—"

Benedict cut her off with a wave of his hand. "It no longer signifies."

Rufus slanted a glance at Ludlowe, who had suddenly taken a great interest in his wineglass. If Revelstoke's tone was any indication, Ludlowe had led those older boys to torment the younger and weaker. Or he'd said nothing and used the excuse to heap abuse on a lad under the guise of punishment. Hardly surprising that Ludlowe had engaged in such behavior as a school boy. The years had done little to change him.

On Rufus's right, Mariah was too engaged in a stiffly polite squabble with Mrs. St. Claire to pay attention to the rest of the conversation.

"Of course, my Sophia must have an entirely new trousseau before we can even think of holding a wedding," her mother grated through a fixed smile. "Won't the trip to Bond Street be diverting, dear?"

Sophia kept her eyes fixed on her plate. "Quite."

Mr. St. Claire muttered, "Bond Street, always Bond Street," and drained his wineglass with a grimace.

Mariah sniffed. "I insist on giving you the name of my modiste. She is more than capable of whipping up something tasteful in no time. None of this vulgar, flimsy stuff that's in fashion now. Why, in my day, a lady had the decency to cover up."

In her day. As if she were in her sixties and not five years Rufus's senior. Of course, when one was built along Mariah's lines, covering up was the only decent option. He considered his wine and decided any further imbibing wasn't worth the damage to his stomach.

"There is nothing wrong with the modiste I currently patronize." Mrs. St. Claire's cheeks took on a rosier cast.

"She always has done wonders for my daughters' wardrobes."

Mariah cast a pointed look at Julia. "So I see."

St. Claire gave a discreet cough and angled his head toward Rufus. "Enough to make you reconsider the special license, isn't it?"

"Enough to make me reconsider the prospect altogether," he replied, lowering his voice, "only circumstances are against me there."

St. Claire leaned back while a footman refilled his glass. "I hear you've an estate in Dorset."

"I do," Rufus agreed. "I spend most of my time there."

"Good man. I expect your efforts at proper management pay off in the form of increased revenues."

"Indeed."

The footmen reappeared, bearing silver-domed platters and placed them about the table. As one, they removed the covers. Rufus bit back a smile. Equidistant between Ludlowe and Mariah sat a heaping platter of tripe. If Ludlowe's fleeting look of disgust was any indication, he hated the stuff as much as Mariah.

Catching Ludlowe's glance, Rufus raised his glass. Ludlowe answered the salute with a benign smile, but the malice that glittered in his eyes was anything but.

Yes, malice. Enough for Ludlowe to take advantage of a fortuitous situation at the Posselthwaite ball, a chance to play a nasty trick on an old rival and, at the same time, rid himself of a besotted Sophia.

CHAPTER EIGHT

SOPHIA POKED at the choice morsel of quail Highgate had placed on her plate. The sole bite she'd managed to swallow had turned to sawdust on her tongue.

The evening was turning out worse than she feared. A tense atmosphere reigned about the table as everyone pretended her mother and Lady Wexford weren't nearly at stiffly polite blows over the wedding plans. They'd both clamped their mouths shut just short of sniping at each other.

Across the table, Ludlowe's laughter rang out, high and false, over some remark Julia had just made—to Benedict, but that didn't matter. Ludlowe had been trying unsuccessfully to attract Julia's attention the entire night. The singular loudness of his booming laugh only proved how desperate he'd become.

He'd barely glanced at Sophia all evening.

Swallowing, she pushed her chair back. Highgate immediately turned in her direction, his eyes sharp, discerning. Beyond a few exchanges with her father, he'd hardly said a word the entire meal, but in all that time, his presence had borne down on her like a weight. He didn't have to make a single observation for her to know he'd taken in every last nuance of the dynamic.

And now he pinned her with his gaze. "Should you be leaving when tonight is partly in your honor?" he murmured.

"I cannot stand this charade another moment."

"Are you all right, Miss St. Claire?" This from Ludlowe. It had taken him several hours, but at last he'd deigned to pay her more than passing heed.

"Forgive me, Mama, Papa. I'm afraid I'm feeling rather ill."

Lady Wexford harrumphed. "No wonder. You've barely eaten enough to keep a bird alive. Sit down and have a proper meal. You'll feel better in no time."

Sophia stared at the chunks of quail swimming in rich sauce, and her stomach lurched. "If you'll excuse me, I really think I ought to lie down."

"Nonsense! In my day, young ladies were brought up with better manners."

To Sophia's left, her mother puffed up, but before she had a chance to explode—in as mannerly a fashion as possible, of course—Highgate intervened.

"That will do."

He pronounced the words quietly, but with such an understated command, Sophia froze in place while an odd shiver crept up her spine. Then he turned back to her, pinning her once again with that fathomless gaze. "Go if you must. Don't let my sister stop you."

Sophia's slippers scarcely made a sound on the risers as she climbed to the library. The tense twitter of the conversation in the dining room faded. Without a doubt, she'd given them a new topic to discuss, or perhaps another reason for her mother and Lady Wexford to continue their dispute.

She breathed in. Even the air, free now of the sickly-sweet scents of overly rich sauce, smelled fresher away from the scrutiny of her family.

The handle turned easily in her hand, and the door's creak echoed through the empty room. At one time, her father's collection of learning lined three walls of shelves. New leather and parchment had filled the room with their distinctive odor. Gilt titles embossed the works of Plato, Aquinas, Shakespeare—anything that might indicate education and culture.

Not that her father had ever cracked the spine of a single volume. At any rate, the shelves lay mainly empty now, the books sold to make up the expenses of several seasons' worth of ball gowns.

Sophia passed them by, experiencing a pang of regret for the loss of Linnaeus's *Species Plantarum*. The pang was fleeting. Tonight she needed to escape, both her family and the reminder that Ludlowe would never look her way.

Padding to the fourth wall, she reached for her copy of *Sense and Sensibility,* its pasteboard covers well thumbed. Even in their reduced circumstances, the Dashwood sisters had managed to find happiness. If only Sophia could hold as much hope for her future.

A sob escaped before she could catch it.

Behind her, hinges groaned. She whirled. A man stood silhouetted on the threshold, his profile singularly unimposing. Highgate. Why must he invade her solitude? Could she not have a moment of peace to cry over Ludlowe?

"What are you doing here?" Her voice wavered, but she pressed onward. "You said it yourself not two days ago—we need to be careful not to put ourselves in a spot where we cannot call things off."

He advanced into the room and shut the door. With the latch's sharp click, the darkness deepened.

Sophia let out a gasp. The sheer and utter gall. She was trapped. If she raised a fuss, the entire household—Ludlowe included—would come running. She and Highgate would be well and truly caught.

"We need to have a discussion." He advanced, his boots thudding closer and closer. She no longer held a clear idea where he was. Why hadn't she thought to bring a branch of candles? On closing the door, he'd cast the library into darkness. The only source of light came from weak moonbeams filtering through the window.

"We already had one before dinner."

"We need to have another." His booted feet thumped to a halt. Heat radiated from her right. If she breathed in deeply, she might scent sandalwood. She tamped down the urge to shrink away. "It is past time you got over your feelings for Ludlowe."

Her fingernails bit into her palms. "That, my lord, is none of your affair."

"I've chosen to make it my affair." A quiet authority laced his tone.

Once more, she shivered. "Why? What does it signify? In two weeks or so I shall cry off our arrangement, and we'll never see each other again. What could you possibly care about my feelings for another man?"

"That man does not deserve your feelings." Such certainty. Such finality.

She attempted to penetrate the shadows to catch a glimpse of his face. "What could you possibly know about it?"

"I know a great deal about Ludlowe, a great deal of which is unsavory." He paused and drew a breath. "Consider what he's done to you. He could have helped extricate us from the situation, but has he acted?"

"He . . . He told me he'd do what he could. He said I could count on him."

"Hmmm." Another pause during which she imagined him nodding. "And have you been able to?"

"I've no way of telling, do I?"

"Convenient, isn't it? I could tell you more, but I see you will not listen. You will not wish to believe the truth."

He pronounced each word with a clipped finality that stole her breath and made her heart quake. A cold foreboding settled into the pit of her stomach. Thank goodness she'd merely picked at her supper. He knew something awful about Ludlowe. No. She thrust the idea aside. She was not ready to admit she'd frittered the last five years away on a sugar-spun fantasy. If she gave up on Ludlowe, she would have to accept spending the rest of her life on the shelf, faded and forgotten, as Mama often reminded her.

She hugged the book to her chest. "I'd rather not hear it right now, if you don't mind." Her voice wobbled horribly on the words.

"Will you accept it on trust then?" His tone softened into a rolling resonance that surrounded her like an old blanket. It conjured a vivid image of a warm, crackling fire on a cold night, of reclining on a settee, her head cradled upon a masculine pair of thighs, listening to that voice read poetry. She could almost feel his fingers sifting through her curls.

No! She had no business imagining him this way, especially not when the fantasy was attainable. All she had to do was refrain from crying off. But she knew nothing about him. Hadn't the last five years taught her the futility of existing in a world of fancy?

Shaking her head, she pressed the novel to her skin.

"What have you got there?" Somehow he'd caught the motion in the low light.

Wordlessly, she gave up her shield.

He moved to the window, and beneath the pale filter of moonlight, his shadow-self coalesced into flesh and bone. "What is this? I cannot read the title."

She swallowed. *"Sense and Sensibility."*

"You'd do better to put more value in sense than sensibility."

"What do you know of it?"

"Perhaps more than you realize."

His words bore little substance, yet his tone was fraught with meaning, as if he were hinting at a past emotional entanglement.

"Is that your answer then? Rely on sense alone? On cool logic to govern your entire life?"

"Isn't that what Elinor Dashwood did? And come to think of it, Ludlowe reminds me of Lucy Steele, although he's not after any particular fortune, only respectability."

She stared at his profile. The moonlight softened its harshness until even his scar faded. "You read novels?"

"I believe in putting a thing to the test before I consign it to feminine frivolity."

"Have you read any other such works? I greatly enjoyed *Pride and Prejudice*."

"I'm afraid I haven't had the pleasure."

She made her way back to the shelves, where leather-bound volumes had once stood in rank after rank like soldiers. Able to locate it in the dark, she reached for another much-thumbed book.

"I think you ought to give it a try. You might even recognize your sister in Lady Catherine." In the process of handing the novel to him, she hesitated. "Unless you've drawn the conclusion such occupations are indeed frivolous."

The corners of his mouth twitched. "Never let it be said that I backed down from a challenge." He took the book, his fingers brushing hers as the exchange took place. "Perhaps we can discuss it once I've read it."

She snatched her hand away. "You mean if you don't find it too frivolous."

"Miss St. Claire, I never proclaimed the other a frivolity. If that is the conclusion you drew, you were in error. And now if we wish to avoid further difficulty, we really ought to rejoin the others, painful as the notion may be. I shall go first. Wait a few minutes and follow."

With a sweeping bow, he turned and left the library, leaving Sophia alone with her thoughts. A third shiver passed through her. How on earth had she managed to challenge this man?

"Miss Julia, if I might have a word."

Julia turned on her heel, but a glance in the direction of the drawing room showed her mother and Lady Wexford already seated, studiously ignoring each other. Thank goodness. Neither had overheard Ludlowe's whispered request.

The silence emanating from the room was so deafening, the prospect of conversation with Ludlowe was nearly tempting. Nearly.

She turned back to him. "Aren't you going to drink port with the gentlemen?"

He grinned. "Highgate's already taken himself off somewhere and your friend Revelstoke doesn't seem to care for my company."

Julia sent him a pointed stare. If the man could discern Benedict's dislike, why couldn't he pick up on her lack of enthusiasm? For that matter, he ought to have noticed Sophia's affection long since. "Would you like to join us in the drawing room, then?"

"I was rather hoping I might speak with you alone."

Thinking of her sister's predicament, she narrowed her eyes. Sophia had mentioned his presence that night. If Ludlowe sought to win her by placing her in a compromising situation, he'd best make other plans. "We are barely acquainted, sir. What could you possibly have to say to me that you cannot say in front of my mother and Lady Wexford?"

He reached out and placed a hand on her forearm. "It would only take a moment of your time."

Arching a brow, she pulled back. "Then, whatever it is, you may state it here."

"Please, I realize this is highly unusual, but it is a most urgent matter."

"Most urgent?" She waved a dismissive hand, the gesture bordering on rudeness. Not that she cared, as long as he cottoned on to the idea she was not interested in his attentions. "Before the Posselthwaite ball, you barely addressed two words to me in your entire life. I cannot imagine what has changed in the days since, as you keep cropping up."

"My station, if I may speak plainly. That is what has changed."

"Ah, yes, the earldom. Have you received word from the Lord Chancellor?"

He shook his head. "It's far too soon. As your friend Revelstoke was so eager to point out the other evening, there's still the matter of the widow."

Julia studied him carefully. While his mild expression barely flinched, his voice had taken on an edge at the mention of Benedict. "Still, I fail to see what that has to do with me."

"My dear, it has everything to do with you. As Clivesden, I shall have a responsibility to assure the future of the line. I shall require a countess."

Even though she had known this was coming, the contents of her stomach churned. The second helping of syllabub threatened to put in a reappearance all over Ludlowe's impeccable tailcoat and embroidered waistcoat. That would be taking rudeness a bit too far.

While she didn't care much for Ludlowe, she took pity on his valet, and swallowed hard. "Surely any number of young ladies out this season might fulfill your requirements. Why, my own sister—"

"Is already betrothed. In any case, I have already made up my mind."

"And the young lady in question?" Julia couldn't help goading. "Is she to have any say in the matter?"

"That is what I wish to determine."

She clutched at her bodice. "You cannot possibly—"

He cocked his head. "Why can't I? You're of good family."

"Not that good," she broke in.

He gave a small cough. "Good enough. Your reputation is spotless. Come now, it is a splendid match."

For her, yes, and she must consider the family's finances. If her mother insisted on pushing her in Ludlowe's direction, he must have the blunt to go along with the title. But was she to be responsible for her father's gambling debts? She was not the one at the card tables night after night, wagering money she didn't have.

And Ludlowe's presumption that she should simply fall into his arms! She inhaled and prayed he would attribute the heat rising in her cheeks to a virginal blush. "I'm afraid I must decline. My sentiments are not engaged."

He laughed, actually laughed, and she stole another glance in the direction of the drawing room. The last thing she needed was her mother's interference. Fortunately for Julia, but perhaps unfortunately for Mama, conversation had renewed between the two ladies. From the looks of things, they had returned to their dinner discussion. Lady Wexford leaned in, quite red in the face, and her finger jabbed the air as she drove a point home.

"You, Miss Julia?" Ludlowe's reply brought her attention back to the matter at hand. "You worry about your sentiments being engaged?"

"It has always been my hope to make a love match," she lied.

His eyes glittered, and he raised a skeptical brow. "A love match? Surely you've had ample opportunity to make one by now. That baronet who offered for you two years ago. What was his name?"

"Brocklehurst," she supplied mechanically.

"Yes, that Brocklehurst fellow. He was utterly taken with you."

Precisely the reason she'd refused his suit. "I had no idea you paid such close attention to my doings."

"Oh, not at the time, certainly, but one hears things."

She dropped her hand from her throat and hid it in her skirts to mask its shaking. Keeping her voice steady became a concerted effort. "What sort of things?"

"Only that certain women have a tendency to guard their hearts and not open them to any man. And you, my dear, you trump them all."

"And men accuse ladies of gossiping," she said faintly. Well-bred young ladies didn't shout, after all. "I suppose you believe yourself to be the man to win such a vaunted prize."

He let out another bark of laughter. "Your heart doesn't interest me in the slightest."

She recoiled from his words. They repulsed her even more than his touch. "You may rest assured you are quite safe from its sentiment." She drew herself up and took a step in the direction of the drawing room.

His hand snaked out and latched onto her wrist. "Don't you see? That's exactly what makes you the ideal bride for a man like me."

She fixed him with a glare. "Unhand me, sir. I no more invite your touch than I do your suit."

"But—"

"You heard the lady. Remove your hand from her person."

Julia let out a breath, as, shoulders set, Benedict

stepped between them. He'd adopted the officious tone he'd perfected in the cavalry.

Ludlowe took the hint immediately. "I hope you'll give due thought to what I've said tonight."

She inclined her head. "Rest assured. I've already given your proposal all the consideration it merits. Now if you'll excuse me, I'm feeling quite unwell."

She backed away. Ludlowe lurched in her direction, but immediately stepped back, as, jaw set hard as granite, Benedict advanced. She headed for the staircase, intending to take herself off for the evening. Halfway up, the thud of booted feet met her ears, descending the flight toward the ground floor. Then from the foyer, rose the echo of Ludlowe's voice grumbling for a footman to call his carriage.

"Miss Julia, wait."

At the sound of Benedict's voice, she turned. He stood at the foot of the staircase, one hand on the newel post, his expression inscrutable.

"Of course," she breathed. "I did not mean to be so rude, but Ludlowe is completely insufferable. I owe you my thanks."

Below them, the front door cracked shut. Her heart lightened.

"Nonsense." He didn't move a muscle—he simply held her gaze captive—but she felt as if he were commanding her without words. Commanding her to come back down the stairs and stand before him.

She clutched at the polished mahogany railing, wanting nothing more than to retreat to her bedchamber and forget every vile word Ludlowe had said. He'd just offered her the sort of match she'd always wanted, but stated in the terms Ludlowe had used—it turned her stomach.

And now Benedict compelled her to stay.

After another moment's hesitation, he mounted two

steps. Julia slanted a glance toward the drawing room. If her mother were to see . . .

"What is it?" she asked, her voice low.

He climbed a few more stairs, far enough to bring his face on a level with hers. "I heard part of what he said."

Her grip on the railing became painful. "I prefer not to discuss it."

He ascended to her riser, forcing her to look up at him. "I want to know everything."

He'd never addressed her in that tone, the one he'd most recently used to get rid of Ludlowe. His captain's tone, brimming with authority.

She swallowed to relieve the dryness in her throat. "I cannot bear to repeat it. It was vile enough having to listen to it the first time."

He reached out, his hand pausing for a moment in midair before settling over hers. Her breath hitched at the contact. He'd touched her any number of times in the past. Why must she be so aware of it now? "That's exactly why I want to know what he said. If he dishonors you, by God, I shall call him out."

Her heart tripped over itself. "Oh, please don't."

He opened his mouth to reply, but shrill voices ringing from the drawing room cut him off.

"I shall be quite relieved when this entire mess is over." Lady Wexford's stentorian tones echoed through the hall. Heavy footfalls announced her imminent appearance.

Mama burst out a reply that Julia didn't catch. Benedict chose that moment to take her hand and pull her noiselessly the rest of the way up the stairs. Reaching the upper corridor, he led her into the first doorway on the left.

Papa's study lay shrouded in darkness. Benedict pushed the door closed until no illumination remained but a tiny wedge of light from the hallway.

"What are you doing?" Julia whispered.

"Making sure we have a chance at a little uninter-rupted conversation." The direction of his voice told her he'd come to stand before her. The thick Axminster car-peting muffled the thud of his shoes. She could not see him, but his presence hovered inches away, a tangible force.

"Do you wish us to be discovered?"

"Little chance there. I've already taken my leave with your father. I thought it prudent not to brave the draw-ing room."

But Julia could think of nothing beyond her sister's situation. Mama might disapprove of Revelstoke, but she'd play the situation into an excuse to push her at Lud-lowe. "What will my mother make of this if she finds us here?"

"One can only hope."

She stiffened. The words had floated from his lips lightly enough, but their long-term friendship had fa-miliarized her with every nuance of his speech. His tone reminded her of their waltz, when she accused him of practicing his flirting. Now she wondered. Had he in-deed been practicing or in earnest?

With her.

"Come," he added, when she didn't respond. "You'd be happier with me than Ludlowe."

"Mama will find a way to let you off the hook. She favors Ludlowe's suit."

"The devil you say!"

She didn't even flinch at his language. Long acquain-tance had inured her to it. At times like this, she envied him the freedom to express himself in such terms. "He's going to be an earl, you see."

"Whereas I'm a mere second son of little enough means." The level of bitterness in his tone shook her far more than his profanity. She'd never before heard him express acrimony for being born the spare.

"There's no need to sacrifice yourself for my sake. I'm perfectly capable of refusing Ludlowe until he gives up. I've had plenty of practice. Although . . ." She chewed her lip for a moment. "Perhaps if I'd had less practice . . ."

He drew breath in an audible hiss. "What do you mean?"

"Nothing, really. Just a remark Ludlowe made."

That was the wrong thing to say, apparently. Strong fingers wrapped about her elbow. "What remark?"

His tone brooked no argument. Drat it all. She wanted to forget the things Ludlowe had said to her, not open them up to Benedict's scrutiny. "Apparently, I have something of a reputation."

His fingers tightened their grip. "How dare he impugn you when your reputation is impeccable?"

"Except when you drag me to a darkened room for a *tête-à-tête*."

He dropped his hand. Cool air wafted over her as he strode away. His shoes thumped toward the far end of the room. "That is a different matter. By God, I *shall* call him out."

"You shall do no such thing. I care nothing for Ludlowe, but this simply isn't important enough for you to risk your life over the truth."

The merest whisper of dull thuds told her he'd marched back. His presence loomed over her. "What exactly did he say to you?"

"He only noted that I've turned down every man who's offered for me. You cannot call him out over such a thing."

"Then what did he say to make you so upset?"

"It seems I've refused so many suitors I'm considered a bit of a cold fish."

"He said that to you?" Fabric rustled. She imagined his tailcoat shifting as he dragged a hand through his hair. No, more thuds. He was marching away—toward the door. "I must contact Upperton. He'll agree to be my second."

A memory surged into her mind. Her nine-year-old self slipping on a stone. That momentary sensation of weightlessness followed by a heavy splash. A white-faced Benedict hesitating only a moment before jumping in after her. His head had disappeared twice under the murky water before she pulled him out. How little he'd changed, flying off half-cocked over a trifle.

"Benedict!"

At the sound of his given name, his footfalls came to an abrupt halt. She felt it in the change of his energy, from movement to complete stillness. Apparently, she also possessed a captain's tone.

"He did not say such a thing to me, not in so many words. I took his meaning well enough. At any rate, it seems he's decided this makes me his ideal bride."

"Ideal bride?" Distaste echoed through his words. "Who would want such a marriage?"

Julia took a deep breath. She'd never imagined making this admission to a man, even if she had known him most of her life. "I do."

A second or two of silenced ensued. "You cannot be serious."

"I'm perfectly serious. I've watched my sister languish for years over a sentiment that is supposed to render a person happy. It's brought her nothing but pain. Why should I open my heart to something like that?"

An image, long suppressed, surfaced in her brain, and she shuddered. *No.* She squeezed her eyes shut and thrust it aside. She would *not* think about that day, even if it had more to do with her refusal of love than anything Sophia had ever done.

"Don't you believe the risk might be worth something?" Stealthily, he'd worked his way closer. His voice rumbled within inches of her ear, the captain's tone completely gone, replaced by something low and velvet and beguiling, something that turned her insides—oh God—to liquid heat. "If your sentiments were returned—"

"I have none to return." She let out a little twitter of laughter.

For a moment, his breathing, shallow, harsh, and agitated, broke the room's silence. "You? Have none to return? I do not believe that for a moment. I recall you climbing trees to put baby birds back in their nests."

She ought to have laughed at that memory. Instead, a shiver passed down her spine at the utter conviction in his tone. "Believe what you will. Only I know the truth of what lies inside me."

"I'm not certain you do." Trembling fingertips fluttered along her neck. Her pulse leaped in response, and she sucked in a breath, the hiss loud in the dark. "You cannot stand there and tell me you feel nothing."

Oh, she felt, certainly—too much and the sensation was altogether too enticing.

"You cannot convince me you'd be willing to enter a marriage with no tender feelings at all."

She reached out, hoping to placate him, but immediately balled her fingers into a fist. Best not to touch him, not while he was in this mood. "I would not be the first to do so." Mama, for one, had entered into just such an arrangement. "Nor would I be the last."

"Then you'd be missing the best life has to offer."

"And I'd save myself a great deal of pain when it all came crashing down."

"Some things are worth the pain. They're most definitely worth the risk."

In the dark, she missed the movement, but the emotion pulsing from him had heightened the rest of her senses. The only warning she received was the whisper of fabric. Before her brain had a chance to process the meaning of that sound, he took her roughly by the shoulders and crushed his lips to hers.

CHAPTER NINE

THE MOMENT their lips made contact, Julia stiffened, and Benedict braced himself for a slap. A slap or a knee to the groin. He deserved both the way he was assaulting her.

Neither came.

Instead, she whimpered into his mouth, the plaintive sound more resonant than a stinging smack. He eased her into a gentler kiss, intended to coax her into softening. He wanted her response.

No, he needed it.

His body screamed for her surrender the way his lungs screamed for air. Over and over, he slanted his mouth against hers, teasing, cajoling, until her breath expelled on a long sigh. He took advantage of her parted lips to sample their lush softness with his tongue.

"Ah!"

That whisper of surprise sent a bolt of heat coursing to his groin, and he caught the back of her head in his palm to hold her in place. He pressed his lips to hers once more and felt a tentative push back. Her hands drifted to his shoulders; her fingers burrowed into the wool of his coat.

Clinging.

Yes.

He wrapped his other arm around her waist to savor the length of her body flush against his. Her lovely breasts, the cradle of her hips, her lithe thighs. She swayed into his embrace, and he pushed their kiss further. Deeper.

Triumph poured through him as her tongue rose to twine with his. A growl surged into his throat, and he pressed his advantage. Her unschooled response, fueled by her awakening passion, aroused him more than a courtesan's practiced caress.

Because this was Julia, his Julia, and he could no longer deny what he felt for her. He pulled her closer, urged even more of a response. He needed more, her taste, her jasmine perfume surrounding them both. Her fingers tangled in his hair, her mouth responsive against his.

Then without warning, she tore her lips from his, planted her palms against his chest and shoved. Benedict froze, and for a long moment, only the sound of their ragged breathing filled the room.

"That cannot happen again." Her words rung with such finality, she might have screamed them.

For an instant, shock held him in an icy grip. Then he stepped forward, intending to capture her once more to put the lie to those words. Now that he'd kissed her once, he couldn't fathom it being a singular occurrence. He quite imagined she'd just ruined every other woman for him.

Somehow in the dark, she eluded his arms, so he settled for a verbal reply. "Why can't it? You'll never have me believe you did not enjoy that."

"It cannot happen again, ever." Her voice quavered oddly on the final syllable. She sounded dangerously near tears, and he wanted nothing more than to pull her back into his embrace and comfort her.

"If I hurt you in the beginning, I apologize."

"You did not hurt me, not in the beginning and not the way you think."

He bit back a curse against the room's darkness. If

only he could see her expression, he'd have a better idea how to respond. "But I have hurt you."

"More like you betrayed me." Something muffled her words. He imagined her, head lowered, speaking around a hand placed along the side of her jaw.

"Betrayed you? Don't you think you're taking matters a bit too far?"

"No, not at all. You're supposed to be my friend." On every successive syllable, her voice strengthened until it reached the crisp chill of accusation. "You're supposed to be the one man I can count on to ask me to dance, and I do not have to concern myself that you'll do anything untoward. I could always depend on you for that, and now you've ruined it."

She turned, and her slippers thudded dully on the carpet as she crossed to the door.

Anger seethed inside him, and he gritted his teeth as if that would hold back the imminent eruption. "I've only ruined your illusions."

She froze on the threshold, her rigid silhouette outlined in the faint light coming from the corridor.

He reached the door in two strides. "You prefer to pretend you have no feeling inside you, that you have nothing to offer a man. And now that I've proven you wrong, you cannot stand to face the truth."

"I have never seen happiness result from such sentiment. Goodnight, Lord Benedict."

He slammed his palm against the door, and it closed with a loud bang.

"What have you done?" She pitched her voice low but could not mask its shaking. She tugged at the door in vain. "Do you *want* us to be caught?"

"Hang it all if we're caught. I want an explanation from you." He leaned his full weight against the oak panel. "Neither of us is leaving this room until I have it."

"What is it you want to know?" The words emerged clipped, as if she'd pronounced them through clenched jaws.

"It's quite simple. I would like to know why you're willing to settle for . . . for such a sterile idea of a marriage."

"I prefer to think of it as sensible." Since he'd closed the door, he'd cast the room in total darkness and once more masked her expression, but he could well picture her chin raised. Defiant, as always, just as she'd been as a child when, that day at the pond, her governess berated her over her soaked and muddied gown. Then, the sensible had preoccupied her far less.

"Then why would you say you've never seen happiness come of love?"

"Have you ever looked at the couples that surround us?" She let out a huff. "My sister, for one. All she's done is suffer for her feelings."

He crossed his arms. "So you've said. I cannot believe that's all there is to it."

"Do not forget my mother. She meant to marry the Earl of Cheltenham, only he abandoned her and she had to settle for my father." For all the good the other match would have done her. Cheltenham had married, produced a daughter, and popped his clogs in short order, leaving the earldom to pass to another branch of the family.

He held in a shout of laughter. "Shouldn't the state of your parents' marriage argue against such a sensible arrangement?"

"But Mama always claimed to love her earl." The words slipped out on a note of desperation. If Mrs. St. Claire had loved anything about her earl, it was his title.

One side of his mouth twisted upward. At least, in the dark, he had no need to mask his expression. "Let's suppose I believe that. Your sister's pain and your mother's—

it comes of their sentiments not being returned. While you . . ."

He let himself trail off. Words tangled with the emotions churning inside him, but he wasn't yet ready to lend them voice, any more than she was ready to listen.

"Benedict, I—Please don't ask too much of me."

"This is about more than Sophia and your mother, isn't it?"

But for the whisper of her breath, silence reigned in the room while he awaited her reply, a silence that became weightier with each passing moment, until it shut out the sounds of the rest of the house.

At last, no longer able to stand it, he groped for her. His hand met hers, their fingers knotted, but she did not pull away. "Tell me who hurt you."

"No one hurt me. Not in the way you think." She paused, and her fingers curled about his. "Do you recall our governess?"

He did, vaguely, as a comic figure, someone they played pranks on, someone they delighted in fooling. "Miss Misery?"

"Miss *Mallory*," she corrected him with surprising vehemence.

"What's she got to do with any of this?"

"She let herself fall in love." Her voice rang hollow. "Sophia and I weren't supposed to know, but we caught her. She'd always blush and get flustered around Smithers."

"Smithers?"

"One of the footmen," she clarified. "Sophia saw them kissing."

"Was she dismissed over that?"

"No." Julia sighed. "We never told Mama. Even then we knew she'd never understand. Miss Mallory was of good family. A footman was far beneath her."

"Surely she did not marry the fellow."

Julia shook her head, a motion he felt more than saw through the connection of their hands. "I do not think, in the end, Smithers felt as strongly. He left us that summer to marry some village girl, and Miss Mallory . . . Miss Mallory . . . she . . ."

"She what?"

"She took too much laudanum."

He slipped a hand to her shoulder, slid it along the nape of her neck, and pulled her head against his chest. Thank God she didn't push away this time. There was worse to come—he sensed as much. He pressed his lips to the top of her head, and breathed in jasmine. "You were so young. How could you have known?"

"I was the one who found her. I went to her rooms. I cannot even recall why now. I thought she was asleep at first, only she didn't"—she shuddered in his arms—"move."

His heart turned over. So young, and he must have been away at school, blithely unaware at the time, barely noticing the replacement when he returned on holiday. He might have lent comfort had he known, the same way her presence had lightened his heart after his parents' demise. Had she even understood the concept of death before the day she was forced to confront it?

He shifted his weight and pulled her closer. "Did . . . Does Sophia know?"

"Mama forbade me from telling her."

Odd that she'd heeded that directive at a time when obedience went against her nature. Even as a child, she must have suspected Sophia was more fragile when it came to matters of the heart. Only that meant Julia bore the burden of her discovery alone.

She'd never been able to share what she'd learned— that love might drive a person to such an extreme, that the pain might become so unbearable it pushed one to take one's own life.

"Have you ever told anyone of this?"

"Mama would not let me speak of it, not even to her. How would it appear if word got out that she'd hired such an unstable sort to look after her daughters? How would that upbringing have affected our ability to catch suitable husbands?"

"To hell with suitable husbands. You needed to tell somebody and not keep that locked inside you." With his fingertips, he traced along her ear to the line of her jaw. "No one ought to bear such burdens alone."

"But don't you see what Miss Mallory's feelings for Smithers drove her to?"

"Her unreturned feelings," he insisted. "It's not the same thing."

She pushed herself away from his embrace, away from him. "Don't ask of me more than I can give. I have never seen love lead to anything like happiness. The so-called love matches of society turn cold after a few years. You've seen it. What of our Prince Regent, forced into marriage with a woman he cannot bear, when by all accounts, he was in love with Mrs. Fitzherbert? And even that passion did not last."

"Then he could not have truly loved her."

"I do not have it in me to return that sort of senti-ment," she insisted. "You have had your explanation, and now I beg you to let me go."

"This isn't over," he growled.

"Yes, I'm afraid it is." She grasped the door handle and pulled. "Goodnight, my lord."

She marched off, closing the door behind her. The click of the latch echoed loudly in his ears along with her dismissal, each cold and perfunctory word a nail driven into his heart.

* * *

JULIA kept her composure until she reached the bed-chamber she shared with her sister. Once surrounded by the familiar—the safe—she let herself go limp, her back pressed to the wall as she slid to the thick padding of the carpet. She touched her fingertips to her lips.

Still swollen, still tingling. And the feel of his arms about her, his chest solid against her breasts . . .

She raised cold hands to clutch her cheeks. What was she going to do now? One touch of Benedict's mouth to hers, and the entire world had tilted on its axis. His lips had slipped so sensually over hers. So compelling. And the smooth glide of his tongue—

The paneled door rattled open, and Julia scrambled to her feet. Too late.

"My goodness, the spectacle in the drawing room." Sophia sailed into the bedchamber. "I was certain Mama and Lady Wexford would come to blows."

"I thought you claimed a headache."

"Highgate convinced me it was prudent to put in an appearance." Sophia looked her over. "But you weren't in the drawing room. What were you doing on the floor? And in your dinner dress?"

"Nothing."

"Then why is your face so pale? Something's happened."

Julia eyed her sister. Roses bloomed in her cheeks. Suspicious roses. "I might ask you the same. Where did you disappear to after dinner?"

"Only the library. That can hardly come as a shock to you." The tips of her ears, just visible through the mass of golden ringlets, turned the same color as her cheeks.

Julia arched a brow. "The library, is it? And what is it about the library that is making you blush?"

"Well." Hands folded primly in front of her, Sophia

cast her eyes to the floor. "Highgate might have managed to track me down."

Of course he had, and further convinced her to rejoin the company.

"Haven't you learned anything from the Posselthwaite ball?" As if she had any right to criticize her sister after what had just happened in Papa's study.

"What more could possibly happen? We're already betrothed."

"If you're not extremely careful, you will not be able to cry off."

Sophia reached up in a habitual gesture to toy with the pendant she wore round her neck. A slight tremor in her fingers made her hand flutter like a bird's wing. "It isn't as if anyone saw us."

"It will not matter whether anyone saw you or not, the way you're behaving."

Her hand came to an abrupt halt. "How am I behaving?"

"Flustered. Why, I haven't seen you this out of sorts since—" Julia clamped her mouth shut. She'd nearly blurted out Ludlowe's name, and Sophia hardly needed the reminder.

Sophia moved to the dressing room and plucked at her curls. Hairpins showered to the floor. "What could I possibly have to be flustered about? We simply had a conversation, and I lent him one of my novels."

"He reads novels?"

"He expressed a liking for *Sense and Sensibility*. I found it rather refreshing that he did not immediately sneer at it as feminine foolishness."

"Oh, indeed."

Sophia whirled, the muscles about her eyelids tight. "Don't think I don't know exactly what you're doing."

"What am I doing?"

"Evading the question by distracting me."

"Oh? What was the question?"

"What were you doing on the floor when I came in?"

Julia focused on the miniature that sat on a rosewood table next to the bed. Out of an ornate gold frame, two young girls, one a golden blonde and the other darker in coloring, gazed serenely on the world. She recalled sitting perfectly still while the artist worked at his sketch pad. Hours and hours she'd sat with Sophia, an arduous task for an eleven-year-old who'd much rather romp through the woods with Benedict. But that was before she'd had her innocence stolen.

She suppressed a shudder at the recollection of Miss Mallory's hand, unnaturally cold and rigid beneath her fingertips. Realization had dawned slowly, but then she was only eleven. She'd washed her hand over and over to remove the sensation of that lifeless skin against hers.

"Thinking."

"Come now." Sophia came over and with a much steadier hand began to remove the pins from Julia's hair. "You're still evading the question."

Julia drew in a breath. "Have you ever permitted a gentleman to kiss you?"

Sophia's hand jerked, jabbing a pin into Julia's scalp. "Of course I haven't. I would have told you, and you know I'd only ever permit one man to take that liberty."

In the ensuing silence, Julia pressed her lips together. What her sister had left unsaid—that Ludlowe was unlikely to ever claim a kiss from her—rang loudly in her consciousness.

"Julia," Sophia said as if she might not like the reply, "did someone kiss you tonight?"

"Benedict," she whispered.

"Oh, Julia, he *is* in love with you!"

She turned to find Sophia grinning from ear to ear. "I'd rather he wasn't."

"Whyever not? You've known each other forever. You

already get on famously. Oh, you must tell me, what was it like?"

"Unexpected." Dark, unsettling, and yet oddly delicious. Not that it would happen again. Not that he would try after her cold dismissal. But surely she could not have acted otherwise. Surely a young lady of good breeding did not demand more.

Not that she wanted more. Oh, no.

Sophia gave her a playful slap on the arm. "Pooh, you're no fun. Now that you're an experienced woman, you could at least advise me on what to expect."

Julia sank onto the bed. "I do not know that I could possibly describe it. Why don't you ask Highgate to kiss you? Then you'll know."

Sophia shook her head. "I could never betray William like that."

Words leapt to Julia's mind and jammed in her throat. Awful, cruel words like, "How could you betray him when he's never truly looked in your direction?" In short, the truth.

But Sophia didn't want the truth. She never did.

Eyes wide, she stared at Julia, expecting encouragement in her fantasies, but tonight Julia could not find encouragement within her. Not in regard to Ludlowe, and not after the vile way he'd attempted to propose. But Julia could never tell Sophia about that.

"No, of course you couldn't betray William like that," she replied in a near monotone, like a pupil reciting a lesson long since learned by rote.

"What if he proposes?"

An awful jolt pierced her stomach, and she snapped her gaze back to Sophia. "Who?"

"Why Benedict, you goose. You could not think I meant William, could you?"

"Please stop."

Sophia raised her eyebrows. "What's the matter?"

"I cannot marry Benedict, and you know it."

Sophia waved a hand. "Mama will get over his lack of a title."

His lack of a title was the least of Julia's concerns, but she'd rather not discuss those matters with her sister. They cut too close to both their hearts. They were part of a past she'd worked so hard to bury. And there it would remain, safely interred. "I'm not sure she will."

"So far as she knows, I've landed myself an earl. She's over the moon about that. Perhaps she'd be willing to overlook Benedict."

"Just how long are you planning to wait before crying off?" Julia swallowed. "Not that it matters. He hasn't offered."

God willing, he never would.

RICH amber liquid swirled in the glass, the movement mesmerizing until it ceased. Benedict tossed back the brandy. It burned a path to his stomach, and for a moment, the buzz of surrounding conversation faded. So much the better. He'd chosen this corner of the club because he'd rather avoid the usual insipid observations about the weather and endless political debate. After yet another unsuccessful day looking at horseflesh, a mere glass wasn't sufficient.

And that wasn't taking into account the disaster kissing Julia had brought about. Three days, and he still couldn't erase the memory of her scent, her curves pressed against him—at least until she pushed him away. Raising a finger, he hailed a footman. He'd need an entire bottle before he'd forget the kiss they'd shared.

For, after her initial hesitation, she *had* shared it with him for a few moments—all too brief, but enough to fuel his imagination at night. Enough to conjure images of her pliant body responding to a far more intimate touch than his lips on hers. He could nearly taste the salt of her skin on his tongue.

He drummed his fingers on the table. Where was that footman?

"You know, you've become downright maudlin these days."

His hand froze mid-drumroll. Upperton stood at the table, his cravat carelessly askew and his hair tousled, as if he'd come straight to the club from his mistress's bed.

"If you ask me," he went on, "it's some bit of muslin that's got under your skin."

Benedict flattened his palm against the table. "I didn't ask you. And how dare you refer to her as some bit of muslin?"

Upperton pulled back a chair and settled himself, arms folded over his chest and his long legs stretched before him. "Perhaps if you told me her name, I mightn't dare."

"I'm barely in my cups as it is. I'd have to be apedrunk before I'd tell you that."

The footman reappeared with a full bottle of Hennessy and a second glass, which Upperton lost no time claiming.

"Shall we make a game of it?" He poured two fingers into each of the glasses. "I shall name a young lady. If I'm wrong about her identity, I shall take a drink. And if I guess it right, you shall drink. Whichever of us is thoroughly foxed first wins."

"What does he win? Unless it's something useful like a broodmare, I'm not interested. I can manage on my own without playing games." To emphasize his point, Benedict downed his measure in one swallow.

Upperton tapped his fingers on his untouched glass. "You realize you're going to wake up tomorrow with the devil dancing on your head and a craving for something vile like kidney and kippers for breakfast?"

"At least I'll have slept."

Arching a brow, Upperton sipped at his drink. "Is it that bad? Let's say we make a wager. I get one guess. Five hundred pounds says I'm right."

Benedict's glass hit the table with a resounding crack. "A wager? Damn you and your wagers. That's what got me into this mess in the first place."

Upperton inspected his nails. "Indeed. And have you let Miss Julia know of your affections?"

Benedict blinked at his friend.

"Don't look so shocked." Upperton leaned forward in his chair. "How could you ever think you were hiding anything with that display the pair of you put on—?"

"What display?"

"When I pulled your leg about making a go of things with her. At the musicale. You cannot be so far gone to have forgotten that. My tone-deaf sisters? Doing horrible injustices to Herr Mozart and various other composers?"

Irritation prickled through the beginnings of a respectable fog of brandy. "Yes, yes. What of it?"

"Well, of course you would not have noticed. You were too busy studying the wallpaper. You could have fried an egg on Miss Julia's face, it was so red."

Benedict fingered the brandy bottle. "Such a poet you are with those images. You ought to give Lord Byron a few lessons. Show the man how it's done."

"Ah, sarcasm. The final refuge of the desperate. I see you're not bothering with denials. That's always a step in the right direction."

"Your point, Upperton, before I give in to the urge to find out what color your hair will turn if I upend this bottle over it."

"You'd never commit the sacrilege of wasting such superior brandy."

Benedict closed his fingers about the bottle's neck. "We can always order another."

"Right," Upperton hurried on, "my point. How does one put this delicately?"

Benedict snorted. "You've no more an idea how to put things delicately than your sisters have an ear for music."

"Conceded." Upperton raised his glass in salute. "I shall barrel straight through it then. You weren't the only one uncomfortable with my teasing. Miss Julia was just as ill at ease. If you want my opinion, she might well accept your suit."

Benedict leaned forward. "How would you like to wager on that?"

"Well, damn."

"What?"

"If you're that confident, I know I've lost ahead of time. What happened?"

Benedict eyed his friend. While they'd certainly passed many agreeable hours—God only knew they'd both nursed the headaches afterward—discussing females, he had never said a word about this particular woman. He refused to consider her alongside opera dancers and actresses and the sorts of women Upperton frequented. In his mind, Julia stood apart from even the higher born daughters of the *ton*. She always had and bloody likely always would. Only, since their kiss, the nature of that distinction had changed. Discussing her with Upperton, as if she were some opera singer he lusted after, was unthinkable.

And yet the brandy warmed his veins and loosened his tongue. "I kissed her."

Upperton's eyebrows disappeared beneath his shaggy fringe. "Indeed? And?"

"Her reaction was not what I'd hoped."

Upperton's laughter earned him a glare from a gentleman a table or two over. "She slapped you, didn't she?"

"No." If only she had. He suspected anger would have been easier to endure.

It was her icy demeanor—understandable, of course, given the secret she'd revealed—that had sent him back to his original purpose of acquiring horseflesh. He recalled too many times they'd laughed together in the past. He wanted the old Julia back.

"Then what?" Upperton prodded.

"She kissed me back."

"And *that's* driven you to this state?"

Benedict lowered his brows. "I'm not in a state."

"Of course you're not."

"Hang it all. She came to her senses."

Upperton tossed back the remainder of his glass. "There's a simple solution to your problem."

Benedict glared at his friend, knowing in advance he was not going to like what Upperton was about to say. "What?"

"Make sure she loses her senses next time."

He studied his glass for a moment before raising it to his lips. "There will not be a next time. She's made that clear enough."

"Where is your courage, man?" Upperton slammed a hand down on the table, drawing more glances from those seated nearby. "You have affection for the girl. You need to bound in and sweep her off her feet. Don't give her time to stop and think. Keep her so occupied, she doesn't realize what's hit her until she wakes up in your bed one morning, and by then she'll be so thoroughly satisfied, it will not matter."

Benedict set his glass down with a thud. "Are you quite through? I cannot believe you've just suggested I seduce a well-bred young lady of an upstanding family."

Upperton slanted him a look. "Wouldn't be the first time it's happened."

"You are assuming the young lady in question is amenable. I can assure you, she is not."

Upperton tipped the bottle and poured them both another glass. "At least things do not bode so well for Ludlowe in that case."

Benedict swallowed his full measure without pause. "He's already proposed."

Upperton's face turned purple as he spluttered and coughed. "Good God, man," he wheezed once he got his breathing under control. "Why didn't you say so in the first place? And, more to the point, what are you planning on doing to stop it?"

Benedict made no reply. A movement out of the corner of his eye caught his attention, and he turned. Shoulders hunched, the candlelight reflecting off his pate, Mr. St. Claire descended the staircase from one of the upper rooms.

Benedict narrowed his eyes. "What do you think he's doing here?"

Following the direction of Benedict's gaze, Upperton perked up. "Speak of the devil."

"We weren't speaking of St. Claire."

"No, but Ludlowe's name came up." Upperton nodded toward a figure strolling in Mr. St. Claire's wake. A tall, impeccably dressed figure, whose walking stick tapped each riser as he advanced. With him was another man, quite average in both height and looks, with only a rather impressive nose to distinguish him.

Before Benedict could react, Upperton pushed himself from his seat and strode toward the elegantly carved curve of the stairs. Benedict groaned. While Upperton hadn't imbibed enough to be even halfway to foxed, he'd consumed sufficient brandy to lose his sense of caution— just enough to make him dangerous.

Benedict scrambled to find his footing. The floor beneath his Hessians listed like a beleaguered ship in a

Channel storm, and he grasped at his chair for support. He'd swallowed more liquor than he'd intended, enough to make navigating the maze of tables and chairs to the door an inhuman feat.

And that was not even negotiating the steps down to the ground floor.

"Where are you off to, Revelstoke?"

Too late. Upperton was back, a gleam of mischief in his eye, Ludlowe and companion in tow. The first time Benedict had ever seen that particular gleam, they'd been first-year students at Eton. After the resulting caning, Benedict had resolved to heed that gleam and run in the opposite direction, but then he'd never been much good with resolve.

"Don't mind Revelstoke," Upperton went on, as he ushered Ludlowe into a chair. "He's had a stroke of bad news and could use a spot of cheer."

"I've got just the thing." Ludlowe's companion pulled a pack of cards from his coat. He proceeded to shuffle them in a flamboyant manner that did nothing to set Benedict at ease. A man that dexterous might easily stack the pack with no one the wiser. "What's your game? Piquet? Vingt-et-un?"

Benedict had not drunk enough to be tempted. He lifted the brandy. "I've got all I need right here, thanks."

Ludlowe eyed the bottle of Hennessy and grinned. "Perhaps you'd like to help me celebrate."

Benedict flopped into his seat, torn between the urge to guzzle the remainder of the brandy and pray for oblivion, or to break the bottle over Ludlowe's thick skull. Either way, it would waste perfectly good brandy, but he was too drunk to care.

"Oh?" Upperton raised his eyebrows. "And what is it we're celebrating tonight?"

Ludlowe's smile widened. Seizing Benedict's glass, he

poured himself a measure and raised it. "A toast, my friends."

Upperton clinked his glass against Ludlowe's. "Cheers! What is it we're drinking to?"

"A successful courtship."

Benedict watched in horror as Ludlowe downed the contents of his glass. He couldn't possibly swallow another drop. As it was, the quantities he'd already taken in were threatening to put in an imminent reappearance.

"Ah." Upperton took a swallow. "And who, pray tell, is the lucky lady?"

"No." Ludlowe set down his glass and wagged an impeccably manicured finger in Upperton's face. From the looks of things, he'd already had as much as was good for him. "No, no, no. If you don't already know, I shan't tell you."

"Then, perhaps more to the point, has she consented to your suit?"

"Upperton," Benedict growled. He really didn't want to hear this. "I think it's best if I leave."

Upperton fixed him with a grin that boded no good at all and clamped a hand on his forearm.

Ludlowe tossed back another shot. "Not yet, she hasn't, but it's only a matter of time. I received word from the Lord Chancellor today. My petition has been accepted."

Upperton gave an exaggerated bow of his head. "My lord. Or might I say my condolences to your bachelorhood. For if you don't soon have every young miss and her mother on your heels, I'll eat my hat."

"Ha! A fate worse than death," added his friend.

Clivesden, for it was thus that Benedict must now think of him, swallowed another few fingers of brandy. "Precisely why I've taken steps to remove myself from the marriage mart posthaste. Before too long, I should manage to get back to the peaceful existence I enjoyed before all this dropped into my lap."

Benedict gripped the bottle, his fingers tightening about the glass as he imagined crushing it in his fist before jamming said fist into Clivesden's overly abundant teeth.

He glanced at Upperton, whose face bore every sign of a man thoroughly enjoying himself. Why'd he invite Clivesden over here? Simply to create mayhem, or did he have a more concrete reason? Watchful and silent, Clivesden's friend continued to fiddle with his cards.

No matter, Benedict was not having any more of this nonsense. He made to stand. "If you'll excuse me, gentlemen."

Upperton reached out an insistent hand and pressed down on his shoulders. "Not going so soon, are you? Not when it's just getting interesting?"

Benedict no longer held a clear notion of the time, but it must be nearing midnight. "I've had all the interest I can take tonight. Any more and I will not be held responsible for my actions."

"Humor me, would you?" Then Upperton turned back to his quarry. "Not letting the small matter of marriage change anything about your life, I see."

"Well, why should it?" the nameless friend remarked.

Clivesden let out a shout of laughter. "I do not see that it's made a difference in the lives of most men of the *ton*. It's a small enough matter to bed one's wife until she gives him an heir and a spare, but after that?" He tipped back his glass and stood. "I fully intend to enjoy myself as I always have."

Once Clivesden and his companion had sauntered off, no doubt in search of an easy mark, Upperton smiled. "There's a true friend for you. As gossip would have it, Ludlowe's swiving his pal's intended on a regular basis."

"What?"

"Keaton. Ludlowe's had biblical knowledge of the man's betrothed."

Benedict fixed his friend with a glare. "Why did you force me to listen to that drivel? I'd just as soon knock the idiot's block off."

Upperton grinned. "Just shoring up my bets."

CHAPTER TEN

"Is IT true what I've been hearing?" Watery eyes narrowed, Lady Epperley surveyed Julia from behind her lorgnette.

Blast it all. She was trapped in the corridor that led to the ladies' retiring room. Of all the times to tread on her hem and require a quick repair. She'd had the chiffon resewn so often already, she doubted there was much material left to work with.

Julia tapped her fingers against her fan. Between Lord Chuddleigh making a nuisance of himself once again and gossip-mongering dragons, she should have stayed far away from the Pendleton ball. Not that she had a real choice, tonight of all nights.

"That depends on what you've been hearing, my lady."

The dowager's frown deepened. "Don't give me such nonsense. You must know. It was all anyone could talk about at the opera last night."

"I'm afraid we did not attend the opera. Too many family matters."

"Humph." Lady Epperley's jowls twitched in cadence with the feathers on her headdress.

Julia cast about for any possible subject of gossip. "Did it have to do with Princess Charlotte's upcoming nuptials?"

"Of course not. Anyone who matters is thoroughly tired of discussing who might be invited to the wedding and whether her royal highness is actually planning on wearing gold."

"I'm afraid I cannot answer your question, then." Julia took a hopeful step in the direction of the retiring room.

"Don't be silly, gel. You most certainly shall."

Did the old dragon intend to infuriate her? "Perhaps if you were a bit more specific."

The dowager leaned so close, the peacock feathers on her fan tickled Julia's nose. "Didn't I have a chat with you at the Posselthwaites'?"

Thoroughly confused, Julia fought off the urge to scream. "A bit of a chat. I believe you had more to say to my sister."

"Your sister, yes. I daresay—"

"Oh, Julia, I've been looking for you everywhere." Face flushed, Sophia came striding down the corridor as fast as her tightly laced stays allowed. "Mama says you must come to the ballroom quickly. They're waiting for you."

"Who is?" *Not Benedict. Please, not Benedict.* Although a few days had passed since their ill-advised kiss, she still was not prepared to face him. Not yet. Perhaps not ever. The mere thought of him turned her palms moist.

"Mama and Papa and Highgate and his sister, of course. They're ready to make the announcement."

Snap! Out came the lorgnette. "Highgate, is it? You'll be the one I want to talk to."

"My lady?"

Julia couldn't blame Sophia for the note of caution in her voice. The dowager's tone carried all the subtlety of a rampaging bull.

"Have you gone and betrothed yourself to the likes of him? Well, gel, speak up. Have you?"

Sophia paled and retreated a pace. "Yes," she squeaked.

"The way I heard it, you did not have a choice but to accept his offer," Lady Epperley went on. "In my day, young ladies approached marriage with a great deal more circumspection."

Sophia stared at the dowager with wide eyes.

"If you'll excuse us," Julia said, "I believe our mother needs us."

Like the figurehead on a warship, Lady Epperley advanced on her quarry. "I am not finished. You young chits. Clearly, you're in need of a better education. Running about, refusing decent proposals and then flinging yourselves on such men as Highgate."

Julia slanted a glance at her sister. Sophia's lower lip trembled, and she sucked it between her teeth.

"What of such men as Highgate?" Julia asked, although she dreaded the reply.

"Please don't," Sophia whispered.

Julia fixed her sister with a hard stare. Why stem the tide of this conversation? By her own admission, Sophia was planning to cry off. Lady Epperley's gossip might well give her the excuse she needed. Unless . . . unless Sophia already knew something.

"Don't what? What have you heard about Highgate?" Lady Epperley lowered her lorgnette and leaned closer.

"It was something Mr. Ludlowe said." Sophia eyed the dowager. "Please do not make me repeat it."

"Mr. Ludlowe?" Lady Epperley frowned. "Heard he's to be called Clivesden now. At any rate, I would not put stock in anything he has to say about Highgate." She stepped closer, mischief dancing in her eyes. "They have a history together, you see."

Sophia blinked once and then again. "They do?"

"Yes, my dear. I should not believe anything one says about the other." Without warning, she snapped her fan closed and took herself off, leaving Julia speechless for a moment.

"What was that all about?"

Sophia's head turned as she surveyed the dowager's progress back toward the ballroom. "I don't know." Her words carried an odd mixture of distraction and relief.

"You have an idea."

"Beyond the fact she's going feebleminded in her old age?"

A feeble mind was likely the least of Lady Epperley's faults. More likely, she acted that way a-purpose to provoke. "If it was mere feeblemindedness, you wouldn't have reacted so strongly."

"There's no time for that now. Mama—"

"Can wait. I need someone to sew my hem." Julia headed toward the ladies' retiring room once more. "You can tell me while the maids fix it."

"I will not repeat what William told me in front of a servant."

Julia stopped in her tracks. "If it's that bad, why haven't you leaped on the excuse to get out of your betrothal before now?"

"I don't suppose I really believed it deep down. William tried to warn me off Highgate the day he came to call on you, but then at dinner, he never spoke a word against the betrothal. If what he told me was true, he would have said something, surely."

Julia paused in front of the door to the retiring room. "And what did he tell you?"

Sophia stared at the toes of her beaded slippers. "He hinted Highgate is responsible for the death of his first wife."

Julia bit back a screech. "Sophia, you knew this before Highgate proposed, and you still accepted?"

"I can't explain, exactly. I did not quite believe it to begin with, and then Highgate was quite persuasive."

Julia opened her mouth to reply, but at that moment, the door opened, and a pretty young brunette emerged. On spotting Julia, she stopped short. Her face twisted itself into such an expression of loathing, Julia felt its impact in her gut. Without a word, the brunette turned the full force of her hatred on Julia, eyeing her from head to toe. She then pushed past Sophia and flounced off down the corridor.

Accustomed to the snub from certain sticklers due to her mother's antecedents, although perhaps not with this level of venom, Julia stared after her. "And who was that, I wonder?"

"The strumpet," Sophia murmured.

Julia gaped. "Sophia! If Mama heard you using such language about a lady of quality, why . . . I don't know what she'd do."

"That is no lady of quality. I tell you, she's no better than a common trollop."

"What makes you say so?"

"At the Posselthwaites', Ludlowe tossed me aside to flirt with her. She carries on so, when she's supposed to be engaged to young Keaton."

"Then why did she look at *me* as if I were some beggar woman dressed in rags?" Julia regretted the question immediately. It might well lead her sister to pose a few of her own—questions with no easy answers, at least if she wanted to preserve Sophia's heart.

Fortunately, Sophia lifted her shoulders in a shrug. "Who knows how the minds of such, ah, ladies operate? Come, we must hurry, or Mama will be along looking for us herself."

She ushered Julia into the room and hailed a maid to see to her sister's trailing hem. While the girl bent and took needle and thread to the silk and chiffon confection, Julia turned the topic back to Highgate.

"Are you really in such a rush to go through with all this, considering what you've heard?"

Sophia cast a glance about the room before replying. Lady Epperley might have taken herself back to the ball, but she was not by any means the *ton*'s only gossip. "What am I going through with, exactly? It's a temporary charade, and when it's finished, we'll part ways and have done." She gave a sharp little nod that set her blond ringlets bobbing.

Julia pressed her lips together. Sophia's scheme sounded like another one of her fancies. The reality was bound to be far different than her sister's imaginings.

"There ye be, miss." The maid pushed herself to her feet. "That ought to do ye until ye get home."

Julia smiled at her absently and started for the door. Sophia clutched at her arm with trembling fingers as they made their way through the cream-paneled corridor and down the stairs. Music swelled from the lower story to greet them.

They met their mother at the entrance to the ballroom. "There you are. You've kept your father and Highgate waiting far too long as it is."

Sophia's nails dug into Julia's arm.

"It was my fault, Mama," Julia put in quickly. "My gown needed a repair."

Mama's brows lowered. "We must hurry. Lady Wexford will want to leave soon."

"But it cannot be midnight yet," Julia protested.

With a smile and nod, Mama angled past a pair of gossiping matrons. "Just so. She's not used to keeping town hours, and I do not want her to miss the announcement."

"I thought she was dead set against any sort of public announcement."

A wicked glint sparkled in Mama's eye—the very same sky blue as Sophia's. "Which is precisely why I want her on hand to witness this."

Sophia slowed her steps until she dragged at Julia like a dead weight. "I don't know, Mama. You know how capable she is of creating a spectacle. Recall what I told you she said in the park."

"Oh, she would not dare. Not in front of the entire *ton*." Mama's observation might not be such an exaggeration. The Pendleton ballroom was packed with guests. Ladies' skirts swirled with color to the lively steps of a reel. Around the room's perimeter, groups stood in conversation. "Besides, it's not as if we're going to stop the orchestra and announce it to the entire assembly. Only a select few will do."

As they pushed their way through the crush, Julia saw that her mother's notion of a select few included Lady Epperley. The peacock plumes drifted above her blue turban as she inspected the crowd.

Beside her, Highgate edged a safer distance from the feathers. Not fast enough. She leaned across him to exchange a few words with Lady Wexford, and, in a sudden, violent motion, he threw back his head in a sneeze.

Julia's gaze passed beyond Lady Wexford, glowering in purple bombazine, to settle on her father—and a distinctly unwelcome sight.

An icy sense of foreboding washed over her, and she pulled up short. "What's Mr. Ludlowe doing there?"

Mama turned. "Come along, dear, we've waited long enough."

At the same moment, Ludlowe caught her eye and smiled, his gaze shrewd, piercing, too perceptive. An urge rose within to spin on her heel and march straight from the ballroom, but the combination of Sophia's gloved fingers digging into her arm and the surrounding crowd made flight impossible.

Bad enough that her parents were about to announce an unwanted betrothal, doomed to failure ahead of time—they were about to do so in front of the one man whose proposal Sophia would accept without hesitation.

What a disaster, with most of the blame laid at her parents' feet.

"Ah, there they are at last." Her father raised a glass of pale liquid to his lips. Bubbles rose to the surface in dizzying spirals. Champagne. "My ladies, each more lovely than the last."

Julia's gaze narrowed in on his nose—suspiciously red, of course. He must have imbibed a great deal of the sparkling wine to make such ebullient pronouncements.

"Come, come." He stepped aside to make room next to Highgate.

Sophia's fingertips threatened to leave bruises on Julia's arm. "You agreed to this," Julia grated to her sister. "Now you must go through with it."

As Sophia trudged to her place next to Highgate, Papa cleared his throat. Fortuitously—for him—the final notes of the reel sounded just then. In the ensuing quiet, his next words rang out loudly.

"My lady." He nodded toward Lady Epperley. "I'm sure you'll be interested to hear this."

The dowager was not alone. Nearby, heads turned.

"It seems I have a rather splendid bit of news. My daughter Sophia has accepted the suit of Highgate, here."

The lorgnette snapped out as Lady Epperley eyed the couple from head to toe. "I knew the gel would get there at last. How many proposals did it take her before she came to her senses?"

A blush crept up Sophia's cheeks, and Julia's heart made a sympathetic flip for her sister's sake. Papa raised his glass to the couple. Around them, the buzz of conversation rose. St. Claire was finally going to marry off a daughter.

One down, one to go.

The buzz grew in intensity until it seemed to fill the ballroom, enough to make the orchestra hold off launching into the next number. Another icy jolt coursed through her. Why couldn't they begin the next set?

And then the unthinkable happened.

Papa held up his hand and cleared his throat once more. In their corner of the room, the buzz died away into silence.

"Seems I have a second bit of news. Most astounding, really."

He phrased his words as if he were addressing Lady Epperley in a private conversation, but all around them bodies strained in their direction. No one wanted to miss this.

"I'll be marrying the other one off, too."

Julia's jaw dropped. Angry words, most of them gleaned from conversations with Benedict and thus unfit for utterance in front of the *ton*, crowded into her mouth, each jumbling into the next until none of them escaped. They jammed together in the base of her throat and formed a knot, impeding both speech and breath.

Her mother's sharp elbow made painful contact with her ribs, and she tripped forward. Ludlowe loomed out of the group to take her arm.

No!

But the denial could not escape. It remained trapped in her throat, joined the knot of words, and held back the scream she so desperately wanted to release over the ballroom.

"My lord Clivesden here has offered for Julia. Well, of course, I accepted."

The buzz started up again, swelling this time into an overwhelming rush. It drowned out all other sound.

Julia's feet remained rooted to the spot. Next to Ludlowe—no, he was Clivesden now. A title, an earl. Her mother's dream for her, a dream whose fingers dug sharply into her flesh, leaving no opportunity for escape.

How Julia wanted to escape. For all she could focus on was the expression of utter betrayal on Sophia's face.

CHAPTER ELEVEN

ALL AROUND Julia, a chorus of congratulations erupted. Well-wishers crowded her toward Clivesden, whose fingers curled about her arm to pull her close. She was too numb to protest, too numb to move from the spot.

Nausea roiled in her gut. If she took so much as a single step, she might double over and spill the contents of her stomach all over the pale rose chiffon of her ball gown.

Mama and Papa glowed with pride, but Julia's most pressing concern was her sister. She threw Sophia a glance of desperation.

Her sister's blue eyes glittered coldly in response. That expression of awful betrayal—rosy cheeks turned to chalk, lips pursed, chin puckered—engraved itself on Julia's heart. "I never meant for this to happen," she wailed, but shock turned her voice thin and reedy. Her words were lost in the uproar.

The news was spreading—it must have already extended to the other side of the ballroom. By morning, word would have reached the ears of even the most reclusive members of society: The infamous St. Claire sisters, both betrothed in a single night.

No doubt her parents had planned the announcement this way so Julia could not say a word against it without creating a scandal. No matter. In the morning, she'd have a talk with her father away from prying eyes, and she'd make him see. She was not about to tolerate this turn of events.

Sophia inhaled through her nose and fought for a calm demeanor—no mean feat when inside her emotions warred. Anger and heartbreak fought for the mastery, but on the exterior, she trembled with cold.

Five years. Five years she'd loved that man in vain, and it all came to this. He'd chosen her sister, who had never paid him a whit of attention.

It was not fair.

She'd have gladly offered him her beating heart on a platter, but he didn't want it.

Black spots danced before her eyes. No. She'd resolved never again to swoon at one of these functions. She would not do it now. Not here with only Highgate to catch her.

Mechanically, she accepted congratulations of one of her mother's acquaintances. She barely noticed who. Faces blurred into one another, and the entire ballroom closed into a single, stifling cell.

Air. She needed air. More than that, she needed to get away from that insipidly grinning idiot she'd cast her heart away on, that idiot who'd taken her sister's arm, who shook hands with all and sundry.

"I say, gel, are you feeling faint?" The words solidified in her ears, the sounds rearranging themselves to make sense. She blinked. Lady Epperley frowned from behind her lorgnette.

"Of course not."

"Of course you are. Don't try to put that past me. I'm too old for the likes of you to fool."

Sophia peeled her fingers away from Highgate's arm. Some instinct warned her that she didn't want him to take heed of this conversation. "Now that you mention it—"

The dowager's sharp nod set her jowls quivering. "The fashion might be all for pale skin, but your complexion is downright sickly. I doubt you've fooled even Lord Pendleton, and he's as blind as a bat."

She slipped farther away from the crowd about her family. "My lady, really—"

"There, there, dear." With surprising strength in one so apparently frail, Lady Epperley clapped her on the shoulder. "Chin up, and all that rot. This, too, shall pass."

For the first time in her life, Sophia looked at Lady Epperley, really looked. Beneath the crusty demeanor and lined countenance lurked a knowing intellect, quite apparent in her glance. While her red-rimmed eyes appeared short-sighted, a spark behind them betrayed the accumulated knowledge of decades of keen observance. Sophia's lower lip trembled, and she clamped down on it with her teeth.

"Got your attention now, haven't I?" the dowager went on. She nodded at Highgate. "You may not believe me at the moment, but one day you might just look back on this evening and realize what a close shave you've had."

Anger blazed to the surface, and Sophia drew in a breath to lend it voice. Lady Epperley knew nothing of her circumstances. Nothing!

"Don't get your feathers so ruffled. You give Highgate a chance and see if I'm not right."

Sophia gripped her fan hard enough to snap several of its ribs. "Give him a chance? Why, not half an hour ago, you asked me why I was throwing myself away on him."

"Perhaps I've changed my mind."

"Changed your mind?" A few more ribs on Sophia's beleaguered fan gave way. Age must have rendered Lady Epperley daft. There was no other explanation. "What gives you the right to pronounce on my future at all?"

Lady Epperley raised her considerable chin. "Experience, my dear. Should you be so fortunate as to reach my years, you might well discover the advantages of becoming a leader of society."

Daft, definitely. Given Mama's background, society would never allow her that sort of power. "I fail to see—"

A cackle cut her off. "You shall, should you have my fortune. Imagine. I can say what I want to whom I please and no one dares gainsay me. I can contradict myself all I like. Why, I'm free to make all the young chits squirm by insisting on all the rules of decorum, even when I think they're utter poppycock."

Sophia wagged her head from side to side. "But—"

"You give your earl a chance, and he'll set you up marvelously for such a place in society one day. Given his age, your chance might come sooner than later. As long as she's discreet, a widow can do as she pleases."

With that, the dowager sailed off through the crowd, leaving Sophia to gape after her towering peacock feathers. Why no one had sent the dowager off to Bedlam ages ago was beyond her.

"What was that about?"

Sophia turned to meet Highgate's keen glance. Here was another who saw entirely too much. While Lady Epperley simply aroused a vague uncomfortable feeling, Highgate stripped her completely naked. She resisted the impulse to cross her arms as a shield.

Unable to stand his scrutiny, she settled for studying his neatly tied cravat. Nothing garish or outrageous in that knot. "I've no idea. I think she's gone a bit soft in her old age."

He ducked his head in an attempt to capture her gaze, and she trained her eyes stubbornly beyond his shoulder. Bad idea. Julia came into view, still standing next to Clivesden as she accepted enthusiastic good wishes from Henrietta Upperton.

"Sophia." Her name hissed through his lips, harsh and low, but powerful enough to cut through the surrounding buzz of conversation.

That did it. Her gaze snapped to his. "I have not given you permission to address me by my given name, *my lord.*"

"I will, nevertheless, use it."

"You shall—"

His hand closed about her wrist in a shackle, and the remains of her fan dropped from her limp fingers. "Come with me."

As much as she wanted to escape this room, she planted her feet.

"Come," he said, his eyes softening.

No. Sophia would not allow herself to give in. She wanted to get away from this nightmare, but not on his orders. Not with him. All she wanted was to go home, where she could give in to her tears in the privacy of her room, as she had so often in the past.

And Julia—

A sob clawed its way to her throat. She wouldn't even be allowed that small comfort. How could her sister console her? From now on whenever she closed her eyes, she would see nothing but Julia standing next to Ludlowe— in Sophia's place.

Bowing her head, Sophia gave in and allowed him to lead her away from the crowded ballroom, vaguely aware of his muttered excuses to passing well-wishers. They were standing in the entrance to the Pendleton town house, Highgate ordering his carriage, before she came to her senses.

"What do you think you're doing?" she grated.

"Taking you home." His tone was unreadable. "You do not look at all well."

She couldn't go home and face the room she shared with her sister, but any other destination was unthinkable. Even his squiring her, betrothed or no, was beyond the pale. Betrothed. Dear God, what had she let herself in for? "You cannot. It's unseemly."

"I am afraid, my dear, you have no choice in the matter. If it's any comfort, I shan't lay a finger on you."

She took a step closer. "Do you not recall our agreement?" she asked, low, allowing her anger to resurface. "You will make it impossible to cry off with any hope of preserving my reputation."

"Did you honestly think you'd come out of this with your reputation intact?"

"Not wholly, no, but why make it worse?"

"Because you insist on making a fool of yourself over a man who does not deserve you."

"How dare you!"

"I dare because I know exactly what sort of man Ludlowe is." Only a slight flush on his cheeks, a reddening that caused his scar to stand out in greater contrast against his skin, betrayed his anger. "With or without his title, you were always far, far above him. Why you should wish to sully yourself—"

"Sully?" She fought to keep her voice from shaking. "But I suppose it's nothing for my sister."

He slid his hand from her wrist to grip above her elbow. A streak of heat coursed along her skin in its wake. "Your sister is not my concern. Your sister can hold her own against the likes of William Ludlowe, because she has no affection for him, while you—"

"While I what?"

"You are far too besotted for your own good. But I intend to remedy that."

RUFUS settled his back against the squabs as his barouche inched along Mayfair's crowded streets. Her shoulders set, Sophia sat opposite him, staring resolutely out the window. Beneath that calm façade, she was seething. Her shallow breaths and clenched fists gave her away, but more than that, Rufus knew from experience the bitterness of betrayal.

He cleared his throat. She flinched in response, but kept her eyes trained on the parade of opulent conveyances and even more opulent town houses outside.

"He would never have been faithful, you know."

There, that got her attention. Her eyes, shadowed to a dull gray in the darkness of the carriage, snapped to his. "I've no idea to whom you are referring, my lord."

"Why, Ludlowe, of course." He stretched his legs and waited for her explosion.

"He is called Clivesden now, I believe. And if I might ask, what do you know of it?"

He pursed his lips. He'd expected fire, not frost. "I know plenty about him. Plenty that you do not."

Her right shoulder jerked upward, and she turned her gaze back to the window. "Lies, rumor and gossip, no doubt."

"Do I strike you, madam, as the sort to bandy gossip about?"

Her gaze returned to his, and her bosom expanded as she took a breath. Just as quickly, she released it, and he knew. She'd puffed herself up for a bald-faced lie, a lie that, in the end, she'd been unable to force past her lips.

"No." The whispered word floated to his ear, barely detectable.

She held her fingers laced together in her lap, the arc of her arms forming a protective wall around her—not about to let anything escape, no anger, no hurt and most certainly no tears. And yet all that and more had to be roiling inside her, longing for escape. He recalled the pain all too well.

"Sophia." He said her name gently, as it was meant to be pronounced, a soft whisper of a name. The eyes she raised to his shimmered with tears. "Sophia, let it out. There's no one here to see."

She swallowed before replying. "No one but you."

"And I shall never tell. Your broken heart is safe in my hands. I know exactly how you feel."

"You do?" she choked out. A lone tear escaped the corner of her eye and traced its way along the contour of her cheek.

"Shall I tell you?"

Her face contorted, her chin crumpled, and her mouth stretched into a grimace. She buried the expression in her hands. His heart turned over to witness such pain.

Easing himself to the seat beside her, he pulled her into an embrace. One hand behind her head, he pressed her face into his chest. Let his eveningwear absorb her piteous sobs.

"How could he?" she gasped. "How could he offer for my sister over me? I loved him."

"He doesn't deserve it, not from you, not from your sister, not from any woman."

He let the motion of the carriage rock them both. He was not worried about arriving at her address in Boulton Row any time soon—he'd instructed his driver to circle the streets of Mayfair until further notice. So much remained to tell Sophia.

She burrowed into his embrace, and he inhaled her scent of roses and woman. Desire unfurled an insistent coil deep in his gut, but he fought to ignore it. After so many years of living alone, he was long used to its unrequited thrum.

The last thing Sophia needed was to fend off his advances. What she needed was his presence, his arms about her, a protected, private oasis where she could spill out her hurt in safety away from curious glances and impertinent questions.

Empathy tugged at his heart, stronger than the pull of

awakening desire. He followed where it led and brushed his lips to her hairline. Fine wisps of blond hair tickled his nose.

She stiffened and raised her head, eyes widening, as if she'd just recalled who was holding her. Her face, still lovely despite the stain of tears and spent emotion, hovered inches from his. An impulse to close the gap, to set his lips to hers and teach her, struck at his gut, but he held firm against it.

It was too soon. If he tried to kiss her now, he might only succeed in frightening her off. He'd driven his wife away with his ardor. He refused to make the same mistake twice.

To cover the moment, he reached into his pocket and offered a handkerchief.

On spying the scrap of linen, ghostly white in the darkened carriage, a thin smile stretched her lips. "I'll have to buy you some new ones. I seem to be in the habit of ruining them."

"If I've lost them, it's to a good cause."

She dabbed at her eyes. "I feel like a silly girl, crying all over you like that."

"Believe me, my dear, I understand. Would you like me to tell you how?"

She blinked and drew back. Uncertainty creased her brow.

He let her go, let her slide back into her corner and put a bit of distance between them. "I will admit up front you will hear things you will not like."

"Tell me the worst of it. What is there between you and Clivesden? There must be something since he insinuated you killed your first wife."

He leaned into the squabs and considered her for a moment. At times—a few minutes ago when she was crying over that blackguard—she seemed so young, but now, when she dared be alone in his presence, despite what she'd been told of him . . . Now she struck him as strong and brave.

"He gave you that idea, did he? I don't suppose I ought to be shocked. Tell me, though, why you accepted my suit if you were under that impression."

"I did not believe it. Not after our talks, and certainly not now. Clivesden must have been mistaken."

"He was not—not completely."

She pressed into her corner, trying to make herself as small as possible.

"I assure you, I am no danger to you. I shall see you home immediately, if you like." He raised a hand to signal the driver.

She straightened and folded her hands in her lap. "No . . . no, I think I'd like to hear what you have to say."

Aware of the risk he took in letting her in, he drew a breath. Best to have it out. He'd ruined one marriage. He liked to think he'd learned from his mistakes. "I loved my wife. When we married, I knew she did not return my feelings. I thought, with time, that might change."

"Why did she marry you then?"

"Her family encouraged the match. They wanted a title for her, you see."

"Yes, I do see."

He nodded. "Not unlike your mother, I daresay."

She looked away. "She might have let me follow my heart and still have seen me a countess."

"You must trust me when I tell you Ludlowe would have broken your heart eventually. Whatever pain you're experiencing now might have been multiplied hundreds of times over had you accepted a suit from him. He would not have been faithful."

"You've said that before." She raised cautious eyes to meet his. "How . . . how do you know?"

"A clever girl like you can guess, like as not."

"Are you telling me he . . . and your wife . . ."

"They had a liaison, yes. I'm certain there were others, but her connection with Ludlowe was one she made sure I knew of. She arranged for me to discover them, you see."

She clutched at her bodice. "Oh. Oh dear."

"Indeed. I now wonder if her aim wasn't to push me to divorce her."

He closed his eyes at the image of the pair of them in bed, naked and disheveled, waiting for him. He'd never seen his wife so satisfied as when he broke down the door to the room they had chosen for their rendezvous.

"I quite understand the anger you must feel right now. The shock. The hurt. The questions. Why couldn't she return my true and honest feelings? Why must she seek comfort with someone else? Why was I not good enough?"

Her breath hitched. Her eyes shone with a fresh spate of tears.

"If it's any comfort, I can tell you the pain dulls with time. As difficult as it may be for you to believe now, one day you will wake up and wonder what you saw in that idiot."

She choked and covered her face with his handkerchief. "How long?"

"How long depends on the depth of your feelings."

"I've loved him for five years."

Five years. Somewhere inside him, his heart hesitated in its steady rhythm. A five-year infatuation was a great deal to recover from. But then his heart raced ahead, his blood hot in his veins, the feeling nearly comforting in its familiarity. He had become acquainted with jealousy long ago.

He tamped down bitter laughter over the irony that Ludlowe should, once again, stand between him and the woman he wanted.

For he wanted Sophia.

He wanted her for all her youth and innocence and capacity to love. He wanted her idealism, wanted to reach out and hold a piece of that wide-eyed certainty that the future would work itself out for the best, and recall how it felt to believe.

She dissolved into a fresh round of sobs, and he couldn't stop himself from reaching for her, from putting his arms around her again and murmuring into her hair, "If you let me, I'll help you get over him."

It took her several minutes to collect herself and respond. Then she raised her head. "How can you possibly?"

A tear trembled on the curve of her cheek. He reached up to brush it away. Her breasts hitched against him on a sharp intake of breath, and she pulled her lower lip between her teeth.

It was his undoing.

"Like this." Holding her gaze, he leaned closer, measuring the movement, giving her a chance to stop him.

Eyes wide, she waited, and he let his lips fall to the corner of her mouth. He tasted the salty bitterness of her tears. For a moment, she sat perfectly still, and he fancied he could hear the pounding of her heart, while he waited for her reaction. If she slapped him, he would take his due without complaint.

With a sigh, she turned her face to the right, and her lips settled against his.

NEVER once, since she'd first set eyes on William Ludlowe, had Sophia imagined kissing another man. She most definitely should not allow her lips to slide together with this man's, but she couldn't stop herself. The tenderness of gentle nips pressed to her skin tugged at her heart and demanded she return in kind, softness for softness, heat for heat.

Highgate's arm snaked about her waist, pulling her flush against his chest. She inhaled the rich scent of sandalwood and spice that hovered in the air about him. An alarming jolt of heat clenched deep in her belly.

With a whimper, she pulled back. His dark eyes studied her for a long moment until the intensity of his gaze sent another bolt blazing through her. She heaved in a ragged breath, aware of her breasts crushed against his chest. She ought to push him away and distance herself.

To her surprise, she didn't want to.

Daring, she reached out a shaky finger to trace the jagged line of the scar that slashed his cheek. The intuitive knowledge of how he'd come by it ought to unnerve her, but in this moment, all she could see in him was the understanding, the stark empathy, the connection created by their mutual heartbreak.

Deep within, something splintered, and a wild, reckless feeling erupted to pour through her veins. Hang them all—her mother, her father. Hang society. Hang Julia and, most especially, hang William Ludlowe. To the devil with him for his blindness.

She fitted her palm to Highgate's cheek, covering the scar, and pressed her lips to his.

A growl rumbled deep in his throat, and he took the mastery. His mouth opened beneath hers, demanded a response, dictated she follow suit. Gone was the tenderness, replaced by searing heat and driving need as the brand of his tongue darted between her teeth.

Compared to the darkness of this assault, their earlier kisses were nothing but the fluttering of a butterfly's wings. This was a battle, and he demanded no less than her complete surrender.

Dear God, how she wanted to give it.

He tore his lips from hers to crush them to her cheeks,

her throat, the ridges of her collarbones. She could do no more than cling to him and tilt her head back in offering—an offering he freely accepted.

He pressed lower to the swell of her breasts above her bodice, and a moan welled up her throat. Parting her lips, she allowed it to escape.

Abruptly, he thrust her away. Her pulse still pounded in her ears. *Thump-thump, thump-thump.* Mind whirling with confusion, she opened her eyes to find him regarding her from beneath half-closed lids.

His normally tidy hair stood in disheveled tufts. Had she done that? *Thump-thump.* She stared down at her hands, half expecting to find dark strands caught between her fingers.

" 'Tis a dangerous game we play, Sophia."

Thump-thump. She should not permit the use of her given name. She should not permit any of this. She opened her mouth to protest, but he set his fingers to her lips before a sound escaped.

"Under the circumstances, I think I can be forgiven the use of your name. Such innocence and yet such passion in you. How I should love to take you home and let you discover your true depths at my leisure."

The promise of those urgent words burned into her soul and raced through her blood. Such forbidden promise. In this moment, she craved the forbidden.

"But you must understand, if we allow this to continue any further, you shall indeed be ruined and our betrothal must then play itself out into marriage."

She let recklessness fuel her response. "I do not give a fig for my reputation. Not after tonight. I shall never marry now, so there is none to know besides me whether or not I've retained my virtue."

He tipped her chin upward. "I should know. I will not risk leaving you with child. I've enough on my conscience."

At the reference to his marriage, she closed her eyes. "I will not believe you killed your wife."

"Your confidence heartens me, but if we are to be completely honest, in a very real sense, I did."

She gasped. "I do not believe it. You couldn't have."

A grim smile twisted his features. "My thanks for your faith."

"But your sister—"

"True, had I actually placed my hands about the woman's neck and strangled her, my sister would have personally seen me in Newgate. Not for murder, mind you, but for bringing scandal on the family." He knocked on the roof, signaling the driver to head for Boulton Row.

"Would . . ." She paused and swallowed. "I know it's none of my affair, but would you tell me how it is you believe yourself responsible for her death?"

"I should never have married her. I should have given her the chance to cry off."

"But you said her family pressured her."

"They did, but they might have relented at a word from me. Alas, I was convinced that with time we might learn to be happy with each other. She resented me from the outset. She was running off once more to meet Ludlowe when her carriage turned over."

She stared at his scar. Gossip proclaimed it a result of that accident.

"Yes, I was there. Like a fool, I went chasing after her. I only wished her to listen to reason. I should have just let her go."

She laid a hand on his sleeve. "She would still have had that accident."

"Perhaps not. If I hadn't been in pursuit, the coachman might not have urged the horses into such a breakneck pace."

He fell silent. Beneath Sophia's gloved fingers, the muscles of his arm stiffened. What had she just forced him to relive? His pain must be infinitely worse than hers. A chilling surge of shyness made her withdraw. She'd no right to touch him.

Wordlessly, he clapped a hand over hers. "Do not pull away. That is what she did."

Good Lord, the heartache behind those words. She could not deny him, but neither could she find an appropriate response. She sat beside him, unmoving, not speaking, while the rumble of the wheels and the steady clop of hooves filled the barouche.

A few moments later, they shuddered to a halt, and he glanced out the window. "We are arrived at your address. I don't believe anyone else has returned from the Pendletons' yet."

Just as well. She couldn't face Julia tonight. Even confronted with the reality of getting over her feelings for William, the future loomed bleak. Married or no, any social event she attended would now mean running into Julia and William, as would any family gathering. There was no escaping him.

And yet Highgate had promised to help her. She could accept that help, but if she did, could she still, in all good conscience cry off?

CHAPTER TWELVE

"I MIGHT'VE KNOWN I'd find you here. Should've thought to look here first."

Benedict raised a bleary eye to find Upperton standing over his table. He no longer had a clear concept of the time. He knew only that the hour was late, perhaps so late he'd return to his family's town house in the predawn twilight.

Without waiting for an invitation, Upperton pulled back a chair and settled into it. Despite the hour, his eveningwear was still in impeccable order. Even his hair remained in artful dishevelment that must have taken his valet an eternity to achieve.

Next to him, Benedict knew he looked like a Whitechapel gin-guzzler. He'd unknotted his cravat hours ago, and his waistcoat hung, half-buttoned, from his shoulders. In short, he was a sodden mess.

Upperton leaned back in his chair, his pose one of practiced nonchalance. "I think you're making rather too much a habit of occupying that particular chair these past few evenings. Have you thought about going out more in society?"

Benedict lifted the brandy decanter to refill his glass, only to find the damned thing was empty. "Sod off."

Upperton ignored him. "I've come straight from the Pendletons'. Well, barring the time I spent combing the gaming hells. Funny things you learn attending balls."

Benedict blinked. An air of expectation settled over the table as Upperton smiled and crossed his arms. Benedict wrinkled his brow into a scowl, but his friend merely continued to wait.

"Oh, all right. Tell me what you heard and have done. I haven't got all night."

"I daresay you haven't. It's nearly five in the morning."

Another pause. Upperton's smile broadened. Such an annoying man. "Why I didn't kick your arse out through your mouth the first day at Eton, I'll never know. Remind me why that is again."

"You were too busy with that Battencliffe idiot." Right. Thank God Upperton had decided to be diplomatic and not remind him that Battencliffe had held the upper hand in that fight. "Fortunately for you, I came along and distracted him with my superior wit."

"Funny, I never knew wit could stand as a synonym for a wicked left hook."

Upperton placed a hand on his chest and inclined his head. "Your servant. And I'm happy to see you're keeping your sense of humor about you. Think you just might need it."

Benedict straightened, a difficult proposition when he'd consumed so much brandy over the course of the evening. He wished for no more than to lay his head in the crook of his elbow and sleep off the effects. Upperton's tone, however, demanded his full, undivided attention, or as close as he could manage, given his condition.

"Am I going to need another bottle?"

"You may want one. Needing one is another question."

"What have you heard?"

"Our friend Clivesden thinks he's won his wager."

Benedict waved a hand. "Well, of course he does. You have to be a right idiot to wager that much without confidence of winning. Julia knows better. She'd never agree—"

"She has."

Benedict slammed his fist to the table. "The devil you say!"

"She has. She's agreed. I saw her with my own eyes at the Pendleton ball, standing there with him. Didn't hear all that was said, but word got round quickly enough. Her father announced the betrothal."

"No. You must've heard wrong. Her sister's betrothed to Highgate. I attended the dinner where the family discussed how they were planning to announce it to society."

"Revelstoke . . . Benedict . . ." Upperton reached across the table and placed his hand on Benedict's forearm. "They announced two engagements tonight."

"No, you're wrong. I will not believe Julia ever agreed to such a thing." But even as he said the words, a sick feeling settled in the pit of his stomach. All the brandy he'd consumed gave an ominous lurch toward his throat. She'd admitted to him she wanted an affectionless marriage. Perhaps she'd thought on it and agreed to Ludlowe's proposal. But that didn't tally with the Julia he knew. The woman he knew was close to her sister. She'd never betray Sophia.

Would she?

"She did not look to be protesting the proceedings. Not from where I was standing."

Apparently so. "You could not have been standing very close if you did not hear what they said."

"I know what I saw. She went along with the entire thing."

Benedict yanked at a fistful of hair. "She refused him. She told me she did."

"She must've had a change of heart then. How long

have we known each other? I swear to you, I would never lie about this."

Shards of ice drove into Benedict's heart. "I know you would not. Only I want very badly for you to be mistaken."

"You'd best accept it. That's not even the reason I'm telling you. What I want to know is what you're going to do about it."

Benedict shot to his feet, steadying himself with a hand on the table as the entire room swayed. "What am I going to do about it?" The answer was obvious enough. He already knew what Julia thought of him. "Not a bloody damned thing."

Upperton stood more slowly. "You're just going to give up? I never thought I'd see the day."

"What do you care about it?" He forced the words through his constricted throat. "It's not as if you've got a personal stake in all this."

"I do if I end up having to pay Clivesden five thousand bloody pounds I haven't got."

"You took that bet?" He seized Upperton by the lapels and gave him a shake. "Then you're an even bigger idiot than Ludlowe . . . Clivesden . . ." He thrust Upperton away. "Whatever the bloody hell we're calling him this week."

OUTSIDE her father's study, Julia drew in a lungful of air and let it out in a measured whoosh. She was about to enter the only wholly masculine domain in this female-dominated house.

Forbidden territory, this inner sanctum of Charles St. Claire. Not even her mother dared enter this part of the town house unless some dire emergency pressed. And if this room had been the site of that kiss with Benedict, well . . . She thrust aside the memory of his lips on hers, his tongue in her mouth, his hands mobile on her body. Papa didn't need to know about that.

Dire emergency pressed Julia now—it had since last night's announcement of her engagement to the Earl of Clivesden, a betrothal that, with any luck, would not endure beyond today.

After another calming breath, she scratched at the door. A faint grunt, muffled by the thick panel, acknowledged her presence, and she stepped over the threshold. Heavy walnut paneled the walls, while forest green draperies covered the windows. The room smelled of cheroot and brandy, the only space in the entire town house where such scents were permissible.

From behind his desk, her father frowned at a ledger. A few sparse wisps of graying hair stood on end. On Julia's approach, he unhooked his spectacles. "What brings you in here so early? Thought you might be expecting callers."

"I've given Billings instructions to inform any callers that I am not at home."

He raised a snowy brow. "Not even that Revelstoke rogue?"

"Especially not him."

"Just as well. Your mother's still got her feathers ruffled over him turning up at Sophia's engagement dinner without an invitation." He paused to mop his forehead with a handkerchief. "Don't know when I'll hear the end of it."

Julia raised her chin. "He had an invitation. From me."

"And yet, you do not want him to wish you well."

"I hardly think if he comes to call, he'll offer best wishes." No, that was the last thing he'd offer. She preferred not to imagine his reaction when the news of her betrothal reached him.

"Why would he not? It's no surprise word has spread,

and those who weren't present last night surely want a chance to wish you happiness." Her father gestured toward a chair opposite, as if she were his man of affairs, but he always had placed his business concerns, such as they were, before his daughters. "Sit."

"I think I'd rather stand." If she had to conduct this conversation in his territory, it gave her a slight sense of control to look down on him.

A line formed between his brows. "Is something amiss?"

She flung up her hands and just as immediately let them drop. "Amiss? You agree to a betrothal without consulting me and ask if anything's amiss when I learn of it. What on earth were you thinking?"

His chest expanded and, with it, his belly below. "Now see here. Between you and your sister, I've put up with enough nonsense. You are two and twenty. It is high time you married."

"At the very least, you could have done me the courtesy of allowing me to choose my suitor."

"I've allowed you and your sister all manner of latitude in that regard, and where has it got me?" He heaved his bulk from his chair and stared down his nose at her. "You've both had ample time to make matches of your own. But you've turned them down, every one. Sophia had a chance with the Marquess of Petherton."

He paused once more to mop his brow. "A marquess, for heaven's sake, and worth ten thousand a year. She refused him. Left me to deal with your mother's fits for weeks, and let me tell you, that was more trouble than I bargained for."

Julia planted her hands on the polished wood of the desk and held his stare. "Do you know why she refused the marquess? She's been in love with Clivesden since she first laid eyes on him."

Papa let out a snort. "That is not love. It is a *tendre*. It is an infatuation."

"It's an infatuation that's lasted five years. Five years, Papa." Of course, he'd missed it. He'd spent the last five years dining at his club and losing at whist. Bankrupting the family. "And I've had to comfort her after every single social occasion where he's ignored her. Or, heaven forbid, he paid her some minor attention. That's when she'd get her hopes up, only to have them dashed when he trotted off to flirt with some other girl. And now you expect me to happily agree to this match, and hang Sophia's feelings?"

She closed her eyes and swallowed. Sophia hadn't addressed a single word to her this morning. "I cannot do it, Papa! I cannot betray her like that!"

He took a step back, the line between his brows becoming more pronounced. "If the girl were in love, as you say, with Clivesden, why'd she accept Highgate's suit?"

She gritted her teeth to hold back the first words that sprung to mind—words she'd overhead Benedict mutter when he pulled her out of scrapes, words her father would certainly not appreciate. "She had no choice. They were caught alone. It's a convenience to avoid scandal."

She clamped her mouth shut before she blurted out the rest—that Sophia planned to cry off. With Papa so bound and determined to marry the pair of them off, no doubt he'd find a way to force Sophia in front of a vicar before she knew what was happening. Most especially if he discovered Highgate might be worth some blunt.

Papa rubbed his chin. "She could not be that much in love with Clivesden, then, if she let herself get into such a situation. No matter. She will be settled, with an earl no less, and so shall you. Your mother is over the moon, and I refuse to let either of you disappoint her after all the heartache she's gone through due to your dithering. I will see the pair of you settled before the season is over, and that's all there is to it."

"Papa, you cannot—"

"I most certainly can. Two titled men, earls no less, have agreed to take you and your sister on and with little dowry to speak of. You will never see another such chance again." He picked up his spectacles, hooked them over his ears, and eased himself back into his chair. Stretching out an arm, he pulled the ledger closer. "Off with you now."

Julia gaped at him. Just like that, he'd dismissed her. He was not going to take her feelings or Sophia's into consideration, as long as they married well and were off his hands. As long as Mama could boast to society that both her daughters were countesses.

Countesses!

"I refuse to marry Clivesden. You cannot force me."

He looked up from his ledger, his mouth working while his cheeks flushed a dull red. "You shall marry him. You owe me that much."

"*Owe* you?" She raised her arms and let them flop to her sides. "In what manner can I possibly owe you such a debt?"

"Do you know how much the pair of you have cost me over the past few seasons? The gowns, the bonnets, the town house?"

"And how much did your latest hand of vingt-et-un cost you?"

He went pale. His hand curled into a fist, and his jaw worked. She'd gone too far. She'd never had cause to hand her father such cheek, mainly because, much of the time, he preferred to let Mama deal with his way-ward daughters, while he hid himself in here and pre-tended his finances were in a better state.

"I did not wish to mention this, but you leave me no choice." He spat each syllable. "I owe Clivesden five thousand pounds."

"Five thou—"

He slammed his fist onto his desk. "Five thousand, I might add, that I do not possess. Clivesden could see me in debtor's prison. And then where would the rest of you be, without the protection of husbands?"

The floor listed beneath Julia's feet, and she clutched at the desk. A husband's protection. A fine job Papa had done protecting his own wife. If he went to debtor's prison, she, Mama, and Sophia would find themselves on the street. "Does Mama know?"

"She does not know the full extent of my debts, and I've arranged to keep it that way."

"How?" Her fingers dug into the wood until they ached. "How could you possibly keep such a matter from her?"

"I've an agreement with Clivesden. He has agreed to overlook the marker if I provide him with a suitable wife."

Julia opened her mouth and closed it again. Her hands turned to ice. For a moment, she could not summon a word for lack of breath. "And you chose *me*?" she asked faintly. "Me? Why not Sophia?"

"It's quite simple. He asked for you."

He asked for her. Of course he had, and she knew why, but was her reputation so widely noised about that her father had heard? And if he had, would he even bother to put the rumormonger in his place? "Did you ask yourself why that was?"

He glared at her from behind his spectacles. "The why does not signify in this matter. Clivesden provided me with a solution, and I took it. Sometimes, we must make sacrifices for the good of all."

Sacrifices. The word echoed through her mind. He wished to sacrifice *her* for a situation of his making.

JULIA made it as far as her bedchamber before giving in to her anger. Her arguments had left her father unmoved. The more she protested, the more adamantly he insisted she do her duty as his daughter.

In four strides, she crossed the chamber—one, two, three, turn; one, two, three, turn—and at each turn she dug her nails into her palms. By the tenth trip across the room, blood welled from little half-moons. She was going to have to do it. She was going to have to accept Clivesden's suit and hang her sister's feelings. And all over five thousand pounds. How appalling.

Her father had as good as sold her.

The backs of her eyes pricked, and she stared across the room to stave off the impending flood. She needed a plan, not tears.

Her gaze lit on the miniature of her and Sophia as children. They were so young then, so innocent. So ignorant of the ugliness of life. She couldn't stand to look at those smiling children another moment.

She marched over to the bedside table, snatched the portrait and hurled it against the wall. The wooden frame splintered with a crash. That time in her life was just as irreparably damaged as the miniature, as the relationship with her sister would ever be.

She choked on a sob that suddenly blocked her throat. Sophia would never forgive her for going through with the marriage, not when her sister would have Clivesden thrown in her face at every turn.

In the end, that was what her choice boiled down to—her sister or her irresponsible wastrel of a father. If he ruined himself, it was through his own folly. Why should she have to pay the price? Why should Sophia and Mama?

Julia drew in a puff of air, and her shaking subsided. She could pay the money back, somehow. Not all at once, of course, but she might manage installments. And if she married, she could manage to secure Mama's and

Sophia's futures. But first she needed to find a way out of her betrothal.

Papa wanted her settled, did he? If she was honest with herself, being settled was the least of her concerns, but if she must marry, then she would—as long as it was not to Clivesden.

CHAPTER THIRTEEN

JULIA CLUTCHED at her cloak as she huddled in the servants' entrance. Outside, rain poured in sheets, buffeted by an icy wind. She'd have to go out in it and soon, even if it meant catching her death of cold.

One ear cocked in the direction of the kitchen, she listened for sounds of impending doom, or in her case, Billings's precise march. Servant or no, he'd haul her straight above stairs and turn her over to her mother if he caught her running off.

Footsteps echoed along the corridor that led to the back stairs. Closer, closer. Nothing for it now. Gathering her courage, she plunged into the weather.

A howling gust whipped stinging droplets of rain into her face and tore the air from her lungs. In spite of a heavy woolen cloak and bonnet, she'd be soaked to the skin in minutes. Ladies did not venture out in such weather, not without a ready carriage and a footman to hold an umbrella and stand as a shield against the elements.

Today, Julia was no lady. Today instead, her behavior was scandalous. Today, she was taking her future into her hands.

Skipping to avoid ankle-deep puddles scattered about the cobblestoned alley, she darted into Boulton Row, headed fast for Curzon Street in the hopes of finding an unoccupied hackney.

What little daylight remained was fast fading. In spite of the deserted streets, she lengthened her stride. Though she might live in the heart of Mayfair, footpads were not unknown, and a lady alone was simply unthinkable.

The clatter of wheels barreling along the cobblestones made her scramble to one side. Her foot sank to the ankle in an icy puddle, while the carriage rumbled past. Her heart leapt into her throat as she caught sight of a crest emblazoned on its doors—for an instant, she was afraid she'd recognized Clivesden's arms.

She hurried on. At the rate the rain was soaking into her cloak, it would soon not matter whether or not she found a hackney. Even if she walked the entire way, she could hardly arrive at her destination any more miserable and bedraggled.

Half an hour later, she arrived, wet to the skin, teeth chattering and her fingers frozen about the strings of her reticule. Letting out a relieved breath, she sloshed up the steps to the imposing oak door, raised the brass knocker and let it fall once. Then she hugged herself in a vain attempt to retain warmth, while praying the butler would not take one look at her and run her off for a ragamuffin.

"Please hurry. Please be home." She muttered the litany between clenched teeth while the wind tore at her wraps.

She was about to reach for the knocker a second time when the door opened. Phipps loomed on the threshold, peering down at her from over his beak of a nose. His brows lowered. "Yes?"

"Please, is Lord Benedict at home?"

"I shall have to inquire. And who might I say is calling at such an odd hour?"

From beneath her cloak, she produced a dripping card. Phipps accepted it with a sniff. A moment later, his eyebrows rose to his hairline. "Miss Julia. Forgive me. I did not recognize you in such a state. But alone? This is highly irregular."

"Please, Phipps, if I could at least get out of the rain."

"Of course, miss, of course."

He stepped aside and allowed her to wade into the foyer of Benedict's town house. Or rather, the house belonging to his older brother, the Marquess of Enfield, who had opted to remain in the country this season.

Phipps's dark eyes went round at the sight of the ever-widening puddle at Julia's feet. "I hardly know what to say, miss. You really ought to put on something dry before you fall ill, but . . ."

"But there's no lady in residence to lend me anything," she completed. There. She'd acknowledged what she was doing—paying a call, alone, on a bachelor. "A warm fire must suffice for the moment."

"I shall send a maid with tea straightaway. Or perhaps Cook can roust up something more bracing. I'm afraid Lord Benedict spends far more time at his club these days than he does here."

Julia's heart gave an awful lurch. "Is he not at home then?"

Half a second's blink and a slight darkening of the butler's cheeks were the only signs that betrayed the man's discomfort. Anyone unfamiliar with the family might have passed the indication by without a second thought. Not Julia. Not when she'd grown up as Benedict's neighbor and been in and out of his house nearly as often as her own.

"I shall inquire. Please wait in the parlor."

Mindful of the thick Persian carpet in that room, Julia cast a rueful glance at her feet. True to form, Phipps's expression remained implacable as he reached for her sodden cloak. "Be off and warm yourself, miss."

The moment Phipps disappeared down the hall, Julia hurried up to the parlor. Standing as close as she dared to the dancing flames, she allowed their warmth to seep into her. Slowly, she began to feel a bit more human and slightly less like an icicle.

But while she thawed, a gale of worries blew about her mind. What if Benedict had already gone out? What if he refused to see her? But then it occurred to her: Her presence here might well be sufficient. If only she could contrive for word to get out. A difficult prospect when the very weather that had provided the perfect cover for her to sneak out of the house also conspired to keep most sensible people indoors and not in a position to catch her.

Sensible.

She'd always thought of herself as a sensible person. Sensible, practical, mindful of her reputation. She'd been all those things up until the moment her father announced her betrothal to a crowded ballroom.

Now she was merely desperate and perhaps even insane. One had to be to venture out in such weather.

The thud of approaching footsteps echoed in the hall. Certain it was a maid arriving with sustenance, she kept her gaze trained on the fire. Booted feet tramped closer. Odd, she heard nothing to indicate a tea cart.

The thumps came to a halt. She turned her head to find Benedict standing on the threshold. His brows lowered as his gaze raked her from head to foot.

"What the devil possessed you to come here?"

At his cold words, Julia whirled, her soaked skirt clinging to her legs.

Benedict propped an elbow against the jamb, his stance casual, his manner dismissive. His black hair flopped onto his brow, more becomingly disheveled than any dandy's whose valet spent hours on artful arrangement. He hadn't bothered with a topcoat or waistcoat. His shirt hung slack, unbuttoned at the neck, displaying a fascinating wedge of skin. The notch at the base of his throat lay shaded by an overhang of unshaven chin.

She caught her breath. No gentleman ought to appear in front of a lady in such a state of undress, and now she understood why. The sight set her heart fluttering and made drawing in air a suddenly difficult proposition. It did more to warm her than any fire.

As she stood gaping, he pushed himself away from the doorframe and advanced on her. His buckskin breeches hugged his powerful thighs like a second skin. Julia caught her lower lip between her teeth. Why had she never before noticed the play of muscles when he prowled toward her?

"Are you going to answer me, or shall I assume you've come to stare?"

She had to swallow before she could reply. "Perhaps I'd be a bit more willing to answer your question if it were phrased more politely."

"You want politesse?" His crack of derisive laughter sent a chill through her. "Yes, I suppose you do. As I recall, your parting words to me were nothing if not de rigueur."

"Are you foxed?"

He stalked closer. "Not yet, no matter how much I'd like to be."

A tuft of hair peeked from the placket of his shirt. She closed her fingers into a fist as her wayward mind urged her to raise her hand and sample its texture. "Have you just got out of bed then?"

He sketched her a mocking bow. "Quite perceptive of you. Yes, the past few days I've found myself keeping rather interesting hours."

A rattle in the corridor announced the tea cart's arrival. The maid cast a fleeting glance at her employer and wheeled it toward the settee, before withdrawing with a quick bob of her mobcapped head.

Benedict raised an eyebrow and strolled to a side table where a cut glass decanter reflected the firelight. Taking a snifter, he poured a measure of deep amber liquid and sipped at it. Julia watched the rise and fall of his Adam's apple as he swallowed.

The glass halfway to his lips, he paused and regarded her over the rim. "No need to look so disapproving. Or perhaps you'd rather drink this than tea. Quite good, but strong if you're not used to it."

Julia slogged to the tea cart. "No, thank you."

"Are you certain? It might help you feel less bedraggled."

She poured a cup of tea, added sugar, and took a bracing swallow. "I did not come here to drink with you."

"Pity. I intend to drink, at any rate." To prove it, he downed his brandy. "But now we've got to the point. Why have you come? More to the point, why have you come unchaperoned to the residence of a confirmed bachelor? Won't your betrothed have something to say about that?"

She tightened her grip on the teacup. "So you've heard."

"Upperton could not wait to tell me. He seemed to think I'd be happy to come rushing to your rescue." Benedict shrugged. "He was quite disappointed to discover otherwise."

Julia's heart plummeted toward her feet. "I do not suppose you'll want to hear why I've come then."

He poured another measure and tipped back his glass. "Indulge me. I've got a few minutes before it's worth heading to my club."

She squared her shoulders and took in a lungful of smoke-tinged air. Part of her recognized that his aloofness was an act. While his posture indicated disinterest, a subtle tension radiated about the set of his shoulders. As earlier with the butler, Julia could thank long acquaintance for allowing her to see past the façade.

"I've a proposition for you."

He studied the olive-and-cross pattern on the crystal. "Do you, now? What is it?"

"I need you to compromise me."

His spine went rigid for a moment, but then he tipped the decanter and a swirl of rich liquid filled the glass, at least two fingers high. "Indeed?" Throwing back his head, he downed the portion. "Ah, wonderful stuff. Are you certain you'd not like any? It's got more of a kick than you're used to, of course, but I highly recommend it."

She lifted her cup. "I'll stick to tea, thanks. And perhaps you'd like to go a bit easier."

"Why? I'm nowhere near the condition I'd like. But perhaps you're concerned about your proposition. Afraid I might get myself into such a state I cannot perform?"

Her mouth dropped open. What on earth was he talking about? "You must be farther gone than I realized if you're going to talk such nonsense."

He set his empty glass aside with a sharp click. In a matter of strides, he closed the distance between them to loom over her. He traced the back of a forefinger along her cheekbone, trailing fire in its wake. At the sensation, she let out a gasp, but his expression remained hard, immovable.

"I assure you I am most definitely not too far gone. Pity I will not be taking you up on your offer."

"What?"

"The answer is no. I will not compromise you."

"If you're concerned for your honor—"

"That is the least of it." He turned away and strode to the window. "Not a week ago, you dismissed me for attentions that, should we have been discovered, would have left you quite thoroughly compromised. That same evening you claim to have turned down Clivesden's proposal. Now I hear you not only accepted that idiot's suit, you've changed your mind about me, as well."

With a sigh, he turned back, coming to stand in front of her. "You are the last person I expected to play fickle female games, and yet, here you are, doing exactly that."

She stepped forward, holding out a placating hand. "You do not understand. I never agreed to his suit."

He thrust her hand aside. "Then why announce it in front of the entire crowd at the Pendleton ball?"

"He worked the arrangement out as a deal with my father. I had no inkling of our engagement until Papa saw fit to announce it."

"And by all accounts, you went along with it."

"I was in shock. They blindsided me, the pair of them. Please—"

His eyes glittered, hard as sapphire. "I find myself singularly unmoved by your pleas."

Julia opened her mouth and closed it again. A sob rose in her throat, but she refused to give it voice. Benedict, her dependable Benedict, refused his assistance when she most needed it. Unbelievable. And yet—it was unbelievable the way he claimed not to care and ranted on at length. He'd clearly cared enough to listen to more than one account of the evening.

Poking up her chin, she drew a steadying breath. "Fine. If you will not help me, I shall find someone who will. Perhaps Upperton will oblige me."

Before she could draw away, his fingers clamped about her wrist, burning into her skin like brands. "You will not offer yourself to the likes of Upperton."

"The likes of Upperton? I thought he was your friend."

"I do not expect you to understand. Let's just say I know more than I'd like about his views on . . . females. Although as a gentleman, he ought to refuse."

Perhaps, but a slight waver in his tone betrayed an uncertainty. She tugged at her wrist, but he held fast. "You leave me with no choice. And if Upperton refuses, I shall have to find a more willing gentleman. Lord Chuddleigh might be interested."

His fingers tightened until she was sure she'd find five parallel bruises the next morning. "You would not dare."

A smile threatened to curl her lips. Ruthlessly, she composed her features. No need to warn him of her imminent victory, or he might dig in his heels. Time, once again, to change tack.

"Revelstoke." She stepped closer and laid her fingers against his forearm. Beneath the fine fabric of his shirt, strong muscles shifted. Tightened. "Benedict, I need you to compromise me."

Tension radiated through the linen. Muscles clenched beneath her touch. The glance he slanted at her was laced with caution—or wariness. Julia's heart gave a painful throb. He would refuse her again, for what she'd just asked of him was more than he was willing to give.

Without warning, he released her wrist. "Have you stopped to consider the consequences of such an action?"

"Of course I have."

"All of them?"

"Of—"

"Stop and think for a moment." He broke away from her grasp and strode to the large mullioned window that overlooked his back garden. Rain lashed against the pane, driven by a harsh wind. Julia shivered. "If I should do this thing, as a gentleman I shall be required to offer for you. Had you thought that far?"

"If I must marry . . ." She swallowed. There. She could no longer deny the fact she would have to wed. "If I must marry, I would prefer it to be to someone I get on with."

He tore his gaze from the scene outside and looked over at her. Framed against the window, he appeared larger than life. "Is that what you believe marriage to be? A matter of people getting on together?"

"Better than a matter of business or a means to a higher position in society. That's all it is to my parents."

He pushed away from the window and came to stand before her. "More to the point, is that how it would be between us?"

His voice had dropped to a lower register than she was used to hearing from him. She'd heard it from the lips of other men, all would-be suitors, and she recognized it for what it was—seduction. An unaccountable shiver raised gooseflesh along her arms, and she wrapped them about herself—a shield.

Never once had she imagined having such a discussion with Benedict, but then she'd never imagined kissing him, either. She thrust aside the memory of his lips sliding over hers, of his tongue pushing into her mouth, of the heat his touch aroused . . .

Two fingers tipped her chin upward. "Answer me, Julia. Is that how it would be?"

Under the force of his gaze, she squared her shoulders. "I do not see why we should not get on together. We always have."

"Have we? Is that why you dismissed me so summarily the other night?"

"I thought a little distance was for the best, under the circumstances."

"Then we are at an impasse, I'm afraid."

"Impasse? I do not understand."

"You and I do not have the same expectations with regard to marriage. Quite plainly, Julia, should you become my wife, I would expect you to perform all the usual duties associated with the role."

Her throat went dry, but she'd long since set aside her teacup. "Duties," she whispered.

He tipped his head to hold her gaze. "You do know which duties I'm referring to?"

Weakly, she nodded. "I—"

"I want you to warm my bed. Willingly, regularly." He leaned closer until she could almost taste the brandy on his lips. "Passionately."

Passionately. The word sent a streak of heat searing straight to the pit of her belly.

"Consider carefully, now," he went on, "whether you truly want me to compromise you or not, because this is the outcome you must live with."

Pulling away, she crossed her arms and tried to make sense of her whirling thoughts. She had no more than a vague notion of what warming his bed entailed. She knew it involved kissing and touching, but beyond that, all she knew was that, under the wrong circumstances, such relations were scandalous. If her experience with kissing him was any indication, they evoked intense feelings.

She closed her eyes and recalled that night in her father's study. Benedict's lips on hers demanded a response, awakened feelings fraught with the promise of pleasure. Dark feelings, overwhelming feelings—like nothing she'd experienced with any other man.

He would demand such a response from her on a regular basis. Could she give him what he wished and yet guard her heart?

She opened her eyes to find him watching her, his gaze intense and alert, as if he hadn't touched a drop of brandy. His expression was unreadable as he awaited her reply, a reply she suddenly could not bring herself to voice.

"Did I frighten you so much when I kissed you?" he murmured.

"The kiss did not frighten me, no." The truth, that. The kiss was the least of it.

"But it was your first, was it not?"

She nodded.

"I thought so. I should have been gentler." In one stride, he closed the gap between them and set his hand at the base of her throat. His fingertips tickled her jawline. He would claim her now. Her lips parted in expectation.

"My God," he murmured, "you're soaked through to the skin. Whatever possessed you to venture out in such weather, and alone?"

"Desperation, I suppose." Her voice croaked the reply. "I walked all the way here because I could not find a hackney."

He growled a string of foul oaths that sent a wave of heat creeping up her cheeks and along her nape. "Do you realize what a risk you took?"

"I imagine all the footpads had enough sense to stay inside."

He shifted his grip until the tips of his fingers bit into the back of her neck. "You will not ever do anything so foolish again. Do you understand me?"

"Then you will agree to compromise me. If you do not, I must find someone who will, for I refuse to marry Clivesden."

"You understand, don't you, that your mere presence here alone with me already compromises you?"

"Only should the matter become known."

"It will become known. How long before you're missed?"

"But who will think to look for me here?"

"Who indeed?" He pulled at a sodden lock of her hair. "You need to get out of those clothes and into a hot bath before you fall ill."

A bolt of liquid heat shot through her at the sudden darkening in his eyes. Without a doubt, he was imagining her naked in her bath.

"I shall have nothing to wear once I've finished." Her cheeks flamed further at the admission.

A ghost of a smile flitted over his features. "I'm afraid I've nothing proper to lend you. I shan't be able to send you back home until your clothes have dried."

He might have been teasing but for the lowered timbre in his voice. It awakened a boldness within her that pushed her to move close enough for her breasts to graze his chest. At the contact, her nipples puckered.

His Adam's apple bobbed on a swallow.

She held his gaze. "Perhaps I do not want to go home."

"Julia—"

Her name on his lips in that low tone caused a frisson of awareness to pass through her. So little separated them—only the fine linen of his shirt and the thin layers of her gown, chemise, and stays, reduced to almost nothing by their recent soaking. The heat of his skin penetrated her and made her crave more, made her crave closer contact.

His arm snaked about her waist, his broad palm flattened against her back, fingers splayed, and pushed upward to settle between her shoulder blades. "We're playing with fire. You realize that, don't you?"

She acknowledged his statement with a nod.

"But you're not going to back away."

She shook her head. "Perhaps I'd like to burn."

With a groan, he pressed his lips to hers. She shuddered and opened to him, her response to the gentle probe of his tongue coming easily, fueled by the recollection of last time. She tasted the bittersweetness of brandy on his lips, breathed in his heady scent, reached to finger the roughness of his stubble.

A growl in his throat, he crushed her in his arms and drew her fully flush with the hard length of his body. His tongue swept deep into her mouth. She pushed her hands up the front of his shirt until her fingers twined into his hair. His unshaven jaw abraded her chin, but still she followed his lead.

She could do this. She could let her body shape itself to his as it would. She could allow him to plumb the depths of her passion and give him all the response he desired. Later, she would sort out the confusion whirling in her brain. For now, all she wanted was to feel.

He pulled away, his breath coming in ragged bursts. His blue eyes darkened to midnight and reflected the flames on the hearth.

The intensity of his gaze drew a whimper to her throat. Good gracious, such naked emotion.

Unable to face it, she closed her eyes and laced her fingers about his neck, drawing him back to her. A husky groan rumbled from his chest, and he renewed their kiss, pressing on her until his weight forced her back.

One step after the other, she ceded beneath the pressure and retreated until something solid pressed into her calves. The settee. Sighing into his mouth, she sank to the cushions.

Once again, he pulled away. Julia caught her lower lip between her teeth and breathed him in. A sharp, masculine tang undercut the brandy. Her wet gown had dampened the fine linen of his shirt until it lay plastered to his skin. Nearly transparent. The firelight gilded his flesh with a cast of gold.

She stretched out a forefinger, and drew it along his neck, past his racing pulse to the fascinating wedge of skin at his open collar. Crisp hair tickled her fingertip, and she flattened her palm to his flesh.

A shudder passed through him, and he settled his

weight over her. Her body responded with an aching throb deep within.

"Julia." He touched his fingertips to her temple, brushing the sodden wisps of hair from her forehead.

That intense, blue gaze filled her vision, and once again she shuttered her eyes against it. As long as she didn't have to see, if she could only feel.

His lips skated along her jaw to the lobe of her ear and the hammering pulse just beneath. She shifted under him, her hips canting into a cradle for his.

He groaned and pressed back, the whole, hard length of him like steel between their bodies. His fingers drifted lower, a gentle caress along her cheek to her throat, and there they halted at the fastenings of her bodice.

With each tug at the tiny buttons, her pulse pattered all the harder. Dear God, he was about to unbutton her. She ought to stop him before he overwhelmed her completely.

Without warning, he froze, his body tense and alert.

"What is it?" Julia managed.

He turned that disturbing gaze toward the door. "I heard something. The servants." With a sigh, he heaved himself to his feet. "Just as well. In another few moments . . ."

She took the hand he offered and let him pull her upright. "In another few moments what?"

He gave her a wan smile. "I'd have done something that would have shocked the maid when she came in to collect the teapot."

"But I've asked you to compromise me."

"I'd like a little more privacy than my sitting room." He took her by the shoulders and brushed kisses to her cheeks and brow before tightening his arms and crushing her to him. "We are about to create such a scandal, you may no longer receive invitations to all the balls and such you attend."

She burrowed her head against his shoulder, marveling at how simple, how easy the gesture seemed. "It does not matter. I only went about in society to please my mother. Since it turns out that pleasing my mother involves becoming the Countess of Clivesden, I fear she shall have to be disappointed in me."

He pulled back and rested his hands on either side of her neck. "I've a house in Kent. My mother left it to me as part of her dower properties. If you like, I'll show it to you."

Kent. The very name called to mind sunny summer days traipsing through the woods in the name of adventure. She and Sophia had spent their girlhood at Clareton House, running wild as often as they could escape Miss Mallory. Julia had first come across Benedict during those years, as their property abutted the Marquess of Enfield's lands. She hadn't been back since Sophia's first season. Her father had sold the property to move the family to Town with the proceeds. He'd traded an idyllic life for ball gowns and social standing.

"Shall we leave tonight?"

"You've nothing to wear," he reminded her. "And you cannot go back out in such weather dressed as you are. Leave matters to me. I'll order you a bath, and Mrs. Brown will prepare a guest room for you."

"And where will you be?"

"I've some business to take care of, and if I put in an appearance at my club, no one will suspect anything is amiss." He leaned in to brush his lips across hers, once, twice. "I swear to you, I will make no demands that you are unwilling to fulfill. Do you trust me in this?"

She blinked. Before her the old Benedict, the one she'd grown up with, had reappeared. "Of course."

"Then I must warn you." He studied his hands. "My estate is in rather poor condition. Most of the rooms in the main house are uninhabitable."

"Oh?" She understood the slow dereliction that came of depleting funds. She'd been living with them since her father sold her childhood home and moved the family to Town.

"There is a place we can stay, only it's very small."

"How small?"

He looked her full in the face. "It has only one bedroom."

CHAPTER FOURTEEN

FRESHLY SHAVEN and dressed, Benedict ducked from his carriage into the entrance of Boodle's. He prayed he'd find Upperton there at this hour and that Upperton was still speaking to him after the way they'd left things. Alert, he strode straight for his usual table, waving off the footman who stepped from the shadows to offer brandy.

Tonight, Benedict wanted to keep all his faculties about him.

"Revelstoke. Thank God!" He turned his head to the right to find Upperton strolling toward him. "I thought you'd never get here."

Benedict consulted his pocket watch. Half past seven—early by his usual standard. "What's happened, man? You look like your mistress's husband just caught you sneaking down the trellis."

Upperton stopped short. "Give me a bit more credit than that. I don't bother with married ladies for good reason."

"Glad I've run into you, at any rate. We need to talk where we will not risk being overheard."

Eyes narrowed, Upperton studied Benedict for a moment. "Miss Julia seems to have turned up missing. You wouldn't happen to know something about that, would you?"

Benedict pressed his lips together. He hadn't expected word to get out quite this fast. "Come with me."

He led Upperton to the third story, where a long corridor flanked by closed doors stretched before them. Private rooms—available to members who wished to pursue more intimate activities.

Upperton hesitated as Benedict pushed the nearest oak panel open. "Don't want anyone getting the wrong idea."

Benedict grabbed him by the collar and dragged him inside. "Then tell them we hired a courtesan who was amenable to the both of us at once. Now tell me, what's this about Julia?"

Upperton cocked his head. "I thought for certain you'd know."

"I *do* know. What I want to know is how *you* know, and, more important, can I expect her family to turn up at my town house and take her back home?"

Worry shifted in his belly. He should never have left her alone. He should have sent her straight to Kent and followed separately in the morning. Surely if the St. Claires had searched for her at the Uppertons', they'd think to check his address as well.

And if they discovered her there, they'd spirit her back home and keep her under close watch until she married Clivesden. No matter how Julia felt about the match, it was clear her parents favored it.

"I do not think her family suspects you have anything to do with it," Upperton said. "I only found out through a stroke of luck. My sister paid a call on Sophia and brought the news back with her. Strict secret, so of course Henrietta came bursting in to tell us."

Benedict released a stream of air. "So I have time."

"I would not say that. The gossip will have made the rounds by tomorrow. So tell me." Upperton nudged him. "What made you change your mind about helping me?"

"Get this straight once and for all. I am not doing a thing to help you win an idiotic bet."

"All right, but if this ensures I win . . ." Upperton shrugged. "Think of the scandal, man. Clivesden will not want to go anywhere near her now."

"I'm about to make doubly certain of that. I'm taking her to Kent in the morning."

"Ah, yes, in the morning, once you've properly ruined her, of course."

Benedict fisted a hand in Upperton's lapel. "I'll thank you to keep your nose where it belongs. I should not even tell you my plans, only I need your assistance."

Upperton pulled himself loose and brushed at his sleeves. "You've got a funny way of asking for favors."

"If you'd learn to keep your gob shut, it would help. But I reckon you'll assist me if only because it will ensure you win that bet."

With a sigh, Upperton stepped back. "What do you want me to do?"

Benedict held up his fingers. "Three things. One, you're going to put it about that you saw me in some gaming hell or other tonight. Doesn't matter which one, as long as people think I did not spend the evening at home."

Upperton nodded. "Easy enough. What are the others?"

"First thing in the morning, you will present yourself at Doctor's Commons and procure me a special license."

"A week or more might pass before the archbishop's office sees fit to grant it. You'd best head straight for Scotland."

Benedict shook his head. "It'll take me a week to get there. More, if this sort of weather holds. No, they'll expect us to go that route once they work out what's happened. We'll be safer in Kent. As soon as you've got the license, I need you to bring it to Shoreford House.

Or rather, the gamesman's cottage, as that's the habitable portion."

Upperton raised a brow. "You know, people might say you abducted her."

"I didn't. She came to me."

"So she's finally worked out what she wants, our Miss Julia?"

Benedict ignored that remark. "Now, there's just one more thing."

HUNCHING his shoulders against an icy wind, Rufus alighted from his carriage in Boulton Row. A grim-faced Billings greeted him at the door.

"I should like to call on Miss St. Claire."

"I shall enquire if she is at home."

Beneath his greatcoat, Rufus shivered as Billings made a precise about-face and left him on the doorstep. "What the devil?"

The hour was past eleven in the morning. Billings had no reason to play this sort of social cat and mouse with him, now that he was officially Sophia's intended. She couldn't be aiming to cry off at this juncture, could she?

Not after the carriage ride and heated embrace they'd shared. She'd left him hungering for the promise of their marriage bed with those guileless kisses and her un-schooled response. If she broke things off at this point—

The door whipped open to reveal Billings, ever implacable. "She will see you in the morning room, my lord."

Letting out a breath, Rufus stepped over the threshold and handed his wet hat and coat to the butler. Sophia met him halfway down the corridor.

"Thank goodness you've come." Her face was paler than usual, a near chalk-white. Purplish rings beneath her eyes stood in contrast to her complexion.

"What's happened?"

"Julia's gone missing, and it's my fault." A tear escaped to course down her cheek.

His arm froze in midair, halfway to brushing it away. Instead, he placed his hand on the small of her back and gently guided her to the morning room. "Your fault? How can it be your fault?"

"I've been awful to her ever since her engagement was announced. I . . ." She sank onto a settee and twisted her hands in her skirts. "I could not bring myself to talk to her, to ask her how she could just stand there and accept her betrothal when she assured me she would turn that man down flat. How can I do it? How can I live the rest of my days with *him* as my brother-in-law?"

Rufus settled himself beside her. His thigh brushed against her skirts. "How do you know that isn't the real reason she's gone? To get out of her betrothal?"

"Surely she would have left word, if only so we would not worry."

"How long has she been gone?"

"Since last night. Mama insisted on taking me to her modiste for my trousseau, and when we returned, Julia was gone. Papa said they had words. We've made inquiries but no one has seen her."

Rufus rubbed his chin. "Since last night, you say? Has no one thought to check the roads heading north?"

"In that awful rainstorm? No one in their right mind would have set out then."

"Or they might have, if they did not want to be caught."

"But north. Why—" She gaped for a moment. "Do you think she's eloped?"

"If I were the gambling sort, I'd lay money on her running off to Scotland with her Lord Benedict." Imagine, that bastard Clivesden a cuckold, or near enough. About time he learned how it felt—not that he would ever know more than the burn of humiliation. He didn't possess enough feeling to understand the depth of grief his peccadilloes had caused others.

A line formed between Sophia's brows. He resisted the urge to flatten it with his forefinger. "Oh, she'd never run off with Lord Benedict. He's in love with her, you see."

"Then it seems perfectly reasonable for them to run off together."

"Not my sister. She doesn't want to marry for love."

Rufus sat back, his shoulder brushing Sophia's, and drummed his fingers on the settee's wooden arm. "Perhaps he's convinced her otherwise."

She leaned into him, prolonging the contact and sending a pleasant rush through his gut. "At any rate, Papa's already made inquiries at his town house."

"And?"

"According to his butler, he was not at home, but . . . Oh, he could not have run off with Julia. If anyone knows of Revelstoke's doings, it's his friend Mr. Upperton, and Mr. Upperton gave his word he saw Revelstoke at their club last night."

Rufus frowned. "And what of Clivesden in all this?"

"What of him?"

"Has he been apprised of his betrothed's sudden disappearance?"

"Papa sent him a message, of course." She curled her fingers about Rufus's forearm, making it difficult for him to attend her next words. "Better he hear it from us than have some gossip tell him at the opera."

BENEDICT swept the curtain aside for a glance at the landscape, now swathed in twilight. All day, low gray clouds had scudded across the sky, driven by an icy wind, but at least the rain had held off. As it was, yesterday's downpour had turned the roads to mire, slowing their progress to a crawl.

After several hours' travel, they were nearing the coast, nearing the cottage. At least the condition of the roads would delay any pursuit—doubly so if Clivesden and St. Claire checked the northerly routes before concluding he'd returned to his lands in Kent.

The warm weight of Julia's head lolled against his shoulder, swaying in time with the movement of the carriage. The constant shiver and rumble had lulled her, childlike, into a doze. If she passed half the day napping, she might well find sleep elusive this evening.

The thought sent a flood of heat to his groin, but he tamped the reaction down. He'd left her untouched last night, and he'd resolved to do so tonight, even if they must occupy the same bed. Once they wed, he'd have years ahead of him to unlock all her secrets. Surely, he could last a few more nights until Upperton arrived with their special license.

Or until she was amenable—whichever came first.

He would wait, even if certain parts of his anatomy were in disagreement with his plans. And until then, nothing prevented him from arranging things so she became amenable more quickly.

Careful not to disturb her, he leaned his head fully out the window, craning his neck for a glimpse of the rutted track behind them. No sign of pursuit. No sign of anything much on the roads this far out. Only Arthur, trotting along behind the carriage on a tether. The gelding tossed his head. Eager for a faster pace, the beast.

Soon they'd arrive at the cottage, where Arthur would have room to stretch his legs. And Benedict, as well, if he were going to keep his hands off Julia during the time it took her to settle in.

The carriage slowed; the team turned. Without looking, he knew they'd just entered the long drive to Shoreford House. They would not follow it to its end where his neglected Tudor pile sat overlooking the Strait of Dover.

No, he'd given his driver instructions to stop at the gamesman's cottage—a bit of added insurance should Clivesden pick up their trail too soon. He'd expect them to stay at the manor itself rather than the whitewashed cottage with its thatched roof and diamond-paned windows.

In years past, in the summer, the gardener would have filled the window boxes with a riot of colorful flowers—when the estate still retained a gardener. Beneath the leafless, dripping branches, it appeared rather mournful.

Already, the carriage was slowing. He tipped a finger beneath Julia's bonnet to trail it along her cheek. "Wake up. We've arrived."

She blinked, and he watched her gaze clear as she shook off the confusion of sleep. Pushing herself into a ladylike sitting position, she broke all physical contact, and cool air rushed into the space between them. "My apologies. I haven't been a very interesting traveling companion."

"If you've rested, it's for the best after the chill you took yesterday."

She pulled her cloak protectively around her—his valet had managed to dry it by the fire overnight and brush it until it looked new. Benedict recognized the gesture for what it was. Now that they'd arrived, she was having an attack of nerves or perhaps even second thoughts about their plans.

He would have to tread lightly.

The coachman opened the door with a rattle and let down the stairs. Benedict alighted and held out his hand. "Come, let me show you our new domain."

Her hand grasped his, overly tight, to cover a tremor, he thought. On reaching the ground, her eyes widened. "Oh."

"A bit rustic, I'm afraid, but better than the main house."

"No, it's charming."

He smiled to himself. She'd meant that. "Will you still say that once you realize you will not have any servants to attend to you here? Not that," he added quickly, "we'll have to cook for ourselves. I'll send the coachman along to the main house with instructions to bring us meals at regular intervals, but beyond that—"

He stopped and ran a hand through his hair. Here he'd meant to distract her from her nerves, and he was rattling on like some schoolboy. "What I mean to say is if you require the assistance of a lady's maid, I suspect I'll have to fulfill the role."

Capital. Now he'd gone and made her blush. That comment hadn't done much for his own predicament, either, as his mind filled with images of him helping her out of her clothes, his fingers brushing against soft, white skin.

"In that case, I suppose I shall have to make do." At least she responded, even if she did keep her eyes firmly trained on the ground.

JULIA hunched her shoulders against the wind's bite. On its back, it carried a raw salt tang that told her this estate lay near the coast. That hint of bitterness unsettled her in its unfamiliarity. The district she'd known in her childhood had lain farther inland, and its scents consisted of the earthier odors of grass and trees and bog.

After yesterday's dousing, she didn't think she'd ever be warm again. Right now, all she wanted was a fire and a hot cup of tea, but the cottage's lone chimney, with its lack of a smoky plume, appeared unpromising on both counts.

She followed Benedict inside. The cottage's interior

consisted mainly of a single room with a large, open-hearth fireplace at one end. Before it stood a rustic table that served as both workspace and dining. Crockery and pewterware sat on shelves; bunches of herbs hanging from the rafters lent a hint of lavender to scent the air.

At the opposite end of the space, a lone door led to what must be the single bedchamber. A bedchamber she would have to share with Benedict soon. A shiver of another sort coursed through her.

Benedict raised an eyebrow at her. "Still think it's charming?"

She cast another glance about. They were most definitely far from the genteel trappings of the *ton* and all its social confinement. With a sharp nod, she decided. "Yes, I do. We shall look after ourselves and make an adventure of it."

He crouched before the stone hearth and peered up the flue. "Well, then the first order of business seems to be getting a fire started."

"The place does feel a bit drafty, and I could do with a cup of tea." She shivered again. The cavernous room would take ages to heat. How long before the warmth reached the opposite end where the bedroom lay? If, indeed, it ever reached so far.

"Why don't you change out of your traveling clothes while I see to the fire?"

"You know how?"

Half his mouth jerked upward. "I'm not completely useless, you know. I learned my first year at school, and I often had to make do in the cavalry."

She pressed her lips together.

"Don't look so skeptical. Go change, and by the time you're through, I shall have a roaring blaze started."

"Did they teach you how to build a fire without wood at school," she teased, "or did you learn that trick in the cavalry?"

His expression went grim. "You'd be surprised." He waved in the direction of the bedchamber. "Now off with you."

She crossed to the door, opened it, and bit back a gasp. Whatever she'd been expecting, this was not it. The thick feather tick with its neat coverlet, a glimmer of white in the deepening twilight, and plump pillows looked inviting enough, but it was so—narrow.

She'd been hoping for something broad, where she could lie on one side and he on the other with a good foot of mattress between them. Then she might pretend she was sharing a bed with her sister.

In this bed, she couldn't pretend. In this bed, they couldn't help but brush up against each other. She shivered in the drafty room. In this bed, they would have to cling together to create any semblance of warmth.

Their baggage stood in the far corner next to the clothespress, where the coachman had set it. She busied herself with unpacking her few items of clothing and storing them next to Benedict's coats and breeches. Yes, he had mentioned the manor house being mainly uninhabitable.

She selected a gown to replace her traveling clothes. Made of pale blue muslin, it was at least two seasons out of fashion. She hadn't stopped to think about where Benedict might have procured her a few changes of clothes on such short notice, but at least she could rest assured he hadn't broken into her house for them. Neither she nor her sister had ever owned such a fussy gown with so many flounces and ruffles.

Come to think of it, this sort of style suited the Upperton sisters' taste to a tee.

Her fingers clumsy and numb from the chill, she made as quick work as she could with the buttons and shimmied out of her traveling clothes and into the mountain of ruffles. At least the excess fabric stood a chance of keeping her warm. When she tried to fasten it, she realized the intention behind all the flounces—to mask a bosom that was less well endowed than hers.

Henrietta Upperton, definitely.

The muslin strained across her breasts and pulled tight at the shoulders. As she struggled with the final button, a stitch gave an ominous pop.

Taking a deep breath—but not too deep, lest she actually tear something—she turned the door handle. By now, at any rate, there ought to be a blaze on the hearth.

She found Benedict down on all fours, puffing into a pile of kindling.

"Is that your secret trick?" She bit down on a smile. "Making fire out of air?"

He glared at her. "Deuced wood is wet. I cannot get it to catch."

She crouched beside him as he sat back on his heels.

"How do you like your adventure so far?" he asked. "We're likely to freeze if we stay here."

"You could always send word to the main house for someone to come and lay a proper fire."

"I have laid a proper fire." He jabbed a finger at his haphazard pile of sticks. "It's not my fault it's been raining so much the entire wood pile is soaked."

"Then whoever you sent for would not do any better a job of it than you." She seated herself on the planks beside him. "Unless you want me to try."

"Have you ever, in your entire life, had to light a fire?"

"No, but I reckon I can strike a flint." She reached for the flint, intending to take it out of his hands. Instead, he tangled her fingers in his. He ran his thumb across the back of her knuckles.

"So cold," he murmured. "We cannot stay here. I do not know what I was thinking."

She thought of that narrow bed they'd have to share,

and her heart thumped. She ought to be glad of the re-
prieve. If removal to the main house were feasible,
they'd each have their own room, as it should be, as it
was even between married couples.

She'd still be compromised, but she would not be
compromised.

But here was a chance to experience the relationship
between a man and a woman. As much as his purported
feelings for her frightened her, she trusted Benedict
above all other men.

While she trusted no man with her heart, she could
trust him with her body. Only him.

"Are you going to give up our adventure so quickly
then? Come. Pretend things are as they used to be—
when we were children," she said.

He considered her, his blue eyes darkening until they
took on an intensity that was anything but childlike.
Spirals of heat uncurled in her midsection. Deeper
within, something felt like it was melting.

Not her heart. Whatever it was, it was located deeper
in her belly, closer to her feminine core.

He adjusted his grip until his fingers wrapped about
her hand. "When we were children, I do not recall
wanting to do this."

Holding her gaze captive, he raised her hand to his
lips. She inhaled as he grazed the back of her hand, the
touch like velvet.

"Or this." He turned her hand over to press a kiss
into the center of her palm.

"Or this." He trailed his lips along her wrist.

Her eyes drifted shut, and she listened to the blood
rushing in her ears and let herself experience. Let herself open. Let herself go.

Over the pounding of her heart, a whisper of movement told her he'd shifted, inched closer, his presence
bright and compelling.

She gravitated toward it as a flower turns its face to the sun. His breath floated over her lips, and she parted them. His lips brushed against hers softly, easily, as light as their first kiss was hard. He pressed, and she pressed back, such a simple give and take.

She sighed into his mouth, and he slipped a hand to the nape of her neck, exerting a gentle pressure, angling her head for a deeper probing of his tongue. She responded to his every move as if they were once again waltzing. He led, and she followed until her head spun like yet another whirl through a ballroom, only this time, instead of dodging other couples, they were completely alone.

He pulled back for an instant, and her heart fluttered with fear he'd stop. Leaning forward, she reached for him. Her fingers dug into the rough wool of his lapels, as she tugged him back to her.

He feathered eager lips to her cheek and temples, swift, joyous little kisses that drew forth a bittersweet burst of emotion. At last, he rested his forehead against hers. For several moments, the only sound was their ragged breathing.

"So sweet a response," he whispered. "How you tempt me to do more."

She raised her hands, and placed them on both sides of his face. His breath hissed through his lips, and she waited for his eyes to flicker open. "I think . . . I know I want more."

He closed his eyes. A tremor seemed to pass through him. She felt the flutter of movement beneath her fingertips, as fleeting as the shiver of a horse's skin as it shakes off a fly. "You are making my resolve to behave like a gentleman extremely difficult to maintain."

She opened her mouth, but before she could utter a single word, he placed a finger across it. "Don't say it. Don't tempt me further."

"What was I about to say?" she teased, in spite of the finger.

"That you don't want me to behave like a gentleman." He knew her too well. She'd wanted to issue a challenge, just as she had so often during the course of their childhood. "Perhaps I don't."

He placed his hands on her shoulders and held her away. "You do not understand. If I give into my passion in this moment, I would take you here and now, and you deserve so much more than a quick tumble on a cold floor."

"Strange, I do not feel the least bit cold." She didn't—not in Benedict's arms.

The corners of his mouth edged into a grim smile. "You might change your mind once it's too late." He settled back on his heels, placing distance between them. "Best we puzzle out how we're to get a fire started. Tomorrow, I'll show you about the place."

CHAPTER FIFTEEN

"I DO NOT understand this insistence on a public spectacle, when the matter of this marriage could just as easily be solved in private." Mariah tugged at a glove. "Away from curious eyes."

Across from her, Mrs. St. Claire puffed herself up, no doubt to retort—as politely as possible, naturally.

Rufus trained his gaze out the window and attempted to ignore them, an impossible feat the way they sat. This was the carriage ride from hell. Not only was he crammed in with his sister, a captive audience to her ongoing—but oh-so-proper—argument with his future mother-in-law, but the crowds on Bond Street had slowed the horses to a standstill. Passersby paused to gawk for a moment or two at the crest emblazoned on his barouche before continuing on their way, at a much greater clip on foot.

Next to her mother, Sophia shifted her weight, flapping one hand ineffectually in an effort to stir the stuffy air. She glanced at him, and he caught himself wishing she would smile, not that she had reason of late.

Julia had been gone for two days; no doubt, her absence would be noticed soon. Clivesden had burst in on the family yesterday evening with some wild notion of going after Julia and her lover. No matter how much the St. Claires and even Clivesden himself might want to keep that information secret, it would get out and make the rounds under cover of raised fans from one ear to the next. Part of Sophia, at least, must agree with Mariah—and Mariah remained blissfully ignorant of the latest developments. The family need not draw attention to itself in the face of the impending scandal.

"Mama, perhaps we ought to go home."

Mariah gave a firm nod. "Finally, the chit has said something sensible. I never thought she had it in her."

"Nonsense!" Mrs. St. Claire broke in before Rufus had a chance to leap to Sophia's defense. "You are to be married. If you're not seen purchasing your trousseau, people are bound to speculate why not."

Sophia caught his eye and paled. If Mrs. St. Claire wasn't careful, Mariah might start asking difficult questions.

He cleared his throat. "I believe we'd arrive at our destination more quickly if we walked."

Sophia sat up a bit straighter. "What a splendid notion."

"Young lady, you will remain right where you are." Mariah leaned forward until her face hovered mere inches from Sophia's. "It is unseemly for you to be seen in Highgate's company unchaperoned, and I most certainly shall not walk."

Rufus turned to her. "Ah, yes, such a danger a man might pose to impressionable young misses in the midst of a crowded street. It isn't as if I'm proposing to spirit her off into the side lanes at Vauxhall."

He tapped on the roof, an absurd action, perhaps, since they'd stood on the same spot for the past five minutes, but it signaled the footman to let down the steps.

Rufus leapt from the carriage to the teeming thoroughfare. "I intend to take some air. Would you care to join me?"

"Don't be ridiculous," Mariah began, but Sophia ignored her.

She laid a hand in his extended palm and alit. Her smile strained slightly at the corners, as if it knew it only existed as a façade to show the world everything was perfectly fine. "Thank goodness," she murmured. "I couldn't bear those two another moment."

"I can't blame you there." He tucked her hand inside his elbow and set off, leaving the barouche where it stood, stalled in the middle of the street.

"I ought to thank you for the outing, but your sister is probably correct. We'd be best staying home."

Rufus touched his hat to a pair of passing ladies. They glanced his way and then turned for a second glimpse. It was the scar, of course. They viewed it as a symbol of his tragic first marriage. "I think the outing will do you good. Better than staying home and worrying over . . . things you cannot change."

She nodded in reply. It was the only possible response on a crowded Mayfair street where any number of eager ears strained to overhear. But he knew what thoughts turned in her mind—concern for her sister and apprehension for the future.

The notion that he could gauge her thoughts on a mere expression and inclination of her head warmed him through. He'd never before reached such a level of sympathy with any woman.

"I still wonder if a shopping expedition is the best idea. Once we reach the milliner's, Mama is certain to forget herself."

He slanted a glance at her. He knew little of ladies' fashions, but even his untrained eye could pick up the air of shabbiness that hung over her costume, the fraying about her hem, the lack of crispness to her spencer, the sagging lace edging her bonnet. She deserved much better than her family could offer. "Should you see anything you'd like, I shall charge it to my account."

She stopped in the middle of the pavement, two spots of rose springing into bloom below her eyes. The river of strollers continued to swell around them.

"I cannot allow you to do that." She kept her voice pitched low, but each word floated distinctly over the rumble of carriages.

"It would be my pleasure. Consider it a gift for the trouble our arrangement has caused you."

The pink in her cheeks darkened, and she bit down on her lip. An image jolted through his mind. She might look just like this under more agreeable circumstances—in his bed, her pleasure spent. Blood pulsed to his groin at the thought of her lying sated in a tangle of white linen sheets, naked, her breathing shallow, and that lovely flush gracing more than her cheeks. It would cover her neck, her breasts . . .

He held her gaze, and her blush deepened. "We . . . we ought to be on our way."

"Yes, we ought. At this rate, your mother and my sister will arrive before we do. I'm sure there's something scandalous to that, although I can't imagine what." Well, beyond his wanton thoughts.

"Your sister might claim you lured me off into some den of sin."

He blinked at her, and a grin tugged at one corner of his mouth. "And what do you know of dens of sin?"

"Absolutely nothing." Surely that wasn't a tinge of disappointment he heard tainting her tone. Surely not.

She turned away before he could be certain. They strode off down the street once more, making fast for the milliner's. More passersby cast him speculative glances. He touched his hat to a young lady who looked as if she ought to still be in the schoolroom. The chit's eyes went round, and her frowning governess chivvied her along.

Sophia's fingers curled into his elbow, and their shoulders brushed, as she leaned close to speak in confidence.

"Why is everyone gaping so? It's enough to make me think I've suddenly burst out in spots."

"They've heard news of our betrothal, my dear, and they're wondering."

"Wondering what?"

"All manner of things that are none of their affair. Whether we'll suit. How much I might have paid your father to take you off his hands. How long after the vows are spoken before you'll cuckold me."

She stopped once more. "But none of that is true. We're not—" She broke off, mindful they stood in an overly interested crowd, but he didn't need her to voice the rest of her thought.

"It's the way they think. They love to imagine the worst of people. Just like my sister. She's forever drawing the worst possible conclusion and embellishing from there. It makes her feel superior."

"What . . ." She glanced around before dropping her voice. "What will she make of me once I've cried off?"

He tamped down a rush of annoyance that she'd brought the subject up and managed to inject a degree of mildness into his response. "She'll be overjoyed at the news. She thinks you quite beneath me. I, however, rarely share her opinions. In fact, I prefer as often as possible to take a contrary view."

There. He'd drawn more color to her cheeks. She looked quite fetching in her shabby bonnet with her complexion aglow. He must remember to compliment her more often.

She cleared her throat. "I believe we've arrived."

They entered the shop, which, for the moment, was blessedly free of his sister. Bonnets, fans, lace, and all manner of ridiculous feminine accoutrements dripped from shelves. The air was tainted with a mixture of heavy perfume, dust, and flecks of feathers.

"My goodness, if it isn't Miss St. Claire." Rufus watched a dark-haired young lady make her way between displays.

The scent of perfume increased, and he searched his memory. Something familiar about her.

In the midst of fingering a length of blue ribbon, Sophia stiffened. "Good afternoon."

Her tone lacked its usual warmth, but the newcomer ignored it. "I don't believe I've been introduced to your . . . Well, I suppose this is your betrothed, isn't it?"

"This is the Earl of Highgate," Sophia murmured, eyes narrowed. On guard.

"My lord." The brunette dropped him a curtsey.

He nodded an acknowledgment, but as Sophia had neglected to tell him the young lady's name, he could not make more of a reply.

At any rate, she turned her attention back to Sophia. "How is your sister? I hope she's well. I haven't seen her at any of the usual gatherings in days."

The color drained from Sophia's cheeks, and her fingers tightened on Rufus's arm. "I . . . Julia . . ."

"I'm afraid she's been ill these past days," Rufus supplied.

"What a pity. I heard the oddest rumor about her." The brunette made a show of straightening the lace cascading from her cuffs. "Someone told me she'd left Town altogether. And she didn't go alone."

Sophia started. "Who told you that?"

The brunette threw back her head and emitted a high-pitched twitter of laughter, the awful keening enough to set any nearby dogs to baying. It triggered a memory. Clivesden's companion from the Posselthwaite ball. His fingernails bit into his palms until the skin stretched tightly over his knuckles.

"Now, now," the brunette replied. "I cannot give away such information. While I'm sure he's in a position to know, the notion is simply too ridiculous. Why should she elope with a younger son when she might have a title?"

Sophia placed a hand to her throat. "Indeed."

Poor thing. She'd give up the truth in another minute. He grasped Sophia's arm. Her shoulders squared, her bosom expanded, and the flesh beneath his fingers firmed, taking confidence from his presence.

"I haven't the time to stand and listen to idle gossip." He thought of Mariah and infused his tone with the contempt only she was capable of—the sort of contempt that froze on contact.

The brunette snapped her eyes to his and immediately slid her gaze along his left cheek.

Releasing Sophia, he closed the distance between him and the interloper. She was small enough that he could loom over her. "You've been given an explanation for Miss Julia's whereabouts. Further speculation is unbecoming to a young lady of your breeding."

One hand over her heart, she retreated, the bloom dropping from her cheeks. "If you'll forgive me, my lord, I seem to have forgotten a pressing engagement."

Her heels beat a rapid tattoo on the floorboards as she exited the shop.

"Gracious, Highgate, you've no call to frighten her half to death."

He turned to find Sophia's eyes wide and shining. Was that admiration? The thought stunned him. Even in his unmarred youth, he could barely recall a woman ever looking on him in such a manner. And she'd called him Highgate, as if they were old acquaintances. Had she even realized?

He allowed himself a smile. "I was merely imitating my sister. I'd no idea I'd be so successful at it. Perhaps I should take to treading the boards."

Her expression softened, but didn't quite melt into the smile he'd hoped to conjure. "This is no time for jokes. She knows, and she'll spread rumors."

Rufus cast a quick glance about the shop. The proprietor was occupied with a pair of society matrons at the opposite end. Good. He placed his hands on Sophia's shoulders and guided her to the very back of the premises, where a towering display of feathered headpieces partially blocked them from view.

Her lips parted on a gasp, and he could think of nothing but the other night when she'd responded to his kisses with such gusto. He stepped closer, breathed in her scent. Roses and sweetness and woman. How she tempted him to relive the experience, but not here in a milliner's shop. Not when his sister and her mother might walk in at any moment. Time was of the essence.

"She knows nothing."

"But she said—"

"She suspects, certainly. She wanted confirmation. In another moment, you would have given it to her."

Sophia pulled her lower lip between her teeth. "I owe you thanks for intervening. She caught me by surprise. But, oh, she must know. She was practically throwing herself at Clivesden at the Posselthwaite ball. She . . . she must have coaxed the story out of him."

Rufus clenched his jaw at the catch in her voice. He knew what she was thinking—that bloody bastard had let the dark-haired chit turn his head. "No, I don't think she has."

"But she said *he*. Her informant was a gentleman."

"She was lying to get you to admit the truth. Clivesden would never have told her about your sister."

"What makes you so certain?"

"Because he's a man. Because he's Clivesden and because he's used to getting whatever he wants. He'd never admit a young lady got the better of him."

She pressed her lips together and stared at the floorboards. "The story will get out."

He reached out and caught her chin in his hand, tipping her head up until he captured her gaze. "Yes, I daresay it will. But you and I will weather the storm." He stopped himself just before adding *together*.

"I'm not thinking of myself," Sophia said slowly. "I'm thinking of Julia."

Twinned red chimneys, dropping crumbs of brick onto a slate roof dotted with missing slabs, topped a massive Tudor pile at the head of the broad, sweeping drive. Diamond-paned windows glinted dully in the watery daylight. The entire place brooded beneath a sad air of neglect.

A sharp breeze bearing the salt tang of the nearby sea whipped at Julia's bonnet. She shivered.

"I never imagined your manor was anything like this," she said, looking at her hands. She'd passed an uneasy night, clinging to her corner of the bed. Ignoring the unfamiliar presence beside her had been difficult. After the kisses she and Benedict had shared, though, he'd been a perfect gentleman and left her untouched.

The thought was frustration and relief combined. While a part of her wanted to get past the hurdle of physical intimacy, another was quite content he hadn't pressed the issue. With each kiss and each touch, she found it harder not to lose herself in him.

"It's been rather forgotten of late. I find myself in want of an estate manager." Benedict placed his hand over hers and tucked it into his elbow. "Come. Let me show you."

Gravel crunched beneath her feet as they advanced. Pale ocher walls glowered at them, as if their arrival had disturbed the manor's rest. Fine, jagged lines veined stone, eroded by salt-bearing winds off the Channel and overgrown with twining ivy.

Julia pressed her free arm against her waist. "And you're planning on making your home here?"

"Few rooms in the main house are fit for human habitation. I leave them to what servants I've retained." Yes, he'd mentioned his estate manager disappearing and others of the staff seeking employment elsewhere.

They reached the front steps. Another gust threatened to snatch the bonnet from her head. "I know it doesn't look like much," Benedict went on, "but the land is good. Excellent pasturage."

When she made no reply, he tugged with his elbow. "At least let me show you the stables."

"The stables. Of course. Where else would you begin a tour of your property but the stables?"

Their footsteps thudded along the pathway, the sound loud in a silence so complete the pounding of nearby surf reached her ears. They skirted weed-rank flower beds, once laid out in a precision years out of fashion, but now the plants trailed dolefully beyond their assigned confines. Sad, leggy bushes that hadn't seen a proper pruning in years choked the paths of an overgrown maze. The state of dereliction was nearly comforting in its familiarity.

Julia began a mental catalog of all the work needed to make the place habitable once again, from shoring up the sagging chimneys to replacing broken panes of glass to bringing the boxwood under control. And that was just on the outside. Goodness only knew what state the interior had been allowed to attain.

By the time they rounded the corner to the stable yard, she added the repaving of the paths with proper flagstones to her list. "Is this why you came to Town?"

Benedict hesitated before taking another step. "What?"

"All this." She swept her arm in an arc to indicate the shabby tableau of his property. "You've come to town to seek a wife to help you cope with all this."

His arm went rigid beneath her hand. "I will not deny making the place habitable is more than I can take on with the staff I've got, but I was not in London to seek a wife. You did not catch me attending many balls, did you?"

She studied him. The raw sea breeze had reddened his cheeks. "Other than the Posselthwaites'."

"I went to the Posselthwaites' to find you and warn you about Ludlowe. That was all. I had no plans to marry."

She stared at him, trying to divine the meaning beneath that last sentence. His tone suggested an "unless." *Unless I could marry you.* She lowered her eyelids to examine the path at her feet and idly kicked a stone. It skittered among the smaller bits of gravel to become lost in a weed-ridden border.

Benedict cleared his throat. "I came to Town in search of bloodstock. I'm sure I told you."

"Ah, yes. Tattersall's. Why hire a gardener when you can throw your money away on cattle?"

"In the event, I did not throw away as much as a farthing." He enunciated each syllable with military precision. Beneath her hand, his arm went rigid. "I know I've neglected my duty here. I do mean to make something of this place, but I cannot breed mares I do not have."

Well, blast. She'd managed to strike at the quick with her blunder. She reached out with her free hand, but he dropped her arm and stalked toward the stables. She hurried after him but came to a halt as an excited chorus of barking shattered the eerie silence.

Several rust-colored hounds came pelting round the corner of an outbuilding. Julia shrunk back, but Benedict strode into their midst, scratching at their ears and patting their flanks, while they leapt at him and smudged his coat with muddy paw prints. His laughter rang over the dogs' yammering. A broad smile spread over his features, and his face took on a boyish expression of mischief, an echo of the sunlit summer days of their childhood.

Something in her heart thawed and swelled at the sight. Suddenly, the ruin and neglect of his estate mattered not at all. He was happy here, happy as she never saw him in Town.

Watching him crouch and take one of the dogs by the loose skin about its neck, rubbing until the beast's tail shook with delight, she caught a sudden vision of him as a father. He would not be content with consigning his children to tutors and governesses. He would chase them across the pastures and through the woods, sharing every discovery. She pictured him crouched beside a dark-haired little boy, poking at the dirt with him, heedless of soiling their clothes.

In her mind, the child suddenly looked up, and his inquisitive gaze met hers. He smiled, an impish little grin that promised nothing but trouble. She returned the sentiment, certain her expression mirrored his exactly.

And then, as realization sank in, her heart turned over. The little boy's eyes, glinting with mischief, matched her own—hazel flecked with gold. Heavens, this was her son. Hers and Benedict's. Upperton's words echoed through her memory. *Any children you produced would be the absolute terrors of their schoolmasters. It'd be perfect revenge. Put their names down for Eton the moment they're born.*

A bittersweet longing for this future rose in her belly, not as insistent as the desire that arose when she and Benedict kissed, but more compelling, somehow. Poignant and aching, nonetheless. She could have this future if only she possessed the courage to risk her heart.

A high-pitched whine caught her attention. One of the hounds had wandered over to stare at her with soulful dark eyes. Its tail, stained white at the tip, gave a hopeful thump against the hard-packed earth of the stable yard.

She crouched to pat its head and scratch behind its ears. "And aren't you a well-behaved fellow? Look at you, patiently waiting for your due, rather than jumping about like the rest of the pack."

The tail pounded a joyous cadence at her praise. She smiled. How long had it been since she'd patted a dog? Years and years, certainly. Not since her childhood at Clareton House. She might have been ten years old when her mother decided she couldn't abide the creatures, not the smell and certainly not the stains and rents the hunting hounds tore in her daughters' skirts.

Julia extended her hand to stroke the animal's flanks and let herself dream. Her children would be allowed to play and explore without sparing a thought to the state of their clothes. *Her children.*

She stole a glance at Benedict. He'd left off romping with the pack of dogs and straightened. He watched her closely, expression serious, his gaze hard and piercing enough to make the hairs on her nape stand on end. The breeze ruffled his hair, causing locks of it to ripple like tattered black banners.

Slowly, she uncurled her fingers from the hound's coat and unfolded herself. Still he watched, gaze intense, leaving her with the impression that he, too, had been imagining their future.

The wind harshened, lashing his hair and tearing at her cloak. An icy drop of rain struck her face. More pattered to the ground about her feet, leaving shallow depressions to mark their passing.

He approached and held out a hand to her. "Best we get inside."

He took her hand and tore off. Julia stumbled after him, one palm pressed into a stitch in her side. The air tore from her lungs in ragged bursts by the time they reached the cottage.

HE watched her through supper, watched her pick at cubes of stewed mutton with shaky fingers, while sipping steadily at a glass of claret. As she drained her goblet for the third time, he laid his fork on the scarred wood. Here they sat in the most rustic of settings, eating simple food, stiffly, one at each end of the table, as if they were separated by twenty feet of polished mahogany, overhung by a crystal chandelier and served by liveried footmen.

Julia blinked at him over the rim of her wineglass, her hazel eyes round and soulful and reflecting the firelight. The claret stained her mouth a becoming cherry red. Her lips parted slightly in an unconscious invitation to taste the lingering remains of wine on her tongue.

Blood pooled in his groin at the thought of the bed that awaited them, the mattress cold, certainly, but they'd warm it soon enough. Not yet, though. He wished to savor the anticipation a little longer. And if he touched her tonight, above all, he wanted her to be sure. While he required her to be his wife in truth after their marriage, she was not his wife yet. If she wanted more time to adjust to the idea of their physical intimacy, he was willing to allow her that much.

"You've hardly touched your supper." He confined his comment to the banal, to the safe, in hopes of curbing his own eagerness.

If, in the end, she refused him, he would pass another night of pure hell. No, best not think about that, either. Whatever depths of passion lurked beneath Julia's surface, she was still a virgin, still sheltered as any young lady of her class. The raw reality of a carnal relationship, even with him, still carried the power to shock her.

With her fork, she poked at a chunk of carrot. "I do

not suppose I've ever been much on mutton. The wine is rather nice."

The words were a hint if he ever heard one. "You might want to take things easy. No one's watered it."

"Oh." Roses bloomed in her cheeks, and then she giggled, a bubbling, joyous sound he didn't think he'd ever heard her emit.

In all their past, he'd heard her laugh, certainly, a deep, throaty gush more suited to the bedroom than the ballroom. He greatly enjoyed coaxing it from her with pointed comments. But such a girlish sound as a giggle? He'd never heard that, even during her childhood.

"It's already affecting you. You sound like your sister."

His remark provoked another outburst, this one long enough to set the halo of curls about her face to swaying. "Oh my. Oh my goodness." She covered the ruffles on her bodice with a hand. "At least I don't sound like the strumpet. Do I?"

Benedict nearly spit out a mouthful of claret. "Strumpet? What do you know of strumpets?"

She shrugged. "I don't know that she really is a strumpet. Only Sophia calls her that because Ludlowe . . . No, I suppose he's Clivesden now."

"Call him whatever you like. Personally, I prefer 'that great bloody idiot.'"

She broke into another fit of giggles, and he smiled to himself. Once they were safely married, he planned on having a great deal of fun plying her with strong wine and provoking her to laughter. Preferably while stark naked in his bed. If her giggling set her curls aflutter in such a way, he could only imagine the effect on her uncorseted breasts.

Ah, yes, once they were married, he would indulge her taste in wine. He'd indulge his own taste for it, as well—sipped straight from her body.

Pop!

The sound, accompanied by a fresh spate of giggles, brought him back to the present. "What the devil?"

Pop, pop.

That hadn't come from the fire. No, it had come from Julia. The rosy glow spread to her forehead. Her lips and chin quivered. Before long, she could no longer hold it in, and she broke into gales of laughter.

Pop, pop, pop.

"What is that?"

"This gown." *Pop.* "It's rather too small." *Pop.* "The stitches keep breaking."

He ought to tell her to stop laughing, but the idea of her giggling her way out of that ridiculous gown was far too appealing. A flounce at her collar gave an ominous lurch. How long before the bodice gave way entirely to expose the creamy upper swells of her breasts? He shifted on the unforgiving wood of the chair, but nothing would relieve his current discomfort, unless it be her hand, her mouth, her soft, yielding body . . .

She paused to collect herself.

Damn.

"Now, where was I? Oh yes. That great bloody idiot threw Sophia over for a girl with the *ton*'s most irritating laugh. Come to think of it, she's a great bloody idiot, as well."

He bit down on his tongue to keep from smiling. He might regret the indulgence at some point in the future, but she really was endearing when she swore. "Why is that?"

"I think she must wish she had the great bloody idiot for herself. Good God, imagine if they produced children. An entire family of bloody idiots. In any case, at the Pendleton ball she gave me the nastiest look. And that was before Papa made the announcement about my betrothal. I had no idea why she would do such a thing, but I suppose she was jealous."

She paused for air and made a sweeping gesture with one hand that threatened to send the congealing remains of her supper crashing to the floor.

Benedict propped his chin on the heel of his hand and stared for a moment. Claret, yes. After their wedding, he would order it by the case. It had surely loosened her tongue. He would have to find a better way to occupy that luscious pink tongue later.

"Now, where was I?"

"Nattering on about strumpets, I believe."

"Nattering? Was I really nattering?"

"A little bit, yes. But do go on. I find it diverting. In fact . . ." He tipped more wine into her glass.

She blinked and took a ladylike sip. The tip of her tongue darted out to catch a stray drop, and lust streaked through his gut at the sight. He'd been about to pour himself another glass but decided against it. Once he had her warm and willing in his bed, he wanted to ensure he enjoyed every second of the experience.

The inviting smile that spread across her features sent another jolt southward. Tipsiness brought a becoming glow to her cheeks. Her hazel eyes sparkled. He held her gaze to memorize her as she was now—still innocent and yet willing to trust him, with her body at least.

If he wanted her heart as well, he'd have to work for it. He would start with the physical, and cultivate her response in the hopes of igniting deeper feelings within her. In unleashing her passion, he might yet foster love in her heart.

The direction of his thoughts must have shown in his expression, for she slanted her eyes downward. Her fingers curled around the stem of her glass, and she took a drink—more than a sip this time, a full swallow that sent a ripple coursing down her neck muscles.

He pushed his plate aside and stood. Her eyes snapped back to his, wariness flashing through them. He knew her to possess an adventurous side, but, he supposed, a few nerves were only natural. Her eyes followed his movement, as he skirted the table and held out a hand to her.

She looked up at him through her lashes. "Don't you want dessert?"

One corner of his mouth edged upward. "Oh yes."

Again that slanting glance, down and away. He'd seen that before. It might mean a woman was interested, as long as—There. Julia's gaze drifted back to meet his. Interest—anticipation, even—warred with the wariness.

He crouched at her knees, bringing his face below the level of hers, allowing her the power. If she wished to refuse him in the end, so be it. Reaching out, he placed a hand on her thigh.

With a gasp, she stiffened beneath his palm, even as warmth welled through her skirt and shift into his skin.

"Are you frightened?"

Her eyes glittered and her nostrils flared, a sure sign she was about to lie, but then she relented and nodded. "Perhaps a little."

"Is it me that frightens you or the act?"

"I think it's mostly the unknown." Her voice broke on the final word.

That response might well apply to her ignorance of what transpired between lovers behind closed doors. Or it might refer to their future.

"I will not force my attentions on you. Not so much as a kiss if you do not want it."

"The kissing is rather nice, actually." The wine-enhanced pink glow on her cheeks deepened to red.

"Then I suggest we start there and see where it leads." He paused. The second half of what he was about to say might prove painful indeed. "Wherever you wish to stop, I swear to you, I will."

Eyes closed, she nodded again.

He leaned in and kissed her. Her lips parted beneath his on contact, her breath drifted into his mouth, and her tongue rose to meet his. She tasted of claret, and the air about her carried the slight salt tang of desire. God help him if her fears overcame her, and she asked him to stop. He would keep his word to her, but it might well kill him.

Not breaking the kiss, he reached up to smooth her hair back from her face, to tangle his fingers in her curls. A popping sound filled the air—a few more of her threads breaking—as her hands sought the support of his shoulders.

He bit back a groan. His mind had just filled with images of ripping that ridiculous too-tight confection from her body, ruffle by ruffle, to expose the porcelain perfection of her breasts. With a growl, he tore his lips from hers before he lost control entirely and laid her out on the table.

Oh God, to seat her firm little bottom at the very edge, lift her skirts and drive himself home. Or perhaps he'd feast on her first. His hand clenched in her hair, and he trembled.

No, too soon. She needed him to take this night slowly. He owed her that much. They'd have the rest of their lives to explore the depths of his passion and hers.

Her breath hitched, and her bodice sagged. "Why did you stop?"

He blinked open his eyes and held her gaze. "Do you feel the pull between us?"

Her eyes, flecked with green and gold, darkened with need, regarded him steadily. "Yes."

"Where do you feel it? Show me."

She slid a hand to cover her belly—just over her womb. "Here."

Triumph surged through him, entwined with a bolt of pure need. Carefully, deliberately, he slipped his hand from her hair, tracing along her neck and down beneath her gaping bodice, until he covered one firm, round breast. It filled the hollow of his palm perfectly. He'd always known it would.

"Oh!" Her eyes drifted shut, her head tilted back in such blatant invitation, while her nipple pebbled into a taut peak.

He leaned in to set his lips just below her ear. Her pulse beat, wild and erratic like the flight of a drunken butterfly. "How you respond to me, my love."

She stiffened. The flutter against his lips increased, and her fingers tightened.

Too late, he realized his mistake. Too late to deny it. She was not so far gone with wine and lust that she missed the ring of truth behind the endearment.

"What is it?"

She pulled away and stared at him. The haze of passion had lifted to give way to fear. Her eyes were round with it.

"Julia?"

"I . . . If we do this . . ." The muscles in her throat rippled as she swallowed. "What . . . what will happen to me?"

He dropped his hands. "What are you talking about? Nothing will happen. Well, no." He rubbed the back of his neck while his thoughts raced. He had no experience with calming a virgin's nerves to know what to say to her at this point. It didn't help clear his mind that certain parts of his anatomy ached with an urgency to finish what they'd started.

"No?"

"I mean, you'll be ruined of course, but you already are. We'll have to marry. You know this."

"Yes, I know that, but that's not what I mean." She stared at her folded hands. "When you look at me, the way you were looking just now. Like you want to devour me. It's just . . . Oh, I don't even know how to say it. I feel as though you might consume me, and there won't be anything left once you're through."

Oh God, she had no idea the images she conjured. He ignored the insistent throb in his groin and reached for her hands. "The last thing I wish to do is hurt you. I want there to be something of you left for next time."

The line of her jaw shifted toward tension. Damn it, why had he thought to make light of the matter, when she was dead serious? "I can't think of next time. I can't think of the future."

"Then don't. Concentrate on how you feel. Relax and let the pleasure take you."

Her brows lowered. "You swore you'd stop if I asked."

The devil take it all. "That I did. Are you asking?"

"I . . ." She nodded. "I think I am."

He released her hands and shot to his feet. His body screamed with unslaked lust. Time to get away from her now, before he broke something.

"Benedict?" She must have caught his expression if the hesitance in her voice was any indication.

He turned away and reached for the wine bottle. "Do me a service, would you?" He kept each word, each syllable tight and precise to hide the shaking that had begun within. "If you want me to keep my word, you will leave this room. Now."

He didn't turn until her footfalls faded and the soft click of the latch told him she'd gone into the bedchamber. The bedchamber, hang it all. He took a healthy swig from the wine bottle, wishing for something stronger to calm the raging need within.

So close. He'd been so close to having her willing beneath him only to ruin it with one unguarded slip of the tongue. Damn it to hell. He threw his head back and drained the bottle.

Coward that he was, he waited a good hour—until he

was sure she was asleep—before entering the bedchamber. If he'd had the foresight to order a bottle of brandy from the main house, he might have lasted rather longer.

But then if he had any foresight, he might have curbed his tongue. At least he'd learned. His honest utterance of emotional truth had brought her back to her senses. She wasn't ready to face the full impact of his feelings for her.

Next time, he'd keep Upperton's advice in mind and not allow her to think until it was too late. As long as he prevented her from thinking, she had no problem with sensual. No, she reveled in his kisses and touch.

Moonlight, unhampered by clouds this night, bathed the room in a silvery glow. The white of the linens and the sheer curtains shone like pearl in its gentle glimmer. Julia sprawled in the center of the bed, arms flung outward, as if, even in sleep, she meant to guard the entire feather tick.

Her breath ebbed and flowed in an even cadence, slow, steady and alive, even if she was dead to the world, helped to that state by the claret.

Air hissed through his teeth, while a surge of renewed lust jolted through him. Next time—soon—he would overwhelm her with sensuality.

Without thought, his fingers unknotted his cravat before going to work on his shirt buttons. He shrugged out of his coat and waistcoat, laying them flat on the clothespress. No doubt his valet would cringe at the notion of leaving them to wrinkle, but this cottage came with no amenities such as a dressing room with places to hang his eveningwear.

In the cavalry, his uniform had survived greater indignities. His civilian clothes would have to adjust.

He stripped off his trousers and stole to the bed naked. Julia might be shocked, but if he played his cards right, they might continue their explorations in the morning—

as long as he was fortunate enough to catch her just as she was awakening so he could distract her with sensual pleasure.

He fully expected to be aware when the moment for action came. He already knew he would not get a wink of sleep as long as he must lie beside her, unsated.

CHAPTER SIXTEEN

BENEDICT LAY in the feeble light of dawn, listening to Julia's breathing. All night long, he'd tried to match his respiration to her even cadence, but her presence in his bed warded off sleep. How could he possibly drift off when all he'd ever wanted was within reach?

Her back to him, she slumbered on, her hair spread across the pillow. Careful not to wake her, he lifted a honey-colored tendril and wound it around his finger.

She let out a sigh and nestled the length of her body against his. Her rounded rump brushed his groin, and he stifled a groan as he stirred to life. Soon. Soon, she would awaken and the seduction would begin.

Warmth radiated from her lithe figure. It flowed through the barrier of her fine lawn shift and permeated his being. Unable to stop himself, he smoothed a palm down the length of her bare arm. The answering quiver that passed over her flesh reminded him of a skittish colt.

He would have to approach her as such, if he wanted to make her his in truth. His Julia deserved better than a rushed coupling that might well leave her in loathing of the act every night hereafter.

Leaning forward, he fitted his arm around her waist. His hand spread across her belly, his fingers brushing the lower curves of her breasts. His. All his.

A sigh escaped her lips. *Yes.* Her mind still wandered the no-man's-land between sleep and waking, while her body reacted instinctively to his touch.

He brushed his lips across her bare shoulder, inhaling her clean scent of jasmine mingled with lavender from the bed linens while he took his first taste of her skin. Tension stiffened her body. He held his breath. There. She was awake now, awake and aware of where she was and in whose bed she lay.

Just as well. He wanted her awake and aware when he took her. He wanted to watch the golden flecks in her eyes darken with desire. He wanted to hold her gaze as, at last, he joined their bodies. He wanted to hear his name fall from her lips as he brought her to completion.

She tried to turn in his embrace. "Benedict?"

"Hush, Julia," he whispered just below her ear. She trembled, and his fingers dug into the soft curve of her belly. "Don't move yet."

"What—"

"Hush. It's early. We've the entire day before us to spend as we like. Should you be agreeable, we do not have to rise for hours yet." Or she didn't, at least.

Her shoulders lifted as she inhaled, the air hissing between her teeth. "Hours?"

He smiled into the silken drape of her hair. "Hours and hours."

"What shall we do with all those hours?"

Laughter rumbled up from his chest. Her innocence amused him as much as it enflamed. "Perhaps . . ." He raised his hand and combed his fingers through her tresses. "Perhaps we'll spend part of them recalling our childhood."

Lord only knew he needed some form of distraction to take his mind off the lust that raged through his veins and set his blood aflame.

"Our childhood?"

"Why not?" He pushed her hair off her neck and ran a fingertip along her nape. "We are in Kent, if not in the homes we knew as children. What better place to think back on more innocent days?"

"Innocent? You were never innocent."

His finger drifted farther, tracing the indent of her spine. "I was more innocent than I am now. Come. Tell me your most cherished childhood memory."

Her legs twitched, a discreet pressing together of her thighs, and he smiled at her responsiveness. For him and him alone. No other man would ever learn that Julia St. Claire possessed a hidden well of passion, infinitely deep, just waiting for him to unleash the flood.

"My most cherished memory. That will require some thought."

He pressed his lips to the angle where her shoulder met her neck.

"I cannot think if you do that." The words floated from her lips, low and throaty.

"Really?" He tightened his embrace. "Then I shall have to do this instead."

He bent his head to the spot and nibbled this time, seeking out her pulse and feeling it accelerate beneath the hot stroke of his tongue. Her breath expelled on an airy rush, while her neck arched. She angled her head until she gazed at him from over her shoulder, her eyes half-lidded and angled sideways. Catlike. A rosy glow infused her cheeks, and her lips parted, full and inviting.

An offering he gladly accepted.

Tipping her chin toward him, he leaned in for a taste. She opened to him immediately, her tongue rising to greet his. Her weight shifted in an attempt to turn into his kiss. He tamped down a surge of need.

Not yet.

Reluctantly, he eased back. With a final, gentle nip at her lower lip, he pulled away.

After a moment, her eyes drifted open, questions mirrored in their depths. Yes. The first pinch of desire held her in its grip. Now to let it simmer for a while until she was mad for the next jolt.

He settled her back to his chest once more. Her rounded backside cradled his erection. A small flinch accompanied the contact, but then she settled in. He inhaled the clean scent of her hair mingled with the merest tang of her arousal.

Dear God, she was already wet for him. He nearly groaned aloud at the thought. Though he dearly wanted to slip his fingers beneath her chemise and test that theory, he forced himself to lie still and listen to her breathing.

The longer he drew this out, the longer he withheld the ultimate pleasure for them both, the greater the reward in the end.

He steeled himself to patience. "How about now?"

"What?"

"Can you think now?"

"What was the question again?"

He smiled into her hair. "I want to hear your fondest childhood memory."

"Will you tell me yours?"

"Yes, if you tell me yours first."

For another moment, silence reigned, giving Benedict ample time to consider other means of distraction. Delicious means. Before this day was out, he meant to discover every last spot on her body that elicited a response.

"Do you remember that hollow tree?" she said at last.

"Yes."

He did, clearly. A giant oak stood near the borders of Clareton House just over the boundary of the family's seat. Its enormous trunk encompassed a space in the center, and a crack large enough to admit a child on hands and knees split its base.

Although Julia had made the initial discovery, he'd always thought of the tree as Sophia's realm. It was her faerie castle. The dried leaves on the hollow's floor stood in place of rushes, the peeling inner bark tapestries to her child's imagination.

The moment their governess learned the source of their tattered hems and stained skirts, the St. Claire girls were forbidden from playing there. Naturally, whenever they could escape her vigilance, they made directly for that tree.

"I thought you hated pretending to be a princess locked in a tower waiting for a prince to come riding to your rescue," he said.

She nodded. "I only played at that because Sophia was older, and she insisted. The days I managed to slip off by myself, she could not tell me what to imagine."

"What did you imagine, then, when you were alone?"

She turned her face into the pillow, so that her next words were muffled. "You'll laugh."

He smoothed a palm along her arm. "I give you my word I won't."

Rolling onto her back, she stared up at the ceiling. "I wanted to fly. I wanted to feel the wind on my face and in my hair. I wanted to soar and be part of the sky."

He propped his head on his hand and looked down on her. The blankets had slipped to her waist. The fine lawn of her chemise was sheer enough to reveal the dusky shadows of her nipples. His throat went dry at the thought of taking one in his mouth, his tongue moistening the fabric to transparency, his lips teasing the peak into a taut bud.

Her eyes slipped to capture his. "Do you remember that day?"

"In the hollow tree? There were so many."

"Not in it, precisely. Up it."

A sudden memory snapped into focus. An eleven-year-old Julia, her pale muslin gown stained beyond repair, inched her way out onto a high branch, and then, carefully, pushed herself upright, her arms flailing for balance.

"You came galloping up on that awful beast of yours."

"I beg to differ. In all my life, I've never ridden anything that could be classified as an awful beast."

She folded her arms, pressing her breasts into two tempting mounds that swelled above the edge of her chemise. "You did when you were fourteen."

"Bucephalus?"

Julia shuddered. "That was its name. It was so poorly behaved."

"He was a handful," Benedict allowed. Too much of a handful for a fourteen-year-old youth, in his father's opinion. Naturally, Benedict had taken his father up on the challenge whenever he could sneak away from his tutor.

"More than a handful. That thing reared the moment you shouted at me to come down. He went up and up until I was certain he'd fall over backward on you."

"But you were the one who fell."

"I was so frightened, I could not help myself."

He recalled heart-pounding fear of his own at the sight of her crumpled form in the path, so close to Bucephalus's deadly hooves. How easily he might have trampled her. "How is this your most cherished memory? You turned your ankle."

"That isn't it. It was what happened next." Was that an actual blush staining her cheeks?

For he remembered, as clearly is if it had been yesterday and not eleven years ago, reining his horse. Scrambling to the ground. Rushing to her side. Those wide hazel eyes had stood out against her pale skin. They seemed to pierce straight through to his soul. Tears welled, magnifying the green and gold flecks of her irises. The muscles of her throat worked to hold in a sob.

Even then she didn't want to display the full range of her emotions. Within the next hour, he planned to cure her of that reserve. He wanted to touch her at such a depth that she could no longer hold her passion in check.

"All I did was pluck you off the ground."

She shook her head. "You made certain I was all right. You checked to see that nothing was broken. You were so gentle."

The thought of touching her somewhere so forbidden as her ankle had scandalized his fourteen-year-old self—it had scandalized him because she was only eleven, still a little girl. He should never have blushed at the notion, nor at lifting her into his arms and settling her on Bucephalus's back.

"I put you on that awful beast, as you call him."

"I know, and that was more frightening than watching him rear."

Her face had gone white as chalk. He'd been afraid she'd faint, until he felt the bite of her fingers on his wrist. Strong as iron, her grip.

He nudged her. "You never were much for horses. That'll have to change."

"You're not getting me up on one of your beasts."

"Not even if I'm there to keep you from falling?"

A blush crept from beneath her chemise. He watched it inch higher until it stained her cheeks. "I might allow it then."

He fitted his palm to her jawline, his fingers grazing the pulse just below her ear. It quickened beneath his touch, as he turned her eyes to meet his. "Is that so?"

"It'd be like that day once more, when you saw me home."

"You were so scared, you couldn't even look." She'd buried her face in his chest the moment he scrambled on behind her.

"You rode so fast."

"You were hurt. I needed to get you home quickly."

The muscles in her throat jumped as she swallowed. "When I closed my eyes, I could almost imagine I was flying."

"Julia." He let his hand slide along her neck and farther. His fingers skimmed the ridges of her collarbones.

"Yes?" The word burst from her lips on an outrush of air.

"Do you still want to fly?" His hand slipped another inch to rest on the upper curve of her breast.

She pressed her shoulders into the mattress, a subtle inclination toward him, a slight arch of her back. A silent, unconscious plea from her body for more. Oh, yes, she wanted to fly, whether or not she knew it.

She covered his hand with her palm, her fingers curling about his. "It was no more than a childish fancy."

"There is more than one way to fly." He leaned in until their lips were a hairsbreadth apart. "Let me show you."

SHE closed the distance between them. Bold of her, yes, but he aroused that feeling. He awakened a sense of fierceness, of recklessness and restlessness entwined. The sort of recklessness that had led her to slip away from both Sophia and Miss Mallory to attempt flight.

Not long afterward, she'd learned to clamp such feelings down, to lock them away in her heart. But sometimes at night when sleep eluded her, she would close her eyes and recall for a few delicious moments what racing home on the back of that ravening beast of a horse had felt like. Locked within Benedict's arms, she'd experienced heart-pounding fear, but mingled with it was a joyous rush that made her stomach clench, flip, and, yes, soar.

For that one brief moment in time, she thought she knew what it felt like to fly. And now he promised her another chance. She had only to let go and seize it.

He pressed his mouth to hers, following her lead. His body stretched over her, his solid weight pushing her into the yielding feather tick. Beneath it, the bed ropes groaned.

She disentangled their fingers and set her hand on his bare shoulder. Corded muscles bunched beneath her touch. His tongue thrust deep into her mouth, but just as quickly, he pulled away to rain kisses across her cheeks.

The hot rush of his breath tickled her chin. His lips trailed lower, his tongue seeking out the delicate ridge of her collarbone before pressing onward. Her fingers pushed into the thick waves of his hair, and he dipped his head farther.

His lips teased along the edge of her chemise. Raising his gaze to capture hers, he paused. Goodness. The sight of him in dawn's glow, looming above her without a stitch of clothing, his black hair falling about his face in wild waves, his eyes darkened to midnight with pure need.

A wild thrill, a rush of terror and fascination en-twined, clawed through her midsection.

His hand slipped up her torso to cup a breast, pushing until it plumped above her chemise. Not far enough. He held her gaze, and his lips descended to close about her fabric-covered nipple, his tongue dampening the lawn to transparency.

He drew the peak between his lips. Fire coursed through her veins, and she arched her back, her head pressing into the pillows.

"You're beautiful," he murmured, before drawing on her once more.

His hand crept down to her hip as his lips continued to tease her breast. His fingers tangled in her chemise, bunching the fabric at her waist.

"This, unfortunately, must go. It's in my way."

At his bidding, she raised her arms and let him sweep the scrap of fabric from her body. Her cheeks burned hot under his scrutiny, and she tugged her lower lip between her teeth.

This was Benedict. She'd known him forever. He'd offered her companionship through the summers of their childhood, relieved the boredom of balls with his pointed jabs at the *ton*, rescued her from the attentions of overzealous suitors.

And now he lay naked with her in bed, all golden skin and steely muscle, his eyes burning with fierce emotion, as he took in the curves of her body. She'd never bared herself in this manner to another soul, and, in this moment, she couldn't imagine allowing any other man to be this intimate with her.

Only Benedict. She trusted no other man with so much.

"Beautiful," he whispered. Gracious, the reverence in his tone. "More than I ever imagined."

He reached out with a finger and circled her nipple. She pressed toward his touch, and he took her in his palm.

"You imagined me?" she whispered.

"Dreamed."

His lips captured hers in a demanding kiss. He held nothing back now. His kiss flooded her with a dark passion that ran burning through her veins. She gave back in kind, her tongue twining with his, her trembling hands gliding over his shoulders and back.

She accepted the full weight of his body, the heat of his skin, his heavy erection, hard and pulsing against her belly. He would complete her, body and soul.

She moaned into his mouth.

He tore his lips from hers to trace a path down her neck once again. With teeth and soothing tongue, he worshipped each of her breasts in turn, teasing her nipples to tight, aching buds, while deep within, she hummed with need.

His hand slid to the curve of her belly, his fingers flexing, and she tensed. How far would he dare touch her? She jerked her hips against the mattress. How he aroused an ache inside her, a hollowness begging to be filled. He suckled hard at a nipple, and a whimper escaped.

"Please."

He raised his head, his eyes dark and intense, while one side of his mouth twitched into a half smile. So wicked, that look. So calculating, so full of plans for her. Such promise of pleasure.

"What do you want, Julia?"

She couldn't possibly express in words where she wanted his touch. Heat blossomed on her cheeks and spread downward. "I . . . I . . ."

His hand slipped another inch. "Tell me."

"I cannot."

"Yes, you can. Let no secrets lie between us."

She looked away, and he ducked his head, maintaining eye contact. "There's nothing forbidden between us." His fingers crept further until they grazed the curls between her legs. "Nothing at all."

She pressed her hips upward in a wordless plea, and her thighs slipped open. His hand inched farther, his fingers curling into her slick folds. She turned her face into his chest and let out a low moan.

And then his fingers moved, parting her, slipping inside, exploring. Short bursts of sharp pleasure pulsed through her in rhythm with each stroke. She inhaled his familiar scent of leather and spice and raw masculinity. And still those fingers petted and probed, testing, searching, at last finding the very center of her need.

She arched her back and cried out. Her nails dug into his shoulders as white-hot pleasure streaked through her, wonderful and yet frustrating as, within, this sense of urgency tightened and tightened again.

Her breath tore from her lungs in ragged spurts, and still those fingers teased in relentless rhythm. They drove her onward, higher and higher, until she could barely tolerate any more, and yet her body danced to his tune, her hips rocking with every stroke.

His eyes were on her, and she did not care. The weight of his gaze pressed upon her, while his breathing quickened in pace with hers.

Her head thrashed on the pillows, and still the pleasure built. He dipped his head to draw on a nipple. His tongue circled the peak in time with his fingers. The tempo increased, and her body gathered itself.

"Reach for it, Julia. Let yourself go."

At his impassioned plea, her entire being convulsed about his fingers in rippling waves of intense pleasure. Another and another and another. The air erupted from her lungs in a high keening.

At last, she collapsed onto the pillows, the occasional renewed jolt still coursing through her.

His touch eased without wholly ceasing. His lips brushed at her hairline. Reaching for him, she traced the contours of his face, his stubble a gentle scrape like sand, until he caught a finger between his teeth.

He pulled her into a searing kiss, wrapped his arms about her, and rolled onto his back. Then he set her above him, his hands smoothing down her spine to curl over her backside.

She tensed in spite of herself at the hardened length of his erection pulsing between them, the invitation clear. "I do not know what to do."

With a smile, he took her hand in his and laid her palm flat against the hard plane of his chest. "You touch, you kiss, you do whatever your heart wishes. I doubt very much any of it would displease me."

She watched his face as she traced a pattern through the scattering of hair across his chest. Amid its crisp texture, her fingertip trailed along a ridge of flesh. Her heart seized. The faint line of white angled across his torso toward his belly.

"When did you receive this?"

He shrugged. "Small skirmish in Belgium."

"But your letters. You never . . ." The occasional messages she'd received during his time with the army had been full of anecdotes about his men and his superiors.

"I saw no point in worrying anybody. The cut was not deep, and I recovered."

"Still, I should like to have known." What if his wound had been grave? She might have lost him and never realized. "This is rather more serious than your colonel who threatened his horse with half rations for misbehavior."

He smiled. "You remembered that?"

She remembered every last one of his letters, she realized with a start. "Of course."

"All that is past. Let's not think on it now."

Her palm still rested on his chest. He pressed his hand over it, a prompt to recall her to the present. She skimmed along his skin and flesh beneath firmed. His eyes fluttered closed, his breathing hitched, and she smiled to herself.

Leaning down, she pressed her lips to his throat. His fingers tangled in her hair and then traced the length of her spine. Her tongue darted out to taste the salt of his skin. He moaned and trembled beneath her. Emboldened, she explored, learning where to touch to elicit a shiver, a tightening of his fingers, a groan of pleasure.

She flicked her tongue across the flat disk of his nipple, and he bucked beneath her, his breath coming now in harsh pants. His hands slid the length of her thighs, down and then up again, until they pressed her open.

"Forgive me, love. I cannot wait any longer." He grasped her hips and raised them, his fingers biting into her flesh in his urgency. He positioned himself at her entrance and flexed his hips. Tender flesh stretched as he began to fill her.

"Easy, now." His voice was strained, anything but easy. Cords stood out in his neck in his effort to hold back.

He withdrew and pressed forward again. This time, something tore within her, and she let out a yelp.

"Oh God, if it hurts you, I'll stop."

It sounded like stopping would hurt *him*. She gritted her teeth, braced her hands on his shoulders and drove her hips down.

"Julia!" Her name was half admonition, half supplication.

"You said I could not do anything to displease you," she panted.

His hands tightened their grip. "Not displeased, but I'd have spared you."

She tilted her hips experimentally. The bright pain of the initial thrust had dulled to an ache.

He let out a strangled cry. "Good God, don't move."

She stiffened. "Am I hurting you?"

The tremor of his laughter radiated through her body from their joining. She shivered as the need within reawakened and surpassed her discomfort.

"God, no." He closed his eyes and inhaled, the movement pushing him deeper. "You are so tight and hot and wet around me. It's paradise, complete and utter paradise."

And his tone, so deep, so passionate, so compelling. It sucked her into him, into his world where she could believe in him and his love and that he'd never harm her. With him, she did not need to guard her heart.

A shudder passed through him that she felt deep within. He raised himself on his elbows to brush her lips with his, once, twice, and with every tiny motion, her tension eased. He'd told her not to move, but, God, how she wanted to. He pressed a kiss to the hollow of her throat, and she whimpered.

"I would give you more time to adjust," he said, voice rough, "but I can hold back no longer."

He lay back and gripped her hips, holding her steady, and withdrew, inch by torturous inch. She sagged against him, torn between the twin sensations of the easing of ravaged flesh and the emptiness at his loss.

He held her gaze, his blue eyes nearly black with need, boring into her, captivating and compelling. And then he thrust, a sharp jerk of his hips that filled her completely and struck at a point deep inside that sent liquid flame through her.

Her eyes closed, and she dug her fingers into his shoulders, holding on for dear life. Again and again, he surged into her, building ecstasy within while she panted above him.

Still he pressed on, and pleasure rose in her, racing toward another peak. It rushed in on her again, like before, only more intense because he raced alongside her.

He released her hips, and she fell on him, driving with him, while he pulled her forward to draw at a nipple. The pleasure redoubled. She threw her head back.

Soon. She'd reach that soaring apex soon. Yes and yes and *yes*.

"God help me." He grated the words, low and harsh.

At the same time, the tempo increased, each surge of his hips harder, deeper, bolder than the last until he bucked off the bed. With a final thrust, he let loose a strangled cry and collapsed into the pillows.

His arms tightened about her, pulling her forward with him into a mindless kiss, while he slipped free of her body. Her pulse still thrummed with the rush of her blood, but at the tightening of his arms about her, she relaxed into his embrace, rested her head on his chest and listened to the vital thump of his heart as it slowed. Peace filled her and surrounded her.

She rubbed her cheek against warm flesh. He could not seem to stop touching her—the arch of her eyebrow, the lobes of her ears, the tendon in her neck—each brush of his fingers a reverence.

She snuggled closer. "You never did tell me your most cherished memory."

"It no longer signifies." His fingers curled against her scalp. "Nothing trumps this moment. I know you do not want to hear of it, but I love you. I always have. Even at the age of fourteen when I had nothing better to do than escape my tutor and run horses that were too wild for me."

She raised her head. "You loved me then?"

He held her gaze and nodded. "That may have been the day I first realized."

An upsurge of emotion swelled within her until it reached her eyes and pricked at their backs. How she wanted to return the sentiment and mean it. "Oh, Benedict—"

A clatter echoed through the still air outside. A shout rang out, and then another. The pounding of fists rattled the door to the cottage. It opened with a crash. Footsteps thudded across the floor of the main room.

Benedict pushed himself up onto his elbows. "What the deuce?"

He yanked the sheets over them as the door to the bedroom burst open. Red-faced, disheveled, cravat askew as he never appeared in public, Clivesden stood on the threshold.

CHAPTER SEVENTEEN

Heedless of his nakedness, Benedict shot to his feet. "How dare you? What the devil are you doing here?"

Clivesden's eyes widened as he took in the scene. Then he lunged at Benedict. "I might ask you the same thing," he roared, before throwing a jab.

Benedict ducked the flying fist and slammed Clivesden into the wall. Before Clivesden could recover his breath, Benedict jammed home an uppercut that smashed the idiot's head into the plaster.

Ignoring the pain in his knuckles, Benedict pulled back his arm for another blow.

"Benedict! Stop!"

At Julia's scream, he hesitated but only for a second as he recalled all of the reasons he was here—the wager, Julia's lost reputation, Amherst's oft-bloodied nose and blackened eyes. No, he couldn't stop. Not now. Again and again his fist smashed into Clivesden's overly pretty, if unshaven, face.

A pair of strong arms halted his next blow and pulled him away. "Stop, man." Upperton's voice sliced through the roar of blood and anger in Benedict's head. "Don't kill him. You don't need that on your conscience."

"Where the hell did you come from?" Benedict unclenched his fist and shook out his hand. His knuckles ached from repeated collisions with Clivesden's face, just enough payment for his inaction as a schoolboy in the face of Amherst's bullies. "For that matter, where the hell did he come from?"

He waved at Clivesden. The bastard slumped against the wall, eyes half-lidded and glassy. Blood poured from his nose, which now sat at an odd angle. The bone and cartilage had yielded to Benedict's blows with a satisfying crunch.

"It seems to me you asked me to come," Upperton said grimly. "I can't say much for the reception."

Too late, Benedict recalled he wasn't wearing a stitch of clothing. Neither, for that matter, was Julia. God, what a spectacle. But a quick glimpse of her showed she'd managed to retrieve her chemise from the tangle of sheets. One hand clutched at the coverlet she'd wrapped about her shoulders. The other twisted in the fabric of his banyan—she must have pulled it from the clothespress while he was pummeling away at Clivesden.

"Here." Round-eyed and red-cheeked, she tossed the deep red brocade at him.

With a nod, he covered himself before turning back to Upperton. "You still haven't told me how the devil he found us."

"They must have followed me. I'm sorry, mate. I thought I'd been careful."

"They?" cried Julia. "Who else is with you?"

Upperton flicked a glance in the direction of her corner, but he was careful not to look full on. Just as well. Even if she had covered herself, Benedict didn't want to beat another man for ogling his intended.

"Your father came along with Clivesden. I convinced him he'd rather wait outside, but I've no idea of his patience."

Benedict ignored Julia's squeak. Clivesden was stirring. With a shake of his blond head, he raised his fingers to probe at a rapidly rising knot on his jaw. When the tips came away red, his brows lowered, and his gaze focused on Benedict, narrow and malevolent.

Clivesden heaved himself to his feet, and Benedict lurched forward, fists balled, ready to wade in once again. Arms outstretched, Upperton stepped between them.

"You can call off your lapdog," Clivesden spat. Blood now stained the once pristine whiteness of his cravat. "I've no intention of settling this matter now."

"You always were afraid to face a man's fists, weren't you?" Benedict grated. "It was easier for you to prey on the weaker."

"I'd call you out for that, only I'd rather not have the gossips twist the story and have us facing each other over a trollop."

The absolute scoundrel. Benedict lunged, only to meet with the implacable barrier of Upperton's shoulder.

"Trollop?" Julia let out a screech of outrage. "Between you and my father, you would have turned me into one!"

Benedict had no chance to react to this pronouncement. Beyond Upperton's shoulder, he caught a glimpse of Clivesden's battered face. The cad might have worn a smirk, only the swelling twisted the expression into a leer. But then his bloodied mouth rounded into shock.

Out of nowhere, another pair of fists seized him by the lapels and bore him backward into the wall. "What did you just call my daughter?"

"Papa!"

Somehow St. Claire had squeezed himself into the crowded bedchamber.

"I called her what she is." A sneer managed to etch itself across Clivesden's ravaged face, as arrogant as he'd ever been at school while taunting the weak. "A trollop. A whore."

St. Claire's belly heaved, his face and pate blotched with red. "Mind your language in front of a lady."

Clivesden straightened and shook off the older man's grip. "I see no ladies present. Only a common trollop. She could improve herself by servicing men in alleyways."

No. He hadn't. The bastard simply hadn't. Pulse pounding in his ears, Benedict thrust himself at Clivesden, but once more, Upperton held him back.

"I swear to God, I'll kill him," Benedict growled. "Here and now."

Upperton tightened his grip. "That's my concern."

A bead of sweat trickled behind the arm of St. Claire's spectacles. "My daughter was perfectly right to run from you, if this is the contempt you show her."

"I'll see you in Fleet Prison."

"I'll do you one better." St. Claire threw his shoulders back, and pinched each finger of his left glove. He yanked the bit of leather free and swatted Clivesden's face. "For the insult to my daughter, I'll see you at a dawn appointment."

Clivesden glared at him for a moment, before a maddening semblance of a smile twisted his bloodied features. "And who would stand with you as a second? One of your creditors?"

"I will." Benedict thrust Upperton's arms aside. "If Mr. St. Claire cannot fulfill his role, it would give me the greatest pleasure to blast you to hell."

A gleam came into Clivesden's eye. "My second will be in touch. Pistols, I presume."

"Naturally," replied St. Claire.

Clivesden nodded, but he kept his gaze fixed on Benedict. If pure hatred might be encapsulated into a single glance, Clivesden had succeeded. After a moment or two, he swept from the cottage.

"Papa!" Julia's cry broke in on Benedict's string of mental curses.

Benedict turned. Her cheeks blazed with heat, more than might be explained by their recent activities, although he caught the telltale wash of pink on her shoulders and neck. The flush of a well-satisfied woman.

Except she was glaring at her father while biting her lip at the same time, the expression an odd mixture of irritation and embarrassment. Hardly the picture of a woman basking in the afterglow.

Damn that bloody idiot Clivesden for spoiling the most perfect moment of his life.

"Papa, you cannot fight a duel over this. I will not have it."

"I most certainly can," he replied. "I'll not stand for a man saying such things about you. Most especially when you were perfectly correct to lay the blame on me."

Julia's face crumpled, and she took a step toward her father, only the bed blocked the way. "I never asked for this outcome."

"Get yourself dressed. Both of you." St. Claire's voice hardened as he addressed Benedict as well. "Any discussion can wait for the ride back to Town."

St. Claire then stalked from the chamber, Upperton in his wake. Julia waited until the door closed behind them before saying anything further. "You have to do something to stop this."

Crossing to the clothespress, Benedict reached for his shirt. "Whether you like it or not, a duel was probably the inevitable outcome of today. I expected he'd challenge me."

She let out a whimper but just as quickly cut the sound off.

"You could not possibly have imagined Clivesden would stand aside and wish us well. Not when—"

He clamped his mouth shut. Damn, he'd nearly blurted the truth. Hoping to cover the moment, he pulled on his trousers.

"Not when what?"

In the midst of tucking in his shirttails, he paused. "No matter. I want to know why you said to him what you did."

She stopped in the midst of shaking out several yards of pale blue muslin. "Said what?"

"When he called you—" His throat constricted with anger. God, he couldn't even bring himself to repeat it. "When he called you a whore. I'd have strangled him for that alone, but you agreed with it. And you blame your father?"

She looked down at the pile of fabric, and twisted it in her hands. "Papa sold me to settle a debt. Apparently, I'm worth five thousand pounds."

"Five thousand?" The exact amount of the bet. His mind whirled. Had Clivesden suspected St. Claire might never pay him back and sought to recoup the loss through the wager at White's? Such assuredness, such confidence, such utter arrogance. "*Five thousand?*"

"I know. It's ridiculous."

"Five thousand." He couldn't fathom it. "The same as—" Damn it, he'd done it again. Blast him and his mouth.

"Same as?"

"It's nothing."

"No, it's not nothing." She accompanied her words with a slashing gesture. "It cannot be nothing. I want to know why, of all the eligible ladies of the *ton,* he settled on me. You know something. It isn't right you've kept it from me."

"Didn't he answer that question when he proposed?" He stared hard, silently pleading with her not to make him repeat any of that vile proposal. It ought to stick in her memory more, at any rate. She'd been a party to the scene.

"There's got to be more to it than that. Why's he so dashed relentless about the whole thing? He could have any chit he wants without lifting a finger. He could have had my sister, for goodness' sake."

Benedict's fingers fumbled with his cravat. Blasted thing. He'd never got the hang of tying it properly without help. "I think he saw you as a challenge. He could've had any number of chits, as you say, but so could most of the other men of the *ton*. I think he wants to be able to claim he's landed the one woman they cannot have."

"Contrary idiots, the lot of you." She pressed her lips into a line and stepped into another of Henrietta Upperton's ruffled confections. Wordlessly, she presented her back, while holding her hair in a pile on her head.

After a moment's confusion, he realized she wanted help with her buttons. His fingers trembled as he pulled the sides of her bodice together and fastened one tiny clasp after the next. His knuckles grazed the warmth of her skin that penetrated the negligible barrier of her chemise. The memory of that skin's softness tingled through him.

He gritted his teeth and thrust the images aside. As much as he'd love to tear off this gown and take her back to bed, now was not the time with her father and his closest friend waiting on the other side of the door.

"You know," she said as he fastened the final closure, "I do not believe you ever told me how you knew that idiot would pursue me in the first place."

He stepped back. "Oh, I'm sure I must have." A blatant lie. He never wanted her to find out she'd been the subject of a wager at White's.

"No, you didn't." She turned to face him. "I distinctly recall you telling me Ludlowe had set his sights on me, but never where that information came from."

An expectant pause ensued. He blinked. She blinked

back and folded her arms. With a growl, he raked a hand through his hair. *Think, man.* But no plausible explanation sprang to mind. In another moment, she'd probably tap her foot.

Fine then. "He wagered five thousand pounds on you."

"He *what?*"

Benedict nodded. "Five thousand pounds that you'd become the next Countess of Clivesden. I did not realize the full import until he told us he was in line for the earldom."

Her lips disappeared ominously into her mouth. "I dearly, dearly hope you had the decency not to sign on that wager."

"Of course I didn't sign. What do you take me for?"

"Someone who hangs about the likes of George Upperton."

Heat crept up the back of Benedict's neck, and he suppressed an urge to tug at his collar. Thank God, he'd never managed to knot his cravat. "Upperton may have, er, signed on that wager."

Julia clapped her palm over her mouth. Then her ruffled bosom gave a mighty heave as she drew in air. Several stitches protested the movement with loud pops.

Benedict held up a hand, hoping it would be sufficient to impede the impending explosion—or prevent her from marching into the next room and confronting the man himself. "I said *may* have. I haven't seen the evidence for myself. I'm only going on a few things he's said."

"I should think those are the sorts of suspicions you'd want to verify." Her tone was as glacial as yesterday's wind—and today's, no doubt.

"Right. We might do that now."

Her glare unwavering, she crossed her arms. The way she was glowering, he'd be fortunate if she allowed him to seduce her again sometime within the next decade.

For that matter, Upperton might well worry about his own possibilities for future progeny. Lucky thing he was in the next room.

He heaved a sigh. "Yes, well, pack your things. And then we'll see about getting this sorted."

BENEDICT was wrong. They didn't get the question sorted, not in the cottage and not halfway through the journey back. Not when a silence reigned in the carriage, so weighty it dulled the clop of the horses' hooves on the road and the clatter of the wheels.

"Bloody great idiot," Benedict grumbled.

Upperton raised his brows.

"I will not refer to him by his title. I find the one I've bestowed on him preferable." Benedict tried to catch Julia's eye, but she refused to meet his gaze. Let him try to wheedle a smile out of her. She was not about to play his games. Let him stew.

"Oh, quite." Upperton stared out the window for a moment. "I say, I'm sorry for this."

"What do you mean?"

"I reckon if he found you so quickly, it's my fault. Thought I slipped out of Town on the sly."

"I suppose it was too much to hope he'd lose time checking the routes to Scotland," Benedict said.

Next to her on the squabs, Papa held himself rigid, his presence more substantial than ever before in her life. He preferred to ignore his daughters in favor of more masculine companions, companions who drank with him and wagered. Companions who fleeced him until he was willing to sell his own children to extract himself from debt.

"You didn't think we'd know who to watch?" His outburst sounded unnaturally loud in the tense air. "The pair of you, thick as thieves. And don't think for a moment you're square with me, young man. Just because you've agreed to step into this duel, doesn't mean we don't have business of our own to take care of."

At the mention of the duel, Julia drummed her fingers against her reticule and bit down on her tongue. She would not say a word. No indeed. She was not speaking to any of them. Foolish men, resolving their differences with violence, if not with fists then at twenty paces. Next thing she knew, Papa would challenge Benedict.

"Who is more reprehensible, sir, the man who antici-pates his wedding night or the man who sells his own daughter for five thousand?" Benedict pronounced each syllable with a careful, clipped precision, as if he were reporting to a superior officer.

Papa twisted his glove between stubby fingers—the same glove he'd used to strike Clivesden and which he'd yet to put back on. "Wedding night?"

Benedict flushed a dull red. "In spite of the way things appeared this morning, my intentions are honorable."

Papa made an incoherent sound in his throat, halfway between a harrumph and a growl.

"I can prove it." Benedict nudged Upperton. "Can't I?"

Upperton tore his gaze away from the passing scen-ery. "What?"

"Do you have it?"

"Right here." Upperton patted his breast. "Didn't realize the Archbishop would come through quite so quickly."

"Have what?" Blast. The words popped out before she could stop them. Useless words, for she knew very well what Benedict would have procured from the Arch-bishop.

"There was no time before we had to leave Town," Benedict said, "so I asked Upperton to get me a special license."

Julia studied her nails. "Looks as if his trip has been a total loss all round then. Perhaps I shall marry Clivesden, after all."

Upperton broke into a violent fit of coughing, while Benedict fixed her with a frightening glare. She suspected he'd used that look to cow junior officers.

"Don't even joke about that." His words came low and lethal, undercutting Upperton's hacking. A frisson passed down her spine. "Not after—"

He cut his thought short when Upperton's coughing came to an abrupt halt. A tense silence fell as Benedict held her gaze, his blue eyes eloquent with rage and confusion. Julia suspected, but for the color, they mirrored her own.

"You will not be able to extract yourself from this marriage," Papa pronounced. "You've determined that by your own actions."

She could make no reply in her defense on that count. Word would get out. If not by the time they returned to Town, then certainly the duel would raise a veritable gale of *on-dits*.

The duel. Why had Papa seen fit to challenge Clivesden over the truth, all over some antiquated notion of honor? No matter the outcome, nothing good could result from the duel. Papa might well carry the blood of another man on his hands for the rest of his life, and that was at best. At worst, he'd die himself.

As if he'd guessed the tenor of her thoughts, Papa leaned forward, hands folded between his knees, and launched into a discussion of the details: weapons, location, ideal conditions.

Julia pressed her lips together and gazed out the window. Poplar trees lined the road. Interesting trees, poplars. Interesting enough, at least, to distract her from a diatribe against masculine idiocy that might rival a fishwife had she lent it voice.

At last, she could stand it no longer. "Papa, have you ever even shot a pistol?"

He settled back, and readjusted his spectacles. "Of course I have."

"Oh?"

"I dueled Cheltenham over your mother."

Julia blinked at her father as if seeing him for the first time. She studied the lines at the corners of his eyes, his furrowed forehead, and, in her mind, willed those marks away. She imagined a less fleshy version of his face and a head covered by more than a mere fringe of hair. She pictured him less as a friar who enjoyed his own ale rather too much and more as a man, still youthful, still full of hope for the future. She'd never before had occasion to think of him as ever being Benedict's age, but he must have been, once.

"You and Cheltenham."

"Shockingly enough, yes. I cannot abide certain words."

His tone left Julia with no doubt what those words were. "He called Mama . . ." She couldn't bring herself to say it.

"Yes, when he jilted her. Someone had to defend her honor." Papa spoke with finality, as if those few words sufficed to explain what must have been quite a scandal at the time. Then he expelled a great sigh that seemed to deflate him. "I couldn't give her what she wanted most. Only Cheltenham could have done that. So I've tried to make up for it by giving her everything else."

Everything else—a town house in Mayfair, ball gowns, parties, season after season for his daughters, titled sons-in-law.

"At least I'll see you settled," he went on, almost to himself. "That devil's bargain I made with Clivesden was just a last, desperate effort. And now it's failed. I've failed her. Whatever becomes of me, you'll make sure you look after your mama."

CHAPTER EIGHTEEN

"AND WHERE do you think you're off to at such an hour?"

At his sister's stentorian tones, Rufus released the brass handle to the front door, and turned on his heel. Damn it. He'd nearly made it to safety. "I am expected at the St. Claires' to escort Miss Sophia to the theater."

Mariah advanced, heels thudding dully on the parquet of the vestibule. "Nonsense! You shall do no such thing."

He raised a brow. What good was a title if he let his sister bully him? God only knew he'd let her get away with it often enough when they were children. Mariah had always taken her role as the eldest to mean she decided the course of his life, even when that extended to such banalities as the disposition of his tin soldiers. "And what, pray tell, is your objection to the theater?"

"None whatsoever. Only you've no chaperone but me, and I have a decided objection to your alliance with that family."

"Do you really? And since when? As I recall, you stood by knowing I had to offer for Miss St. Claire."

Mariah's graying curls swayed about her sagging cheeks. "Had I realized the potential for scandal, I would have objected more vehemently from the beginning. As things now stand, you'd besmirch your title by marrying into that family."

He slapped his gloves against his palm. "As things stand now? What has changed?"

"You haven't heard?"

Slap! Any more of this and the first act would have started by the time they reached Drury Lane. "Listening to gossip again?"

"The younger sister has run off. Does that mean nothing to you?"

"Yes, I was aware."

"Aware?"

"Naturally. Miss St. Claire has been worried sick over her sister's disappearance." He knew as much firsthand. He'd spent yesterday evening at the St. Claire town house, lending Sophia his shoulder, while they waited for her father to return with news. As of very late last night, he hadn't. "I was hoping an outing might provide a distraction."

The loose skin at Mariah's neck trembled with rage. "You knew of this scandal and you did nothing? You did not even see fit to inform me."

"Looks as if I did not have to, did I? It seems you've found out all on your own. I'd congratulate you on your adeptness at listening to the latest *on-dit,* but I'm afraid I'm running rather late."

"And it means nothing to you that the sister's tossed her betrothed aside to run off with some former cavalry officer? What's more, they were caught."

Rufus studied his sister. That last bit came as a surprise. He'd already worked out the rest of it on his own. Granted, the bit about being caught might not actually be true. That young shrew they'd run into might have spread all manner of rumor. On the other hand, St. Claire may well have returned to Town. "Well, that's a charming piece of news. Now, if you don't mind, I really must be off."

"You cannot continue with this engagement."

"I can, and I most certainly will. Even if I no longer wished to pursue a marriage with Miss St. Claire, a gentleman does not cry off."

She advanced another step. "A gentleman can arrange matters so a lady cries off. But she'd never dream of it, would she? She had no hope of landing a title, in spite of her looks. Come to think of it, how can you be certain she really fainted that night at the Posselthwaites'?"

With a sigh, Rufus pulled his gloves on. "I plan to spend an evening at the theater with a young lady who, no matter what her background, I've decided suits me most ideally as a wife. To put things plainly, I do not give a tinker's damn what the *ton* thinks of the match, as I plan to retire to my estates as soon as the vows are said. If my connection to her family is an embarrassment to you, that is no problem of mine."

Mariah's quivering turned into an outright tremor. "I shall make it your problem if you cannot choose a more suitable young lady."

"Then you shall no longer be welcome on my estate."

"You cannot expect me to spend the summers in Town with no society to speak of."

He cast a glance about the vestibule. All imported Italian marble and gilt wallpaper, the entryway announced its inhabitants' impeccable breeding. The town house had belonged to the late Lord Wexford, and had not been included in the entail. Mariah had never borne her husband an heir, and his holdings had passed to a distant cousin. If she wanted to escape the heat and grime of summer in London, she was beholden to her brother and whatever invitations she could manage.

Rufus jerked a leather glove over his hand. "As I see things, you have two alternatives. Tolerate my choice of spouse and, above all, treat her with respect or seek yourself a new husband."

"What? At my age?"

He allowed himself a smile. She was in her early forties, endowed with no particular beauty and likely barren. "A husband might do something to improve your temper."

"Husband indeed," she harrumphed.

He recognized her near constant trembling for what it was. More than excess weight put on over the years, more than moral superiority. No, it was fear. Fear that if she lost her grip on the tiller of her standards, she might lose her heading, her purpose, her position altogether.

But he could never remark on such a thing. In the history of their interactions as siblings it was not the done thing, any more than it would have behooved him to propose marriage to the scullery maid. So he settled on the expected response—the kind that had ever characterized their relationship since their childhood when he discovered her fear of spiders and delighted in answering her screams by crushing the offending arachnid and tormenting her with the remains.

"You need a man to reform," he needled. "I hear Lord Chuddleigh is in dire need of it."

Her bosom expanded with an impending explosion.

"If you refuse to undertake such a daunting task, there's a novel in the study. *Pride and Prejudice,* I believe the title is. You might find it edifying. Now if you'll excuse me, I'm going to be late."

He left her spluttering on the threshold and leapt into his waiting barouche. The horses' hooves clopped loudly on wet cobblestones as he set off for Boulton Row. Bone-chilling wind accompanied another rainy evening.

As much as he hated to give Mariah credit, she was right about one thing. He couldn't attend the theater tonight, with or without a chaperone. While the outing might prove a welcome distraction for Sophia, he preferred not to expose her to the *ton*'s speculative glances.

His carriage rumbled to a halt outside the St. Claires' town house. The moment the stairs were lowered, he bounded from the vehicle into a misty drizzle and up the front steps. In response to his knock, Billings whipped the door open almost immediately.

"I believe Miss St. Claire is expecting me," he said when the butler remained in the doorway, blocking his entrance.

"I shall have to inquire to make sure her plans haven't changed."

"I see." He didn't, but he had no choice but to wait in the foyer while the butler made his inquiry.

After a few moments, a white-faced Sophia, still clad in a muslin day dress, drifted down the staircase. "I'm dreadfully sorry, my lord. I cannot possibly attend the theater tonight. Not after what's happened."

He tugged off a glove, finger by finger. "I'd drawn the same conclusion myself."

"But you do not know the whole of it. Once Julia comes home, there's going to be a horrible scandal."

"Hadn't we already worked that out?"

"I'm sure it will be far worse than expected. Julia will never be able to show her face in society again. Not after the kinds of rumors Eleanor is certain to spread."

He stared for a beat. "Eleanor?"

"Yes, from the shop yesterday. Lady Whitby's niece. I'm afraid that under the circumstances . . ."

The hair on the back of his neck rose as she trailed off and cast her eyes to the floor. "Under the circumstances what?"

With shaking fingers, she reached out and plucked at his sleeve. "You must see that our alliance is impossible now. Surely you do not wish to connect your title to . . . Well, the likes of the St. Claires."

He hoisted a brow. "You're crying off now? With no witness about to make it stick?"

"Please."

To his astonishment, he noted a tremor in her lower lip. This was no act, no fit of pique carried out before others for form's sake. She was serious and, if he didn't miss his guess, unhappy at the prospect of carrying out her duty.

He took her chin in his hand, raising her gaze to his. Her wide blue eyes swam with tears. "What's this now?"

"Isn't it what you wanted? It was our agreement that I would cry off. It's only happened sooner than expected, but under the circumstances—"

"Hang the circumstances. Get your wrap."

She cast a despondent glance at her limp dress. "I cannot possibly go out in society. Not now and not like this. Not unaccompanied."

"Where I'm taking you, there will be no one to see."

She stepped away from him, breaking their physical contact. His hand dropped to his side. She turned her head to the left, watching him from the corner of one eye, wary. "Where are you taking me?"

"For a ride in my carriage. I'd like to discuss our agreement if you're amenable."

SOPHIA hunched in her cloak as they rattled off. She could barely believe she'd left with him, and without so much as informing anyone of her whereabouts. Why, she was as bold and as brazen as Julia.

Guilt over her sister settled uncomfortably in her stomach. Julia, whom she'd consigned to silence in her jealousy.

Across from her, Highgate cleared his throat. "Let me make one thing clear from the outset. Do not concern yourself for my sake about attaching scandal to my name. For one thing, I have already weathered worse than this. For another, you have done nothing scandalous."

She glanced at their surroundings, acutely aware they were alone. The memory of what had happened the last time they rode alone together in this carriage lingered in her mind. Her lips tingled with the recalled sensation of his mouth moving over hers.

"Not unless you count the circumstances of our first meeting."

He waved a hand, a shadow flitting through the darkness. "Society's rules are ridiculous, are they not, when a man can be said to have compromised a lady in coming to her aid?"

"You and I both know nothing untoward happened, but—"

"Vicious tongues with nothing better to do than invent lies about decent young ladies for their own amusement have always existed and will continue to do so. You and I cannot stop them, but we can ignore them."

She studied him from beneath her lashes. "Are you planning on ignoring your own sister?"

His mouth stretched into a wicked grin that dropped the weight of years from his face. It didn't make him look young, exactly—only young enough, and yet experienced, wise to the ways of the world. A finger of flame burrowed deep into her belly. Just in time, she stopped herself from pressing a hand to the spot.

"For years, I've made a habit of ignoring my sister whenever possible. I see no reason to stop now."

Laughter bubbled up inside her, and she gave it free rein. As she subsided, his dark eyes captured hers. He still wore that wicked grin. "You're quite beautiful when you laugh. I'm sorry I haven't had occasion to see that expression on your face more often."

Heat crept up her cheeks, even as her smile faded. She ducked her head. "Thank you. I'm afraid I haven't had much reason to smile lately."

"Have you ever?"

She looked him full in the face, trying to gauge his expression. He watched her with a raw intensity she'd only ever seen on the faces of her suitors. Her breath hitched at the thought, while her heart raced ahead. "Yes, of course I have."

"Tell me about one of them."

She opened her mouth to reply, but he held up a hand. "Wait. I have a condition. None of them can concern Clivesden."

She pressed her lips together. "You've no worries there. He's never given me occasion to smile. Not really, and not for long. It's easy enough to smile at a man if you want to capture his attention, but once you realize he's not really looking at you, that perhaps he never really *saw* you, smiling becomes much more difficult."

To her horror, she found herself forcing the last of her words out through a thickening throat. "I'm sorry. Here you're trying to distract me with happy thoughts, and I'm going all maudlin on you. Why can't I get over this?"

"It will take time. It's like mourning a loved one." He shifted his glance to the window, and she knew he was thinking of his dead wife. "Some days you cannot get past the overwhelming anger. Others, all you feel is a pervasive sadness that tinges everything with a hint of gray. Still others, you catch yourself thinking about that person and all you ask yourself is why it happened to them."

He turned his head to face her. "I am a patient man. I am willing to give you all the time you need."

Her heart gave an odd sort of leap, something akin to shock intermingled with another emotion. But it couldn't be hope. She'd nothing left to hope for. "What's that supposed to mean?"

"I've already told you. I'd like for you to reconsider our agreement."

"Which part of our agreement?" Although, even as she asked the question, suspicion grew within her—suspicion of his intentions. He was on the verge of proposing again, only this time he was in earnest. Her pulse throbbed in her neck.

"I think you must know, but if you prefer, I shall be plain. I should like you to seriously consider becoming my wife."

"Why? You must know I do not love you. Why should you put yourself through another unhappy marriage?"

"Because, my dear, I do not believe our union would turn into a mismatch. On the contrary, you and I get on quite well together. We can talk to each other. We share an affection for books and gardening. You would enjoy my estate in Dorset."

"Your talk is all of sense. What of sensibility?"

"With cultivation, with nurturing, that will come. I'm already aware of the means of arousing your passions."

She drew her cloak more tightly about her—a shield. "The other night was an aberration. I was upset."

"Ah." He shifted his gaze to the street. "But then I suppose you prefer a man's looks over everything else."

She sat up straighter. "I never said anything of the sort."

He leaned toward her until his face hovered a few inches from hers. "And you expect me to believe I could not draw the same reaction from you again?"

She raised her chin, fully aware of the gauntlet he'd just cast at her feet. "Yes."

"Perhaps then, we should put it to the test."

He gave her no chance to reply, no chance to protest. Like a hawk, he swooped, closing the distance between them and sweeping her into an embrace. His lips covered hers with an urgency that brooked no denial.

His tongue pressed at the seam of her lips, demanding entry, and all thought of denial fled. He sucked her into a whirlwind of sensation where desire and need reigned supreme.

She melted into the circle of his arms, her fingers creeping along the breadth of his shoulders to enlace at the back of his neck, while deep within, an insistent pulse thrummed its own demands—shocking demands that conjured visions in her mind of the pair of them with nothing between them, not even clothes.

At the thought, she tore her mouth from his, gasping for air. He pressed his point home, his lips seeking her jaw, the lobe of her ear, her throat.

Her breasts.

She pushed the back of her head into the seat as his warm breath caressed their upper curves exposed above her bodice. An airy moan escaped her throat. His hand skated along her ribs to capture her breast. It swelled to fill his palm, and her nipple hardened to a tight peak beneath his seeking thumb.

His touch made her fidget on the seat, made her thighs rub against each other, the pressure bringing no relief from the relentless ache inside her.

He brushed kisses back up the column of her throat before claiming her mouth once more in a searing possession. Boneless, she slumped against velvet squabs until he half lay over her. Exactly where she wanted him.

Exactly where he should be.

"So tell me, my dear," he whispered, easing back to rest his forehead against hers, "are you upset tonight?"

"Yes."

Laughter, low and sensual, rumbled from his chest. Its tremor passed through her like a flaming arrow. "Liar."

"No, I am upset."

"Only because I have the right of it, and you do not wish to admit it. I shall concede one point to you, though." He kneaded her breast, and her eyes drifted closed. He could have her so easily, and she didn't care at all.

"What?" The word floated from her lips on a sigh.

"I have not drawn the same response from you as the other night."

"You haven't?"

"No." He lowered his head and nibbled a path from her earlobe to the base of her throat. "Your passion is so much deeper tonight. So much richer. What have I awakened in you?"

What indeed? Hunger of a sort she'd never before experienced, hunger that lay deeper in her belly, hunger for him.

With a whimper, she speared her fingers through his hair, holding him to the spot. A growl erupted from him, deep and feral. His teeth rasped delicate skin followed by the soothing brand of his tongue.

Oh, she was lost entirely in a world of Highgate's making, a world that encompassed no more than this carriage, this seat.

Him.

He was sensuality, pure and white-hot. She tilted her head back and gave over to him. Deft fingers skimmed across the bare skin above her bodice. They played along her collarbones, before sliding to her neck and onward to her nape—to the clasps of her gown.

In a few swift movements, he made short work of them. His fingers curled beneath soft muslin to peel it away from her shoulders, bringing her chemise and stays along with it. Cool air rushed over her bare breasts, raising gooseflesh, tightening her nipples to aching buds.

He drew in a sharp breath. Sophia's eyelids fluttered

open to find him staring at her body, his eyes black with need, his expression hungry like that of a starving man faced with a sumptuous feast.

He slipped his hands over her flesh until he captured a breast in each palm, testing their weight, squeezing gently. Sophia watched in fascination. His tanned hands stood in stark contrast to pale skin that had never once been exposed to any eyes but hers.

His gaze flicked to hers, caught her watching, and held, as a sinful smile stretched his lips. "Such a sensuous creature you are, my Sophia. And to think I am the fortunate man to make that discovery."

And then he lowered his head to draw a nipple into his mouth. Desire vibrated through her, and her lips parted on a sigh. He responded with firmer pressure, suckling her, while his hand occupied her other breast. The fire in her belly roared higher, melting her until she sagged against the seat, limp and languid and willing.

Waiting for the next wanton pleasure, the next sensation.

Gathering her in his arms, he drew her into his lap, where he pressed urgent kisses to her heated skin, tweaked a nipple here, nuzzled a sensitive spot there, until she could barely imagine his next move.

Her fingers dug into his shoulder for purchase, and she simply held on and let him lead where he would. Some small spark of rationality in her brain warned that if she was not completely ruined yet, she soon would be if she did not call a halt.

Indeed, she should have stopped him long before this. But the sensations he aroused were too delicious, too overwhelming. They were utterly wicked but her body craved every kiss, every touch, and she was more than inclined to give herself over to wantonness.

More cool air rushed over bared skin—her thighs this

time. If he'd managed to push up her skirts, she really ought to make him stop. His hand smoothed a path along her inner thigh, and of their own accord, her legs fell wide to accommodate his searching fingers.

She drew in a breath to protest, but it released on an airy note as he probed her most intimate flesh. "Highgate?"

He studied her face with an odd intensity—as if he expected something of her.

"You cannot convince me you do not desire my touch. The reaction of your body tells me otherwise." Shallow breaths clipped his words.

His fingers slipped into her, oh God, so easily. They parted slick folds of flesh and examined, searched until she let out a cry.

He groaned in triumph, and then his fingers became relentless in their circling of that one spot. She trembled beneath him. Oh how she ached, just there, where his knowing fingers touched, over and over in an unforgiving rhythm.

She panted and gasped to its tempo, her hips straining against him, the jostling of the carriage adding counterpoint to each movement. In the midst of all this sensual assault, he was leading her somewhere—along a path to sin without doubt, but somewhere more immediate.

Her body recognized it if her mind and experience did not. Internal muscles gathered and clenched. She writhed and arched and shook. Her breath tore from her in ragged spurts. And in the midst of it all, pleasure mounted toward a peak high above her. She spiraled upward with it.

And then, without warning, it crashed in on her. Her body convulsed about his fingers. His lips descended to swallow her moans.

She returned his kiss obliviously until he eased back. She opened her eyes to find him staring down at her.

Gradually, her senses returned until she was trundling through the streets of Mayfair in a barouche, sprawled across the seat with her gown undone and her hair in wanton disarray. A blush crept up her cheeks, and she crossed her arms to hide herself.

Gently, Highgate took her wrists in his hands. "A pity to hide such perfection, but I'm afraid we must."

She shook her head in confusion, as he helped her up and set her gown to rights.

"But—" She couldn't go on. She had no experience on which to base this encounter, but a vague feeling grew inside her that they'd left things rather unfinished. Powerful as it was, the pleasure belonged to her alone.

She watched Highgate closely, in search of some indication of what she ought to do next. His expression was unreadable, guarded somehow, as if he were holding himself back. She raised a hand to brush her fingertips along his cheek, but he wrapped his fingers about hers before the touch landed.

"I should take you home now."

"But—Is that it? Am I ruined now?"

He gave a strangled laugh. "I am trying very hard *not* to ruin you—" A tremor racked him, tangible through the fingers laced with hers. "At the moment, the prospect is chancy at best. I beg you not to make it worse by touching me."

She focused on their joined hands. "Oh."

Placing two fingers beneath her chin, he tipped her face up. "It is not my intent to coerce you into marriage, no matter how pleasurable it would be for us both."

His fingertip traced her throat, ending where her pulse jumped. A small tremor passed from it to her skin. His nostrils flared, and his lips tightened in a grimace of agony and restraint combined.

"I want nothing more than to make you my wife indeed." His hoarse words burned into her. Never in her life had she heard such stark *hunger.* "Your sweet response to my touch has left me aching to share the ultimate pleasure of your body."

The longing in his voice reawakened the need within her, made her want, made her ache. *Ultimate pleasure.* How could anything possibly surmount what she'd just experienced? And yet his eyes blazed with such promise.

She could have all he offered. All she had to do was say yes.

TALK of the duel endured for several hours until they reached the cobblestoned streets of Mayfair. Normally bustling thoroughfares lay dreary under a leaden sky that any moment threatened to unleash an icy torrent.

Julia hugged herself to ward off the chill, as Benedict and Upperton attempted to find a means to extract Papa from his financial difficulties once honor had been served. Apparently Clivesden had behaved in a less than upright fashion during his years at school, delighting in setting the stronger on the weaker and cheating at sports.

Papa, however, snapped his fingers in the face of the evidence. "You won't get him to call off a debt over such trifles. Most of the titled gentlemen of the *ton* have done similar." His shoulders slumped. "I can do no better than to see my daughters settled and my wife looked after. After that, I must pay the penalty."

No amount of argument could persuade him otherwise, and so they turned to the tedious details of the evening Papa had given Ludlowe, as he was known then, a marker for five thousand pounds. Who had been present? How deep the play? How much had anyone been drinking? Might Ludlowe have done anything untoward, and if so, could anyone else vouch for it?

Julia did her best to shut them out. The name Keaton came up among the participants. Keaton. Why did that sound familiar? No, she would not let them draw her into their brand of foolishness. They'd still not resolved the matter of Upperton signing on the wager. Above all, why did men insist on settling disputes by means that could see them dead?

They let Upperton out at his family's town house before proceeding to Boulton Row. Benedict descended the steps, and leaned his head into the carriage. "Sir, if I could have a private word with your daughter. I shall not keep you long."

At Papa's assent, Julia took his hand and followed him up the steps to her front door—far enough away to ensure whatever they said remained between them but not out of sight.

"You've been awfully quiet the entire journey." He studied her, his eyes wary and watchful. "Is there anything you'd like to tell me?"

She stared down at her hands, folded as demurely before her as any miss. "It's nothing."

It wasn't, but neither of them could do anything to stop the course of future events. No point in hashing it over. The men had done enough of that on the journey home.

"Look at me, Julia." His voice carried such a note of command that she was compelled to obey. "You must choose how you intend to go forward, my dear. Either talk to me and tell me what's made you so deuced angry, or risk destroying everything we've ever been to each other. But consider carefully. We have no alternative but to marry now. Whichever you choose, it shall determine our lives for the next forty years."

Each ice-encased word stabbed her in the gut. She blinked back tears, even though she deserved his contempt for the way she'd treated him ever since—Well, with the exception of a very pleasant hour or so this morning, ever since the previous evening.

"Why can't we remain friends as we once were?" To her own ears, her voice sounded unnatural, twisted and thick.

"We can never go back to the way we were."

"But why?"

"Because I cannot go back now that I've had intimate knowledge of you. I cannot conceive of marrying another, because every time I go to her bed, I will close my eyes and see you, Julia. You. *Nothing* can erase that from my mind."

His words now rang with the same conviction as what he'd said this morning. *I love you. I always have.* She closed her eyes and swallowed.

The conviction and the confidence. He'd calmly and blithely placed his heart in her hands. He'd given her a power she never wanted, a power to destroy, intentionally or otherwise. And in return, he demanded nothing—yet.

But he would. He'd marry her and, over time, come to expect such openness from her. He'd overwhelm her with his passion and demand a response from her at every turn. A response he'd pulled from her so easily this morning. In the moment, as it was happening, surrendering to passion had seemed as natural as breathing. But now, thinking back . . . Could she open herself to him on a regular basis, could she let herself embrace the utter vulnerability?

She trusted him, certainly, but the sheer intensity he evoked reached frightening levels. At times, it was too much.

"And, as you say, we must marry," she whispered, acknowledging that truth.

She might find herself increasing as a result of this

morning. Even if she did not, there would be no covering up the scandal.

"I'm sorry for the remark about Clivesden. It's just . . ." She searched for the words. "Think about Papa, having to face him. Think of how I feel to be made the subject of a wager."

"That was not my doing."

"I know. But couldn't you have told me? And Upperton! What were you thinking, encouraging him with his part in that bet?"

"That night . . ." He dragged a hand through his hair, pulling it into wild tufts.

She took a good look at him, and his haggard appearance struck her in the gut. He'd barely slept last night, if at all. Guilt swamped her.

"The night of the Posselthwaite ball," he went on, "we were at White's. I cannot even remember what I was about to put down in the book. I saw that idiot dragging your name into a wager, and all I could think of was warning you away from him."

"Were you really so concerned he'd turn my head? You ought to know I'd never do such a thing to my sister."

"I do know, only . . . You will not like this, but there it is. Since all this began, I've been unable to think straight where you're concerned. I left Upperton behind to track you down at the ball. If he signed on that bet, it happened after I left."

"So you haven't done any of this to help your friend win some blunt?"

"Julia, what do you take me for?" The left side of his mouth hitched. "Actually, he wanted me to. He came and told me of your engagement. I told him no. But then, you'd have to agree he was quite good at helping us get out of town."

"Except the clothes he dug up for me are all a bit small."

A sardonic smile spread over his face. Julia's heart tripped a bit faster at the sight. "If he'd found you gowns that fit properly, I'd have had to call him out, too."

An answering smile had begun to broaden across her face in reply, but at the mention of the duel, it faded before it had a chance to bloom. "Please don't make light of that. Bad enough Papa must face Clivesden."

"There's no getting around it. Even if not for your father, he'd have called me out, no matter what he said earlier. In running off with you, I've cost him a great deal of money. Upperton cannot be the only one who took that bet."

"That's his own fault for being so arrogant and wagering so much. Five thousand. How ridiculous! He shall have to find himself an heiress if he wishes to pay everyone back."

"Perhaps he hopes your father will shoot him and put him out of his misery."

It was just the sort of sarcastic comment that made her laugh aloud under normal circumstances. Not today. Not when Papa stood an equal chance of dying. "Please." Her voice caught, and she had to swallow before continuing. "Please don't say such things."

"You're not actually worried for Clivesden, are you?"

"I was thinking of Papa," she croaked. As angry as she'd been with him for his part in this mess, she still didn't want to see him risk his life.

He leaned across and picked up her hand, sandwiching it between both of his. Warmth flowed up her arm from his touch. "It will not be the first time he's faced enemy fire, by his own admission."

"Well, yes, but I know the outcome there. He survived."

"You realize, don't you, that in most of these affairs of honor, no one actually tries to kill his opponent?"

How she wanted to believe him, but doubt shone in

his eyes and deadened his tone. Whatever Benedict's past experience with Clivesden, it was enough to tell him that Clivesden was quite capable of resorting to violence to achieve his ends.

"I cannot stop the duel," he said, as if trying to convince himself that everything would turn out fine. "You know that. But I'll do my damnedest to ensure everyone survives."

CHAPTER NINETEEN

MAMA POUNCED on Julia the moment she came in the front door. She screeched while Billings took Julia's wrap. She railed as she took Julia by the arm and marched her up three flights of stairs to the bedchamber. Once behind closed doors, Mama planted her feet, placed her hands on her hips, and settled in for a nice, long harangue.

Julia sat on the bed, rubbed what would likely show in the morning as five oval bruises, and took the tongue-lashing as her due, but all the while, she waited for Mama to pause for air. In no time, she lost count how many times Mama pronounced the words "scandal," "ruined," "shameful," and "utter, arrant catastrophe."

At one point, she uttered something that sounded suspiciously like a question. "Do you realize how hard I've worked toward this end, only to have you throw it away?"

Julia didn't bother with a reply. No excuse was possible, and at any rate, Mama didn't stop long enough to allow a response.

Half an hour or more must have passed before Mama finally reached "Well? What have you to say for yourself?"

"Nothing."

Mama blinked, her hair long since fallen out of its

coiffure to straggle about her reddened cheeks. Clearly, she expected some form of justification. "Nothing?"

"There is nothing I can say that I haven't already said," Julia explained, as if she were addressing a young child. Indeed, as if she were the parent. "So I say 'nothing.'"

"And what is to become of us? Do you realize we're ruined as a family? Bankrupt? Do you?" Mama's voice strained toward notes usually only obtained by famous sopranos. "You might have saved us."

"Begging your pardon, Mama, but it wasn't my place."

"Not your place? Not your place?" Mama puffed herself up once more. A fresh eruption was imminent, one likely to be punctuated with all the possible variations on "ungrateful."

Right. Time to head her off. Time for Julia to see if her captain's tone worked on anyone besides Benedict. "No, it was not my place. Papa should never have put himself in that position."

She thought of the bleakness underlying his words when he'd despaired over ever giving Mama what she wanted. Good heavens, Papa must have loved Mama at one time. Perhaps he still did in his way. After more than twenty-five years of marriage, he was still struggling to attain the unattainable for his wife. Still trying to gain her approval.

Was she even aware?

"Of course he shouldn't," Mama said. "But what's to become of us now?"

"I shall be settled, certainly. Benedict intends to marry me."

"I should think so." Then she narrowed her eyes. "I had best not hear of you turning him aside. Not after such brazen behavior."

"I shall not turn him down. I'm as good as settled."

"And Sophia is settled."

Sophia had better be settled. Blast. Sophia had plans

to cry off, but Julia couldn't mention that to Mama now. She was going to have to find a way to convince Sophia to marry Highgate, in spite of the impending scandal. "Where is Sophia?"

"She's gone with Highgate to the theater. But don't try to distract me with trifles. You may think nothing of our predicament since the two of you have finally managed to find husbands, but have you stopped to think of your father and me?"

"Papa made me promise to see to your future."

"My future?" A line formed between her brows. "Why my future as if he doesn't plan on being there?"

Julia looked her mother in the eye. Best to face the truth head on. "He may not be."

"What is that supposed to mean?" In contrast to her earlier outbursts, Mama posed the question faintly, almost delicately, as if the answer might break her.

"He's challenged Clivesden over this."

"He? Challenged Clivesden?" She drew herself up and found her voice once more. "What sort of nonsense is that? If anyone should have issued a challenge, it should have been Clivesden to Revelstoke."

Well. Mama might prefer that scenario, since it would still offer her a chance at getting what she wanted. "Are you really so mercenary as to wish Benedict to face a pistol?"

"What? No." She threw her arms in the air, but they just as immediately flopped back to her sides. "I don't want anyone to face that. And your father . . ." She waved her arms again.

Long observance of her mother, both in society and in private, had always revealed a composed woman. Every move calculated, every gesture, every expression. Even earlier when she'd berated Julia for running off, her words had purpose—to arouse guilt.

Mama knew where she wanted to be and behaved as

if she'd already attained a lofty position in society. She couldn't even disagree over wedding plans with a long-term acquaintance in any but a rational, civilized manner. She'd long ago ingested and embodied the rules of proper conduct.

To witness such discomfiture now was unsettling.

"Mama." Julia rose from the bed and laid a hand on Mama's shoulder. Beneath her fingertips, the skin of Mama's neck was cold and damp. "Mama, it'll be all right. Benedict has agreed to act as Papa's second, and Papa's done this before."

Mama laid her spread thumb and forefinger across her brow. "That old duel. He told you of that?"

Julia leaned closer. "He told me he called out Cheltenham."

Was that an actual blush spreading over Mama's cheeks? The heightened color dropped years from her face, until Julia could picture her as a young girl making her first foray into society. Her beauty must have turned all the men's heads and sent the other young ladies into fits of jealousy. Not at all unlike Sophia.

"How much did he tell you?"

At the wariness in Mama's tone, Julia pricked up her ears. "Only that he felt he had to defend your honor."

Mama's cheeks turned crimson, and the wash of pink crept toward her forehead. "That romantic old fool," she muttered.

Julia let her hand fall. In all her years of observing her parents, she'd never imagined anything like this. They'd always treated each other with a stiff courtesy—when they had to interact at all. But to see Mama pinken like a schoolgirl over the memory . . .

"Mama, what happened?"

"No one was hurt, if that's your worry. A small miracle, that. Neither one of them could shoot straight in their condition. They were both thoroughly foxed."

Julia pressed her lips together and tried to imagine a younger version of her father, swaying with intoxication and pointing a dueling pistol vaguely in another man's direction. "Why do you think he did it?"

She had her own ideas, but how much did Mama suspect?

"The man was besotted with me."

The man. Not your father, not Charles, but the man. The wrong man. And Mama was still bitter after a quarter century.

"Do you ever wonder if he still is?"

"What sort of question is that?" Mama snapped.

"An important one." Yes, very important. A week ago, she wouldn't have thought to ask.

"After all this time? I doubt it." She heaved a sigh. "I suppose I might have remedied that in the beginning. It's too late now. Too late for everything." She closed her eyes for a moment and swallowed. Then she raised her fingers to Julia's cheek, the touch fleeting and cool like the passage of a ghost. "You take after your papa, you know."

"How so?"

"Your looks, your temperament. He was never one to let his feelings show, either." And with that, Mama swept from the room.

Mind abuzz, Julia sank to the mattress. *I do not want to turn out like her.* An echo of her statement to Sophia floated through her head. Those words had taken on an even more fundamental truth. She did not wish to become a replica of her mother, her beauty fading with the years, yet still pleasant to look at, but inside still seething with acrimony over a past she could not change.

But Julia did not have to become that person. She had her future before her, a future with Benedict, and, as he'd pointed out to her earlier, she had only to make the choice of how she intended to conduct their marriage. She need only open her heart.

By the time Sophia waltzed into the bedchamber, Julia had changed into her night rail and snuggled beneath the covers. She pushed herself into a sitting position and hugged her knees. And what sort of reception would Sophia give her? A row with her sister would only serve as a capital end to a perfectly miserable evening.

"How was the theater?" she ventured as a means of testing the waters.

Sophia went rigid for a moment. "You're home." Her tone betrayed only surprise.

"Yes, I'm home."

"Oh, Julia." Sophia's face crumpled. "I'm so sorry for the way I acted the other night. I was so worried when you ran off, and thought at first it might be my fault—"

"No, it wasn't your fault." Julia threw back the covers and ran to pull her sister into an embrace. "I left because I wanted to make certain I'd never marry Clivesden."

"Yes, but . . ." Sophia shuddered in Julia's arms. In spite of all reassurances, it seemed her sister was about to give in to a spate of crying.

"No buts. Tell me about the theater."

"Theater?" Sophia raised her head and swiped at red-rimmed eyes. "Oh yes, the theater."

Julia studied her sister. Sophia's cheeks burned bright red, and her normally neat curls lay in tangles about her ears. A suspicious-looking purplish mark stood in contrast to the porcelain skin at the base of her throat.

"Mama said you were to attend the theater tonight with Highgate."

At the name, Sophia let out an airy sigh and leaned back against the wall, her arms about her waist. Her blue eyes held a faraway expression.

"Did you even make it as far as the theater?"

"What?" Sophia gave herself a shake. "Oh, no. Highgate thought it preferable not to appear in public, considering . . ." With a wave of her hand, she trailed off.

"Where did you go then? You'll forgive me the indiscretion, but you look as if—" She didn't want to come out and say Sophia looked as if she'd just been tumbled, except that was exactly how she looked. Julia recognized the symptoms of afterglow.

Sophia floated to the bed and, arms outflung, cast herself to the mattress.

Julia stiffened in alarm. "Who, exactly, were you with just now?"

Sophia's eyelids fluttered open. "Why, Highgate, of course."

"And what were you doing all this time?"

A wicked little smile revealed the tips of Sophia's teeth. So worldly, that smile. "Having a discussion, among other things."

"Oh, Sophia, what have you done?" Julia rubbed her moist palms against the white lawn of her night rail. Virginal white. How ironic now.

Sophia pushed herself up on her elbows. "Nothing to ruin me, precisely . . . Oh, it was delicious and sinful, but I imagine you must know that."

With a wan smile, Julia sank onto the bed, relief washing through her that she'd have someone to talk to, someone who would not berate her for throwing away a chance at a title and, worse, dragging the entire family down into scandal.

"Oh, Sophia, what have *I* done? Mama must already be making plans to send us off to molder in the country. If we're lucky, we might be able to show our faces in Town sometime in the next ten years."

"I thought you liked the country."

"I do, but I've ruined your future as well."

"How? You're not going to marry Clivesden now, are you?"

"Of course not. You must know he came after us."
With a forefinger, she traced a wrinkle in the counter-
pane. "After what he saw . . ."

"What did he see, precisely?"

"Benedict and me . . . in bed . . . together."

Sophia let out a squeal.

"Once word of that gets out, and you know it will, no
one will have me."

"But isn't that what you want? And don't say no one.
If Benedict has ruined you, he'll be gentleman enough
to make you an offer."

"He's already arranged for a special license."

Sophia reached out and patted her hand. "Well, there
you are then."

Struck by the irony of the situation, Julia stared at her
sister. Here was Sophia, dreamy, flighty Sophia, being
practical about the entire scandalous mess, when a few
minutes earlier she'd nearly given in to another one of
her tearful spells.

"Sophia, about the wedding . . ."

"If Benedict has a special license, you can marry
whenever you please."

"No, I mean your wedding. You cannot cry off."

"But Highgate assured me I wasn't ruined." Sophia
ducked her head to study her folded hands. "Although
he did ask me to reconsider our plan."

"You must. It has nothing to do with whatever just
happened with Highgate and everything to do with the
wager."

SOPHIA's hands went suddenly cold, and she fisted them
in her skirts in a vain attempt to bring the feeling back.
"Wager?" Even her voice sounded faint. "What wager?"

"Clivesden was so confident he'd win my hand, he

wagered I'd become his countess—before he ever proposed and before I even knew his intentions."

Sophia looked up sharply. "He proposed? When?"

"He did. The night of your engagement dinner. Sophia?" Alarm sharpened her sister's tone.

Of course, Julia thought she was about to burst into a flood of tears, as she'd often done in the past over Clivesden's slights. No more. She would waste no more of them on him.

"I never asked for any of this, you know." Julia jumped to her feet. "I never once encouraged him. I did not even know he was interested until the night at the Posselthwaites', and you know—you *know*, Sophia—I did all I could to encourage him in your direction."

"I know," Sophia whispered. Her voice refused to go any louder.

Julia took a step forward. Her chin trembled. "It's not as if he ever loved me or planned to. Do you want to know why he chose me over you?"

She paused, pacing across the room and back, but Sophia couldn't bring herself to answer. Morbid curiosity prodded her to learn the reason. Whatever it was, she could withstand it.

"He doesn't want a wife who loves him. He told me he wanted me specifically because I did not love him, and what's more, I did not seem to love anybody. Apparently, I have a reputation among the men of the *ton*. They think I'm made of ice."

"And so he proposed to you?" Her words emerged flat, when, like a dam bursting, the years of built-up pain within her ought to have shattered in a violent eruption of heat, as rage seethed to life. Instead, calm pervaded her. Imagine, she was actually discussing Clivesden proposing to another woman—her own sister, no less—and the prospect didn't bother her in the least.

"I'm sorry. I did not think I ought to tell you. I knew you'd be upset."

"I'm not upset, honestly."

"I turned him down flat," Julia went on as if Sophia hadn't spoken. "Papa and Clivesden blindsided me that night. They made an arrangement behind my back, because I never suspected a thing. I could not very well make a scene in the middle of a ballroom in front of the entire *ton*. And part of it was shock. I could barely believe what was happening."

"Julia, I'm not going to cry this time. Truly."

But Julia hadn't finished her speech. She leaned over and placed a hand on Sophia's shoulder. "I'm sorry you've been hurt in all this, but please understand one thing. Any of the hurt comes from Clivesden's doings, not mine. It's always been him. For the past five years."

"I know," Sophia whispered. "I understand that now." She understood even more, an unpleasant truth, perhaps even more profound than the one Julia had just voiced. Clivesden hadn't spent the last five years hurting her— not intentionally. He couldn't have when he'd barely acknowledged her existence. If anyone had hurt Sophia, it was Sophia herself in allowing her fantasies and her illusions to take root to such an extent they blurred reality. "But what does any of this have to do with my betrothal to Highgate?"

"Papa owes Clivesden a great deal of money." Julia sat beside her once again and looked her in the eye. "If he can't pay, the family is bankrupt. Clivesden was willing to forgive the debt in exchange for, well, me."

"*No!*"

"It's true. It's all true. Papa admitted as much. Can you imagine if Mama knew? She'd have preferred I went through with it as a duty to the family."

"But how . . . how *could* they?" Sophia couldn't say more. The eruption of fury she'd expected much earlier seethed through her now. And yet her eyes remained strangely dry, as if the spate of heated emotion had evaporated all her tears.

"For what it's worth, I mainly blame Clivesden. It had to be his idea. The wager he made, claiming he would marry me—the amount of the wager was the same amount Papa owes him. I think . . . No, I'm sure, he meant to find a way to recoup his losses."

"The cad. The utter, utter cad!" Sophia gulped in cool air, in hopes of calming the inferno within. "To think," she said when she could go on, "only a week ago, I'd have done anything to be standing in your shoes—or at least to have caught his eye in time."

"Yes, well, because I've managed things so he no longer wants me, he's determined to send Papa to prison over the debt. This is why you must marry Highgate. If you are settled, this cannot hurt you."

"And what of Mama?"

"I've already promised to look after her. Papa is satisfied with the arrangement."

"What will become of him then?"

"That remains to be seen. He has to survive a duel with Clivesden first."

Sophia reached for her throat to tug at her locket. "A duel? Papa means to fight a duel?"

"Yes, with Benedict as his second. Sophia"—Julia's brow puckered—"Sophia I just remembered. This talk of the wager. Does the name Keaton mean anything to you?"

"He's betrothed to that strumpet."

Julia looked as if she might laugh at that, but really, what could she possibly laugh about under the circumstances? "Truly? I wonder what he knows about Clivesden."

"I've no idea, but Highgate knows a great deal. But why do you ask about Keaton?"

Julia's forehead wrinkled, an expression Sophia recognized as an indication her sister was turning something over in her mind. A plan of some sort. A plan that might well mean trouble—for somebody. "Keaton was there the night Papa lost all that money. And now you tell me Highgate knows something."

"They have a great deal of history together, it turns out. It's not pretty."

"Then you'd best tell me everything. Perhaps we can stop the proceedings."

RUFUS just happened to be passing through the corridor that bisected the town house from the foyer to the conservatory when Hastings replied to a knock. He didn't even need to glance at the case clock to realize the hour was unfashionably early for callers.

Curious, he slipped closer. Hastings seemed to be in serious discussion with somebody—somebody too small for Rufus to make out over the butler's stocky frame.

"This is highly irregular." Hastings infused his tone with the censorious manner of his employer. No doubt, Mariah had chosen him for the ability.

"But—"

At the sound of the feminine voice, Rufus froze. Sophia stood on the doorstep, alone from all appearances.

"Miss," Hastings went on, "it is simply not done."

Right, then. Time to intervene. Rufus strode into the foyer, his Hessians thudding sharply on the parquet. "Whatever isn't done, an exception can be made."

Sophia shivered on the threshold, clutching a midnight-blue cloak about her shoulders. A broad-brimmed bonnet shadowed her face, but not enough to hide her rounded eyes or her pallor. At the sight of him, the tension about her lips eased.

Those lips. He'd tasted them last night, merely sipped

from them, but not enough to quench his thirst for her—not when his fingers tingled at the recollection of her body melting about them, contracting in shuddering release.

"My lord." Hastings's protest broke in on his memory. "The young lady is alone."

"The young lady is my betrothed, and furthermore, my sister's presence in this house fulfills the requirement for an appropriate chaperone."

He stopped just short of ordering Hastings off, but the butler took the hint all the same. With a sniff that bordered on insubordination, he turned on his heel and stalked down the corridor. No doubt, Mariah would have a full report before the hour was out.

"Fortunately," he added once Hastings was out of earshot, "my sister is still abed. With any luck, she will not disturb us. Now what has led you to risk your reputation in coming here?"

She laid a gloved hand on the superfine sleeve of his coat, and he fancied warmth seeping into his forearm at four precise points, each the exact size of her fingertips. His heart gave a thump. Perhaps she'd come to a decision about their future.

"Oh, Highgate." Her voice trembled on his name. "Might we talk somewhere a bit more private?"

His heart gave another thud. Something in her tone hinted at ominous news. In spite of all that had passed between them, in spite of all she'd learned of Clivesden, would she refuse him in the end?

"Yes, of course," he replied mechanically, while his mind searched for the ideal venue. He didn't want to take her to the morning room and risk his sister interrupting Sophia's set-down. Mariah would be as insufferable as ever about the entire situation. He didn't want to deal with her gloating on top of his disappointment over not marrying Sophia.

He led her along the corridor to a little-used room. The late Lord Wexford's study had stood untouched since his demise, a masculine space enclosed with dark-paneled walls and heavy wooden furnishings. Draperies of heavy velvet shut out the morning's feeble sunlight. A fitting scene for the end of Highgate's renewed hope for the future.

He took up a spot by the window and watched Sophia out of the corner of his eye. Her teeth tugged at her lower lip as she surveyed her surroundings.

"I've come to ask your help," she said at last.

He snapped his head about to face her. "Help?"

"Yes, please. You must agree. We cannot do this without a man's perspective."

He arched a brow, as relief flooded his body. Best to appear intrigued than to reveal his concern that she'd come to cry off. "I think you'd better start at the beginning."

"There's to be a duel, you see. Papa has challenged Clivesden."

Rufus straightened his spine. "Your father and Clivesden? Not Revelstoke?"

"No," Sophia said. "Julia knows better how it all came about, but that's not what's important. We must discover when and where it will be held."

He opened his mouth to ask why she wanted such information and just as immediately closed it again. He knew why. Sophia, or perhaps her sister—or, worse, the pair of them—were scheming to stop the proceedings. "No."

"No?" She stepped toward him. "You cannot mean that."

"I'm afraid I do."

"But—"

"You cannot stop this. It's a matter of honor." He put

his hands on her shoulders. "Once honor has been satisfied, everyone will get back to their lives."

"Those who survive, you mean. And what if it's Papa
who gets shot?"

He allowed his thumbs to trace the ridges of her collarbones. At least she wasn't pulling away. "These things
rarely end in an actual injury."

Sophia lifted her gaze to the ceiling for moment. There
was nothing she could say to that. Nothing whatsoever.
"Why do men have to be so stupid about things?"

"Pride, my dear, pure and simple."

"But . . ." She paused. "You had very good reason to
call Clivesden out, and . . . you never did."

Sophia watched him run a hand through his hair, causing it to stand out in spiky disarray. It made him look
boyish, somehow, endearingly so. She wanted to smooth
it back into place.

"My wife was already gone, so what was the point?
Shooting Ludlowe, as he was known then, would not
have brought her back, and it would not have changed
her feelings. Besides, she was more at fault than Ludlowe
ever was. He was convenient for her. If she hadn't chosen
him, she'd have chosen another."

A sudden chill passed through her, and she clutched
her cloak about her throat, seeking warmth. She wanted
his warmth, she realized, wanted his arms about her,
one hand smoothing along her back. She wanted to rest
her head on his shoulder, to breathe him in and forget
everything else.

No, that was not quite true, either. In reality, she
wanted to make *him* forget, to erase his past and leave
him with a future. "You've given this a great deal of
consideration, haven't you?"

"I haven't had a great deal else to think about in the

last few years. In a way, it's been convenient. Whenever Mariah started badgering me about my duty to my title, I merely had to remind her of my past scandal. What good family would want someone with my past staining their reputation?"

"And yet you came to Town this season."

A mirthless smile tugged at his lips. "Mariah can wear you down after a while. She started claiming people will have forgotten after ten years. I partly came as a means to shut her up, reckoning the *ton*'s daughters would take one look at my face and shun me. That would only prove my point."

"And instead you've become embroiled in our affairs."

He shifted his grip to place his hands beneath her cloak. Long fingers curled about her waist. The simple warmth of his ungloved palms through the thin muslin of her day dress radiated from the point of contact to pool deep within. The recollection of those knowing hands on her body set that liquid heat to simmering.

"I've weathered worse. I reckon it's been worth it, if only that I've been permitted to touch your purity and innocence for a few brief moments."

Heat flooded her cheeks. "Oh."

"Oh, indeed." His whispered words hung in the air, fairly echoed off the paneled walls. Then he leaned closer.

Heavens, what he could do with that mouth of his. Before meeting him, she'd never have expected such thin lips to be capable of such sensuous kisses. She shivered at the recollection of their easy slide over hers, coaxing, demanding that she open to him.

He was about to do so again. Oh, how she wanted him to. But she couldn't. He'd already flustered her into nearly forgetting why she'd come.

At the last moment, she tipped her chin down and

ducked away. "No, I'll not let you distract me from my purpose."

His darkened gaze focused on her lips. "Did you have a purpose in coming here then?"

"Yes." His hands still held her by the waist, and she twisted out of their grip. The longer she remained in physical contact, the greater the chance she'd surrender to temptation. "Please, Highgate . . . Rufus . . ."

At the use of his given name, his breath hissed between his teeth. Sophia blinked. Could something as simple as his name affect him so?

"Rufus, you must tell me."

"What?" The question emerged in a hoarse whisper.

"I need to know where the duel will take place."

He reached out and curled his fingers about her jaw. "You and your sister cannot stop this."

"We must try." Taking courage from his reaction, she closed the distance between them and placed her hands on his chest.

Beneath her palms, muscles quivered. "Sophia."

"We must try." She let her voice drop until she barely recognized its register. "If not to stop the duel, then at least to stop Clivesden." She held his gaze. "You cannot deny me that."

THE frosty ground of Hyde Park crunched beneath Arthur's hooves. Beyond a fitful breeze that set naked branches creaking and stirred the threads of mist into ghostly swirls, nothing else moved in the predawn air.

Benedict squinted into the twilight ahead. No one else had arrived yet, not even Clivesden's second. With a click of his tongue, he urged his mount onward.

He might have taken a more fashionable conveyance to the meeting place and arrived by carriage, but it would not have felt right. Arthur had always accompanied him to battle. Together they'd survived Boney's worst. Now that the stakes were merely personal, Benedict saw no reason to change tradition.

Sensing his master's tension, Arthur snorted and danced sideways off the path. A squeeze of Benedict's thighs brought his mount under control. He shifted his weight back and reined Arthur to a halt, straining his eyes toward the trees ahead.

A figure materialized out of the fog. At the newcomer's approach, Arthur ducked his head and pawed the ground.

"Still determined to go through with this?" Upperton's voice reached his ears, riding the back of a sharp gust.

Benedict gave a curt nod in reply and dismounted. "I have no choice. I gave my word."

"I know that, man. I mean the rest of it."

"One way or another, I'll see it through."

Upperton threw him a glare of disapproval. "If it were me—"

"It isn't you. Have you taken care of St. Claire?"

"I tipped some laudanum into his drink last night and brought him home. Told the butler he'd had all that was good for him. By the time he wakes up, the gossip might even have died down." Thank God St. Claire was such a creature of habit. Sending Upperton to find the man at his club had been a simple enough matter.

"Although . . ." Upperton shifted his weight from one booted foot to the other and eyed him. "Are you sure you want to start your marriage on an off note? St. Claire won't be happy his own son-in-law cheated him out of his chance to redeem himself. People will say he was a coward."

Perhaps, but Benedict would find a way to return himself to St. Claire's good graces later. "Have you brought the pistols?"

"Right here."

Upperton produced a dark wooden case from beneath his arm. He flicked the brass clasp to display a brace of guns. Their polished wood and metal barrels gleamed dully in the low light. Benedict took one in his hand to test its unfamiliar weight, imagining his fingers curled about the hilt of his cavalry saber. He missed its balance and the lethal whoosh as he swung it.

Much more subtle a weapon, his saber. With careful handling, it killed silently.

"Sure you know how to fire one of those?" Upperton asked.

"I know well enough."

"But can you hit anything?"

Benedict returned the pistol to its mate. "It will not matter. Clivesden shall have his satisfaction, and we shall all move on with our lives."

"Indeed. And what of Miss Julia?"

"Much will depend on today's outcome, won't it?" He'd rather not think of Julia right now. He didn't need the distraction.

The rumble of carriage wheels saved Upperton the need to reply. Benedict turned in time to see a fashionable barouche shudder to a halt. A liveried footman leapt from the back to lower the steps.

Clivesden, impeccable in a hunting jacket and starched linen, strolled from the conveyance, followed by a familiar figure. Keaton, according to the signature on the messages Benedict had exchanged with Clivesden's second—a second Clivesden had apparently been cuckolding. Keaton, surprisingly adept with a pack of cards. Suspiciously so. Keaton who had been a party to that infamous card game the night St. Claire lost five thousand. Benedict might turn the situation around yet, but only once honor had been satisfied.

Upon catching sight of Benedict, Clivesden's expression hardened to granite. He might have narrowed his eyes, except they were already swollen from the beating he'd taken the other morning.

A chill passed through Benedict. He'd seen such grim determination on the faces of Napoleon's troops—the expression of men who were ready to kill lest they be killed, men who had nothing left to lose.

Upperton nudged him. "You sure about this?"

"Nothing we can do to stop it now."

At their approach, Clivesden studied Upperton as if he were some ragged pauper come to call on the Prince Regent. "What is he doing here? And where is St. Claire?"

"St. Claire isn't feeling quite up to the proceedings this morning. I'm taking his place. Upperton, here, will act as my second. Now let's get this over with."

But time conspired against him, almost as if the morning mist had thickened to a tangible force that slowed movement. Benedict stood apart from the proceedings as Upperton sluggishly trudged off to meet Clivesden's second. He barely listened while the two went over the terms and approved the weapons, barely noticed four pistols loaded, the extra pair left with the seconds.

Clivesden would be satisfied with no less than blood.

After an eternity, he stood with his back to Clivesden, the loaded pistol an anchor in his hand, a burden that would increase with every step of the twenty paces.

"One."

At Upperton's proclamation, he took his first step, then another and another. At ten, he tensed in spite of himself, half expecting to feel the bite of lead in his back with each successive stride toward his fate.

"Nineteen, twenty."

He turned to face Clivesden. Even at this distance, he could make out the glitter of his adversary's eyes, the set to his jaw, the determination. He'd always imagined the face of death to resemble a skull or a specter or something equally horrific. At the very least, he'd expected to see it on the face of a French soldier. Never, once the war had ended and he sold his commission, had he thought to confront death again, and certainly not at twenty paces from an old school rival.

Damn it all, so much for noble intentions. If he stood any chance of coming out of this alive, he'd have to shoot to kill.

Drawing a breath, he raised his pistol.

CHAPTER TWENTY

JULIA HELD her breath as Highgate's barouche clattered to a halt in a remote section of Hyde Park. Sophia's fingers tightened around her hand. Thank goodness for her sister. Without Sophia, her hand would tremble, and if her hand trembled, her legs were sure to follow. And then she'd never get out of the carriage.

"Do you see anything?" she asked. She couldn't bear to look.

"No, it's too misty."

"Perfect weather for passing undetected." This from Highgate, who sat in grim-faced disapproval on the opposite seat. He'd insisted on accompanying them, of course.

"We shall have to get out," Sophia said.

"You shall do no such thing. Ladies have no business witnessing such proceedings. Why I let you come this far—"

A stern glance from Sophia cut him off, adding another layer of worry to Julia's already frayed nerves. What Sophia might have promised him to secure his cooperation, Julia preferred not to speculate. With his face set in rigid lines, he might as well have been the devil.

The devil turned his eye on Julia. "He will not want you here. He will not wish for you to see."

"I, nevertheless, feel it's my place to bear witness." The strength of her voice surprised her. How could she sound so steady when, inside, everything churned? "If it weren't for me, none of this would have happened."

"Oh, Julia, do not say such things," Sophia implored. "Lay the blame on Clivesden if you must, but never yourself."

Highgate unfolded himself, stooping as he accommodated his form to the carriage's interior. "I shall have a look. The pair of you stay right where you are."

The idea that Papa was out there facing injury or death set Julia's heart pounding. She couldn't sit idly by. That they had come to this at all, that they faced each other with loaded pistols was her fault. With luck, she still might stop it. Exchanging a look with Sophia, she stood.

The moment she stepped from the carriage, she saw them. Perhaps a hundred yards distant, Clivesden faced another man across forty yards of open ground. Where on earth was Papa? For the man opposing Clivesden was much younger, tall, broad-shouldered. The wind whipped his black hair about his face.

Not Benedict. Never Benedict.

The ground beneath her feet gave an awful lurch.

"*No!*"

She lunged, but Highgate grabbed her and pinned her arm in a surprisingly strong grip. "The last thing he needs is a distraction," he grated. "If you cannot bring yourself to obey, at least heed me in this."

Her heart slammed into her throat. Both men raised their arms, deadly barrels pointing at each other, aiming for the kill.

"*Stop!*"

Julia shouted the order too late. At the last moment, Benedict's arm snapped upward. Smoke and flames exploded from the barrel, and the report echoed through the dawn silence.

Highgate's fingers tightened about her shoulders.

Neither man blinked in their direction. Across from

Benedict, Clivesden still stood, pistol aimed. From this vista, it looked to be pointing straight at Benedict's heart.

Firearm still loaded and deadly, Clivesden seemed determined to draw out proceedings now that Benedict's shot had missed.

With a violent tug, she yanked herself from Highgate's grip and launched herself toward Benedict. Highgate gave a shout, and his feet came pounding behind her, but she ignored him. She must get to Benedict. All her attention focused on him.

If Clivesden noticed, he gave no sign. His face contorted, and he pulled the trigger. The pistol roared to life, and before Julia's eyes, Benedict crumpled to the ground.

"*No!*"

Julia's scream split the cold morning silence and echoed through the trees. The firm thuds of booted feet joined the *slap-slap* of her slippers against the frostbitten grass, as all converged on the fallen.

Tears blurred her vision. To her left, a form loomed out of nowhere to block her way. Clivesden. The bloody, bloody murderer.

With a force she did not know she possessed, fueled by white-hot rage, she shouldered past him and flung herself to the ground beside Benedict. Next to his slack hand, still warm from his shot, lay his discharged pistol. Deep red blood oozed from a jagged tear in his waistcoat, soaking his garments with an ever-widening stain. So much of it. She carried a handkerchief in her reticule, but staunching the wound with a small scrap of linen was like attempting to hold back a spring freshet with a twig.

Fighting the memories and the crawling fear of dead flesh, she touched his face—cold, clammy. His normally healthy complexion had gone a chalky gray.

"No, no." She squeezed her eyes closed, but the image

of him lying on the ground, deathly pale, remained imprinted upon her brain.

Another face hovered into view, a portly man with graying hair and deep creases about his eyes. "Miss, you must stand aside. I must see to him."

A hand alit on her shoulder. With a violent jerk, she flung it off. Still crouching, she turned. Clivesden looked down on the pair of them, his expression unreadable. Indeed, the only hint of emotion came from the increased speed at which his breath billowed in white clouds from his nostrils.

Rage erupted inside her. She shot to her feet. "You! Don't you dare touch me. Not now, not ever. This entire mess is your fault!"

"Miss Julia, I—" He reached out a placating hand.

"You heard her. Don't touch her."

Julia looked up in shock. Those words, spoken in such a commanding, confident tone had come from her sister. Her sister, who had somehow managed to wrap her hands around one of the extra pistols and was now pointing it at Clivesden's head.

Julia blinked, but the scene didn't change. While the doctor fussed over Benedict, Upperton stared, white-faced, his eyes darting between Clivesden and Sophia. Farther back, Clivesden's second froze in his tracks. Highgate stood, a little apart, his body coiled with tension, his jaw set.

Sophia's expression hardened into something Julia had never seen before. Her blue eyes glittered with determination, and her outstretched arm never once wavered. The barrel of the pistol pointed straight and true, directly between Clivesden's blackened eyes. Her knuckles whitened as the standoff stretched out, and still she never faltered.

Slowly, Clivesden raised his hands in the air. "Now . . . now, Miss St. Claire."

"I'll thank you to keep your mouth closed." Sophia's tone held such steel.

"Could . . . could you at least put the gun down?"

"No."

"What's the matter?" Highgate drawled. "Afraid it's loaded?"

"I know it's loaded, man." Out of the corner of her eye, Julia caught the tremor in Clivesden's hands. "We brought two each, in case one shot was not enough."

"What?" Julia shrieked.

"I would not have been satisfied without blood." The words emerged dull and flat, as if he were still wrapping his mind around the concept himself. "Our seconds agreed. It wasn't even supposed to be him. I never thought he'd miss."

"Perhaps he reckoned you weren't worth the lead," Highgate drawled in a tone more suited to a drawing room than a deserted corner of Hyde Park at dawn.

Clivesden's trembling increased. "Do you think you might call your betrothed to heel?"

Highgate folded his arms. "Why should I? I'm quite enjoying this. Besides, she has a point. Perhaps honor hasn't yet been satisfied."

Clivesden shot his second a telling glance. "As the injured party, I declare myself satisfied."

"Injured party?" Julia cried. "How dare you? You're the one who set all this in motion. If my sister would like to claim satisfaction, I say let her."

"A woman? Dueling?" In another moment Clivesden would be on his knees. "Highgate, you cannot stand for this. Unless you mean to make up for past grievances, as well?"

"I might if I thought it would change anything," Highgate said. "Honor will never be satisfied for a man who has none. Why society ought to tolerate such behavior simply because a man holds a title is beyond me.

Proper bloodlines be damned. You, sir, are a disgrace to the concept of nobility."

Clivesden flinched, his head snapping backward as if he'd been physically struck. He'd be well within his rights to call out Highgate over such a pronouncement. Part of Julia hoped he would, but another part had seen bloodshed enough for one day.

God, Benedict. She crushed icy fingers to her lips and turned to his inert form. The doctor had peeled back his shirt and waistcoat to reveal blood still seeping from a ragged hole. She gritted her teeth, crouched over his body and placed her hands on his shoulders. The least she could do was hold him and pray.

THE wood of the dueling pistol was surprisingly warm in Sophia's palm. She'd have expected an instrument of murder to be cold and unforgiving. It was heavy, though—heavy as the responsibility of another's life. Before long, her hand would begin to shake with the unfamiliar weight. She tightened her grip and waited for Clivesden to respond to Highgate's insult.

"Do you feel safe with your betrothed holding me at gunpoint?"

"I feel safe knowing the truth is on my side." She couldn't see Highgate from where she was standing, but she imagined his lips curving into a grim smile. "I can easily put the past aside and point to your current actions. What does it say about a man that he pushes another into a position where he feels he must sell his own daughter?"

At Benedict's side, Julia looked up. "What does it say, further, that he wagers on the situation?"

Then Upperton, who had stood quietly through the entire scene, stepped forward, one arm outstretched toward Clivesden. "And what of this man's behavior with a certain person's intended bride?"

Clivesden whipped his head in Upperton's direction. "What are you insinuating?"

"Only that I've heard from numerous sources that you've become quite friendly with your second's betrothed. But perhaps Keaton's luck will change now that your face isn't quite so pretty."

"Gossip." Clivesden waved a hand. "You cannot prove anything."

"I saw you," Sophia said. "The night of Lady Posselthwaite's ball. You were sneaking off with her."

"What?" Keaton marched up to Clivesden and bunched the lapels of his erstwhile friend in his fists.

Sophia lowered the pistol. No one was focused on her now. A hand settled on her shoulder, the grip familiar and comforting. Highgate.

"You're going to take their word over mine?" Clivesden was saying.

"I believe I will." Keaton gave him a shake. "I've had my own suspicions. They've only just been confirmed. And you can find yourself a new partner at cards. See if you win as often."

Upperton shouldered his way between the men. "Should we take that as an admission?"

"There has been no admission." Clivesden looked from one to the other, his face turning a rather interesting shade of purple. Sophia would never have imagined such a deep shade from such a fair-skinned man. It may have matched his bruises but otherwise didn't do a thing for him. "Of anything."

"Perhaps not," Upperton said, cool as ever, "but if we were to question a few other gentlemen who have lost to the pair of you recently, I daresay we might find a pattern of incredible luck."

Highgate squeezed Sophia's shoulder before joining

Upperton. "Of course, if you forgive St. Claire's debt to you, we might see our way clear to keeping quiet about all this."

At that, Clivesden let out a mirthless bark of laughter. "And who would listen to you? You've all brought such scandal on yourselves the hostesses of the *ton* would never tolerate your presence."

Sophia's eyes flicked to Julia for a fleeting second. "I find I do not much mind. You?"

"No," Julia croaked.

"Be that as it may," Highgate said, "my sister wields a certain influence. Word still has a way of getting out."

Clivesden shoved himself away from Upperton and stalked toward his carriage. "I'm through with the lot of you."

"You can expect my marker for the five thousand pounds," Upperton called after him.

"A surgery is no place for a woman." Dr. Campbell's white hair clung in wisps to his reddened pate. "Most especially not a young, unmarried miss."

Julia exchanged a glance with a grim-faced Upperton and held herself firm next to Benedict's bed. She'd be damned if she was about to give in. "I wasn't aware this was a surgery." She gestured to the masculine furnishings—heavy, dark woods and deep burgundy wallpaper with nary a bit of frippery in sight.

"Even worse," the doctor spluttered. "Neither do you belong in a gentleman's bedroom."

She bit down on her tongue, but she could hardly blurt out that it was too late. Besides, with Upperton present and Highgate waiting downstairs with her sister, her virtue was hardly at risk. "There's no time to argue."

She curled her fingers into a fist to stop their shaking. Benedict's complexion fairly matched the bed linens. The doctor had staunched the flow of blood on-site, but the ball still remained embedded in Benedict's chest. God, she might still lose him.

Dr. Campbell glanced at his patient and pressed his lips into a line. "You're right, there. You'll be leaving now."

She clutched at Benedict's hand. So cold, it lay like a dead weight in hers—just like Miss Mallory. *No.* He could not die. She would not allow it.

"I stay." Astounding how her voice remained so steady when, inside, her heart fluttered in her throat. "Tell me how I can help."

"You'll stand well out of the way. And if you swoon, God help you for I shall not."

Julia poked her chin higher. "I won't swoon."

It was a near thing, however. Unable to look away, she stood aside and watched Dr. Campbell strip Benedict's shirt entirely away. Fresh blood blossomed across his chest and stained the doctor's fingers as he probed for the ball, and her knees turned watery.

With a groan, Benedict rolled his head against the pillow. At the doctor's nod, Upperton pressed down on Benedict's shoulders, while Julia bit back a cry of sympathy. *Don't let him wake up. Not now. Not when the pain must be unbearable. But dear God, don't let him die, either.* The idea of living out the rest of her years without him sank into her stomach and lay like a block of ice.

Deep in concentration, Dr. Campbell muttered a string of oaths under his breath. He pulled a pair of forceps from his bag and thrust them into Benedict's chest. Something small and hard emerged in their grasp and plunked to the floor as he slackened the instrument's grip.

Julia swallowed, and she released a fistful of skirt. "Was that it?"

The doctor looked up sharply, as if he'd forgotten she was there. Drops of perspiration beaded his weathered brow. "Yes, but I'm not finished yet. A wound like this introduces other material into the body. Bits of fabric. Bone fragments."

She shuddered.

"If I do not clean the wound properly, infection is bound to set in."

He lowered the forceps for another probing. Julia closed her eyes, but she couldn't shut out the image of that obscene hole in Benedict's chest. Amid the blood, it blighted the lovely stretch of muscle just above his heart.

His heart. So close.

The devil take Clivesden for his aim. He'd nearly taken Benedict from her. He might yet succeed.

At a low moan of pain, she dared look once more. Benedict's eyes were still closed, but he strained against Upperton's grip. His breath came in shallow puffs.

"You'll have to add your weight, miss," the doctor grated. "If he doesn't lie still, I'll never get everything out."

Straightening her spine, she approached the bed. This close, the blood tainted the air with a faint metallic smell. She could nearly taste the copper on her tongue.

"Put your hands on his shoulders and hold him down."

While Upperton moved to the far side of the bed, she laid her hands on the knot of muscle that capped his right arm and pressed. Thank God, the skin under her fingers was still warm and vital. Beneath the skin, steely muscles, accustomed to wrestling hundreds of pounds of horseflesh, fought her grip.

"Not much longer," she murmured, unsure of whom she was trying to convince. "You have to lie still so the doctor can finish."

Dr. Campbell brushed against her as he continued to extract tiny bits of lead, but she paid no heed. She didn't care, as long as Benedict came through this. The doctor poked once more, and Benedict heaved under her weight, nearly throwing her off.

She pushed until her arms strained with the effort. "Do it. Do it for me. Do it for our future." She choked on the word and bent over his face until they were nose to nose. "Do it because I cannot face life without you."

"You realize that pistol was loaded, don't you?" Highgate's smooth voice sent a ripple of pleasure through Sophia.

She shoved aside her untouched cup of tea. As the gray morning passed to a dull afternoon, they waited in the sitting room. The doctor had descended with Upperton hours ago. Julia was still upstairs at Benedict's side. Sophia recognized his comment for what it was—a distraction.

She turned on the settee to find his eyes sparkling with admiration. Admiration! She couldn't recall a man ever gazing on her in admiration before, not admiration of this whole and utter sort, reserved for her entire being, and not just her face or her body. Warmth bloomed in her beneath the fire of his gaze.

"Well, yes, that's what Clivesden admitted," she replied faintly. "I don't suppose I gave the matter any thought when I grabbed it. I would not have known how to fire it at any rate."

The scene from the park crowded her mind. "Gracious! Pray Benedict will be all right."

The warm weight of Highgate's arm settled about her shoulder, and she leaned into his embrace. "It quite depends on how deep he was hit." His tone betrayed nothing, but a stolen glance at his face revealed a set jaw.

"He cannot die, not over something so stupid. He simply cannot." Her voice wobbled on the final syllable. Her throat constricted painfully.

Heedless of any servants who might pass in the corridor beyond the sitting room, Highgate pulled her against his chest. She rested her head on his shoulder. "If Benedict dies, I'm going to wish I'd shot that miserable man."

His lips brushed her hairline. "No, you won't. You would not want that on your conscience. You ought to be comforted in the knowledge you have one and do not allow self-interest to rule your every action."

She raised her head. "But I have. For the past five years—"

"Hush." He cut her protests off with a swift kiss. Then he held her gaze. "There's acting in self-interest, and there's acting in self-interest."

Watching him, she felt suddenly lighter, as if a great weight had lifted from her shoulders.

"Would it have been in your best interest to marry one of your other suitors?"

"I cannot really say. I never gave any of them the consideration they deserved. I . . . I suppose I might have learned to be happy with one or another of them."

Highgate stretched his legs in front of him and leaned back against the stiff settee, watching her from the corner of his eye. "And would that have been enough for someone like you?"

She turned her head to peer at him. "What does that mean, someone like me?"

He angled his legs about until he faced her. Reaching out, he curled his fingers about her upper arm, his grip strong. "Someone admirable and brave."

Brave? No one had ever called her brave before. All her suitors had taken great pains to compliment her beauty. None ever bothered to exclaim over anything substantial like bravery.

But that was the problem. She, the essential Sophia, was not anything substantial—not to the men of the *ton*. She was window dressing, something pretty for them to look at over the breakfast table, someone presentable to show on their arm at balls, someone lovely enough to grace their beds, but none of them had taken the time to see beyond the surface and to know her, to learn her likes and dislikes. To ask her opinion.

"Someone," he whispered, "with a great deal of love in her heart to bestow on some fortunate soul."

She caught her breath at the longing, the yearning in his tone. *He* wished to be that fortunate soul. Rufus Frederick Shelburne, Earl of Highgate, he of the tortured, broken heart. He, too, possessed a wealth of love, emotions he'd squandered on an undeserving wife. He deserved a partner who could return his feelings.

No longer able to withstand the intensity of his gaze, she focused on his cravat. "Only I've just wasted five years of my life on someone who did not deserve it. I can see that now."

He slipped a hand to her chin and tipped it upward, compelling her to face the truth. "In light of that knowledge, can you say you loved him?"

"I couldn't have, could I, when I did not know him." No, she'd supposed him a paragon based on looks and charm alone.

As she spoke, she awaited the familiar pain, but it didn't materialize. Its nature had changed from sharp and bright into more of a dull ache, tinged with the heat of shame that she'd allowed herself to be caught up in someone so unworthy for so long. It no longer held her in thrall. In fact, she had only to gaze on Highgate, and he eclipsed it.

He reached out and pulled her into an embrace. "I know. Believe me, I know. I have stood where you are now and forced myself to look reality in the eye. In spite of the few months of our marriage, I doubt I ever got to know my wife any better than you got to know Clivesden. She refused to let me in. We were strangers inhabiting the same house."

Sophia closed her eyes, leaned into him, and listened to the words rumble from his chest. She breathed them in, took them into herself, made them part of her. Their low-pitched rhythm soothed her, as did his hand skimming along her spine.

"After all these years," he went on, "I believe I've come to understand something. Love isn't always big and dramatic. It's big, it's deep, but it's also quiet and calm."

Quiet, calm, just as the two of them were now. She eased back, needing to look into his eyes, wanting to see what was written there. "I think it's easy to imagine all manner of strong feelings," she said thickly, "but in the end, they're quite baseless when what they're built on has no substance."

He nodded. "That's it, exactly."

"It's more like Benedict and Julia. They've both loved each other for years, and they're only now coming to believe it."

He trailed his fingertips along her cheek. "And what of you, who sees everyone else so clearly? What is it you know? Might you ever find it in your heart to let me in?"

In the face of such raw emotion, Sophia's throat constricted. Even now a hint of wariness edged his expression; at least part of him dreaded her reply. He'd suffered so long. He deserved a gentle hand and a measure of happiness. Unable to voice her reply, she nodded.

He slipped his hand to the back of her neck and drew her to within a hairsbreadth of his lips. "Then would you do me the great honor of becoming my wife?"

HE woke with a groan. His chest burned as if someone had shoved a red-hot poker into his ribs. The entire area throbbed with a pulse that mimicked a heartbeat.

"Benedict?"

The scrape of chair legs against the wooden floor accompanied the anxious sound of his name. He opened his eyes to the familiar sight of the ceiling just above his bed. His bed. How had he got back to his town house? The last thing he recalled was Hyde Park and fire streaking close to his heart. An instant later, Julia's wan face filled his vision. Julia. Thank God.

"What happened?" he croaked.

"You let yourself get shot, you great, bloody idiot, that's what happened." A flush rose from her bodice to stain her cheeks.

"Ah." A grin pulled at his parched lips. If she could natter at him like a fishwife, his injury couldn't be all that serious.

Julia's breasts rose as her chest expanded; then she let out a huff. "Is that all you have to say for yourself? You found a way to replace Papa, you allowed yourself to become a target, and all you can say is 'ah'?"

"If you gave me some water, perhaps."

With a tiny shake of her head, she turned away. A moment later, she reappeared, glass in hand. The mattress sagged as she sat beside him. With surprising gentleness considering her mood, she eased an arm around his shoulders. His injury throbbed a protest at the movement, and he gritted his teeth against the pain.

Leaning against her softness, he inhaled the sweet scent of jasmine. Her perfume soothed him as much as the cooling draught of water she pressed to his lips. He covered her hand with his, helping to support the glass, for the simple excuse to touch her more.

"Do you know how fortunate you are to be alive?" she asked as he swallowed. "He was aiming to kill you, you know."

"I know. I saw it in his eyes." He would not tell her the rest—that there'd been a second set of loaded pistols in case satisfaction was not obtained in the initial volley.

"And yet, you still shot into the air."

"I thought he'd miss." He'd never let on that her shout at the last possible moment had distracted him.

She let out another little huff, another rise and fall of those perfect breasts. "He did, if you want to see it that way. The ball hit a rib. Half an inch in the wrong direction, and you would have died."

She choked on the last word. Head sagging, she pressed a fist to her lips. Blood stained the ruffle that edged her sleeve.

"What have you done?" Gritting his teeth, he reached for her hand. "That's my blood, isn't it?"

"The doctor needed help extracting the ball," she replied thickly. "I had to hold you steady."

He gave her half a smile. "At least I could have been awake for that."

Her gaze hardened. "I'm glad you weren't."

She looked away, and he didn't press the issue. More than anything else, her tone told him what a close scrape he'd had. His heart swelled with sympathy. Inwardly, he railed against the weakness and pain that prevented him from drawing her into his arms. "Julia—"

"It would have been my fault," she burst out. "Do you realize that?"

"Julia, no."

"Yes!" Her hand sliced through the air above him. "It was my idea that you compromise me. I cried out at the wrong moment. I brought this on you. I brought so much on you, and you never said a word." A tear escaped the corner of her eye and traced a salty path along the curve of her cheek.

Benedict swallowed. "I reckoned Clivesden would call me out. I expected that from the beginning. When he didn't, I arranged things as they should have been."

"Why didn't you say anything when you asked me to consider the consequences?"

Gritting his teeth against the throbbing in his chest, he opened his arms. She eased herself into his embrace, and he sifted his fingers through her hair. "If I mentioned the possibility, would you have gone through with it? Would you have come with me to Kent?"

She raised her head to face him. A single droplet quivered on her cheekbone. "Would I have risked your life? No, of course not."

"Then I'm glad I never said anything."

"But if we'd never gone to Kent, I wouldn't have seen . . ."

He drew his hand through her hair, sifting the fine strands through his fingers. "What did you see?"

"Don't laugh."

He didn't feel like laughing in the least. "I won't."

"I saw our child. I saw our future."

"We will have it."

She sniffed, an unladylike, yet endearing sound. "I've put you through hell, haven't I?"

He skimmed his knuckles along her temple and down, brushing away that clinging teardrop. "You sent me to heaven as well. As I told you the other morning, that moment trumped all. Anything that preceded it is forgotten."

"My God, what have I put you through? Years of waiting." She pressed her fingers to her lips for a moment and inhaled, a single, trembling breath. "Years. I watched Sophia go through it, and I put you through the same. I never realized—"

He held up a shaky hand. "There's a huge difference between you and Clivesden. You know me, and, more important, I know you. Whatever you've put me through, it's been a waiting game more than anything." Reaching up, he drew a finger along her cheek. "But I have you now. I will not let you go."

"What . . . what if my feelings never match the depth of yours?" At least she acknowledged their existence. It was a start.

"I do not believe that for a moment. You've already opened yourself to me." He reached for her hand and entwined their fingers. "I do not just mean in my bed. When you told me of Miss Mallory. Now. You would not be so upset if you did not care."

"Of course I care. You're my friend."

"We are more than friends, Julia. We're lovers. We'll become husband and wife as soon as I recover."

He studied her reaction, caught the tension around her mouth as she contemplated their future.

"It's like with kissing, Julia. We start there and see where it leads. You told me you quite liked the kissing."

She ducked her head. "I liked more than that."

A grin tugged at his lips. "You should not admit such things to me when I'm in no condition to act on them." He raised her hand and pressed his lips to the soft skin on its back. "Never fear, I shall make it up to you."

SHE woke cradled against Benedict's shoulder. The light filtering through the curtains indicated early evening. She couldn't even remember drifting off, but considering the long hours passed in vigil by his side, her exhaustion came as no shock. She closed her eyes against the image of him lying, pale and bleeding, on the dead grass. She'd carry it with her forever, but for now, at least, she could blanket herself in his warmth and listen to the even rhythm of his breathing.

In and out, a steady rise and fall that soothed in its constancy. He would survive, and she could lock away the blinding fear that she'd lose him.

She nestled as close as she dared, wary of disturbing the white bands of linen wrapped about his torso. Peace surrounded her. It filled her. If not for her stubborn heart, they might have slept this way in Kent, wrapped in each other.

They could still sleep this way, for years on end. All she had to do was let him in. But she had—ages ago, whether or not she'd realized it, and never once had she lost herself. She could give herself to him in marriage and trust him with her heart. He was a good, honorable man, and he loved her. And it was long past time she let go her reservations and childish fears. She had only to free herself and follow her heart.

She slipped an arm about his waist, and he shifted in his sleep, turning into the embrace. One of his hands pressed over hers, the fingers tightening into a firm grip.

"I'll have to send you back home again," he murmured. His eyelids fluttered, but he kept them closed.

"I cannot leave yet."

"I'm sure your sister will have something to say about that." The sleep-induced roughness of his voice settled deep in her belly. "Haven't you left her to cool her heels long enough?"

"She and Highgate left yesterday."

"Yesterday?" He blinked. "How long have I been insensible?"

"Over a day."

"And you've been here the entire time?" His voice deepened on the words, sending a shiver along her spine.

"I can hardly make the scandal any worse than it is already."

"Still, you ought to go home before your father decides to come after you."

"I cannot leave until I tell you something." She turned their hands over and entwined her fingers with his. "I've made my choice."

He arched a brow. "Your choice? You mean to tell me you're running off with Clivesden, after all?"

She gave his hand a warning squeeze but could do nothing to prevent the grin that stretched her cheeks until they ached. The moment she admitted to having made up her mind, a burst of emotion released inside her to race along every vein and every nerve ending.

Happiness. Pure joy. Love—love that she was ready to claim and acclaim buoyed her up until she felt as if she was about to float off the bed like one of the Montgolfier brothers' contraptions.

"I ought to, just for that. No, you told me when we came back from Kent that I had to choose how I meant to conduct our marriage."

She leaned over and pressed her mouth to his, her fingertips tracing through the stubble on his cheek. When she pulled back, her lips broadened into a smile that he mirrored, as if he knew what was coming.

"I love you," she whispered. "I love you, and I want you to be happy. I want *us* to be happy."

He gave her hand an answering squeeze. "Then we will be."

CHAPTER TWENTY-ONE

THE SANCTUARY of St. George's Hanover Square soared to heights made all the more cavernous by the size of the gathering. Really, why such a huge space to solemnify nuptials with such a tiny attendance?

Sophia suppressed the urge to waltz up the nave. Her glance skipped past Benedict, standing stiffly before the altar, to settle on Highgate. Heavens, she'd spent hours dreaming of her wedding day, and for the most part, reality mirrored those fantasies. The church was the same, the rector in his ceremonial vestments, her parents in attendance and happy.

Goodness only knew Mama spent the morning beaming while fussing at Sophia to hurry along. Papa, too, walked ahead of her with an actual bob in his step, as if he were thirty years younger. The forgiveness of a five-thousand-pound debt would do that to a man.

The one deviation from the plan was the groom. Highgate, if not as tall and broad-shouldered as the fairy-tale prince of her dreams, acquitted himself quite well in a black coat, brocade waistcoat of silver gray, his cravat fashionably knotted. How long would it take her to untie that intricate tangle of pristine linen? Her fingers tingled, as if they already battled starched fabric, her knuckles brushing the heated skin of his throat.

Thank God those dreams had never come completely

true. She would never trade solid reality for something so insubstantial again.

As she tucked her hand into the crook of his elbow, he gave her a broad smile that crinkled the corners of his eyes. She couldn't help but answer with a grin of her own.

"Shall we?" As if he were asking her for a walk in the park. Or a ride in his carriage.

"Absolutely." How could she hesitate before the glimmer of promise in his dark eyes?

He leaned in to speak low in her ear. "I confess I'm in a bit of a hurry to get through the ceremony. We've quite a long journey ahead of us."

"I am certain we shall find a way to pass the time." She had no idea how she carried off such an air of nonchalance when, inside, her blood hummed in anticipation. The thought of their pervious jaunts alone in his barouche flooded her mind with scandalous images. Images that were most definitely inappropriate in church.

His smile broadened until the creases in his cheeks masked his scar. "I've had a few thoughts on the matter myself, only I fear I cannot discuss them in such a setting."

She slipped her fingers from his elbow and slid them along his sleeve to catch his hand in hers. "I believe that makes us of one mind, my lord."

Julia smoothed her palms down her silk skirts as she made her way up the nave to where the rector stood, ready to preside over the vows—both Sophia and Highgate's and hers with Benedict. She focused on her sister's suspicious radiance. The pale gold of her gown, an echo of her curls, explained only a small part of it. Most of it emanated from the roses blooming in her cheeks, the spark in her eye, the wicked little grin playing about her lips that proclaimed she knew some enticing secret.

If Julia didn't know better, she might suspect Sophia was in love. What a preposterous notion. After five years of pining over the wrong man, she couldn't possibly have got over her *tendre* this quickly.

Could she?

The manner in which she gazed at Highgate—as if William Ludlowe, Earl of Clivesden had never existed, as if no other man had ever existed—put lie to the thought. All the tears shed through countless evenings during which she'd been overlooked were seemingly erased. And from all appearances, Highgate returned the sentiment, fully, openly, unabashedly.

Julia trained her gaze on her hands folded demurely in front of her. Benedict looked at *her* that way, with such an ease and an intensity, it left her fluttery with a yearning that melted her insides. She paused to give herself a mental shake. Surely such thoughts were forbidden in church.

A delicate cough interrupted her musings. Her mother stood at her elbow. "Come, Julia. They're ready."

Julia lowered her lashes, not wanting to see the recrimination, the judgment, the disappointment. She'd borne the weight of her mother's shattered hopes since her return from Kent as a just punishment for her waywardness, but no more. The sooner she laid her hand in Benedict's, the better. With a nod, she started for the altar.

"Wait."

Eyes wide, she turned. "Oughtn't we get the matter settled?"

She left the rest of the thought unspoken, but the words hovered in the air between them, nonetheless. *Then you can go on pretending you have only one daughter.*

"In a moment." Mama flipped her hand in an impatient gesture. Lines of tension formed about her lips. "They'll allow us a little time before they start."

Julia cast a suspicious glance past her mother's shoulder to determine if Lady Wexford had deigned to put in an appearance. Vexing Highgate's sister by holding up the proceedings was the only reason Julia could imagine behind her mother's actions. But no, Lady Wexford had decided to deprive them all of her presence.

Thank the heavens.

"I . . ." The decisiveness in Mama's tone gave way to a wobble. "I thought we should discuss your choice of husbands."

Julia kept her gaze trained on Mama's forehead so she could give the appearance of looking into her eyes without actually doing so. She'd had enough of judgment. "It's rather late for that, don't you think?"

"Yes, I realize . . ." Mama stopped and pulled in a breath. "I did not wish to begin an argument."

Julia shifted her weight in the direction of the canopied pulpit. The rector stood beside it, impatient to begin. Sophia and Highgate had stopped gazing on each other to cast curious glances over their shoulders, while Benedict . . . Benedict held himself rigid, his fingers beating a slow but tense tattoo against his thigh.

"Then perhaps this isn't the ideal topic. Nor is it the time."

"For heaven's sake, I mean to apologize." Mama spit out the words between gritted teeth, the sound low enough to split the expectant silence and carry into the far corners of the sanctuary.

Julia balanced herself on both feet, shoulders dropping to their usual position. "Apologize?"

"For pushing you at Clivesden. I had my heart set on you—both of you—gaining titles. But I understand now."

"Understand what? That I could not hurt Sophia by allowing myself to follow along like a sheep and bend to your wishes?" The words were harsh, but they only mirrored Julia's feelings. How could her mother be so blind to such a simple truth?

"Well, yes." Mama cast her eyes downward. "No, there's more than that."

"What else could there be?"

"I've been so incredibly blind. I ought to be happy for you. If you can't have a title, at least you've made a love match."

At last, she dared meet her mother's gaze. Sincerity shone in Mama's blue irises, and Julia felt suddenly buoyant. Her heels lifted from the floorboards, and she touched the back of Mama's gloved hand. "I'm glad you finally see."

She cast a longing glance up the aisle at Benedict, who raised questioning brows. "I must go. They're waiting for me."

The pale peach silk skirts of an old ball gown rustled as she made her way to Benedict's side. She arrived at the front of the church and laid her hand in the crook of his elbow, delighting in the warmth and vitality that emanated from him.

He leaned over to murmur directly into her ear. "What did your mother want? Trying to talk you into changing your mind at the last minute?"

Julia suppressed a smile at the delicious shiver his warm breath stirred to life. "And cause even more of a scandal? Heaven forfend."

JULIA watched as Benedict dipped the quill into the ink. Her eye followed each swoop as he scratched his name onto the parish register. Such a strong, firm hand to match the strength and starkness of his name.

A name which now belonged to her.

Their fingers brushed as he handed the quill over, and heat streaked up her arm. Awareness of the slightest casual touch consumed her and filled her mind with thoughts of the coming night, and all the other nights stretching ahead of her, one after the other, to fill out the years of their future.

The quill trembled in her fingers as she signed her name below his. She blinked at the register, at the glistening of the drying ink on the page. It was done now. Julia and Benedict, forever united in matrimony.

His fingers slid along her wrist, searching to twine with hers. He lifted her hand and laid it in its proper place—on his arm. "Ready to face the crowd?"

She lifted her eyes to his. "What crowd?"

"You cannot imagine the gossip hasn't made the rounds, can you? I'm sure more than one member of the *ton* has decided to take a constitutional this morning and wander past Hanover Square. Mere chance, of course."

"Of course." She fell into step beside him, following her sister and her parents in the direction of the door. "They'll want to catch a glimpse of Highgate."

"And the young lady some idiot threw five thousand pounds away on."

"You mean that scandalous trollop?"

"Hush, you're still in church." He grinned at her and lowered his voice. "You might want to use a milder term. I recall a certain affinity for the word strumpet."

She waved a hand. "Never to refer to myself."

His grin broadened, taking on a rather evil bent. "If you take it into your head to act the strumpet on occasion—just for me—I don't think I'll mind."

She raised both brows and assumed what she hoped was an appropriate expression of innocence. "Hush, you're still in church."

But at that moment, they stepped over the threshold and onto the columned portico. "Not anymore."

* * *

Such a crowd of gawkers. Not that the size of the gathering ought to have shocked him. Benedict had lived his whole life among these people, long enough to know how quickly word spread through the *ton* and how much its members enjoyed a spectacle.

After all, it wasn't every day a man married off two such notoriously reluctant daughters as the St. Claire sisters—and under such scandalous circumstances. The gossips would have enough fodder to last them until Christmas.

Too bad the weather had decided to cooperate for once. A few rays of weak sunlight, their warmth nearly palpable, broke through the clouds to cast their benediction on the nuptials. Given his choice, Benedict would have preferred a drenching downpour.

He scowled at Lady Epperley, who held court firmly at the front, peering at them through her lorgnette. Lady Posselthwaite craned her neck to see past the dowager's bonnet. In the next instant, she let out a squawk, as Lady Epperley's elbow made contact with her ribs, the movement so rapid, Benedict was not quite sure he'd actually seen anything.

Suppressing a grin, he ushered Julia past the columns of the façade toward the waiting carriage. He had plans for her, none of which involved exchanging insincere pleasantries with various and sundry passing acquaintances. Julia had expressed a desire for their future happiness, and he intended to start with her happiness.

Or at the very least, her pleasure.

A ripple passed through the onlookers. Some sort of commotion erupted farther down the street. Heads turned. Even Lady Epperley directed her attention away from a beaming Sophia to face the disturbance. Good.

Perhaps they could make their escape from Town without any further ado while the *ton* found something new to talk about.

"I say, Revelstoke!" Upperton's voice carried over the heads of the assembly. Nudging the gathering aside, he made his way to Benedict's carriage. "You cannot leave without your wedding present."

"What present?"

Beside him, Julia craned her neck. Upperton clutched a length of rope in his fist, a lead, actually. Benedict followed it with this eye to the source of the commotion. Standing behind Upperton, Nefertari tossed her proud head. With a snuffle, she took an ambling step forward to nose at Upperton's pockets.

"What's this?" Benedict asked, disbelieving.

Upperton held out the lead. "It's your wedding present."

"What have you done? You cannot expect me to believe Clivesden, of all people, has sent me a token of his esteem to mark the day."

"Of course he hasn't. He was, however, all too happy to part with this nag in lieu of paying his debt to me. Beyond what he owed, she was costing him a fortune in oats."

Benedict swallowed and then swallowed again. It would not do for him to put on a display of emotion in front of the *ton*'s premiere gossips.

Julia leaned across him, the better to take in the proceedings, and the softness of her breast pressed against his arm. "What's this?"

He had to clear his throat before he could reply. "Remember when we were in Kent, and I told you I was in the market for bloodstock?" At her nod, he gestured toward Nefertari. "There's my bloodstock."

"But what does Clivesden have to do with any of it?"

"He outbid me in the auction. It seems he took it into his head to present you with a saddle horse."

Julia's laughter rang out over the scene. Nefertari snorted and pawed the ground. "After I told him horses made me sneeze, you'd think he'd have taken the hint."

Benedict's cheeks stretched in a grin. "You told him that?"

"He wanted to take me riding in the park. It was all I could think of to get rid of him."

Benedict held her gaze. Such a lovely smile she had. It spread across the whole of her face until she glowed with happiness. "You could have told him the truth, that you don't ride."

"And have him offer me lessons?"

He cleared his throat. "You're absolutely right there. I'm the only one who ought to give you riding lessons."

A discreet cough forced him to look away. Upperton thrust the lead into his hand. "If the pair of you want to get on with . . . things, I suggest you take your wedding present and be off."

"Thank you, my friend."

Upperton shrugged. "The least I could do." He made a shooing motion with his hands. "Now off with you. I expect there to be a little Revelstoke before this time next year. Don't forget to put him down for Eton."

With a wink, Upperton melted back into the crowd. Benedict handed Nefertari off to a footman with orders to attach her to their carriage and turned to find roses blooming in Julia's cheeks. He cast a glance at the crowd and grinned down at her. Taking her by the waist, he pulled her into a lazy kiss. A collective gasp rose from the gawkers, punctuated by the inevitable *snap* of a lorgnette.

"I don't know when I've ever seen a more disgraceful display of affection," Lady Epperley grumbled. "In my day, husbands and wives showed each other a suitable level of indifference."

When he released his bride, the color in her cheeks had deepened, but her eyes sparkled with promise. He ushered her toward the conveyance, but he had to wait while she pulled her sister into a warm hug. He tamped down his impatience and shook Highgate's hand, but his mind was elsewhere.

A little Revelstoke. Yes. For once, Upperton had come up with a good scheme, one Benedict intended on putting into immediate action.

ACKNOWLEDGMENTS

A project of the breadth of a full-length novel is never undertaken alone. I owe a huge debt of thanks and love to the following:

To Carrie, Caryl, Clemence, Lizzie, and Marian for being my first readers and telling me when my ideas are worth pursuing.

To the members of the Hearts Through History Romance Writers critique group for catching my stupid typos, constant repetition, and extra spaces, and for making me push myself to improve.

To the Lalalas, sisters and brother, for unfailing encouragement and support. More specifically to Valerie Bowman for bringing us together, and to Carla Kempert, aka God, for kicking my behind when it most needed it.

To Vanessa Kelly for challenging me.

To Sara Megibow for being the most awesome, enthusiastic agent an author could ask for.

To Caitlin and Junessa for all your help and encouragement.

To my husband and daughters for putting up with a messy house and less-than-inspired suppers (why, yes, we are having spaghetti again) so I can write.

Read on for an exciting preview of

A Most Devilish Rogue

By Ashlyn Macnamara

Published by Ballantine Books

LONDON, 1820

IF THE key to announcing bad news lay in the timing, George Upperton's mistress knew when to deliver.

"What's that?" Some odd emotion invaded the haze of post-coital bliss, and he rolled to his side. "For a moment there, I could have sworn you told me you were with child."

Lucy Padgett closed her long-lashed eyelids. Strawberry blond hair tumbled over her bare shoulders and breasts as she ducked her head. "I did."

Like a fist to the gut, her affirmation sent the air rushing from his lungs. He frowned and pushed himself up on one elbow. "Are you certain? This could make for a very bad joke."

She shifted to her back, arms crossed, and her eyes snapped open, sparkling with blue fire. "Joke?" Her usual melodic tones hardened to ice. "This isn't a joke. How could you be so cold-hearted as to question me?"

"I only . . ." The fist was still planted in his gut. It settled into the pit of his stomach, hard and leaden, yet managed to expand until breathing became a chore. He pulled a lungful of air in through his nose and tried again. "I thought it took a while before a woman knew."

"It's been two months since I last had my courses. They've never been late before."

George counted back the days in his head. Two months . . . eight weeks . . . A lot could happen to a man in that time. In his particular case, a lot *had* happened. Quite enough to drive from his mind thoughts of Lucy claiming she was indisposed.

Watching, stunned, while an old school chum put a pistol in his mouth tended to do that to a man.

"I thought . . ."

She wasn't going to like his next comment, but damn it, he had to say it. They weren't likely to pass the rest of the evening in more agreeable fashion. Not after her announcement. The mere thought of engaging in additional bed sport now made that weight in his gut twist until he rather felt like casting up his accounts.

"I thought you'd taken the usual precautions."

"Precautions?" She yanked the sheet free of the mattress and wrapped herself in it, the same way she draped herself in indignation. "Precautions?" She squeaked a high note on the final syllable. "You know very well the usual precautions are no guarantee. Last I looked, I didn't create a brat all on my own. I had help."

George had no clue how to reply to this. She was right, of course, but truth was, he'd never considered the matter. He'd assumed she'd protected herself because that's what wise women of her standing did—ensured no unpleasant consequences might cost them their protector.

The heavy sensation intensified until beads of sweat broke out on his brow. How cold-hearted he'd become. How cynical. He thrust aside an image of Lucy cradling a tiny, gray-eyed boy with waves of light brown hair. His son. Who'd have thought? Of course, he couldn't cast the poor woman off at a time like this. Bitter experience had taught him just how that felt.

"No sense in arguing over the matter now that it's too late." He was amazed at how reasonable he sounded, voice low, steady, almost comforting. It nearly set *him* at ease.

Nearly.

The idea of raising a child made him want to carve out a neat hiding spot in his liquor cabinet and remain there for the next few decades.

Blast it all, he couldn't afford this. He could barely afford Lucy, especially since she'd revealed quite extravagant taste where her wardrobe was concerned. The latest bill from her modiste had sent him straight to his club.

She glared at him. "What do you plan on doing about this?"

"Doing?" Damned if he knew. The bottle of brandy in the sitting room was calling at the moment. A deuced siren it was, just as seductive as the Lorelei.

"You . . . you don't want me to raise it, do you?" She sniffed. "I shall require some form of compensation. How else will I live? I certainly won't find another gentleman once I'm fat with your get."

"No, no, of course not." He swung his legs over the side of the bed and plucked his dressing gown from the heap of clothing on the floor. How blithely he'd shed it an hour before. How blindly. "When you mention compensation, what did you have in mind?"

He paid close attention to his dressing gown as he awaited her reply. He slipped his arms through heavy velvet sleeves. Easier to concentrate on the weight of the fabric on his shoulders than to witness her calculated assessment of what she might gain from him.

But he owed her now, didn't he? He'd taken his pleasure in her body and now he must pay a much heftier price than he'd ever imagined.

"I'll need the house, of course."

"Of course," he echoed. He was already behind on rent.

"And I'll need to keep on the cook and my maid. Oh, and a new wardrobe." He imagined her ticking items off on her fingers. He couldn't bring himself to look. "In a few months, I won't possibly be able to wear my gowns."

The weight in his stomach plummeted, and he sank to the mattress. He covered his mouth with one hand until he was certain his dinner would stay where it belonged, then slid his fingers down his chin. "Lucy, my dear, I meant to tell you . . . I mean, I really ought to have said something before now. That's entirely my fault. But honestly . . ."

The words wouldn't come. George Upperton was known among his circle of cronies as a prime wit, but now, when it mattered most, he couldn't summon the means to reveal the truth.

"How dare you!" She leapt from the bed, dragging the sheet along with her. "You utter, utter cad. How could you possibly?"

He glanced sideways at her. Her face had gone a deep crimson that clashed horribly with her red-gold hair. "How dare I what?"

"I've just announced to you that I'm in a delicate condition and you have the colossal nerve to hand me my congé?"

At 'delicate,' he almost snorted. The notes she'd just hit with that shriek were nearly pure enough to shatter crystal or set nearby dogs to howling. Lucy was anything but delicate. But then the rest of her accusation struck him in the gut. "Congé? I'm not as cold-hearted as all that. What I was trying to tell you—"

A pounding on the bedroom door cut him off. "What the devil?"

Lucy stared at him, round-eyed, and drew the sheet more firmly about her breasts. The pounding increased until the heavy oak plank rattled on its hinges.

George tightened his belt, rose, and strode across the room. "Here now. What is the meaning—"

He whipped the door open and found himself face-to-face with a tall, dark-haired man. His pristine collar and impeccably tied cravat bespoke his wealth.

Behind the intruder, Lucy's maid cowered. "Beggin' yer pardon, sir, but he insisted."

George narrowed his eyes and glanced over his shoulder at Lucy. "Might I ask what another gentleman is doing, demanding entrance to your private chambers?"

"I didn't come here looking for her," the newcomer growled. He grabbed George by the front of his dressing gown and whipped him about. "I came here looking for you."

Him? What the devil? George forced a grin to his lips. "You could just as easily have found me at my town house during regular calling hours. Now you've caught me completely unprepared for company. Suppose we might persuade the maid to put the kettle on, but I'm afraid we've finished the biscuits."

As he clattered on, he sized up the stranger—an old strategy of his that had extricated him from any number of tight situations. The man's face was squarish, topped by a slash of dark brows and with a firm line of a mouth at its base. Nothing familiar about it. Certainly not one of his creditors. And yet the man's accent suggested breeding just as much as his clothes.

The stranger gave George a shake. "I didn't come to pay my respects."

"Yes, I'm getting that impression." He allowed nonchalance to infuse his tone. It was too difficult to inspect one's nails when a great oaf had one by the lapels. "But suppose, before you beat the stuffing out of me, you tell me who you are and explain why. Then I may or may not take it like a man, depending on whether or not I agree with you."

Another shake, this one hard enough to rattle his back teeth. "You talk too much."

"So I've been told." He grinned—winningly, he hoped—while balling his hand into a fist. He'd learned the trick as a schoolboy. Make the opponent think he'd try to charm his way out of a fight until said opponent succumbed to a false sense of security. That strategy, combined with an innate sense of when to duck, had saved his nose on more than one occasion. "Can't seem to help myself, though. I have a tendency to natter on when threatened. See? There I go again."

"Shut your gob and listen. You've put my sister in a delicate condition, and I'm here to see you pay."

"Sister?" In spite of himself, he glanced over his shoulder at Lucy. "You never once intimated you had any family." Well-born, possibly well-connected family to judge by her brother's appearance. "My dear, you've been holding out on me."

The instant the words were out, something akin to a sledgehammer slammed into his jaw. His head snapped back. Pain exploded from the point of contact and rattled through his body. The floor tilted, and he stumbled back to land in a heap at the foot of the bed.

Right. Lucy could wait. Time to concentrate on the danger at hand.

He scrambled to his feet, ignoring the ringing in his ears, and waded in, but his opponent was clearly in better practice when it came to fisticuffs. Lucy's brother danced lightly on the balls of his feet, left fist raised to block, while the right hovered menacingly at chin height.

George feinted left before jabbing with his right, but his opponent anticipated the move and weaved out of range. The blow met with mere air, and George staggered once more, off balance, his guard dropping. Another punch whizzed past his ear, but the second jab caught him squarely on the chin.

Stars danced before his eyes, and the room reeled. He

stumbled sideways into something soft and yielding. Lucy steadied him, but he wouldn't make the same mistake twice. He kept his gaze pinned on his opponent, who stood back for the moment, red in the face, perhaps, but his breathing steady and even.

The arrogant bastard.

With a roar, George lunged.

"Roger!" Lucy screamed.

George ignored the ungrateful wench and went for Roger's throat. The ape dodged, but George anticipated as much and mirrored the move, grasping his enemy about the waist and hauling him to the floor. He applied his weight to the other man's belly, planted a hand on his throat and pulled back his fist.

"George! Stop it! Now!"

Lucy's terrified cry made him hesitate a moment too long. Roger heaved his bulk and George's hand slipped. The next thing he knew, the back of his head struck unforgiving oak floorboards. Roger's weight bore him down and forced the air from his lungs. He gasped but pulled in nothing. Blackness shrouded the edges of his vision.

"Stop," he croaked. The weight on his chest eased just enough. "What do you want from me?"

"That's simple enough," Roger growled. Not even winded, the scoundrel. "You're to do right by my sister."

A raw jolt of panic speared his gut. Roger couldn't possibly insist on a marriage, not when any number of protectors had preceded him in Lucy's bed. "What's that supposed to mean?"

"Simple. You got her into trouble. You're going to get her out. The proper compensation ought to hush things up."

"That's blackmail."

Roger smiled, an evil sort of leer that disrupted the

square lines of his face. "That's good business. And you might have avoided the matter entirely if you'd kept your prick in your pocket."

"If *I'd* kept . . . What about all—"

Roger tightened his grip on George's throat and gave him a shake. "The others didn't get caught, now, did they?"

"She can have the house, and I'll settle a sum on her to see to her upkeep. Beyond that . . ." He couldn't admit to his true financial situation. Not with an ape sitting on his chest.

"Beyond that, you'll cough up a tidy sum. My sister deserves a decent life."

"Chin up, dear, we've almost arrived."

George suppressed the urge to roll his eyes at his mother. Gads, how could the woman beam so after hours of jostling in a carriage through the Kentish countryside, crammed in with his sisters?

He exchanged a glance with Henrietta. "And not a moment too soon," he said. "I can barely stand the excitement. We'll go from being packed into this carriage to being packed into a house with entirely too many people."

How he dreaded the thought of a house party, even if the host was his oldest friend. Worse than a ball, because the blasted things lasted days rather than mere hours. He could only escape to the card room in the evenings, while the rest of the day he'd have to find more creative means of avoiding his mother's attempts at matchmaking.

Mama's smile wavered not at all. "Sarcasm does not become you. How many times must I tell you? You'd do better to put on a bright outlook. I imagine you'd attract a bride if you did that."

His left eye twitched, as it always did when his mother brought up the topic of matrimony. "I'll keep that in mind, should I wish to attract one. What do you recommend? Something like this?"

He pulled an exaggerated face that doubtless exposed his back teeth. God knew his cheeks would ache soon enough if he maintained the expression. It didn't help matters that he'd tweaked a few bruises in the process.

"Stop this instant," Mama scolded, but the woman, Lord help her, could never manage to sound stern. "Pity you had to turn up with your face all beaten. Why you men insist on pounding each other is beyond me."

"It's sport." He'd explained the state of his face away with a minor lie about an incident at his boxing club. The truth would only give Mama the vapors.

"Be that as it may, I am certain you will meet your future wife at this party. See if you don't."

"Ah yes, and Henny"—he winked at his sister—"will announce her engagement to the head groom at the same time. Why, I think a double wedding at Christmas will be just the thing."

Mama made a valiant attempt at creasing her brows, but an eruption of laughter quite ruined the effect. "You are completely incorrigible."

"But endlessly diverting."

"And if you turned that charm on a few young ladies . . ."

He held up a hand. "Madam, I believe I'm not the only incorrigible one in this conveyance."

"Nonsense." Mama tossed her head, and the feathers on her bonnet scrubbed across his sister Catherine's face. "I'm simply determined. There's a difference."

Single-minded and obsessed were the terms that immediately leapt to George's tongue, but he swallowed them back. Of course his mother wanted to see him wed. It was what mothers did once their children reached an appropriate age. Unfortunately, his idea of an appropriate age didn't agree with hers by at least ten years.

He caught Henrietta's eye. Her mouth twitched into a smirk that spoke volumes. *Better you than me.* But Mama would turn her attention back to her eldest daughter soon enough. No doubt the moment they reached the conservatory where Revelstoke housed his pianoforte. Coupled with what Catherine passed off as singing . . .

In spite of himself, he winced. He prayed Revelstoke had laid in a good supply of brandy. He was going to need it in vast quantities if Mama insisted on her daughters being part of the entertainment.

The carriage rumbled to a halt at the head of a sweeping drive. The stone bulk of Shoreford House rose gray against a backdrop of blue sky. Shouts hailed from the yard, followed by a heavy *thunk* as the steps were let down. George leapt from his seat, ready to hand his mother and sisters out of the conveyance.

A gentle breeze bore the salty tang of the Channel, mingled with an earthy heaviness that wafted from the stables. The late-August sun beat a gentle warmth on the back of his neck.

"I can't believe you've actually come."

George turned to find Benedict Revelstoke approaching from the main house, a grin across his face. As he came closer, he frowned as his gaze glanced over the bruises on George's face. "I was about to ask how far your mother twisted your arm to convince you to come, but I see she's resorted to more drastic means of persuasion."

George reached for his hand. "Do me a favor and don't call attention to it. If I have to put up with any more cold compresses and female twittering, I may as well take to my bed permanently."

"I don't know how you'll avoid it. Once Julia gets a good look at you . . ."

"I thought I heard my name." Benedict's wife appeared just beyond his shoulder, waddling from the house in the wake of a prominent belly. "Gossiping about me behind my back, are you?"

Revelstoke caught her hand and pulled her close. Their fingers entwined as if they couldn't bear as much as an instant apart. For a moment, they stared into each other's eyes, and in that brief expanse of time, they disappeared into their own realm where only the pair of them existed. It lasted less than two seconds, but an entire conversation seemed to pass between them.

Fighting the urge to roll his eyes, George cleared his throat. God help him if he ever became that love struck.

Julia stepped forward to inspect him more closely. "My goodness, what have you done to your face?"

Revelstoke raised his brows and shrugged.

George glanced over his shoulder to make sure his mother was well occupied in directing the servants with the baggage before responding. "Came out on the wrong end of a rather vigorous discussion, but never fear. It looks worse than it is."

"I shall ask Cook to make you a poultice to draw out the bruising."

He shook his head. "Don't trouble yourself on my account. I'm sure she's got enough to oversee with a houseful of guests for the next week."

"It's no trouble at all. She knows the most wonderful recipes. One of our yearlings got himself into a scrape a while back, but Cook worked her magic, and he's back as good as new. Outstrips the rest of them from one end of the pasture to the other, and barely blows at all."

"You want to dose me with a remedy that you use on livestock? I think I'll pass, thank you. Only, do me the service of not mentioning your ideas to my mother."

With a laugh, Julia excused herself and trundled off to greet the Upperton sisters. Soon the air filled with high-pitched chatter.

George tilted his head in the direction of the main house. "You look disgustingly happy."

Revelstoke shook his head. "Ever the one for a flowery turn of phrase, I see." He took a few steps in the direction of the house. "Are you planning on telling me what you're really doing here?"

"I'm attending this house party at your invitation. Why else would I have come except to pass a few days rusticating here with your guests? Can't think of anything I'd rather be doing."

Revelstoke cast him a sidelong look. "Pull the other one. From all appearances, you've got yourself into some scrape or other, so you've either come here to hide or you want me to get you out of it."

George blew out a breath. "Don't you have some horseflesh you'd like to show off?" He waved a hand in the direction of the stables. "A new broodmare? Perhaps one that's produced the next champion at Ascot?"

Revelstoke clapped him on the shoulder. "That bad, is it? Perhaps you'd rather we have a drink in my study while the ladies settle in. And if you've got any particular sins you'd like to confess, I'll have a listen."

"I never held much with religion. Too many diversions count against you, you know. But if the priest offered brandy in the confessional, he might find he had a more faithful flock." They tramped up the front steps in the wake of two footmen juggling a trunk. The sight reminded him of his sisters and their mother's advice to pack their entire wardrobe. "I say, who all have you invited to this gathering?"

"Entirely too many, but Julia thought we ought to show a bit of hospitality. If I can interest some of the men in acquiring some horseflesh while they're here, it may all be worth it. She's invited her sister, of course, and my brother, and since we'll be entertaining an earl and a marquess, naturally half the *ton* saw fit to finagle an invitation whether we wished to see them or not."

George suppressed a groan. "That means my mother will insist on putting my sisters on display. Tell me your pianoforte's out of tune. They might actually sound decent for once."

"As a matter of fact, Julia just had someone look at it."

"Better order another case of brandy, one I can reserve for my own personal use."

Revelstoke closed the door to his study and strode to a side table where a cut crystal decanter stood full of rich amber liquid. He poured two healthy measures and handed George a glass. George stared into the swirling depths and considered downing the alcohol in one go. No, best not to overimbibe or else he might confess more than necessary.

Revelstoke clinked glasses and raised his snifter. "Come now. What's brought you here and in this state?"

"Seems my mistress forgot to tell me a thing or two. Like the fact she has a brother who doesn't quite appreciate his sister being a kept woman."

"It's not as if you're the man who ruined her." Revelstoke raised a brow. "Are you?"

"Of course not, and you shouldn't even have to ask. I draw the line at leading innocents astray." He stared out the window to the greenery beyond the crosshatch of the mullions. Along a whitewashed fence, mares grazed surrounded by their cavorting foals. "I'm not Lucy's first protector, and I certainly won't be her last."

"Then why would her brother have a problem with you in particular?"

George sipped at his brandy to play for time. "I didn't come here to discuss my problems with my mistress."

The look Revelstoke gave him clearly communicated his skepticism. "Then why are you here?"

"I can't visit an old school chum, especially considering you never come into Town?" He set his glass on a burnished oak table. "Why, you practically forced me to make the trek out to this godforsaken corner of Kent."

"The last thing I'd expect of you is to attend something so respectable as a house party, especially considering chances are quite high your sisters will torture us with their musical talent. So what is it?"

Revelstoke knew him too well, damn the man. "How's the horse breeding business going?"

"It's flourishing." He nodded toward the pastoral scene just beyond the window. "Ask Julia to show you about the place later, and you'll see all the improvements we've made with the profits. But you're no more interested in acquiring a horse than you are in attending a house party."

George snatched up his glass for a fortifying drink. "I was wondering, since you're doing so well, if it was possible to spot me a loan."

Revelstoke tore his attention away from the window. "How much do you need?"

Another mouthful. His last. "Five thousand pounds."

Revelstoke spit out his brandy. "Five thousand? Good God, man. What makes you think I can afford to hand you that sort of blunt?"

"Could you see your way clear to lending me a thousand, say, or five hundred?"

"I daresay you stand a better chance, yes." He marched back to the sideboard in search of the cut-glass decanter. "But what on earth have you been up to that you need those kinds of funds?"

George studied the pattern in the Axminster carpeting. "This and that. I may have got myself in a bit too deep at cards, on top of everything else."

Revelstoke eyed his freshly poured glass, before slowly setting it aside. "Dare I ask what everything else comprises?"

George shrugged. "A mistress whose tastes run to the expensive, mostly. She insisted on a fairly fashionable address, and I've fallen behind on the rent."

Revelstoke fixed his gaze on George. "Don't you think it's time you gave up that sort of living and settled down?"

George glanced toward the ceiling beams. Dark and heavy, like the rest of the room. "Oh no. Don't you start, too. Bad enough my mother's planning on throwing every eligible young miss in attendance in my direction; I don't need you waxing poetic on the virtues of married life. Besides, you can't tell me keeping a wife and child isn't any less expensive than keeping a mistress."

"But it is. No need to maintain separate addresses, for one thing. No need to staff two houses."

George wagged his head from side to side. "You've come over all practical since you became leg-shackled. It's downright boring."

"With the right woman—"

"There you go, sounding like my mother again. I will be the first to commend you on your excellent taste in brides. At least you had the foresight to choose one with wit and cleverness. I'm afraid there aren't many others like your Julia, though. You'll have to understand this mere mortal doesn't possess your luck in that department."

Revelstoke rolled his eyes. "Now you're just being absurd."

"Absurd or not, a betrothal is not going to solve my financial problems. Not unless you've invited an heiress or two who might be willing to overlook my long list of shortcomings." He paused just long enough to allow Revelstoke to reply, knowing full well his friend didn't maintain the proper social connections to attract such an heiress.

In the face of Revelstoke's silence, he went on. "Since no heiresses seem to be in the offing, you might tell me which gentlemen among your guests might be persuaded to play a few hands of whist."

"Have you learned nothing at all from your current predicament?" Revelstoke pushed his glass away. "You're in trouble because you played a few hands too many. Another game isn't going to get you out. It may even put you in deeper."

"Then how do you propose I get my hands on five thousand? I need blunt and soon."

A line etched itself between Revelstoke's brows. "This is about more than a demanding mistress."

"What makes you say that?"

"Because if that were your only problem, you'd hand her her congé and be done with it. So perhaps you tell me the real reason you need so much money, and I'll consider a small loan."

"You're right." George took the decanter and topped off Revelstoke's glass before pouring himself another measure. Talking about that night inevitably called nightmarish visions to mind. "Do you remember Summersby?"

Revelstoke paused, glass halfway to his lips. "I heard. Damned tragedy, that."

"Do you know why he did it?" When Revelstoke shook his head, George went on. "Creditors hounding him. He got in too deep and couldn't pay."

"And him with a wife and young child." Revelstoke shook his head once more, this time in censure. "This is the sort of thing I mean. You get in too far—"

"The debts aren't mine," George cut in. "They're Summersby's. I mean to pay every last one. No reason his family should suffer. They've been through enough."

Revelstoke set his glass aside with a clunk and clapped George on the shoulder. "Commendable of you. Never thought I'd say this, but it's noble."

"Hardly." George let out a harsh bark. Some other man might have thought it laughter, but Revelstoke knew him too well to mistake the sound. It was pain, pure and simple. "I mean to ruin every last one of them, starting with Marshall."

Revelstoke let out a low whistle. "Aiming rather high, aren't you? If you came here with the intention of meeting him, I'm afraid the family is too well connected for the likes of us."

George had suspected as much. "No matter. If you can spot me some funds, I can work on turning them into more. That way when I go back to Town, I'll be ready for the bastards."

"I'm afraid you're in for some difficulty there." Revelstoke clapped him on the shoulder once more. "Julia's father, you see. She doesn't want him tempted, so she's asked me to let all the gentlemen know she's prohibited deep play for the duration of the party."